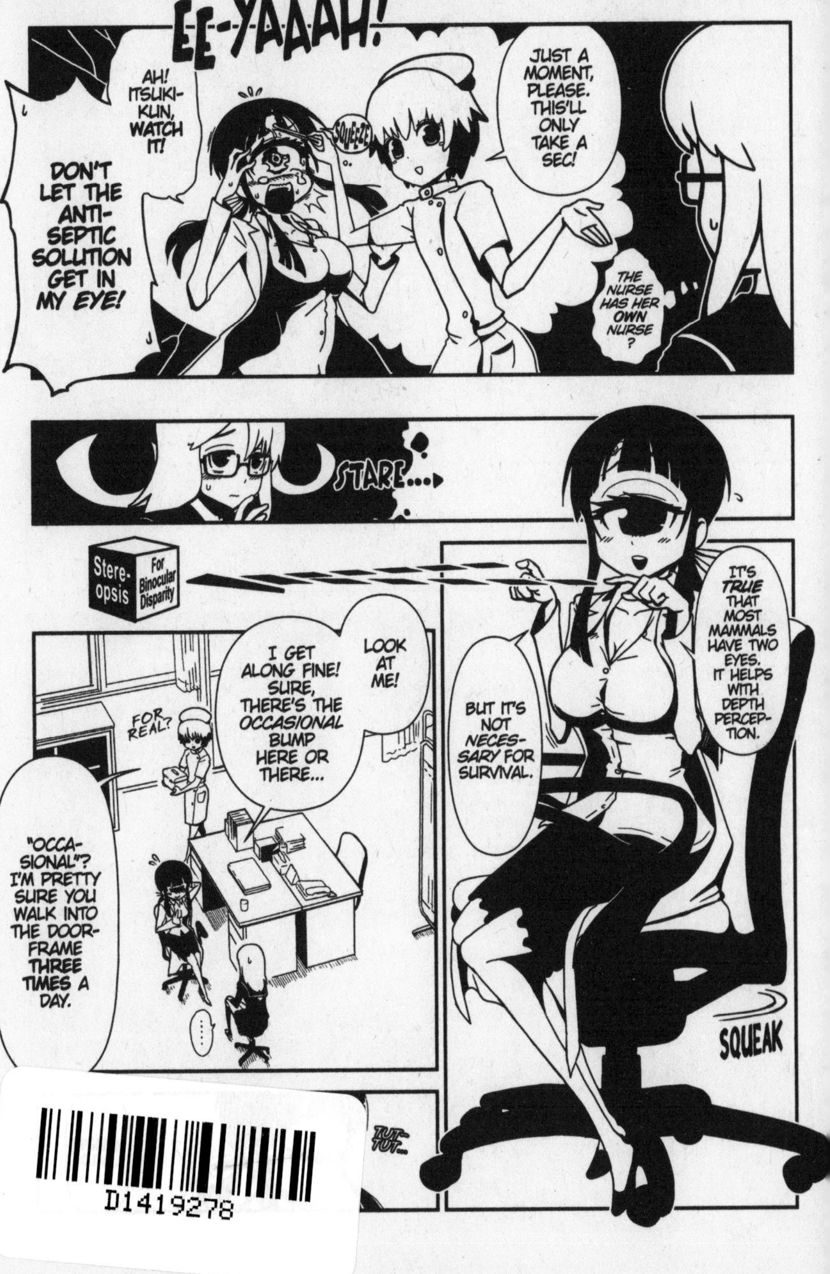
JUST A MOMENT, PLEASE. THIS'LL ONLY TAKE A SEC!
EE-YAAAH!
AH! ITSUKI-KUN, WATCH IT!
SQUEEZE
THE NURSE HAS HER OWN NURSE?
DON'T LET THE ANTI-SEPTIC SOLUTION GET IN MY EYE!
STARE...
IT'S TRUE THAT MOST MAMMALS HAVE TWO EYES. IT HELPS WITH DEPTH PERCEP-TION.
BUT IT'S NOT NECES-SARY FOR SURVIVAL.
Stere-opsis
For Binocular Disparity
SQUEAK
LOOK AT ME!
I GET ALONG FINE! SURE, THERE'S THE OCCASIONAL BUMP HERE OR THERE...
FOR REAL?
"OCCA-SIONAL"? I'M PRETTY SURE YOU WALK INTO THE DOOR-FRAME THREE TIMES A DAY.
......
TUT-TUT...
D1419278

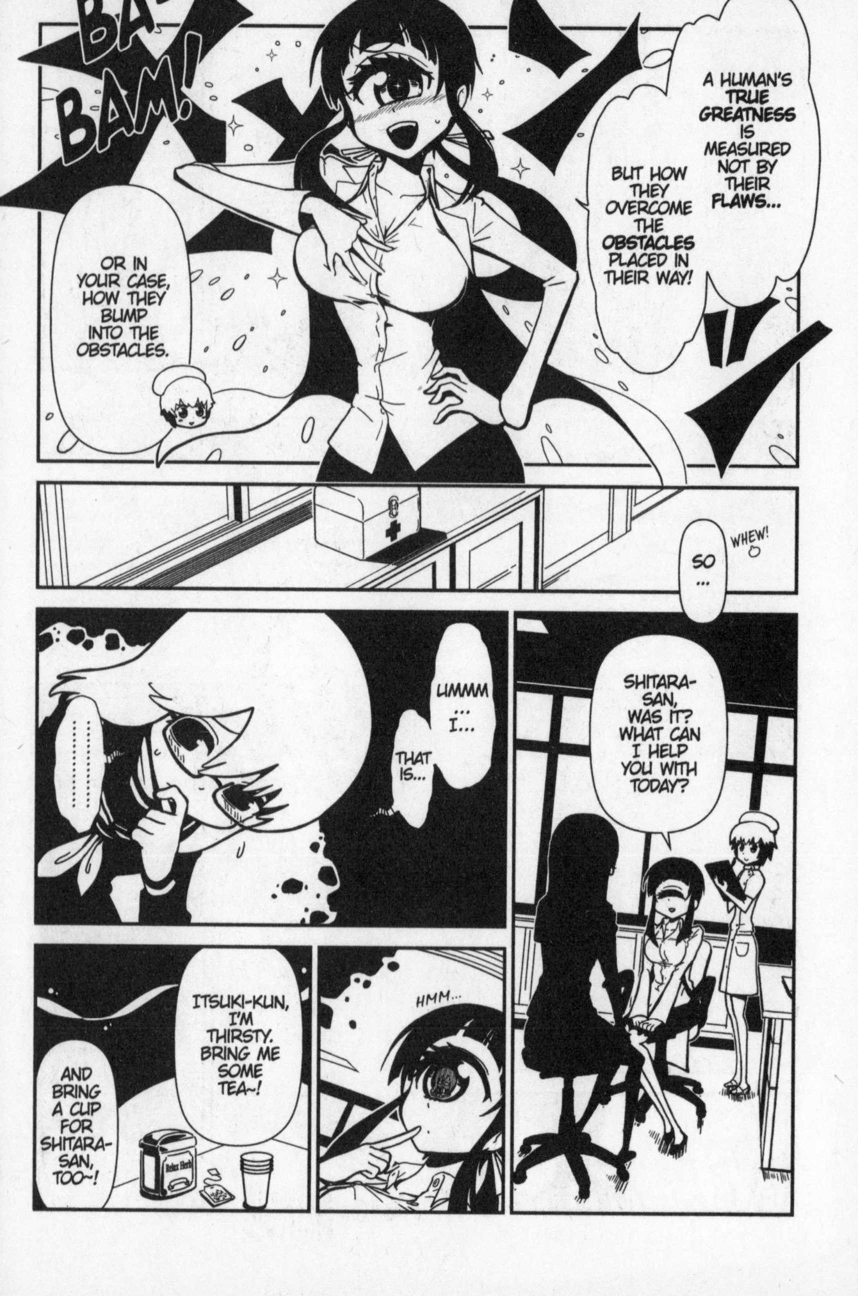
A HUMAN'S TRUE GREATNESS IS MEASURED NOT BY THEIR FLAWS...
BUT HOW THEY OVERCOME THE OBSTACLES PLACED IN THEIR WAY!
BA-BAM!
OR IN YOUR CASE, HOW THEY BUMP INTO THE OBSTACLES.
WHEW!
SO...
SHITARA-SAN, WAS IT? WHAT CAN I HELP YOU WITH TODAY?
UMMM... I...
THAT IS...
......
HMM...
ITSUKI-KUN, I'M THIRSTY. BRING ME SOME TEA~!
AND BRING A CUP FOR SHITARA-SAN, TOO~!
Relax Herb

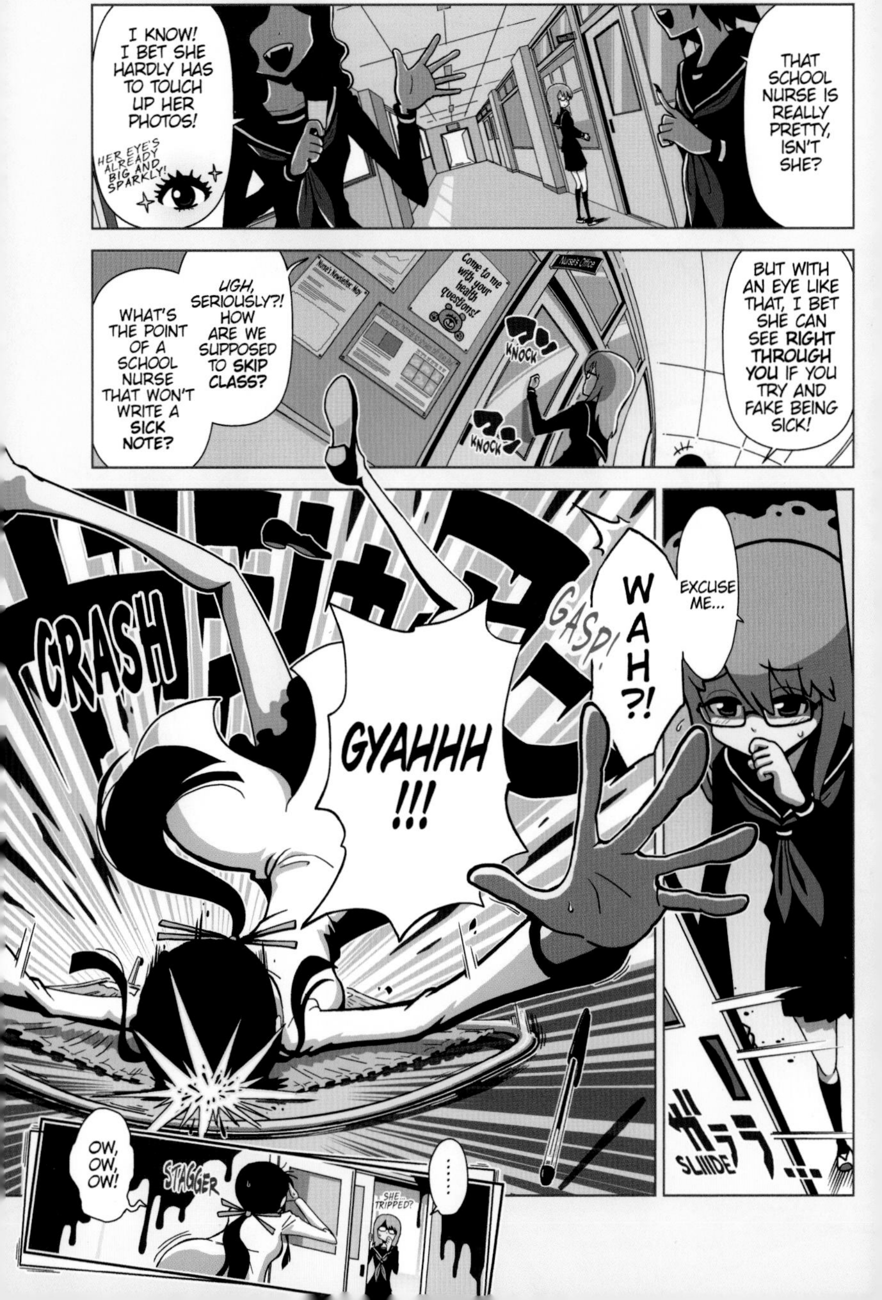
THAT SCHOOL NURSE IS REALLY PRETTY, ISN'T SHE?
I KNOW! I BET SHE HARDLY HAS TO TOUCH UP HER PHOTOS!
HER EYE'S ALREADY BIG AND SPARKLY!
BUT WITH AN EYE LIKE THAT, I BET SHE CAN SEE RIGHT THROUGH YOU IF YOU TRY AND FAKE BEING SICK!
Nurse's Office
KNOCK
KNOCK
Come to me with your health questions!
Nurse's Newsletter: May
UGH, SERIOUSLY?! HOW ARE WE SUPPOSED TO SKIP CLASS?
WHAT'S THE POINT OF A SCHOOL NURSE THAT WON'T WRITE A SICK NOTE?
EXCUSE ME...
SLIIIDE
WAH?!
GASP!
GYAHHH!!!
CRASH
......
SHE... TRIPPED?
STAGGER
OW, OW, OW!

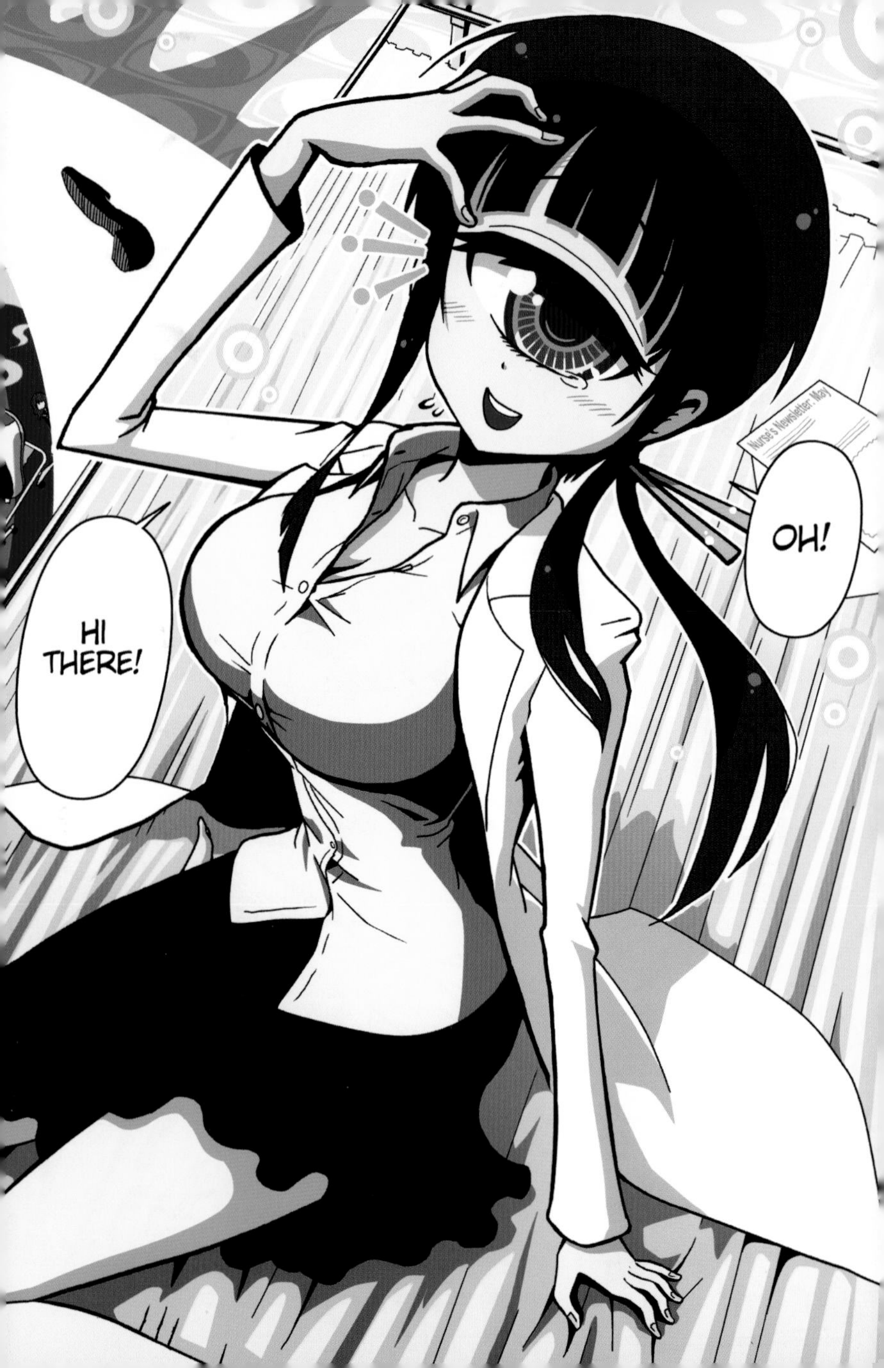
Nurse's Newsletter: May
OH!
HI THERE!

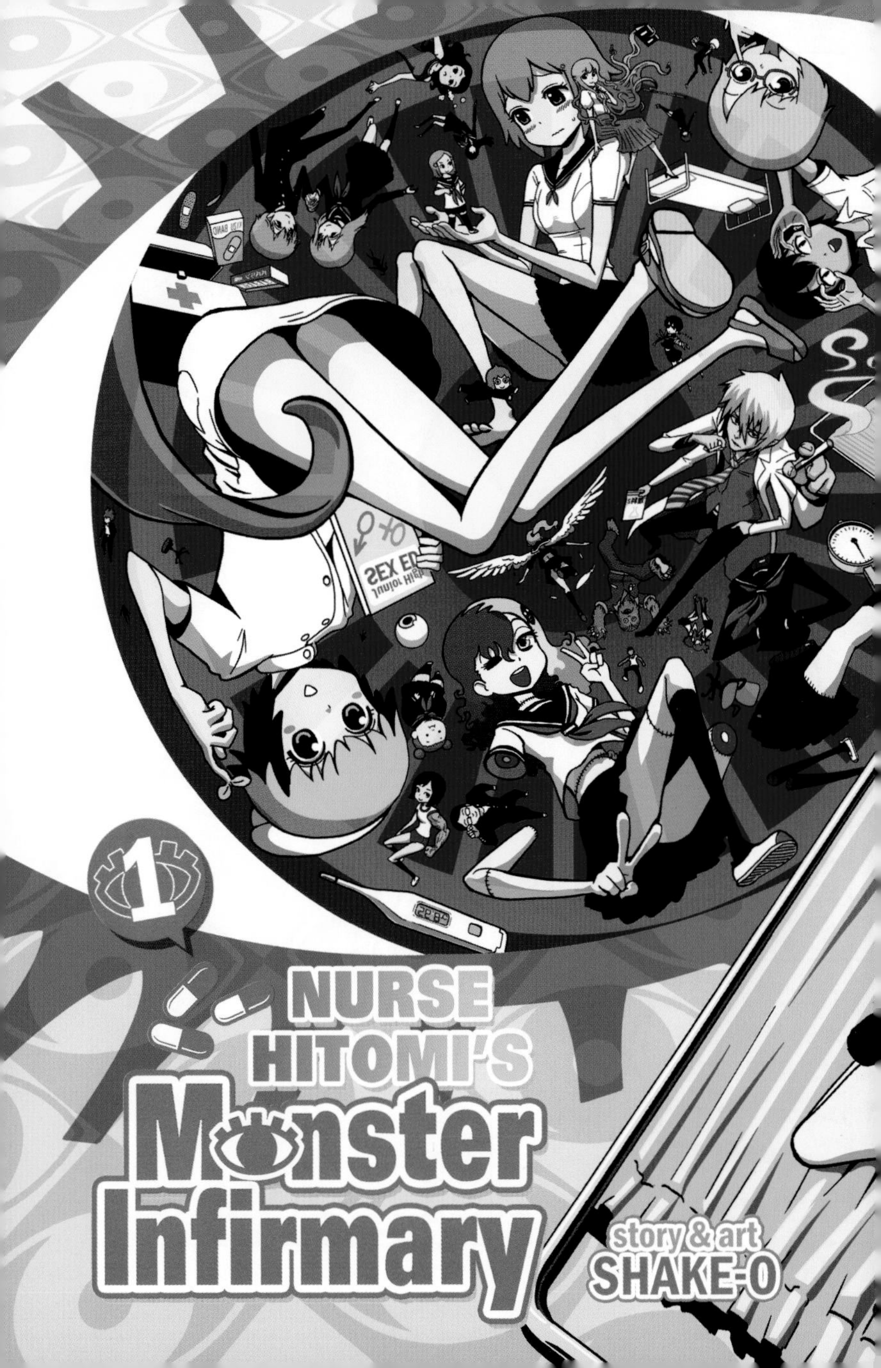
1
NURSE HITOMI'S Monster Infirmary
story & art
SHAKE-O

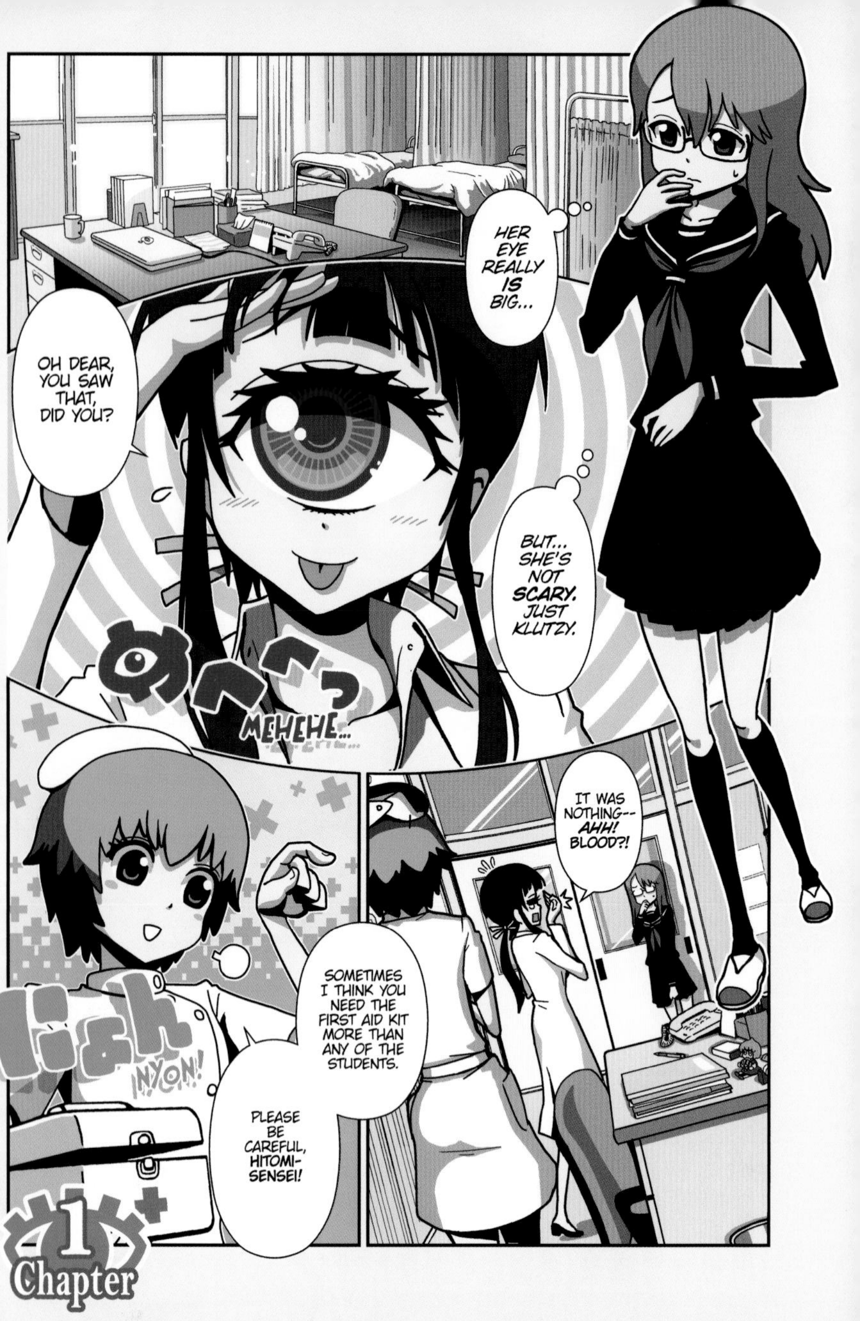
HER EYE REALLY IS BIG...
OH DEAR, YOU SAW THAT, DID YOU?
BUT... SHE'S NOT SCARY. JUST KLUTZY.
MEHEHE...
IT WAS NOTHING-- AHH! BLOOD?!
SOMETIMES I THINK YOU NEED THE FIRST AID KIT MORE THAN ANY OF THE STUDENTS.
PLEASE BE CAREFUL, HITOMI-SENSEI!
NYON!
Chapter 1

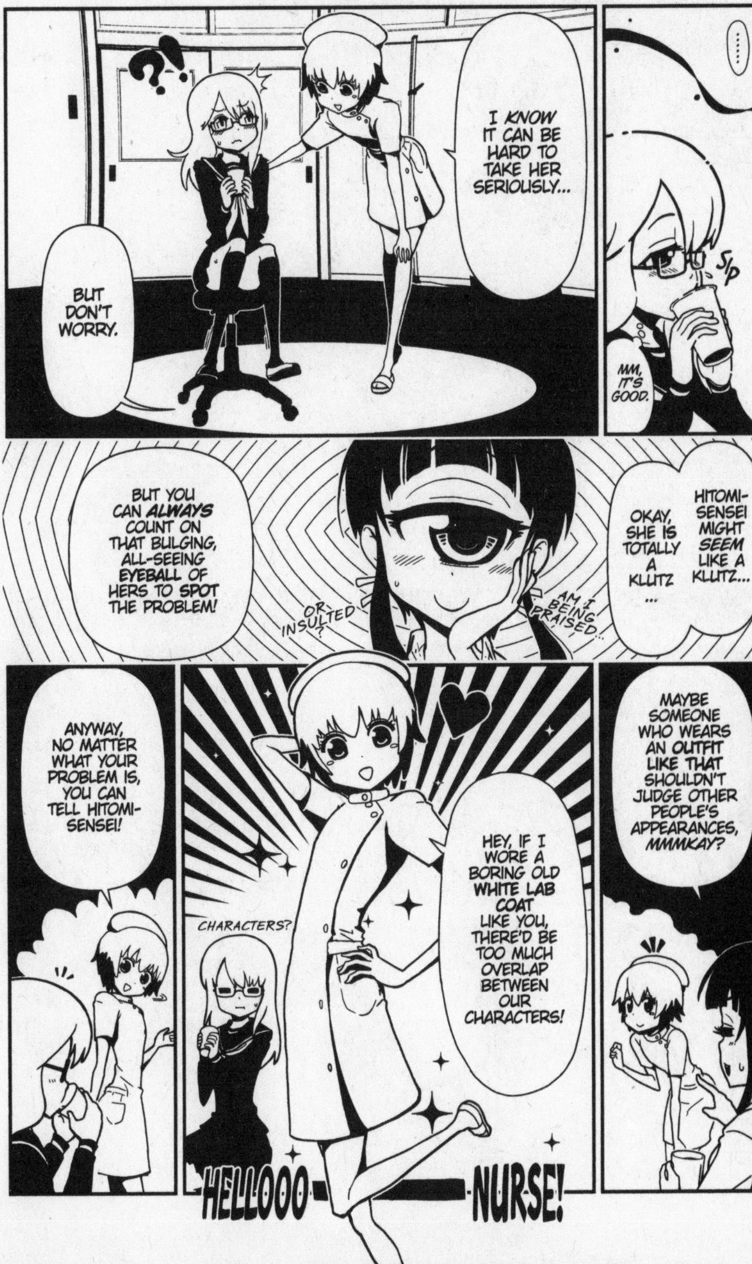
......
SIP
MM, IT'S GOOD.
I KNOW IT CAN BE HARD TO TAKE HER SERIOUSLY...
BUT DON'T WORRY.
HITOMI-SENSEI MIGHT SEEM LIKE A KLUTZ...
OKAY, SHE IS TOTALLY A KLUTZ ...
AM I BEING PRAISED...
OR INSULTED?
BUT YOU CAN ALWAYS COUNT ON THAT BULGING, ALL-SEEING EYEBALL OF HERS TO SPOT THE PROBLEM!
MAYBE SOMEONE WHO WEARS AN OUTFIT LIKE THAT SHOULDN'T JUDGE OTHER PEOPLE'S APPEARANCES, MMMKAY?
HEY, IF I WORE A BORING OLD WHITE LAB COAT LIKE YOU, THERE'D BE TOO MUCH OVERLAP BETWEEN OUR CHARACTERS!
CHARACTERS?
HELLOOO-NURSE!
ANYWAY, NO MATTER WHAT YOUR PROBLEM IS, YOU CAN TELL HITOMI-SENSEI!

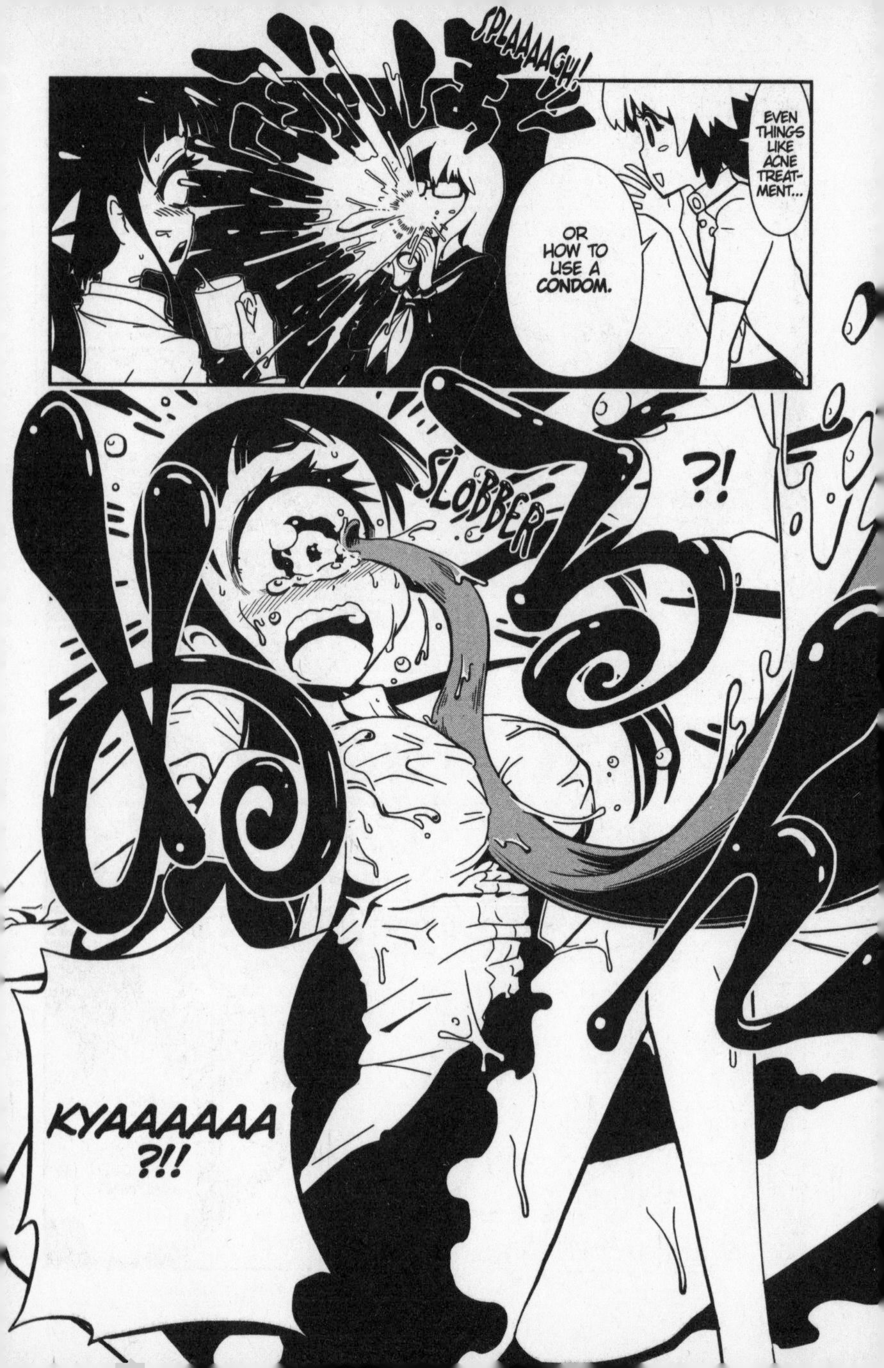
EVEN THINGS LIKE ACNE TREAT-MENT...
OR HOW TO USE A CONDOM.
SPLAAAAGH!
?!
SLOBBER
KYAAAAAA ?!!

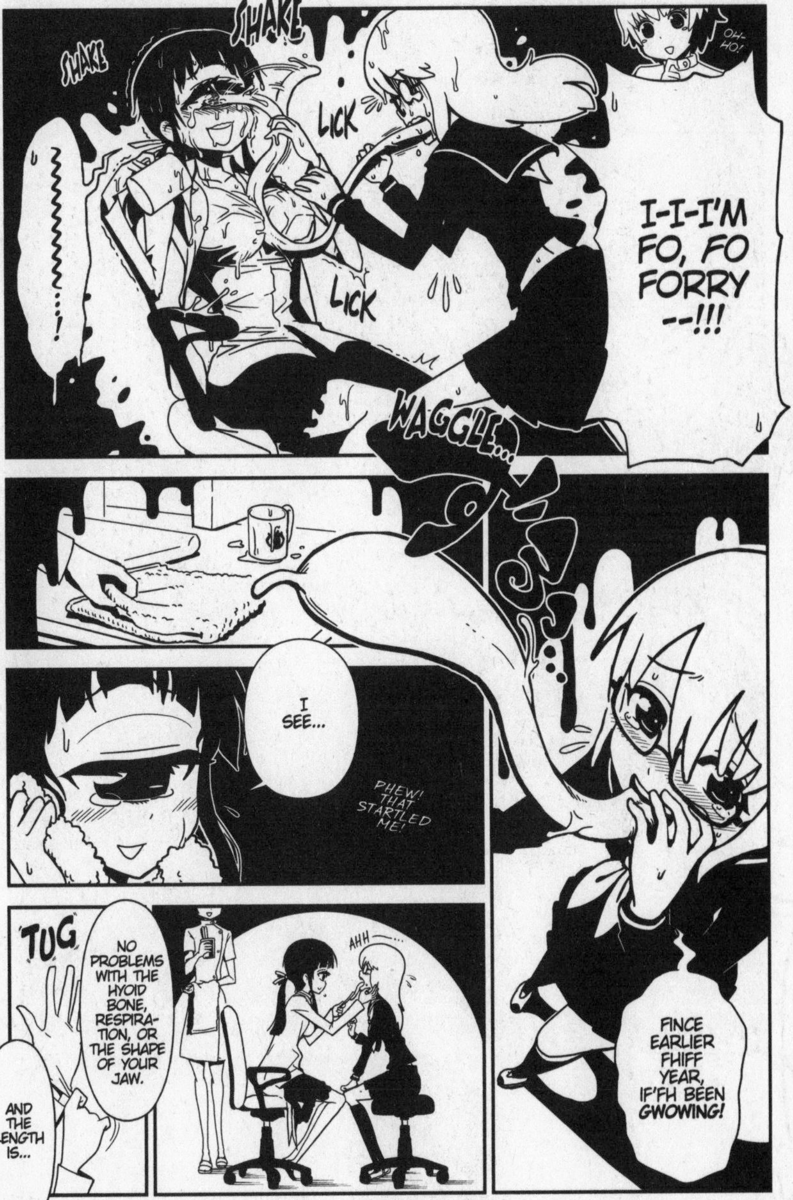
OH-HO!
I-I-I'M FO, FO FORRY --!!!
SHAKE
SHAKE
LICK
LICK
WAGGLE...
FINCE EARLIER FHIFF YEAR, IF'FH BEEN GWOWING!
I SEE...
PHEW! THAT STARTLED ME!
AHH—...
NO PROBLEMS WITH THE HYOID BONE, RESPIRATION, OR THE SHAPE OF YOUR JAW.
TUG
AND THE LENGTH IS...

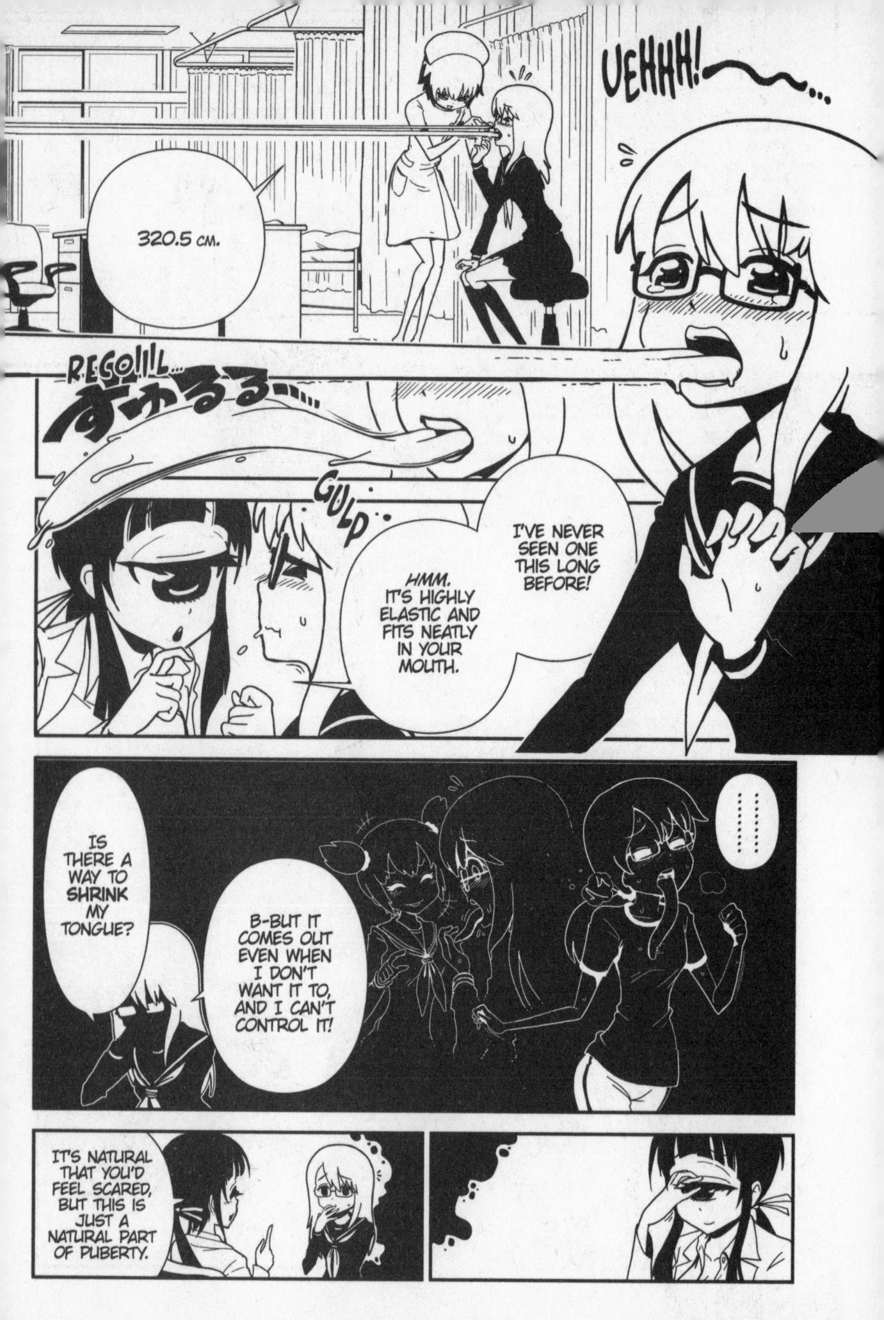
UEHHH!~~~...
320.5 CM.
RECOIL...
すゅるる…
GULP
I'VE NEVER SEEN ONE THIS LONG BEFORE!
HMM. IT'S HIGHLY ELASTIC AND FITS NEATLY IN YOUR MOUTH.
......
B-BUT IT COMES OUT EVEN WHEN I DON'T WANT IT TO, AND I CAN'T CONTROL IT!
IS THERE A WAY TO SHRINK MY TONGUE?
IT'S NATURAL THAT YOU'D FEEL SCARED, BUT THIS IS JUST A NATURAL PART OF PUBERTY.

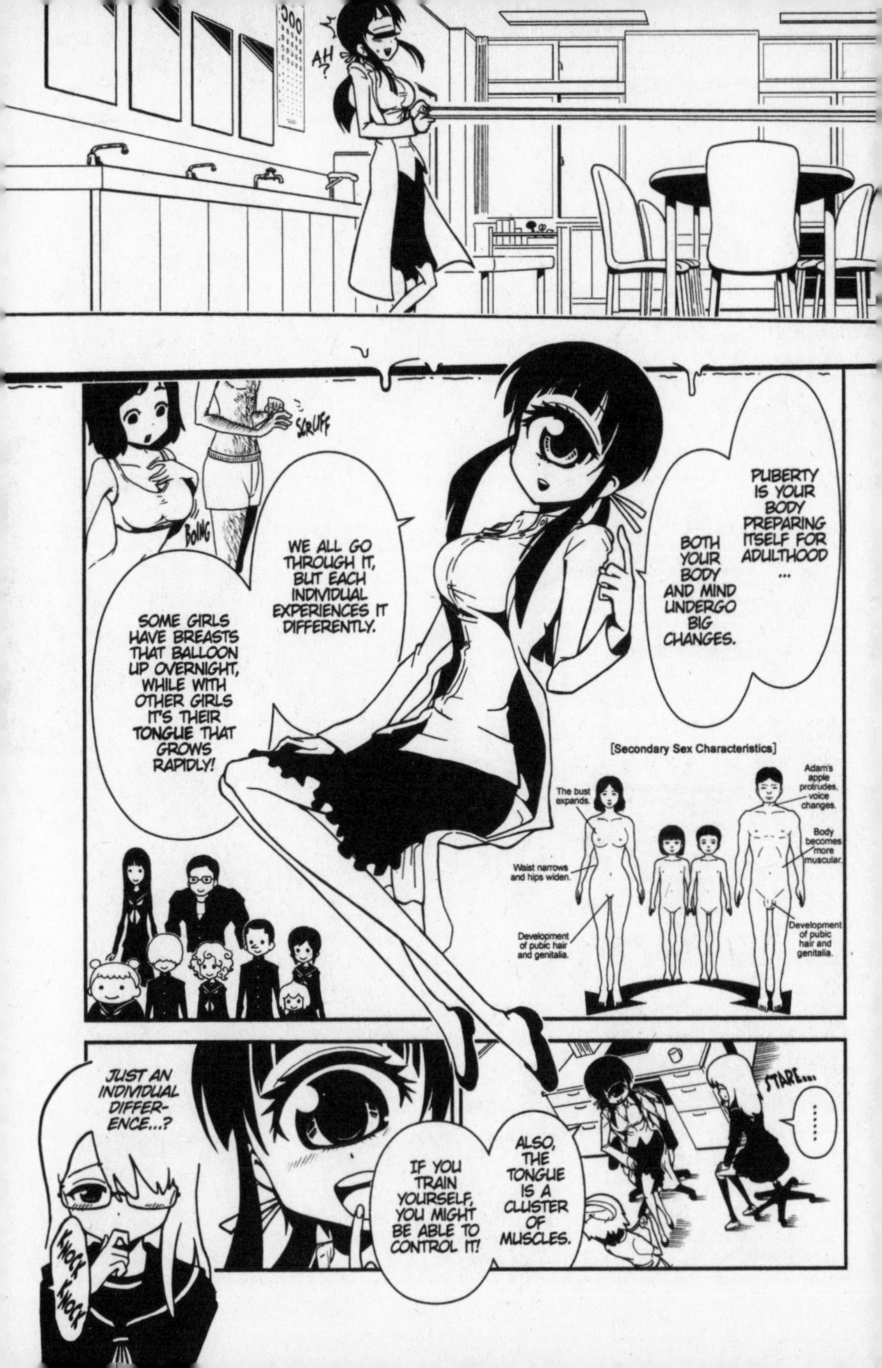
AH ?
PUBERTY IS YOUR BODY PREPARING ITSELF FOR ADULTHOOD ...
BOTH YOUR BODY AND MIND UNDERGO BIG CHANGES.
WE ALL GO THROUGH IT, BUT EACH INDIVIDUAL EXPERIENCES IT DIFFERENTLY.
[Secondary Sex Characteristics]
Adam's apple protrudes, voice changes.
Body becomes more muscular.
Development of pubic hair and genitalia.
The bust expands.
Waist narrows and hips widen.
Development of pubic hair and genitalia.
SCRUFF
BOING
SOME GIRLS HAVE BREASTS THAT BALLOON UP OVERNIGHT, WHILE WITH OTHER GIRLS IT'S THEIR TONGUE THAT GROWS RAPIDLY!
STARE...
......
ALSO, THE TONGUE IS A CLUSTER OF MUSCLES.
IF YOU TRAIN YOURSELF, YOU MIGHT BE ABLE TO CONTROL IT!
JUST AN INDIVIDUAL DIFFERENCE...?
KNOCK KNOCK

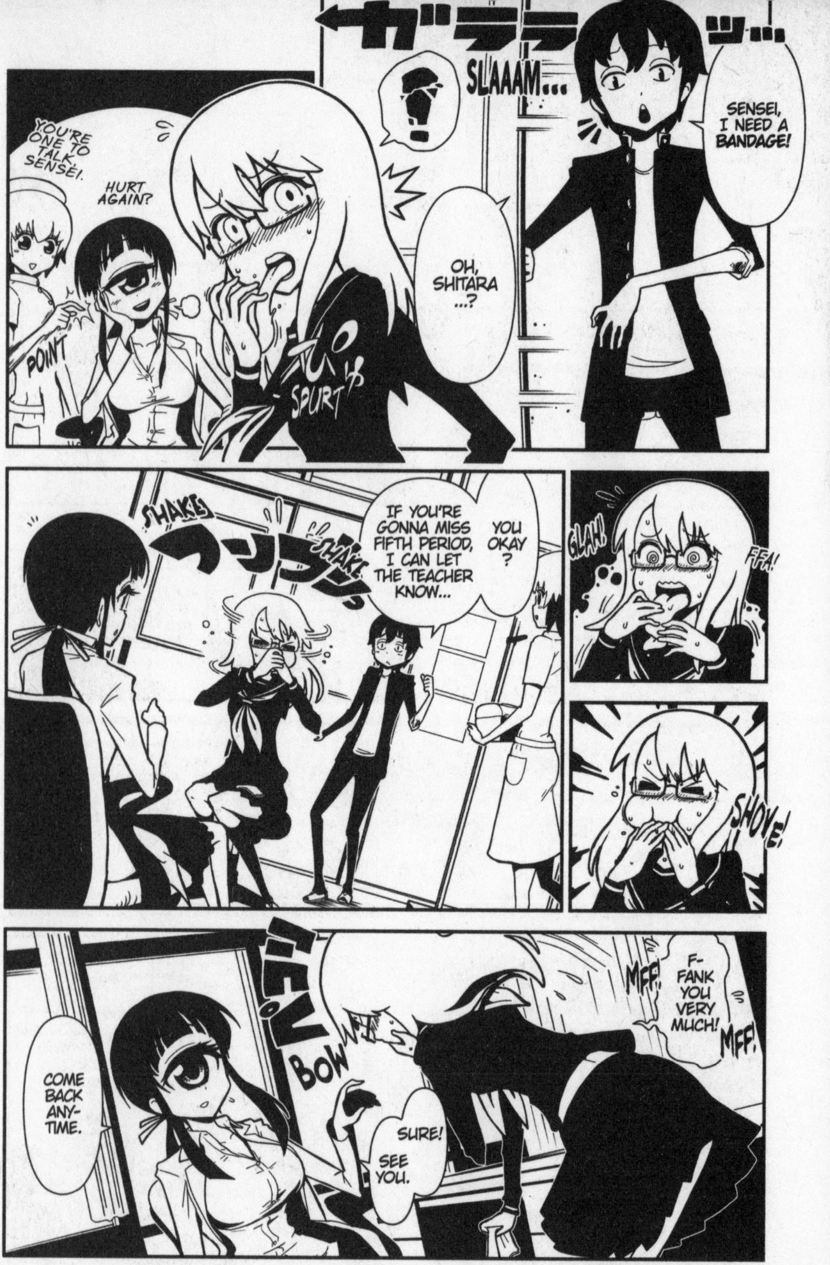
ガラララッ...
SLAAAM...
SENSEI, I NEED A BANDAGE!
!
OH, SHITARA ...?
SPURT
HURT AGAIN?
YOU'RE ONE TO TALK, SENSEI.
POINT
GLAH!
FFA!
SHOVE!
YOU OKAY?
IF YOU'RE GONNA MISS FIFTH PERIOD, I CAN LET THE TEACHER KNOW...
SHAKE
SHAKE
MFF
F-FANK YOU VERY MUCH!
MFF
BOW
SURE!
SEE YOU.
COME BACK ANY-TIME.

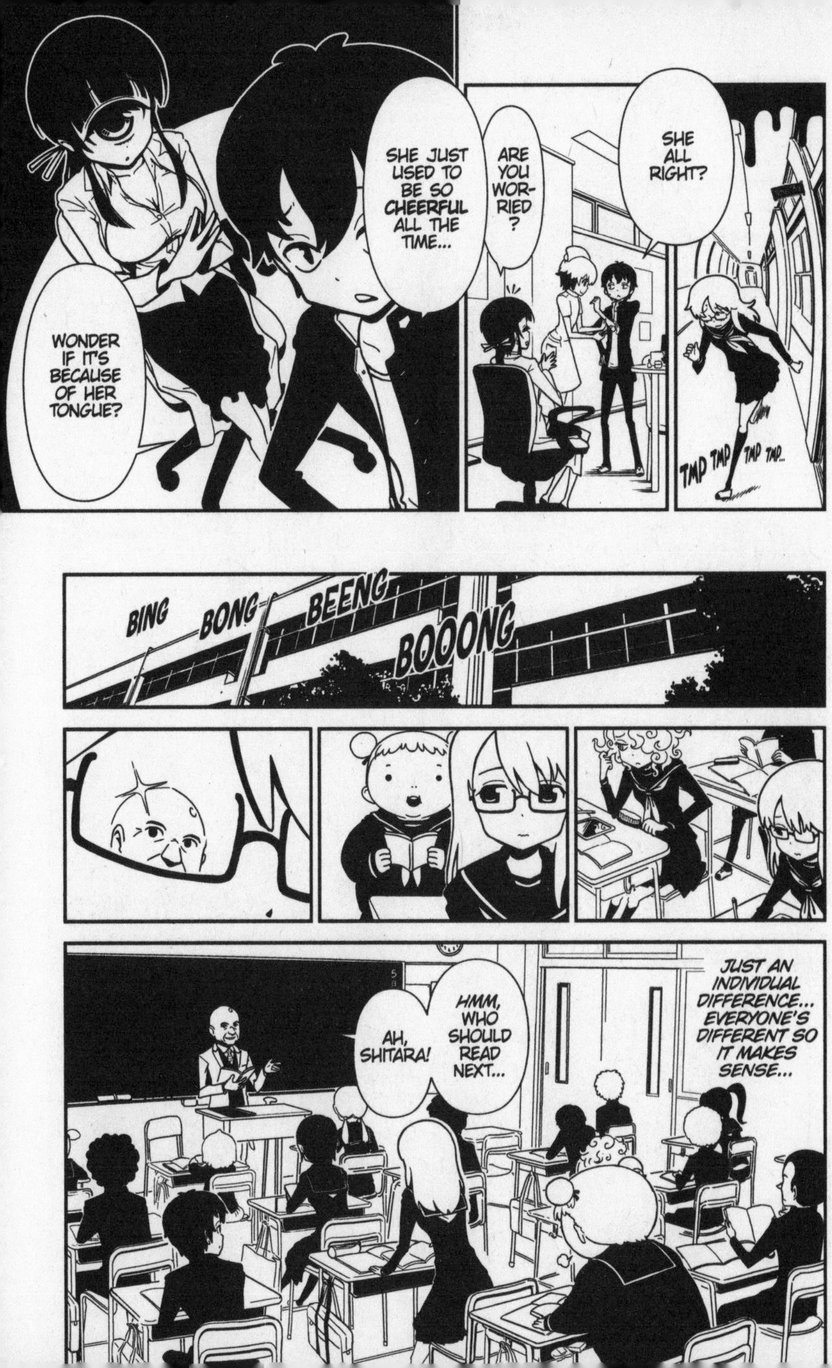
SHE ALL RIGHT?
TMP TMP TMP TMP...
ARE YOU WOR-RIED?
SHE JUST USED TO BE SO CHEERFUL ALL THE TIME...
WONDER IF IT'S BECAUSE OF HER TONGUE?
BING BONG BEENG BOOONG
JUST AN INDIVIDUAL DIFFERENCE... EVERYONE'S DIFFERENT SO IT MAKES SENSE...
HMM, WHO SHOULD READ NEXT...
AH, SHITARA!

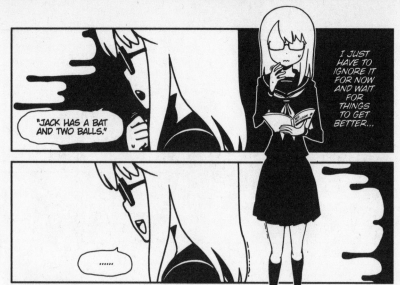

I JUST HAVE TO IGNORE IT FOR NOW AND WAIT FOR THINGS TO GET BETTER...
"JACK HAS A BAT AND TWO BALLS."
......
EVEN IF IT COMES OUT...
I JUST HAVE TO LIVE WITH IT.
DON'T HIDE YOUR FACE. WE CAN'T HEAR YOU!

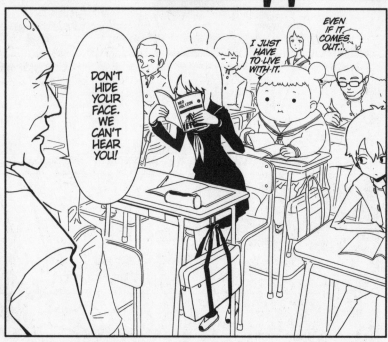

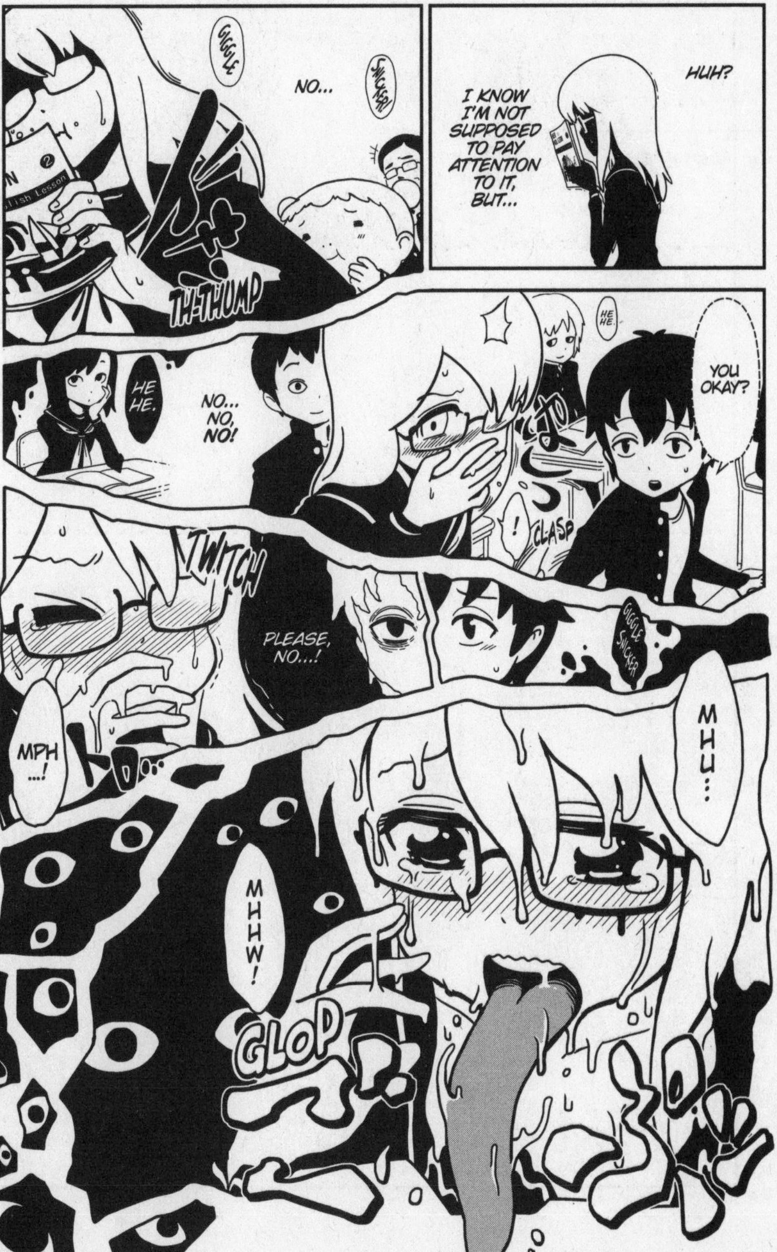
HUH?
I KNOW I'M NOT SUPPOSED TO PAY ATTENTION TO IT, BUT...
SNICKER!
NO...
GIGGLE
TH-THUMP
YOU OKAY?
HE HE.
CLASP
!
NO... NO, NO!
HE HE.
GIGGLE SNICKER
PLEASE, NO...!
TWITCH
MPH ...!
MHU...
MHHW!
GLOP

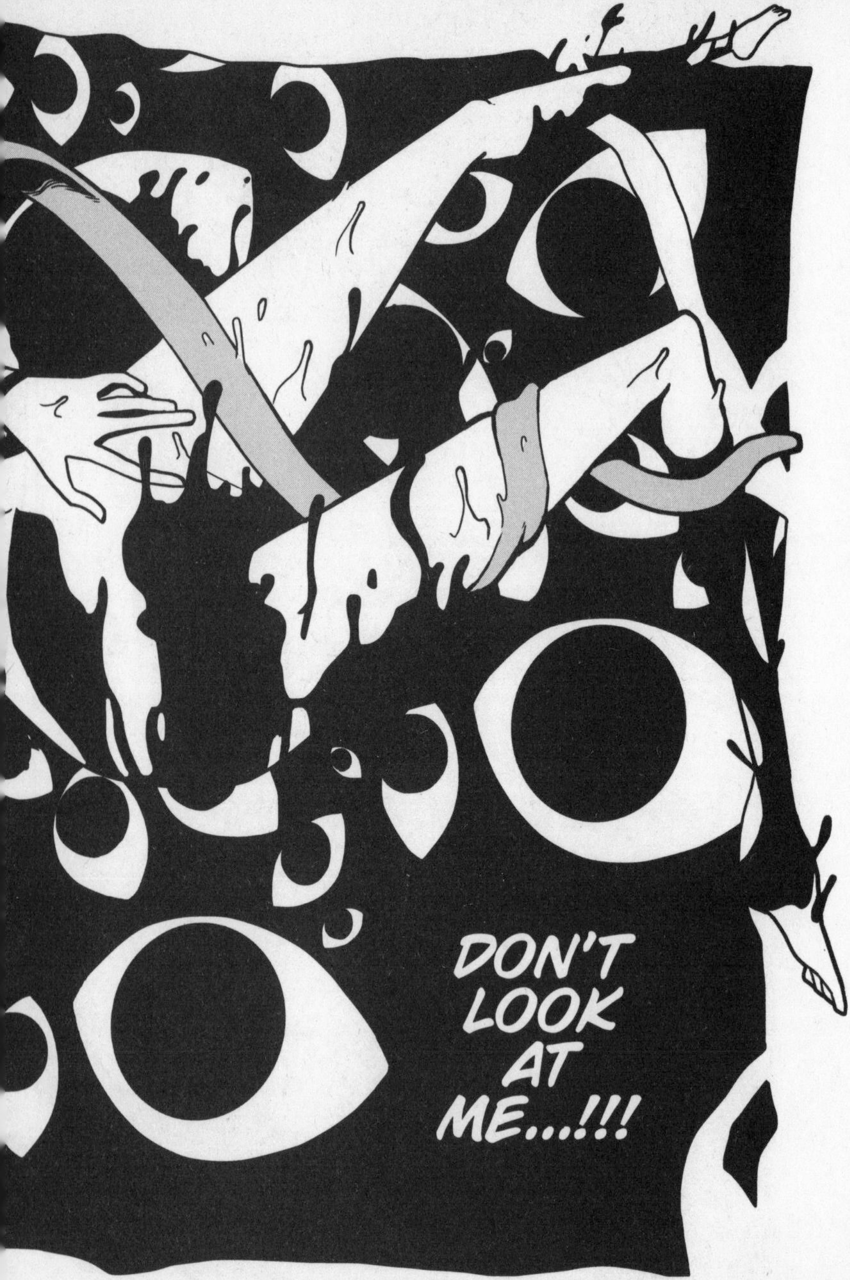
DON'T LOOK AT ME...!!!

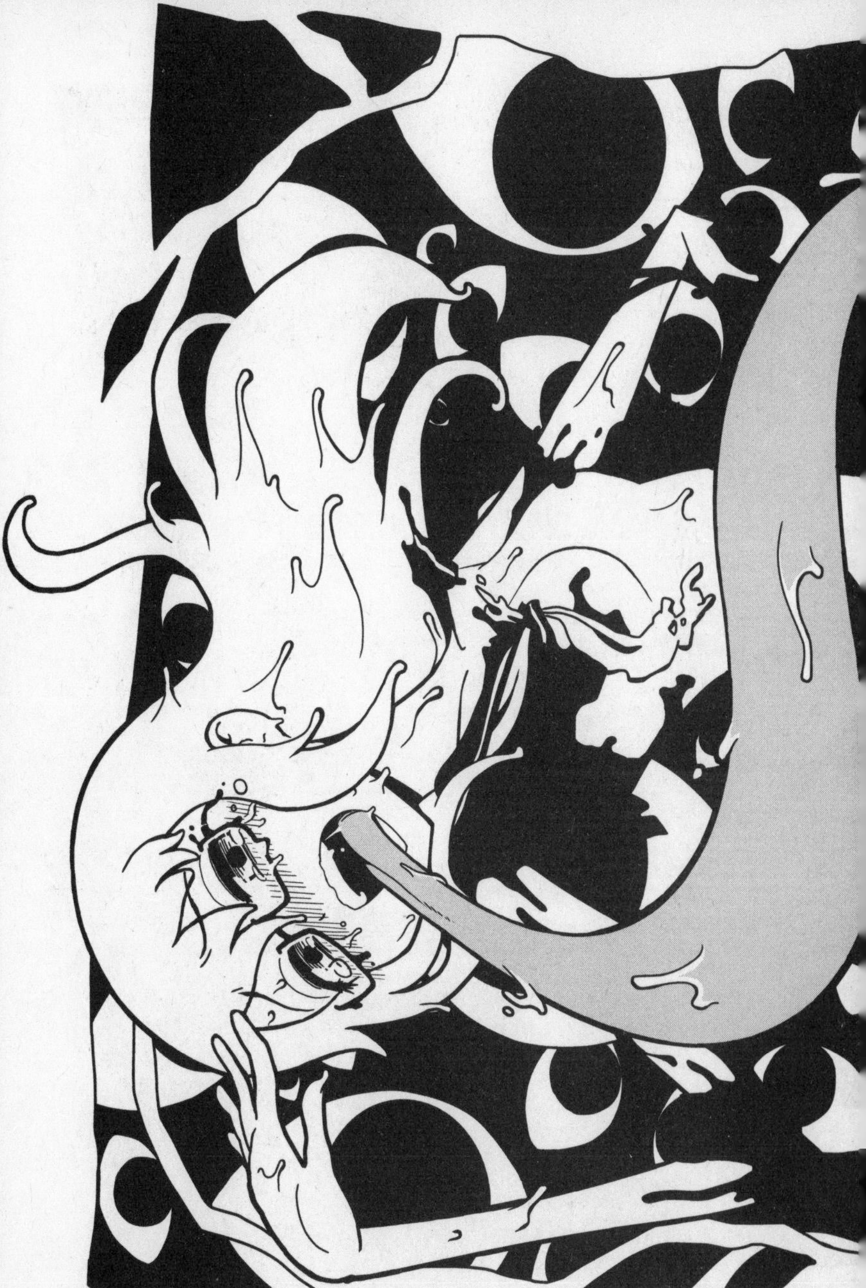

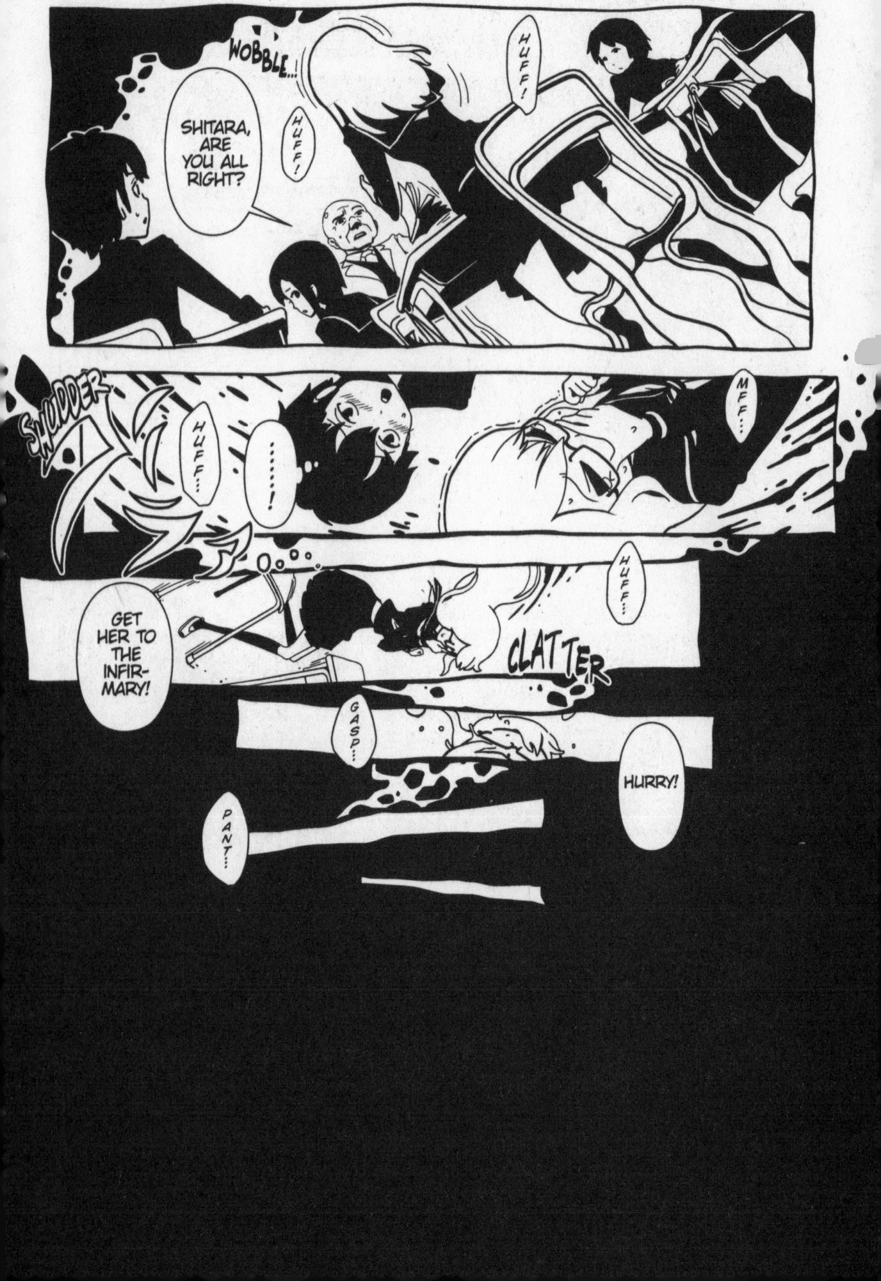
HUFF!
WOBBLE...!
HUFF!
SHITARA, ARE YOU ALL RIGHT?
MFF...
......!
HUFF...
SHUDDER
HUFF...
CLATTER
GET HER TO THE INFIRMARY!
HURRY!
GASP...
PANT...

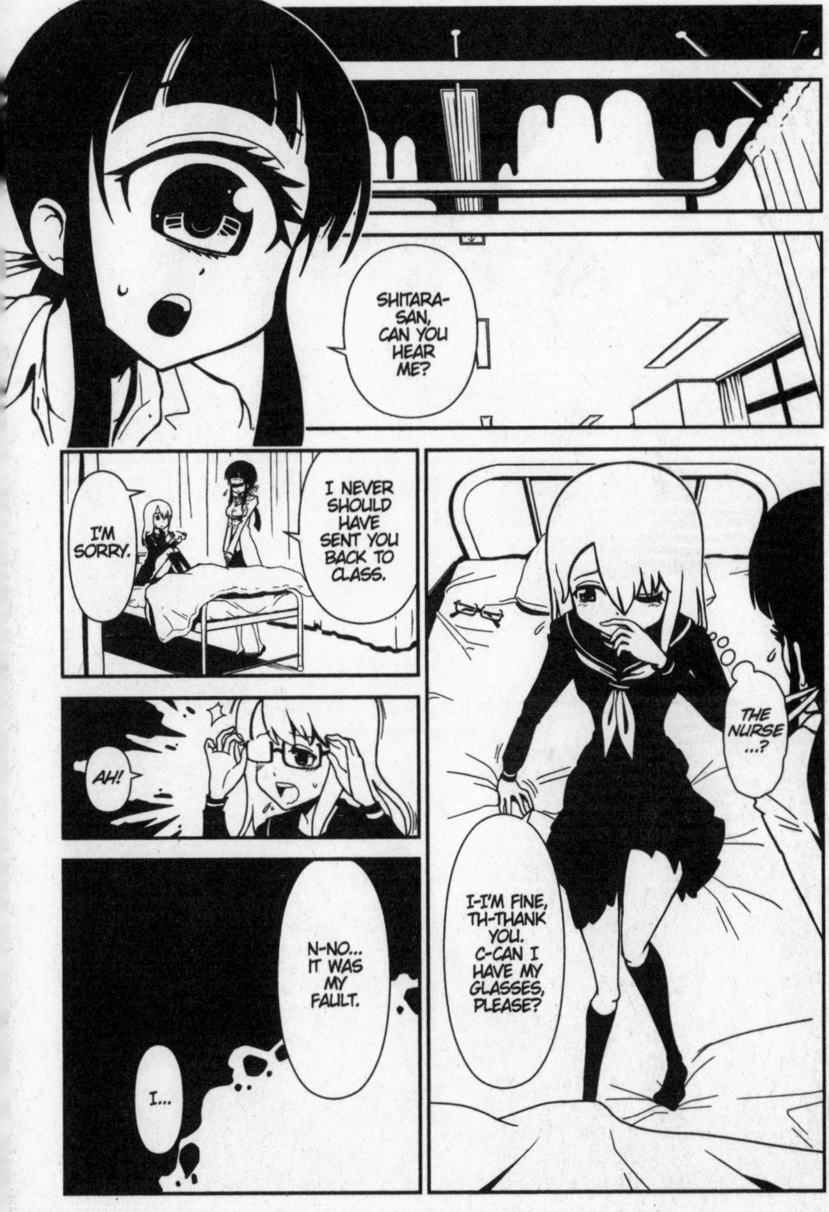
SHITARA-SAN, CAN YOU HEAR ME?
THE NURSE...?
I-I'M FINE, TH-THANK YOU. C-CAN I HAVE MY GLASSES, PLEASE?
I NEVER SHOULD HAVE SENT YOU BACK TO CLASS.
I'M SORRY.
AH!
N-NO... IT WAS MY FAULT.
I...

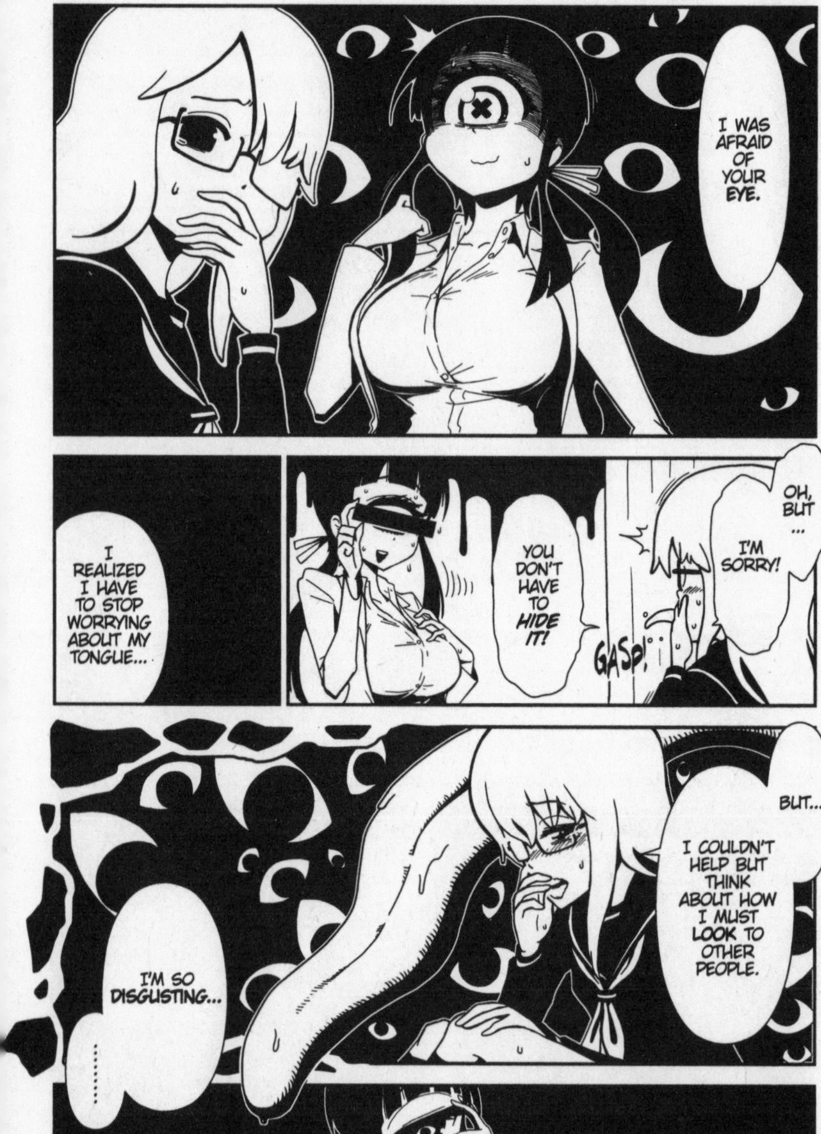
I WAS AFRAID OF YOUR EYE.
OH, BUT ...
I'M SORRY!
GASP!
YOU DON'T HAVE TO HIDE IT!
I REALIZED I HAVE TO STOP WORRYING ABOUT MY TONGUE...
BUT...
I COULDN'T HELP BUT THINK ABOUT HOW I MUST LOOK TO OTHER PEOPLE.
I'M SO DISGUSTING...
......

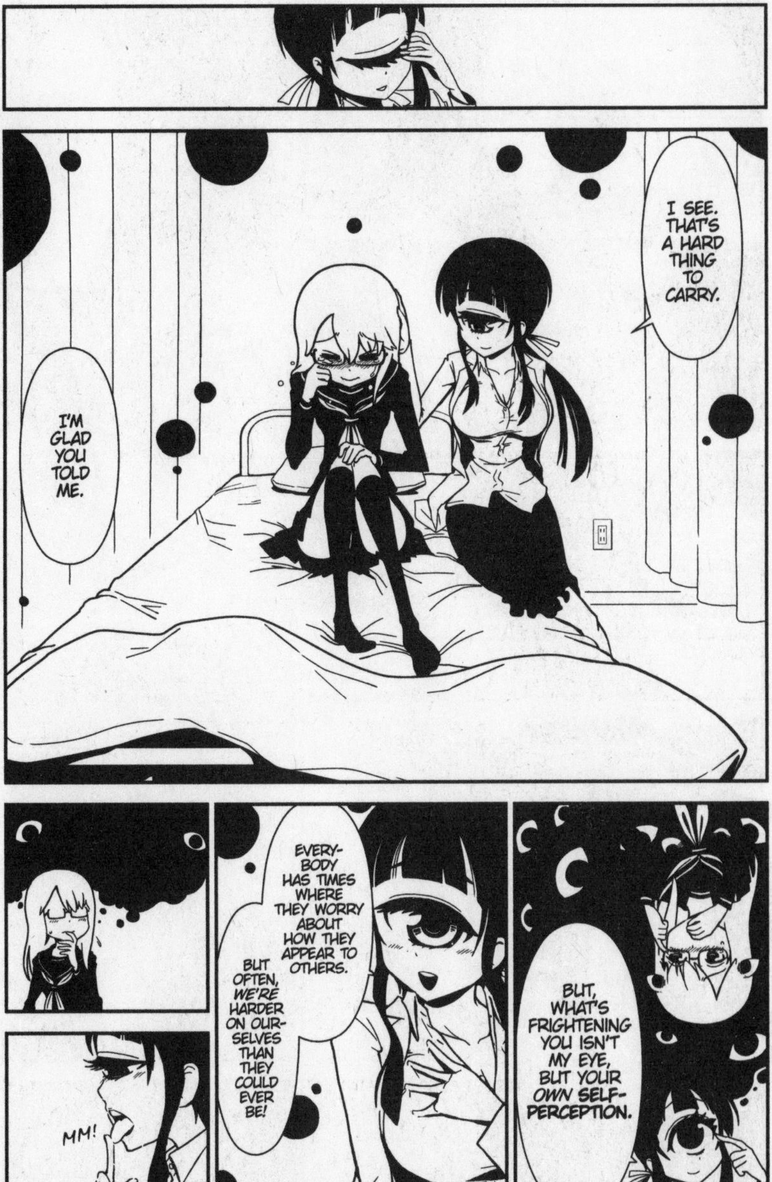
I SEE. THAT'S A HARD THING TO CARRY.
I'M GLAD YOU TOLD ME.
BUT, WHAT'S FRIGHTENING YOU ISN'T MY EYE, BUT YOUR *OWN* SELF-PERCEPTION.
EVERY-BODY HAS TIMES WHERE THEY WORRY ABOUT HOW THEY APPEAR TO OTHERS.
BUT OFTEN, *WE'RE* HARDER ON OUR-SELVES THAN THEY COULD EVER BE!
MM!

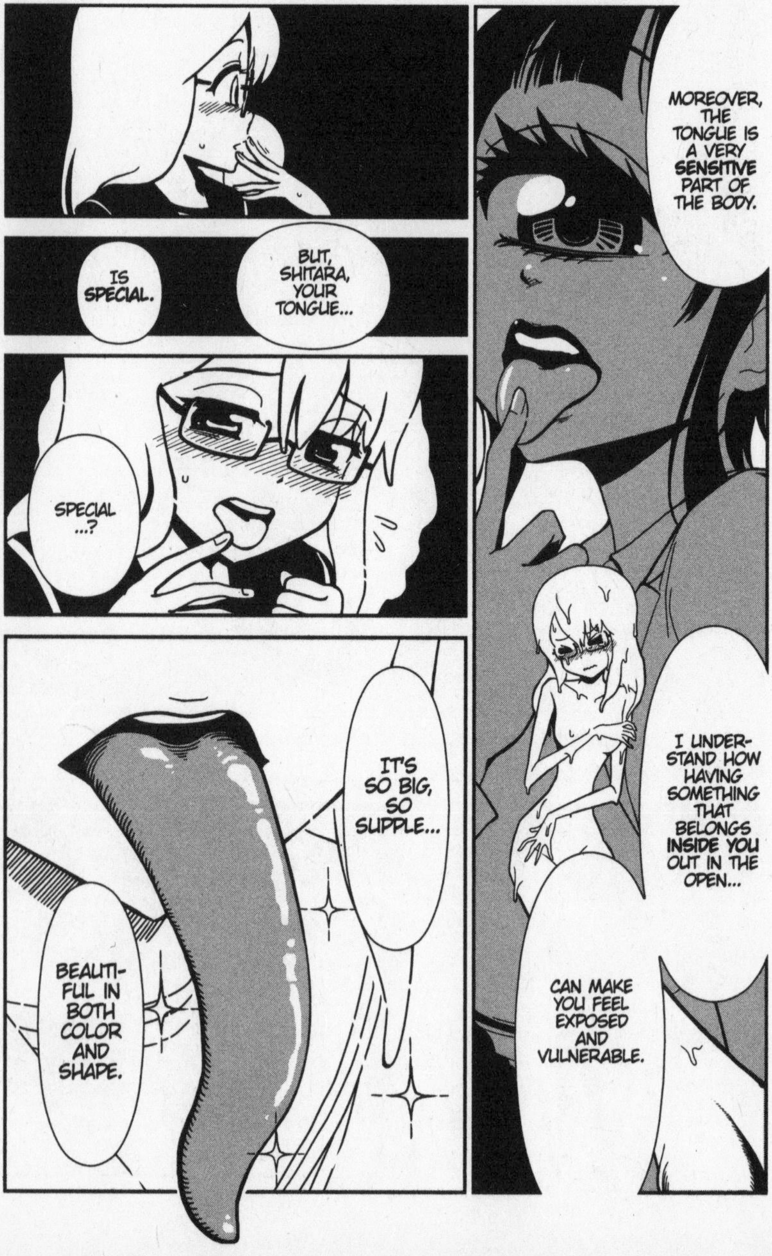
MOREOVER, THE TONGUE IS A VERY SENSITIVE PART OF THE BODY.
I UNDER-STAND HOW HAVING SOMETHING THAT BELONGS INSIDE YOU OUT IN THE OPEN...
CAN MAKE YOU FEEL EXPOSED AND VULNERABLE.
BUT, SHITARA, YOUR TONGUE...
IS SPECIAL.
SPECIAL ...?
IT'S SO BIG, SO SUPPLE...
BEAUTI-FUL IN BOTH COLOR AND SHAPE.

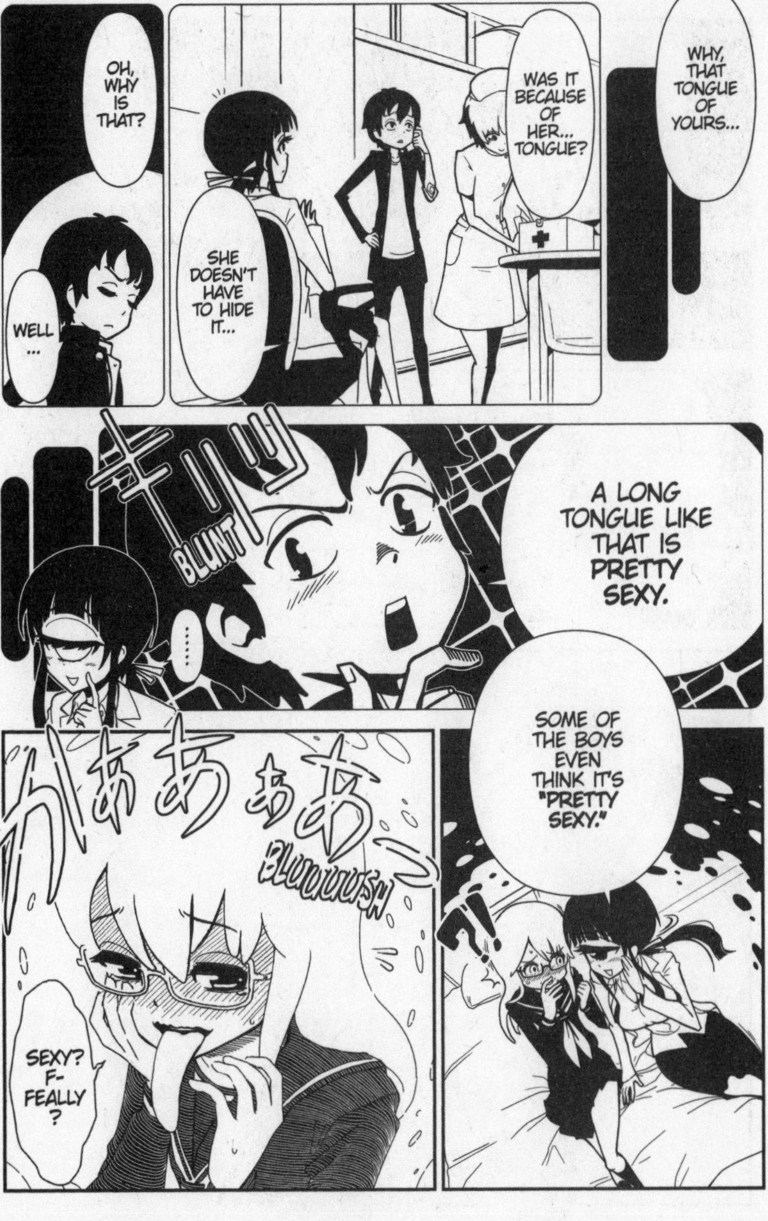

WHY, THAT TONGUE OF YOURS...
WAS IT BECAUSE OF HER... TONGUE?
SHE DOESN'T HAVE TO HIDE IT...
OH, WHY IS THAT?
WELL ...
A LONG TONGUE LIKE THAT IS PRETTY SEXY.
BLUNT
......
SOME OF THE BOYS EVEN THINK IT'S "PRETTY SEXY."
BLUUUUUSH
SEXY? F-FEALLY?

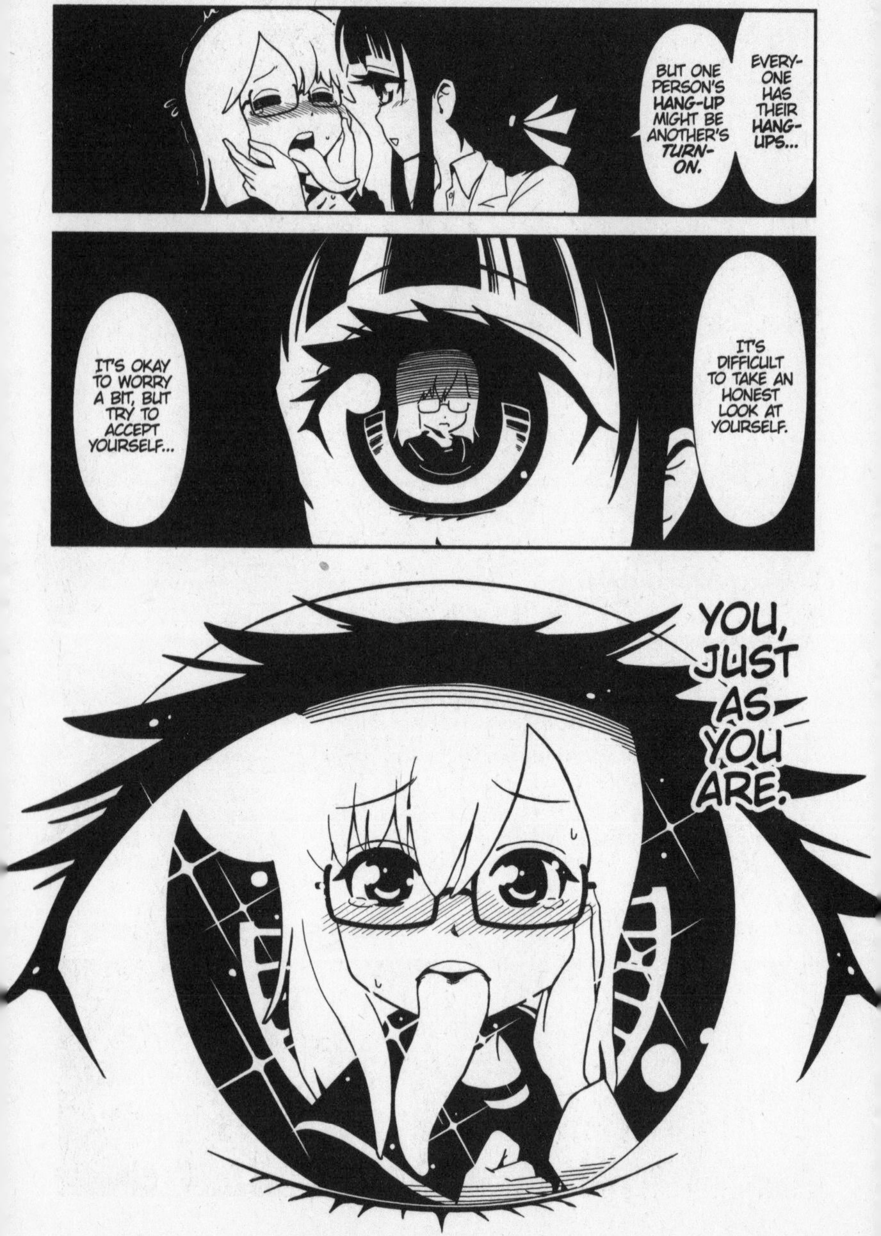
EVERY-ONE HAS THEIR HANG-UPS...
BUT ONE PERSON'S HANG-UP MIGHT BE ANOTHER'S *TURN-ON.*
IT'S DIFFICULT TO TAKE AN HONEST LOOK AT YOURSELF.
IT'S OKAY TO WORRY A BIT, BUT TRY TO ACCEPT YOURSELF...
YOU, JUST AS YOU ARE.

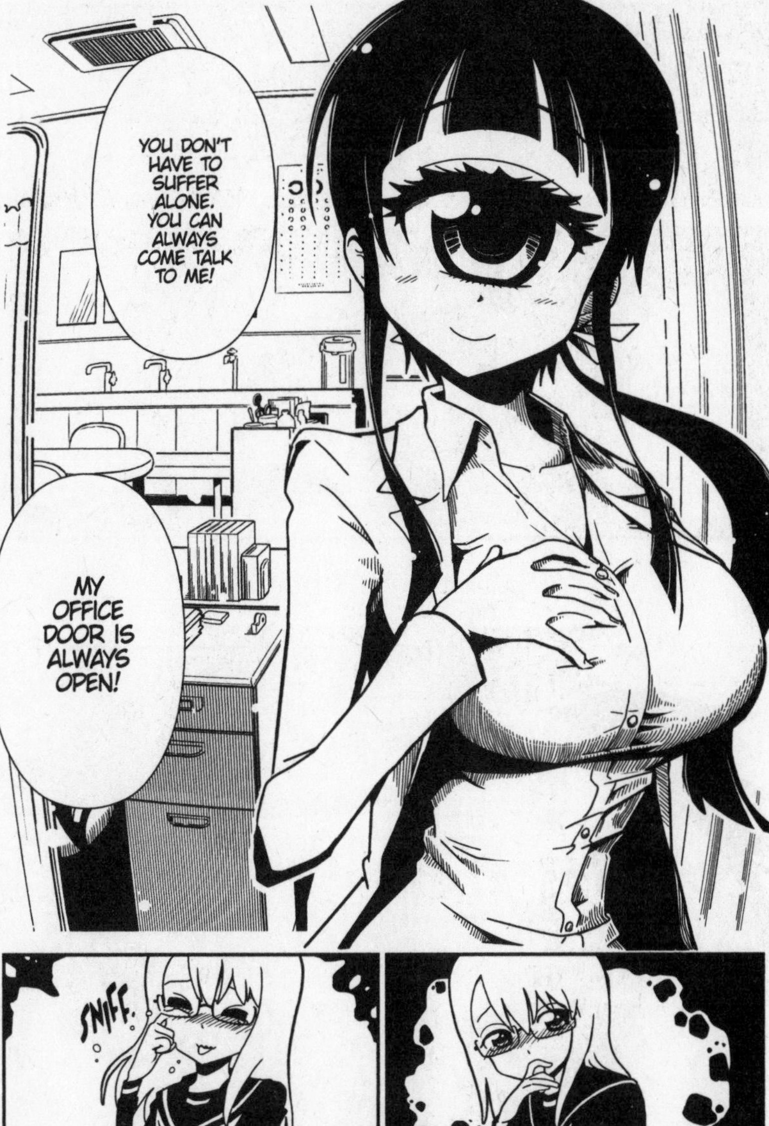
YOU DON'T HAVE TO SUFFER ALONE. YOU CAN ALWAYS COME TALK TO ME!
MY OFFICE DOOR IS ALWAYS OPEN!
SNIFF.

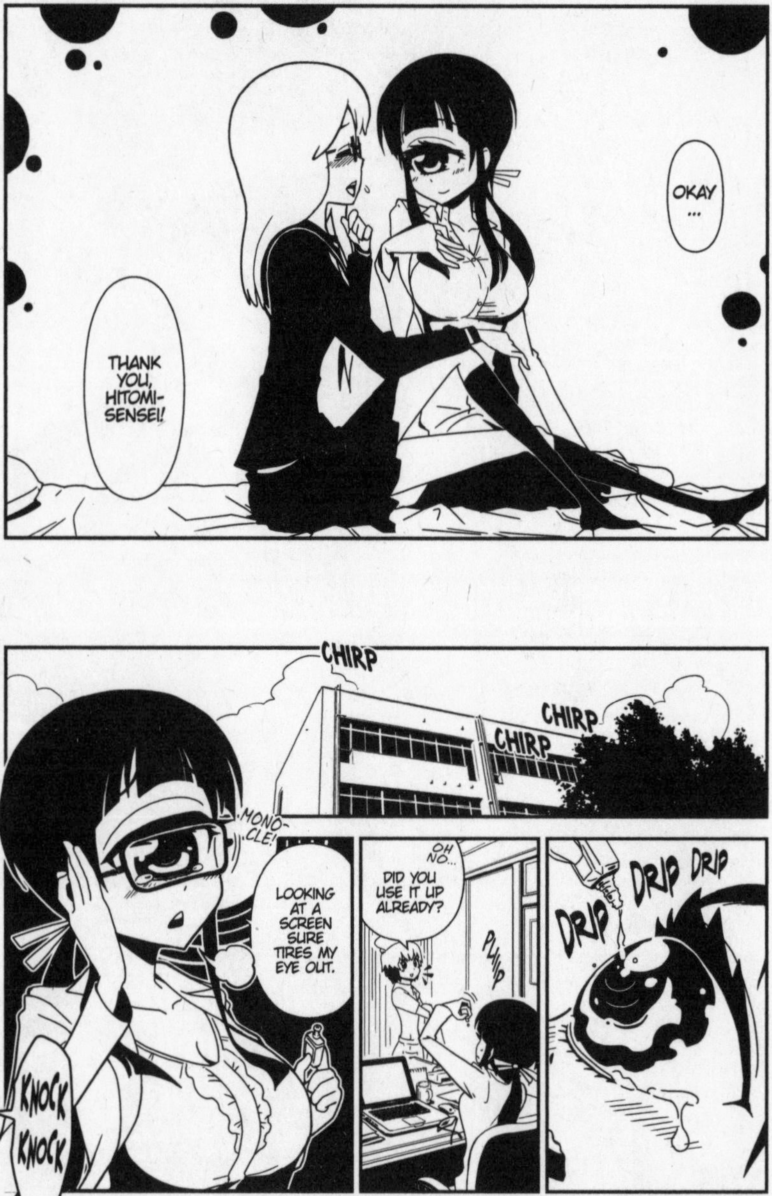
OKAY ...
THANK YOU, HITOMI-SENSEI!
CHIRP
CHIRP
CHIRP
DRIP DRIP DRIP
PLIP
OH NO...
DID YOU USE IT UP ALREADY?
MONO-CLE!
LOOKING AT A SCREEN SURE TIRES MY EYE OUT.
KNOCK KNOCK

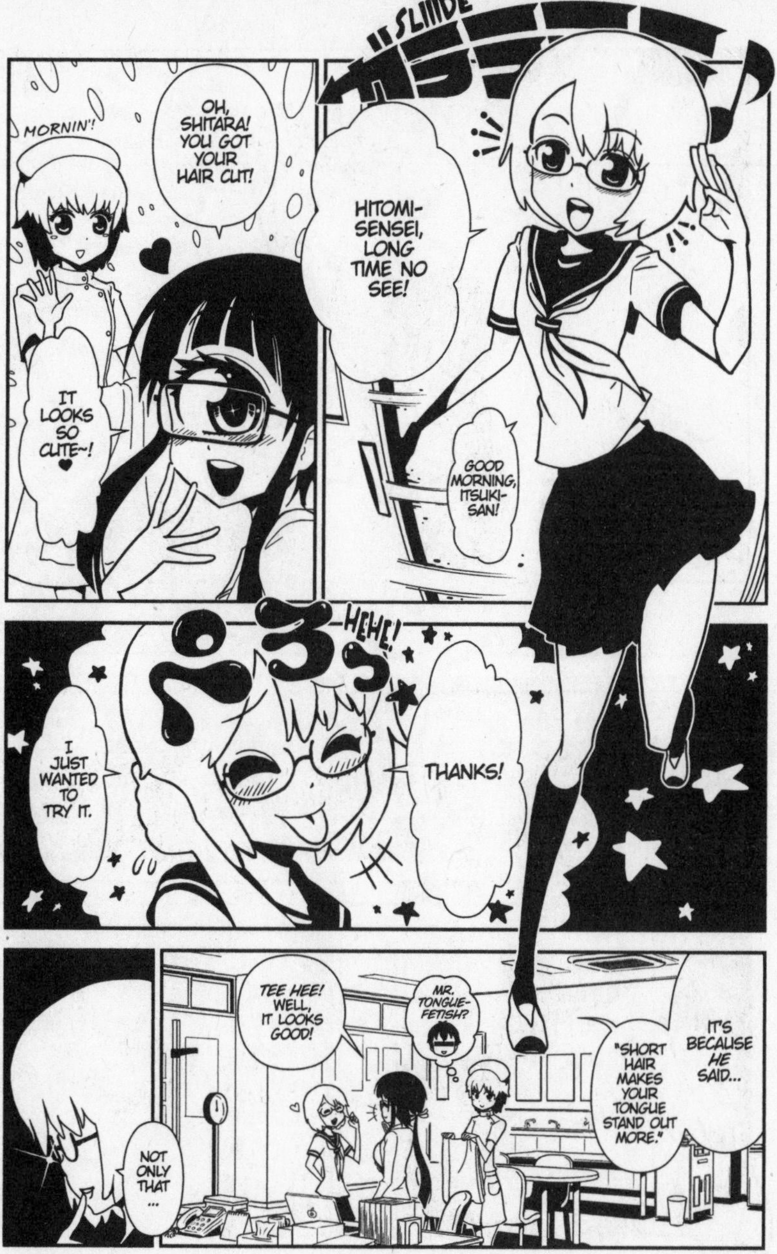
SLIIIDE
HITOMI-SENSEI, LONG TIME NO SEE!
GOOD MORNING, ITSUKI-SAN!
OH, SHITARA! YOU GOT YOUR HAIR CUT!
MORNIN'!
IT LOOKS SO CUTE~! ♥
HEHE!
THANKS!
I JUST WANTED TO TRY IT.
IT'S BECAUSE HE SAID...
"SHORT HAIR MAKES YOUR TONGUE STAND OUT MORE."
MR. TONGUE-FETISH?
TEE HEE! WELL, IT LOOKS GOOD!
NOT ONLY THAT ...

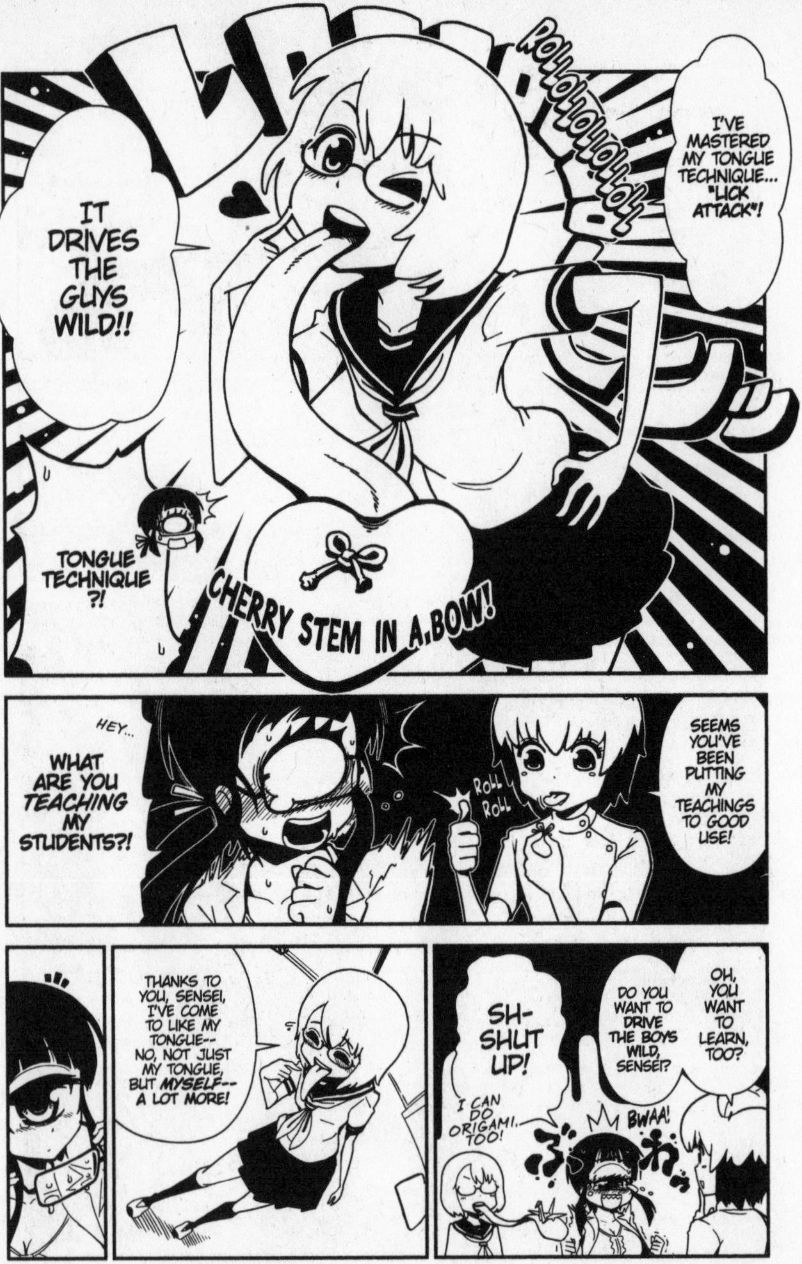
I'VE MASTERED MY TONGUE TECHNIQUE... "LICK ATTACK"!
IT DRIVES THE GUYS WILD!!
CHERRY STEM IN A.BOW!
TONGUE TECHNIQUE ?!
SEEMS YOU'VE BEEN PUTTING MY TEACHINGS TO GOOD USE!
ROLL ROLL
HEY...
WHAT ARE YOU TEACHING MY STUDENTS?!
OH, YOU WANT TO LEARN, TOO?
DO YOU WANT TO DRIVE THE BOYS WILD, SENSEI?
SH- SHUT UP!
BWAA!
I CAN DO ORIGAMI, TOO!
THANKS TO YOU, SENSEI, I'VE COME TO LIKE MY TONGUE-- NO, NOT JUST MY TONGUE, BUT MYSELF-- A LOT MORE!

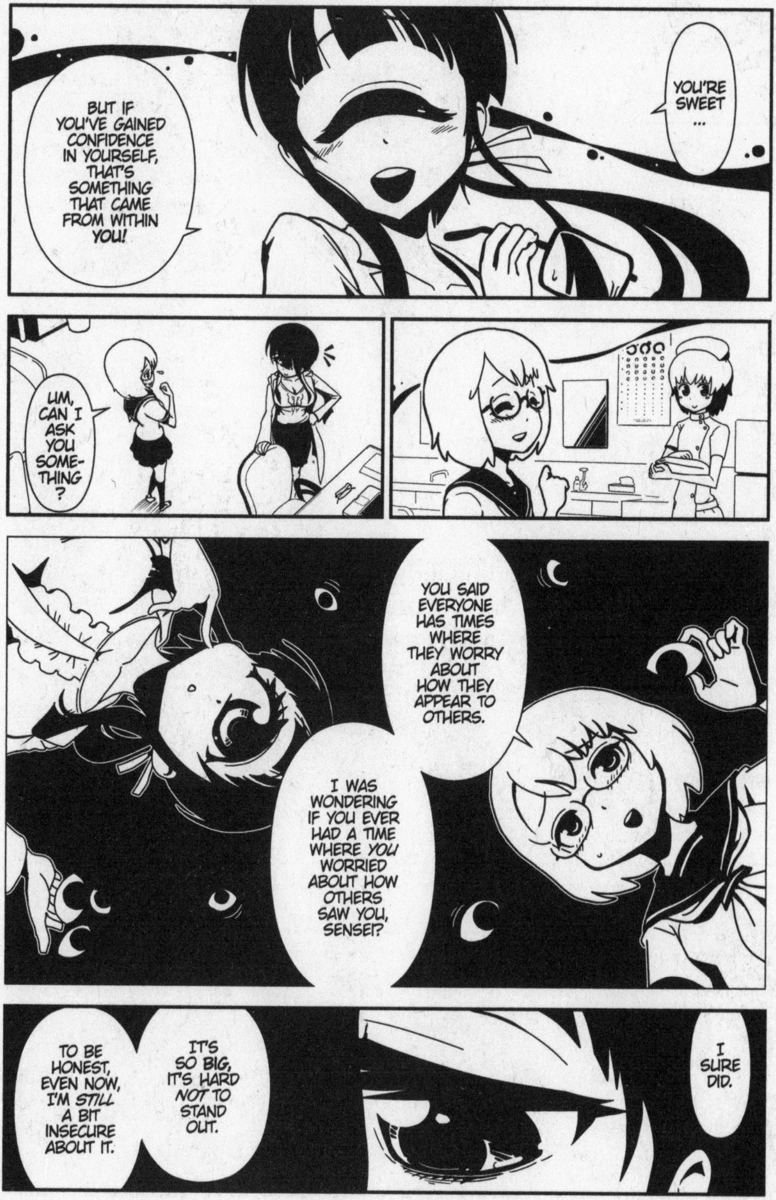
YOU'RE SWEET ...
BUT IF YOU'VE GAINED CONFIDENCE IN YOURSELF, THAT'S SOMETHING THAT CAME FROM WITHIN *YOU!*
UM, CAN I ASK YOU SOME-THING?
YOU SAID EVERYONE HAS TIMES WHERE THEY WORRY ABOUT HOW THEY APPEAR TO OTHERS.
I WAS WONDERING IF YOU EVER HAD A TIME WHERE *YOU* WORRIED ABOUT HOW OTHERS SAW YOU, SENSEI?
I SURE DID.
IT'S SO BIG, IT'S HARD *NOT* TO STAND OUT.
TO BE HONEST, EVEN NOW, I'M *STILL* A BIT INSECURE ABOUT IT.

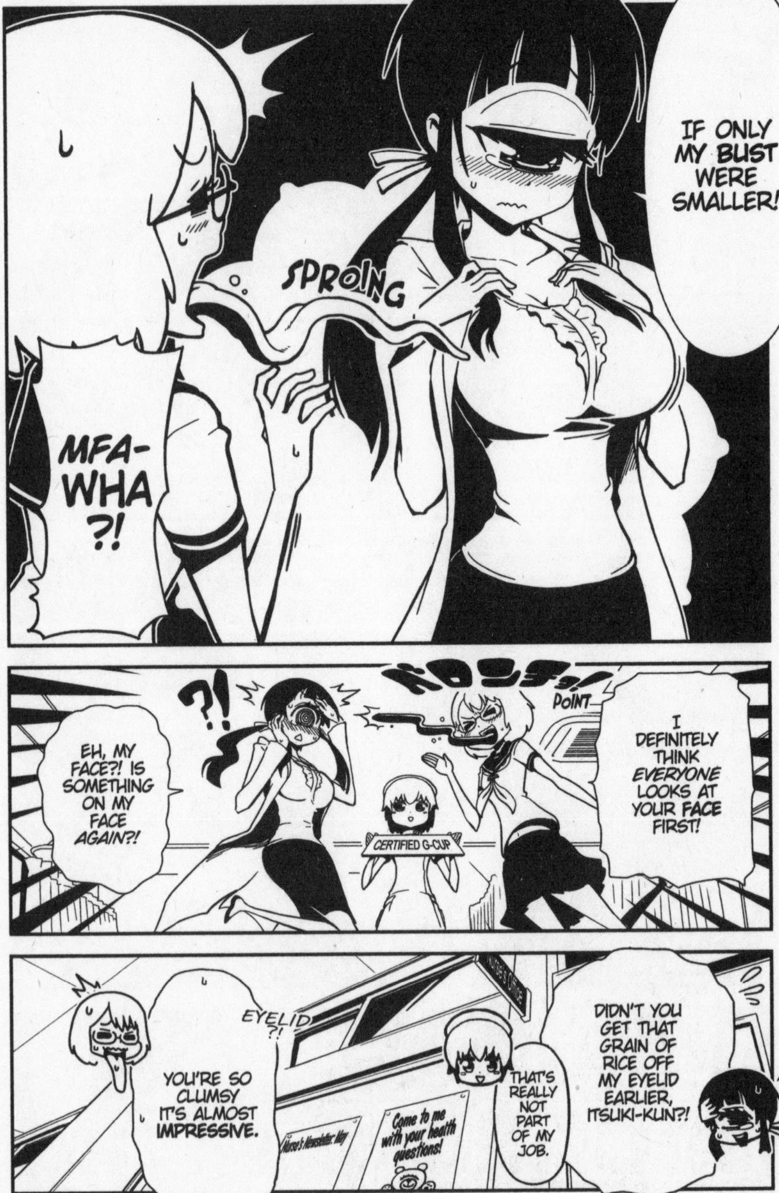
IF ONLY MY BUST WERE SMALLER!
SPROING
MFA-WHA?!
I DEFINITELY THINK EVERYONE LOOKS AT YOUR FACE FIRST!
POINT
?!
EH, MY FACE?! IS SOMETHING ON MY FACE AGAIN?!
CERTIFIED G-CUP
DIDN'T YOU GET THAT GRAIN OF RICE OFF MY EYELID EARLIER, ITSUKI-KUN?!
THAT'S REALLY NOT PART OF MY JOB.
Come to me with your health questions!
Nurse's Newsletter: May
EYELID?!
YOU'RE SO CLUMSY IT'S ALMOST IMPRESSIVE.

NURSE HITOMI'S Monster Infirmary

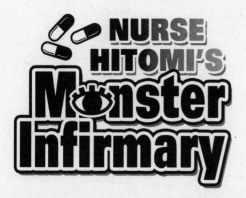

Student Health Record

May 201X

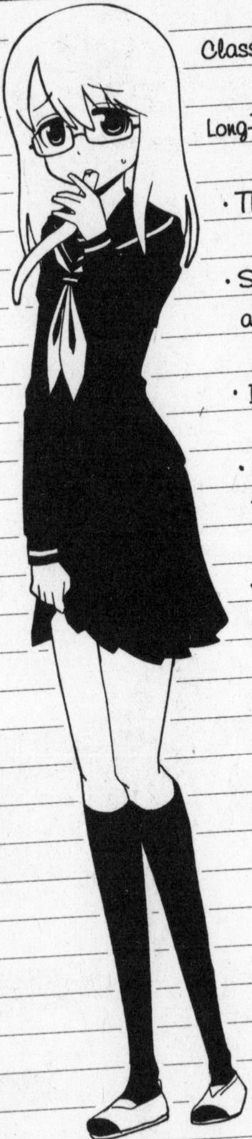

Class 2-A Shitara Nobuko

Long-Tongued Girl

- The length of her tongue was approximately 320 cm.
- Shitara-san's tongue is a long cluster of muscles with a formidable elasticity.
- It has a delicate sensitivity and is vervy agile.
- Used to be very cheerful and relatively talkative. Does not like hot foods.
- July Update: Shitara-san cut her hair and has gained a reputation for being very cute. Everyone seems to like her better now, except for the art teacher Shakeo-sensei who grumbles about her chatting in class.

She also changed her glasses.★

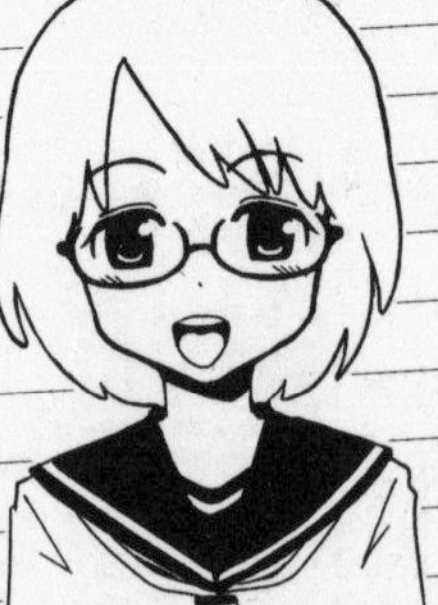

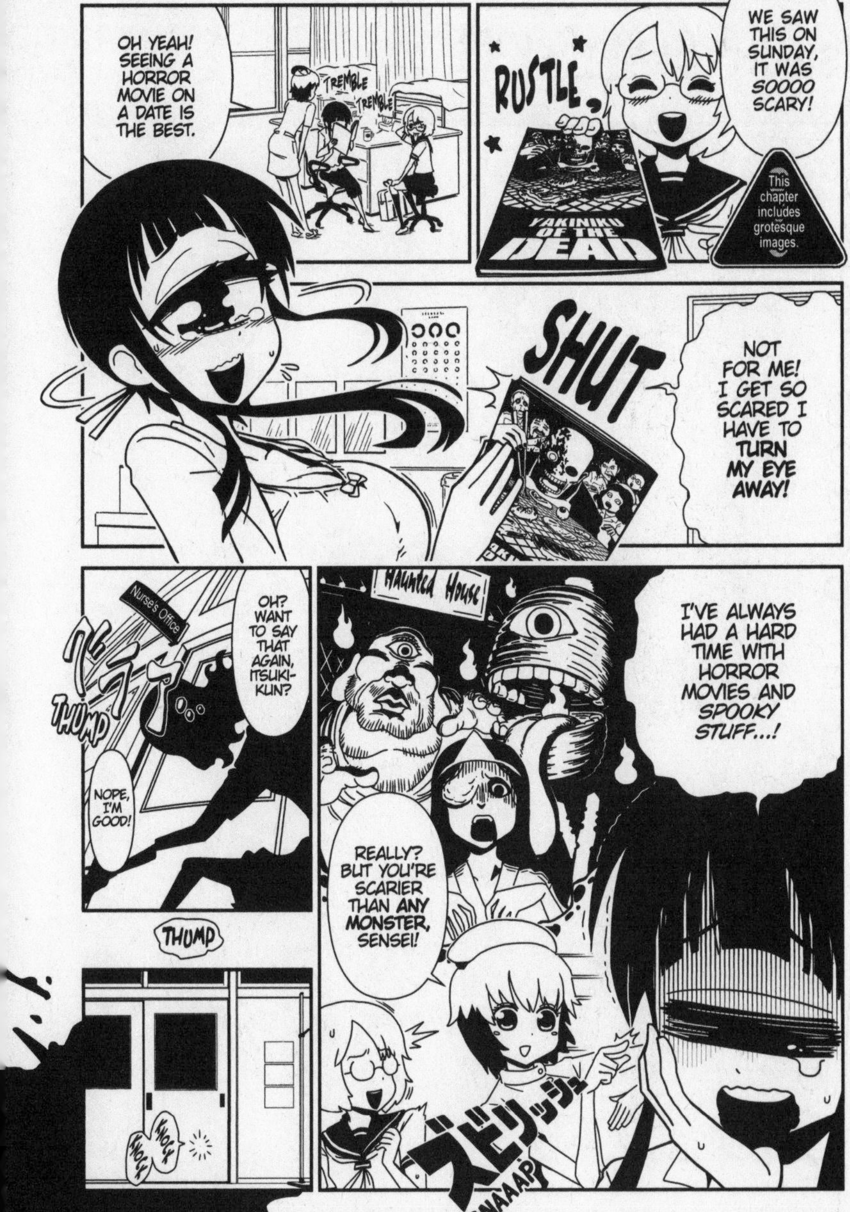
RUSTLE
WE SAW THIS ON SUNDAY, IT WAS SOOOO SCARY!
YAKINIKU OF THE DEAD
This chapter includes grotesque images.
OH YEAH! SEEING A HORROR MOVIE ON A DATE IS THE BEST.
TREMBLE TREMBLE
SHUT
NOT FOR ME! I GET SO SCARED I HAVE TO TURN MY EYE AWAY!
Haunted House
I'VE ALWAYS HAD A HARD TIME WITH HORROR MOVIES AND SPOOKY STUFF...!
REALLY? BUT YOU'RE SCARIER THAN ANY MONSTER, SENSEI!
SNAAAP
Nurse's Office
OH? WANT TO SAY THAT AGAIN, ITSUKI-KUN?
THUMP
NOPE, I'M GOOD!
THUMP
KNOCK KNOCK

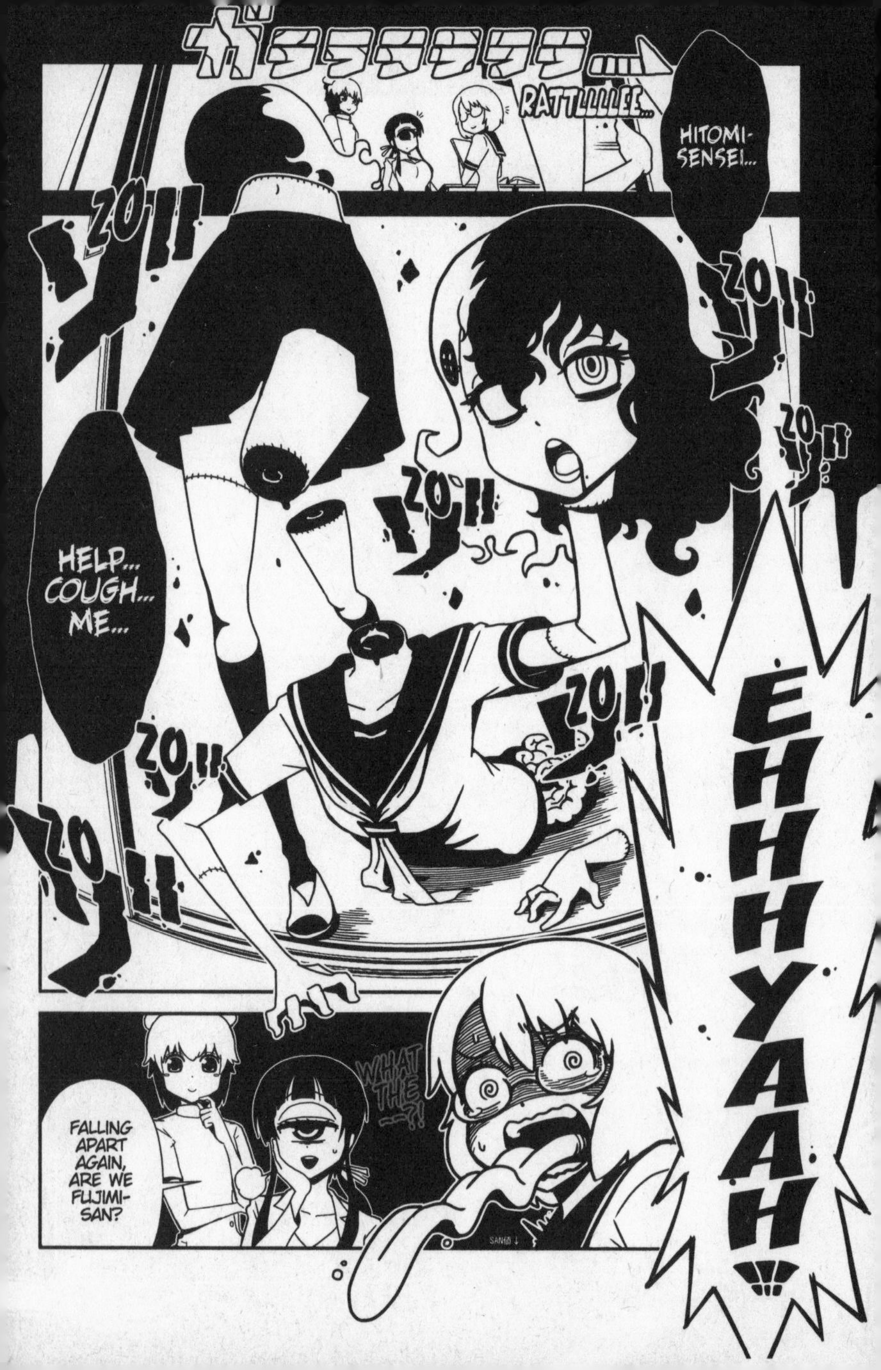
ガララララララ...
RATTLLLLEE...
HITOMI-SENSEI...
ZO!!
ZO!!
ZO!!
ZO!!
ZO!!
ZO!!
ZO!!
HELP... COUGH... ME...
EHHHYAAH!!
WHAT THE--?!
FALLING APART AGAIN, ARE WE FUJIMI-SAN?
SAN値↓

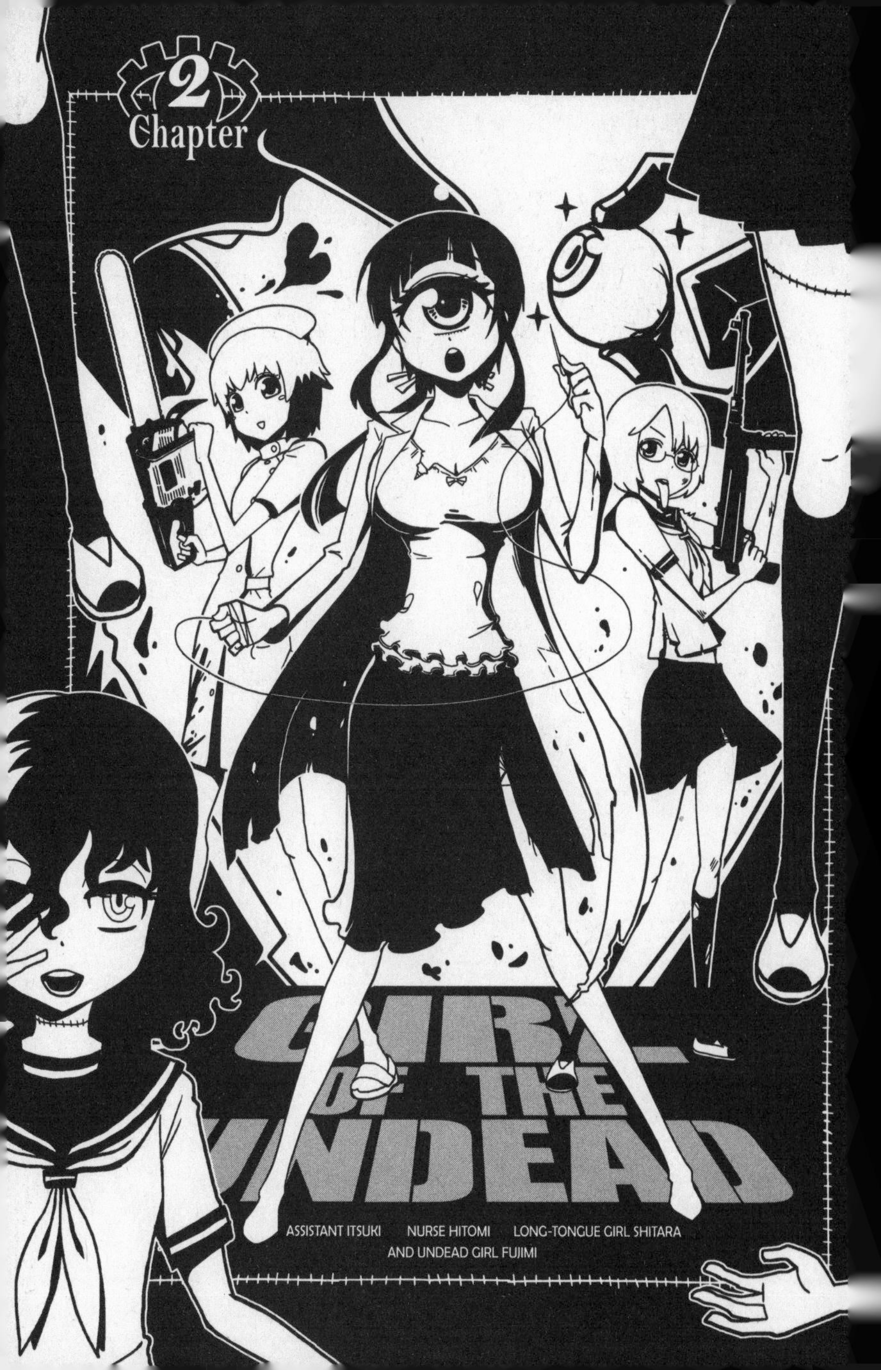
2
Chapter
ASSISTANT ITSUKI
NURSE HITOMI
LONG-TONGUE GIRL SHITARA
AND UNDEAD GIRL FUJIMI

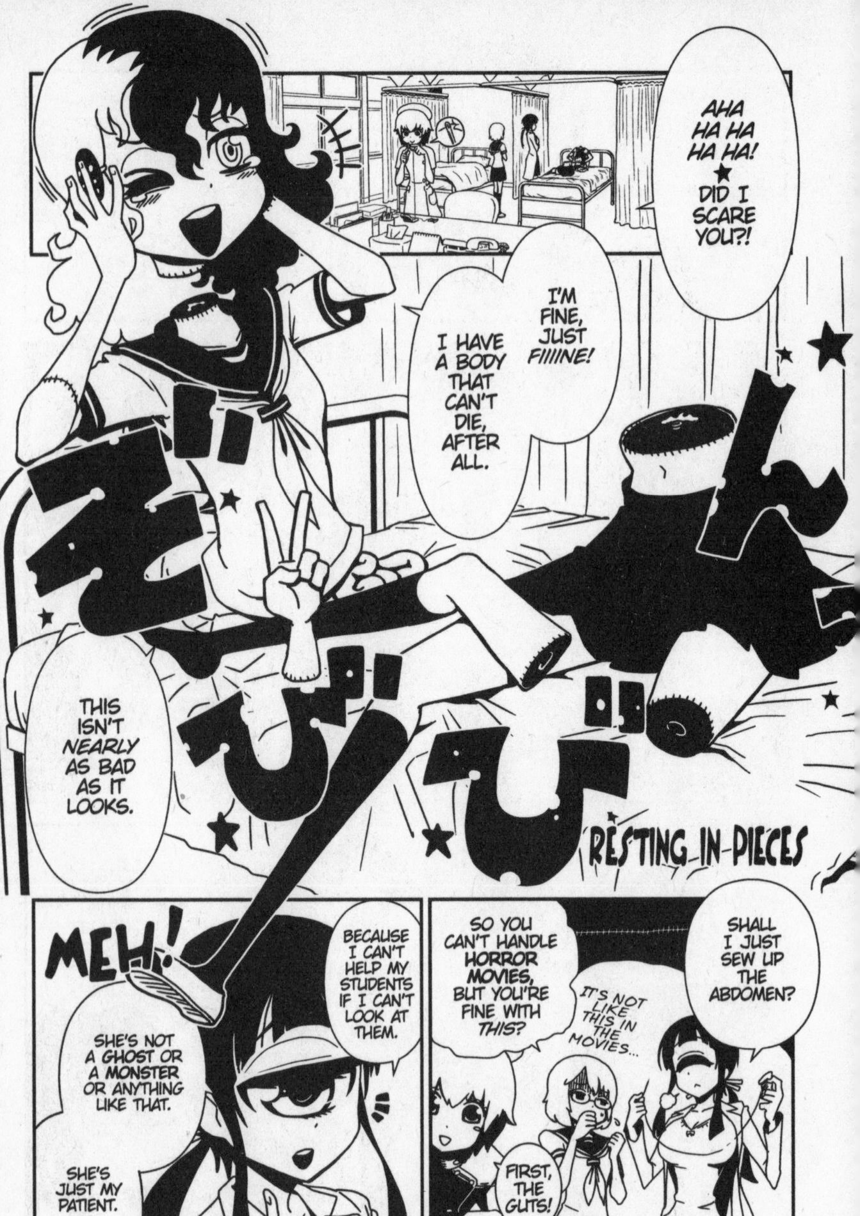
AHA HA HA HA HA! ★ DID I SCARE YOU?!
I'M FINE, JUST FIIIINE!
I HAVE A BODY THAT CAN'T DIE, AFTER ALL.
THIS ISN'T NEARLY AS BAD AS IT LOOKS.
RESTING IN PIECES
SHALL I JUST SEW UP THE ABDOMEN?
IT'S NOT LIKE THIS IN THE MOVIES...
SO YOU CAN'T HANDLE HORROR MOVIES, BUT YOU'RE FINE WITH THIS?
FIRST, THE GUTS!
BECAUSE I CAN'T HELP MY STUDENTS IF I CAN'T LOOK AT THEM.
MEH!
SHE'S NOT A GHOST OR A MONSTER OR ANYTHING LIKE THAT.
SHE'S JUST MY PATIENT.

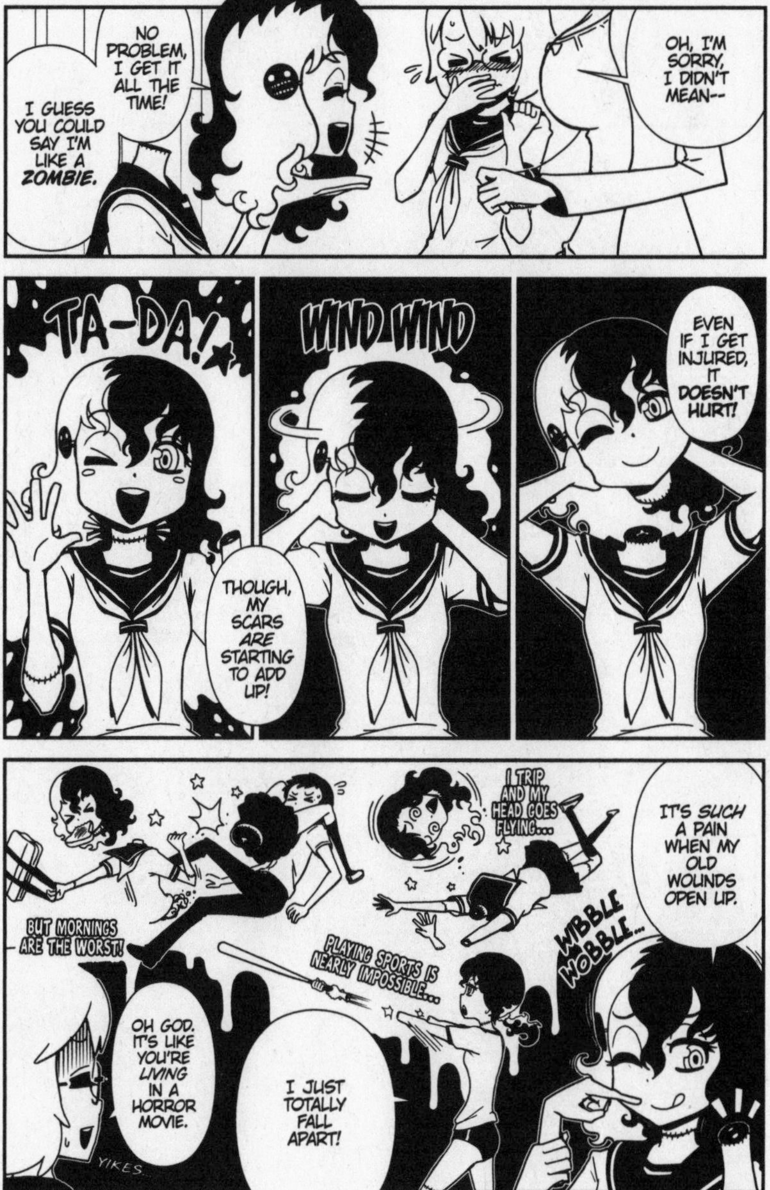
OH, I'M SORRY, I DIDN'T MEAN--
NO PROBLEM, I GET IT ALL THE TIME!
I GUESS YOU COULD SAY I'M LIKE A **ZOMBIE.**
EVEN IF I GET INJURED, IT **DOESN'T** HURT!
WIND WIND
TA-DA!
THOUGH, MY SCARS *ARE* STARTING TO ADD UP!
IT'S *SUCH* A PAIN WHEN MY OLD WOUNDS OPEN UP.
I TRIP AND MY HEAD GOES FLYING...
WIBBLE WOBBLE...
PLAYING SPORTS IS NEARLY IMPOSSIBLE...
BUT MORNINGS ARE THE WORST!
I JUST TOTALLY FALL APART!
OH GOD. IT'S LIKE YOU'RE *LIVING* IN A HORROR MOVIE.
YIKES...

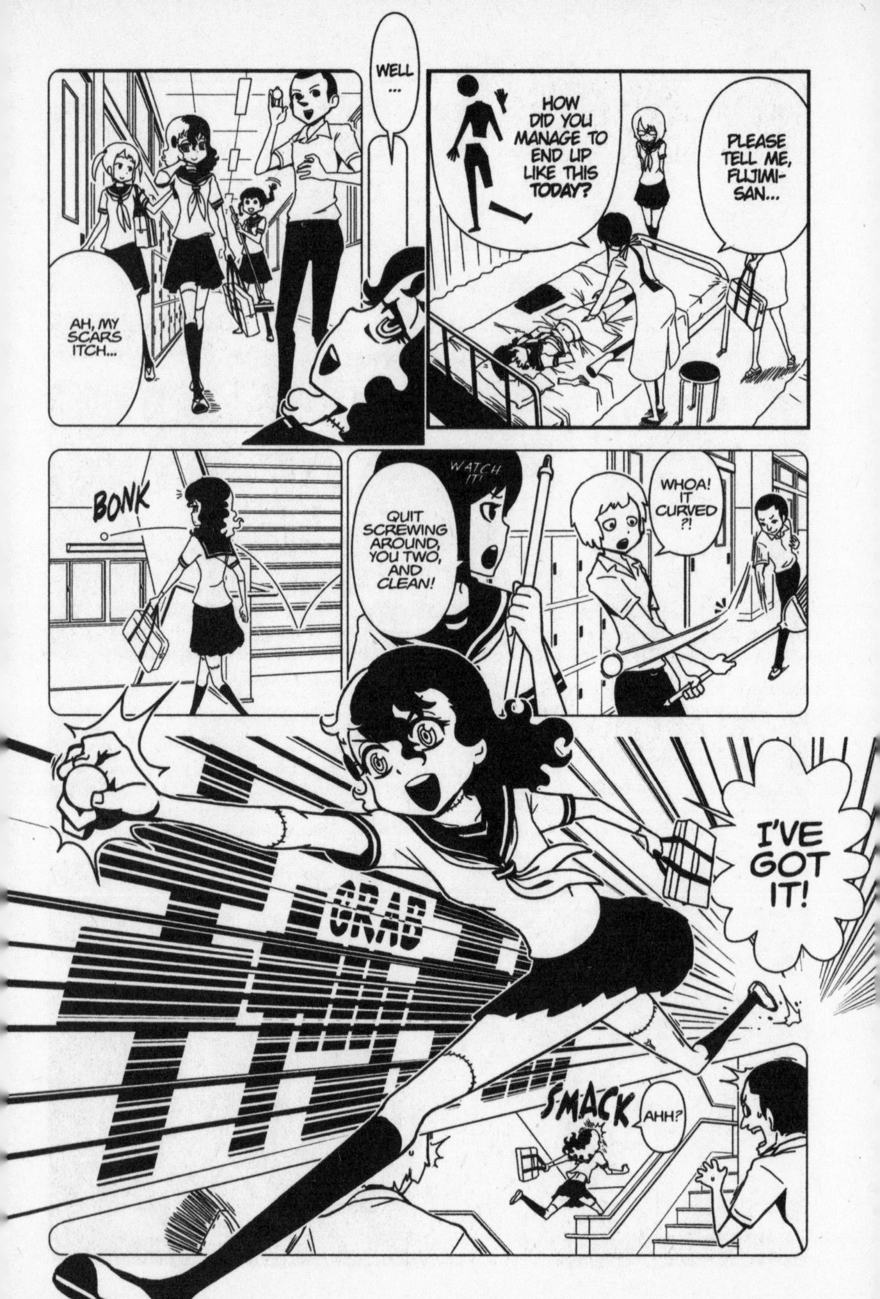
PLEASE TELL ME, FUJIMI-SAN...
HOW DID YOU MANAGE TO END UP LIKE THIS TODAY?
WELL ...
AH, MY SCARS ITCH...
WHOA! IT CURVED?!
WATCH IT!
QUIT SCREWING AROUND, YOU TWO, AND CLEAN!
BONK
I'VE GOT IT!
GRAB
AHH?
SMACK

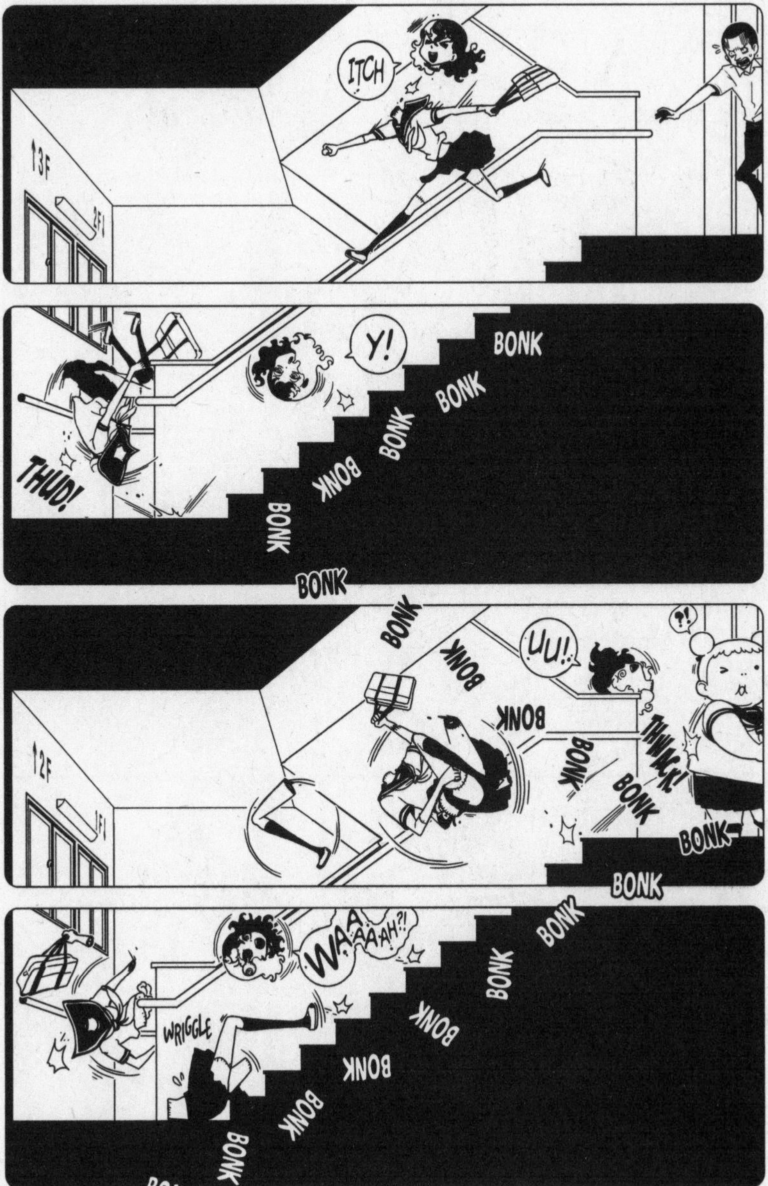
ITCH
3F
2F
Y!
BONK
BONK
BONK
BONK
BONK
BONK
THUD!
?!
UU!
THWACK!
BONK
BONK
BONK
BONK
BONK
BONK
BONK
2F
1F
WAAAAAH?!
BONK
BONK
BONK
BONK
BONK
BONK
BONK
WRIGGLE

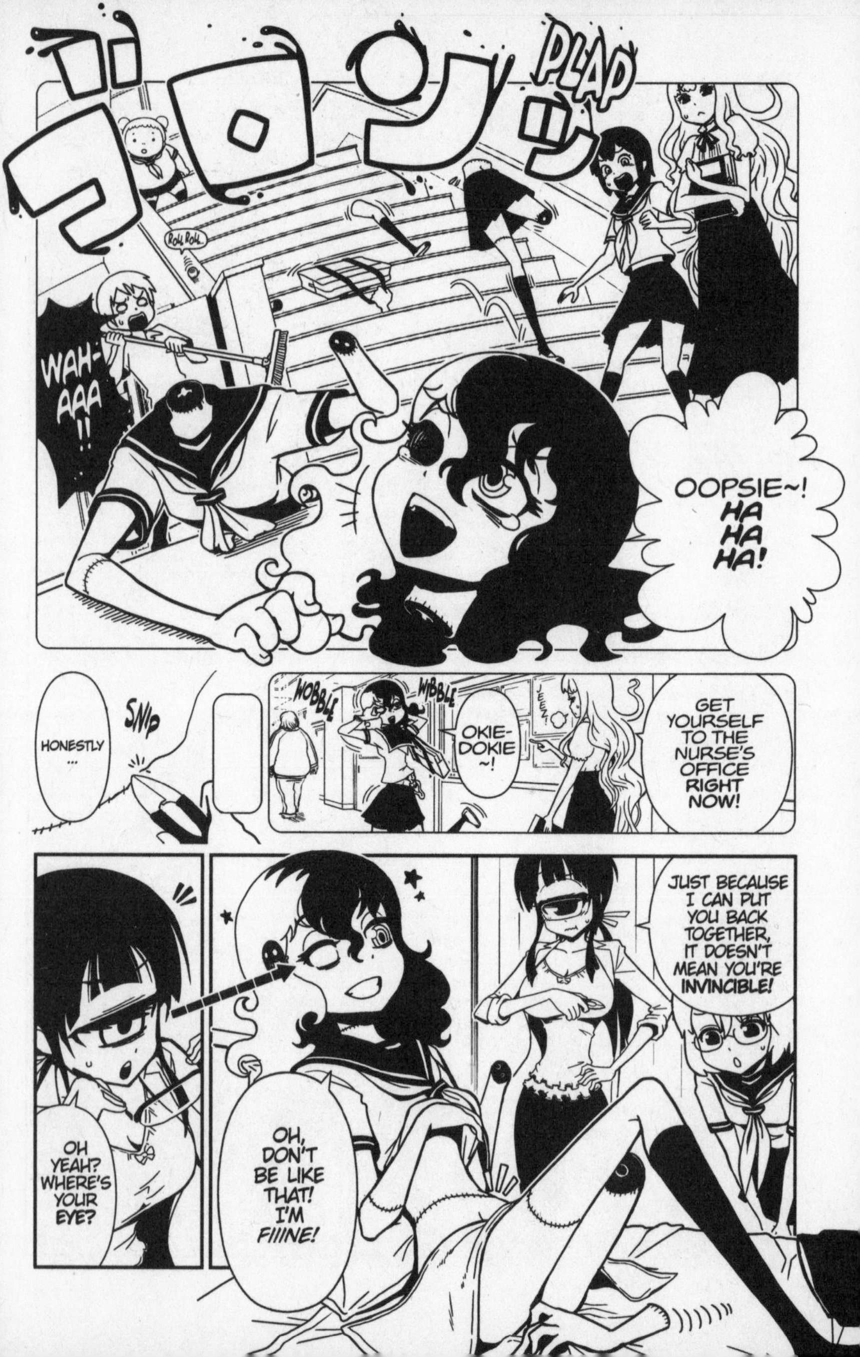
PLAP
ゴロンッ
OOPSIE~! HA HA HA!
ROLL ROLL
WAH-AAA!!
GET YOURSELF TO THE NURSE'S OFFICE RIGHT NOW!
JEEZ
OKIE-DOKIE ~!
WIBBLE
WOBBLE
SNIP
HONESTLY ...
JUST BECAUSE I CAN PUT YOU BACK TOGETHER, IT DOESN'T MEAN YOU'RE INVINCIBLE!
OH, DON'T BE LIKE THAT! I'M FIIINE!
OH YEAH? WHERE'S YOUR EYE?

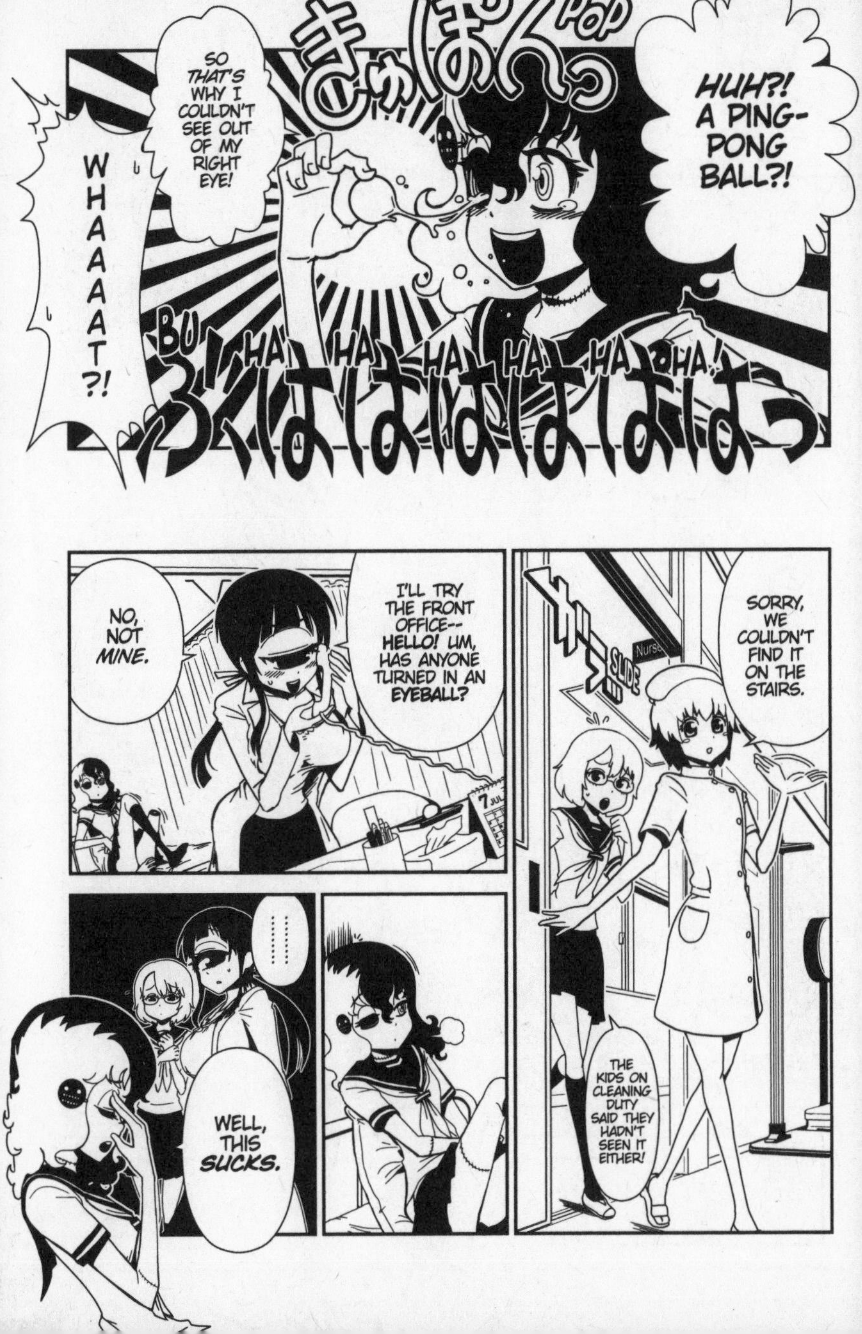
HUH?! A PING-PONG BALL?!
POP
きゅぽんっ
SO THAT'S WHY I COULDN'T SEE OUT OF MY RIGHT EYE!
WHAAAAAT?!
BU HA HA HA HA HA HA!
ぶはははははは
SORRY, WE COULDN'T FIND IT ON THE STAIRS.
SLIDE
Nurse
THE KIDS ON CLEANING DUTY SAID THEY HADN'T SEEN IT EITHER!
I'LL TRY THE FRONT OFFICE-- HELLO! UM, HAS ANYONE TURNED IN AN EYEBALL?
NO, NOT MINE.
7 JUL
......
WELL, THIS SUCKS.

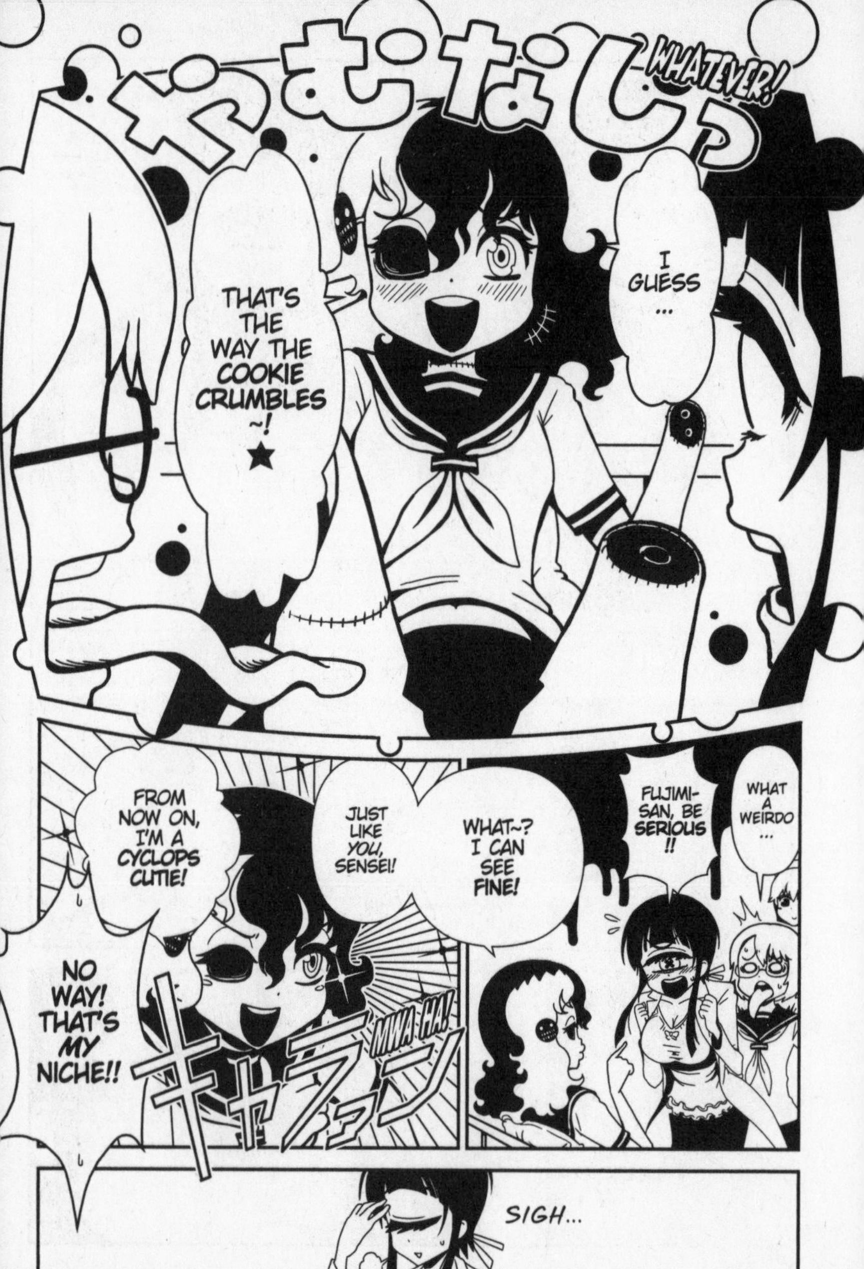
やむなしっ
WHATEVER!
I GUESS ...
THAT'S THE WAY THE COOKIE CRUMBLES ~! ★
WHAT A WEIRDO ...
FUJIMI-SAN, BE SERIOUS !!
WHAT~? I CAN SEE FINE!
JUST LIKE YOU, SENSEI!
FROM NOW ON, I'M A CYCLOPS CUTIE!
MWA HA!
NO WAY! THAT'S MY NICHE!!
SIGH...

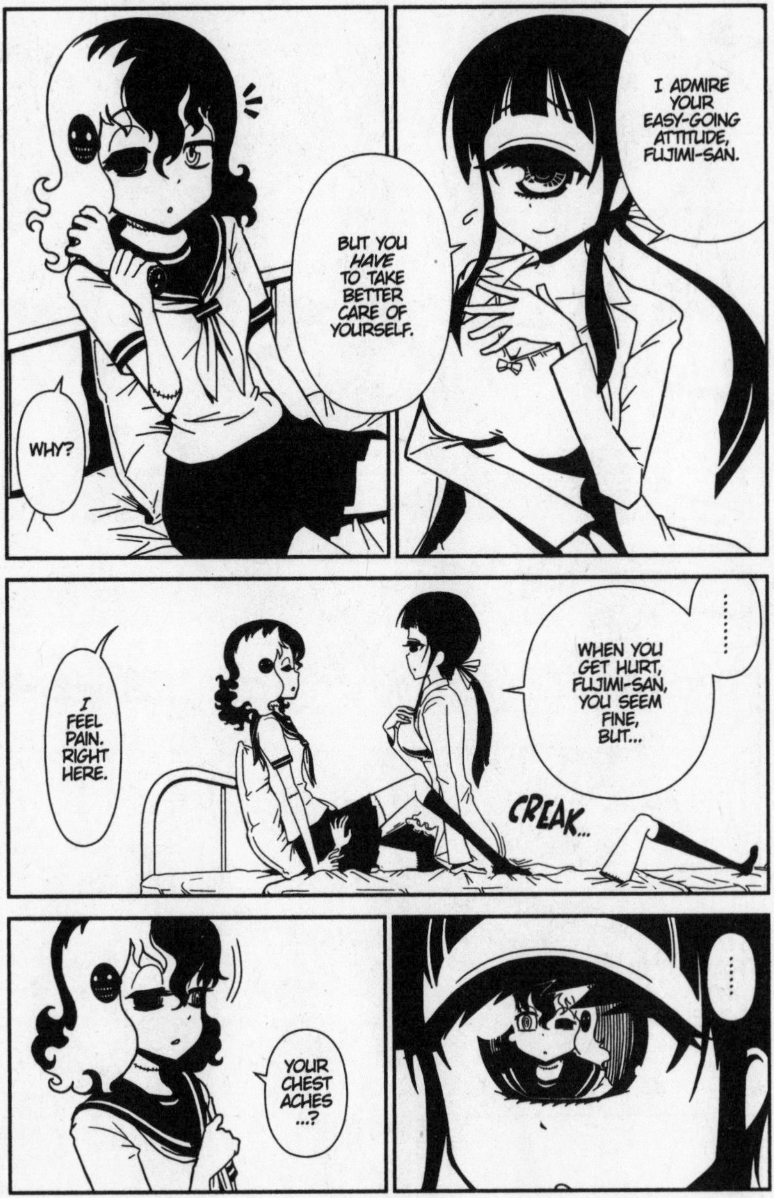
I ADMIRE YOUR EASY-GOING ATTITUDE, FUJIMI-SAN.
BUT YOU *HAVE* TO TAKE BETTER CARE OF YOURSELF.
WHY?
....
WHEN YOU GET HURT, FUJIMI-SAN, YOU SEEM FINE, BUT...
CREAK...
I FEEL PAIN. RIGHT HERE.
......
YOUR CHEST ACHES ...?

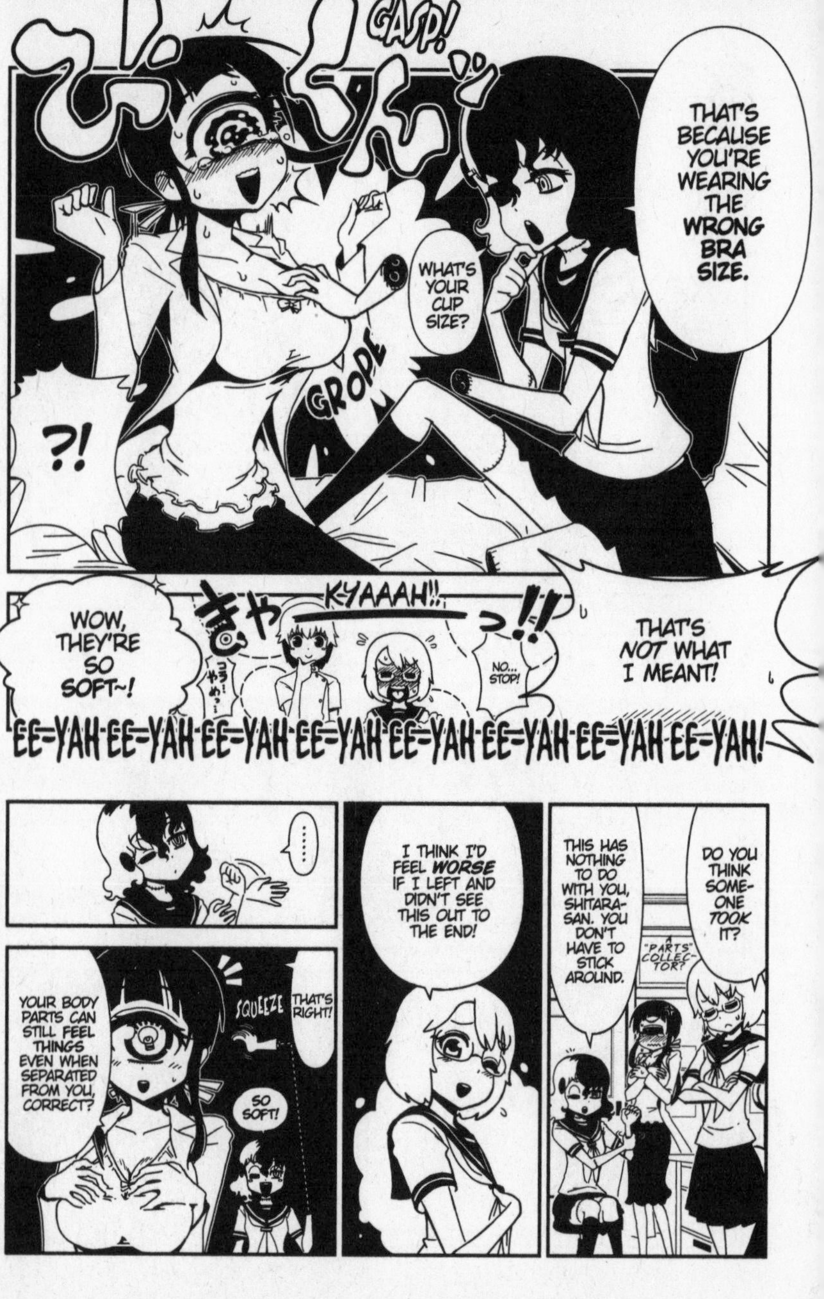
THAT'S BECAUSE YOU'RE WEARING THE WRONG BRA SIZE.
GASP!
WHAT'S YOUR CUP SIZE?
GROPE
?!
THAT'S NOT WHAT I MEANT!
NO... STOP!
KYAAAH!!
WOW, THEY'RE SO SOFT~!
EE-YAH EE-YAH EE-YAH EE-YAH EE-YAH EE-YAH EE-YAH EE-YAH!
DO YOU THINK SOME-ONE TOOK IT?
"PARTS" COLLEC-TOR?
THIS HAS NOTHING TO DO WITH YOU, SHITARA-SAN. YOU DON'T HAVE TO STICK AROUND.
I THINK I'D FEEL WORSE IF I LEFT AND DIDN'T SEE THIS OUT TO THE END!
......
THAT'S RIGHT!
SQUEEZE
YOUR BODY PARTS CAN STILL FEEL THINGS EVEN WHEN SEPARATED FROM YOU, CORRECT?
SO SOFT!

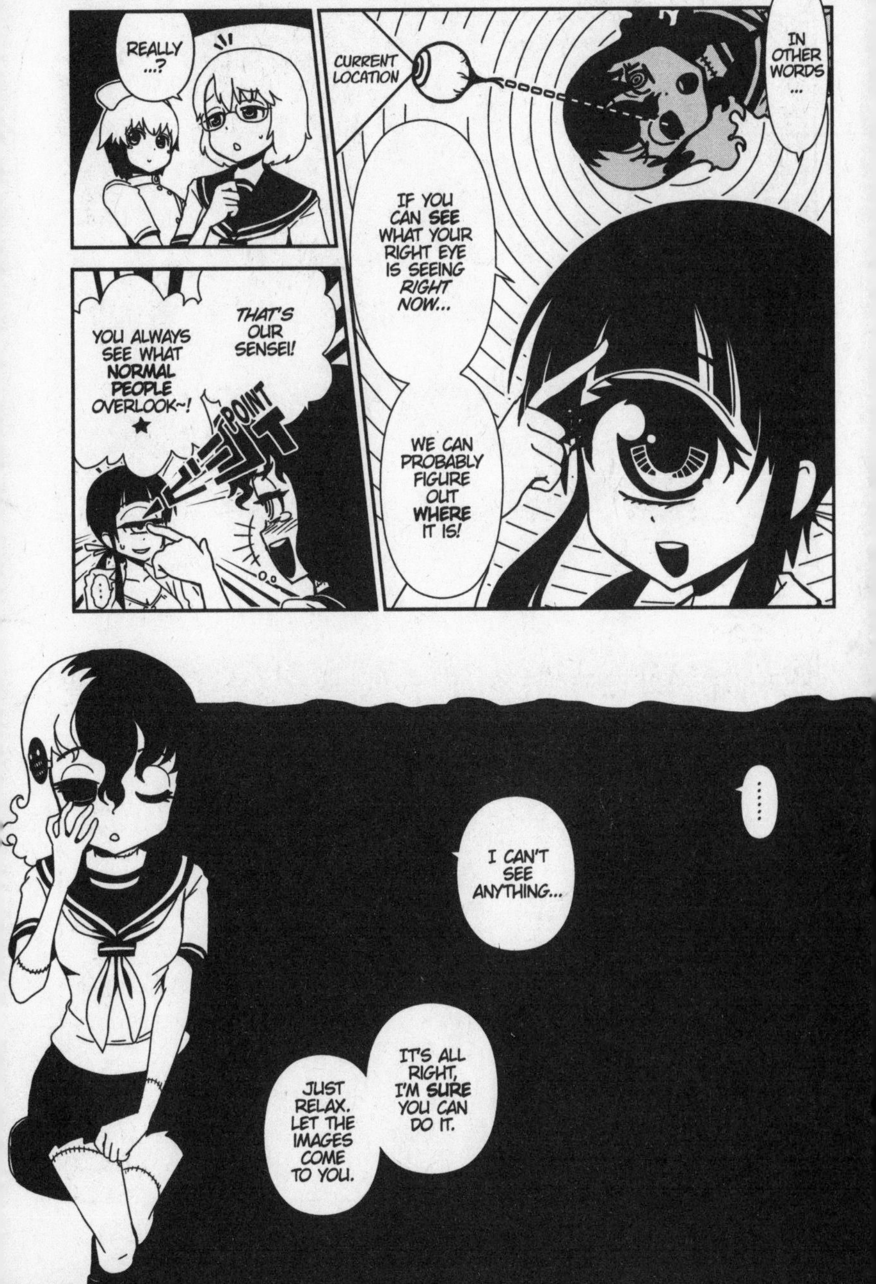
IN OTHER WORDS ...
CURRENT LOCATION
IF YOU CAN SEE WHAT YOUR RIGHT EYE IS SEEING *RIGHT NOW*...
WE CAN PROBABLY FIGURE OUT WHERE IT IS!
REALLY ...?
THAT'S OUR SENSEI!
YOU ALWAYS SEE WHAT NORMAL PEOPLE OVERLOOK~! ★
POINT
......
I CAN'T SEE ANYTHING...
IT'S ALL RIGHT, I'M SURE YOU CAN DO IT.
JUST RELAX. LET THE IMAGES COME TO YOU.

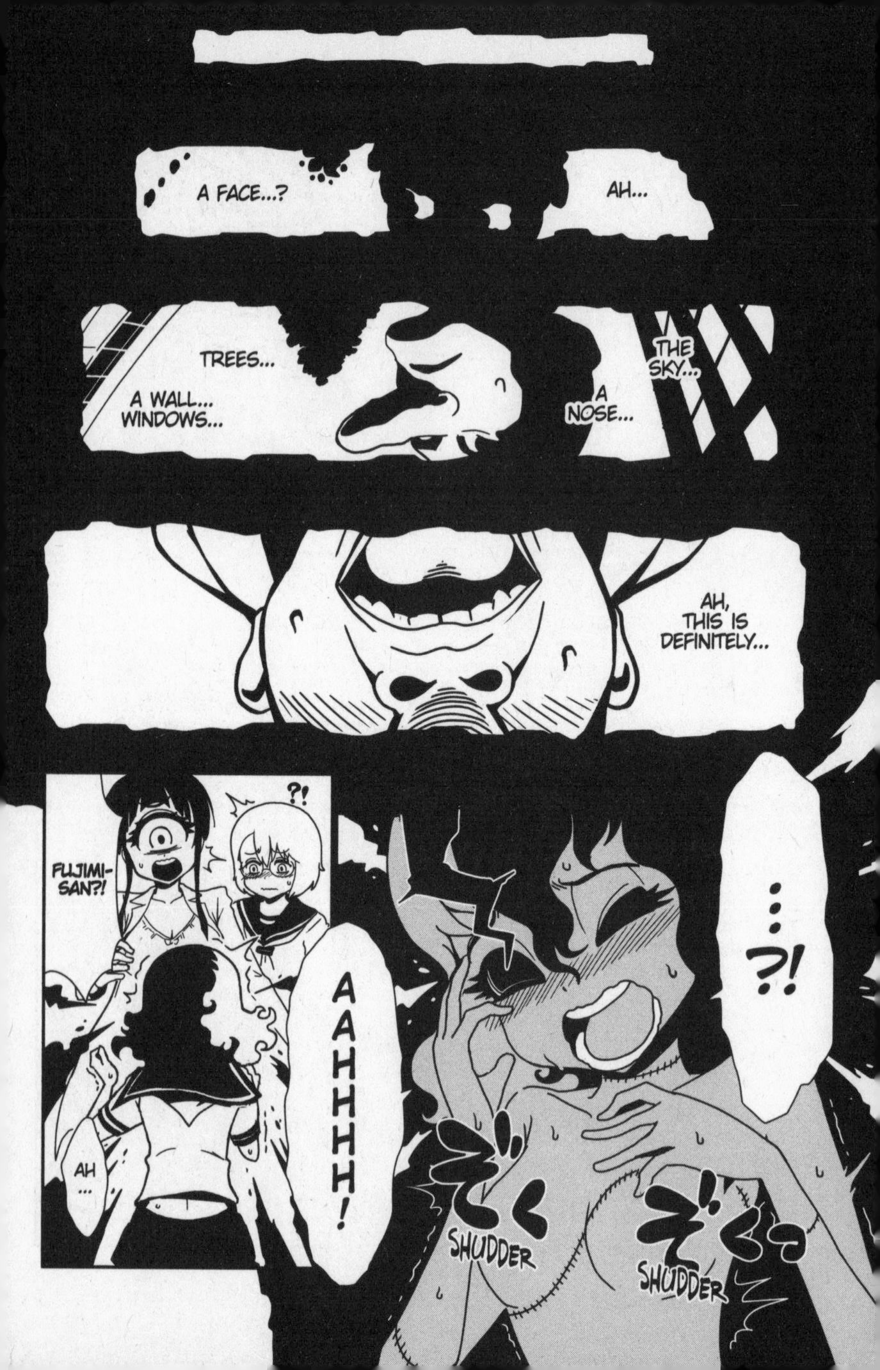
AH...
A FACE...?
THE SKY...
A NOSE...
TREES...
A WALL... WINDOWS...
AH, THIS IS DEFINITELY...
...?!
AAHHHH!
SHUDDER
SHUDDER
?!
FUJIMI-SAN?!
AH ...

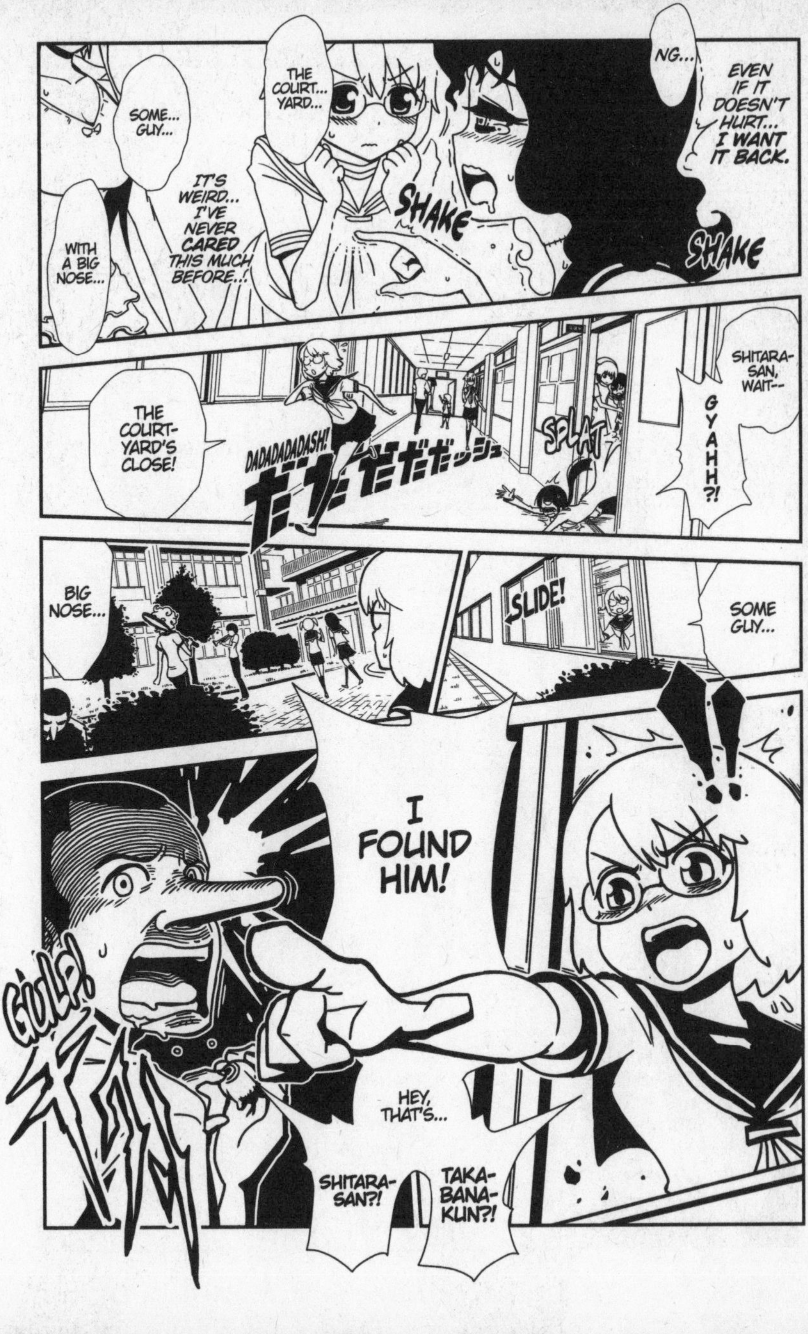
NG...
EVEN IF IT DOESN'T HURT... I WANT IT BACK.
SHAKE
SHAKE
THE COURT... YARD...
IT'S WEIRD... I'VE NEVER CARED THIS MUCH BEFORE...
SOME... GUY...
WITH A BIG NOSE...
SHITARA-SAN, WAIT--
GYAHHH?!
SPLAT
DADADADADASH!
だだだだダッシュ
THE COURT-YARD'S CLOSE!
SOME GUY...
SLIDE!
BIG NOSE...
I FOUND HIM!
TAKA-BANA-KUN?!
SHITARA-SAN?!
HEY, THAT'S...
GULP!

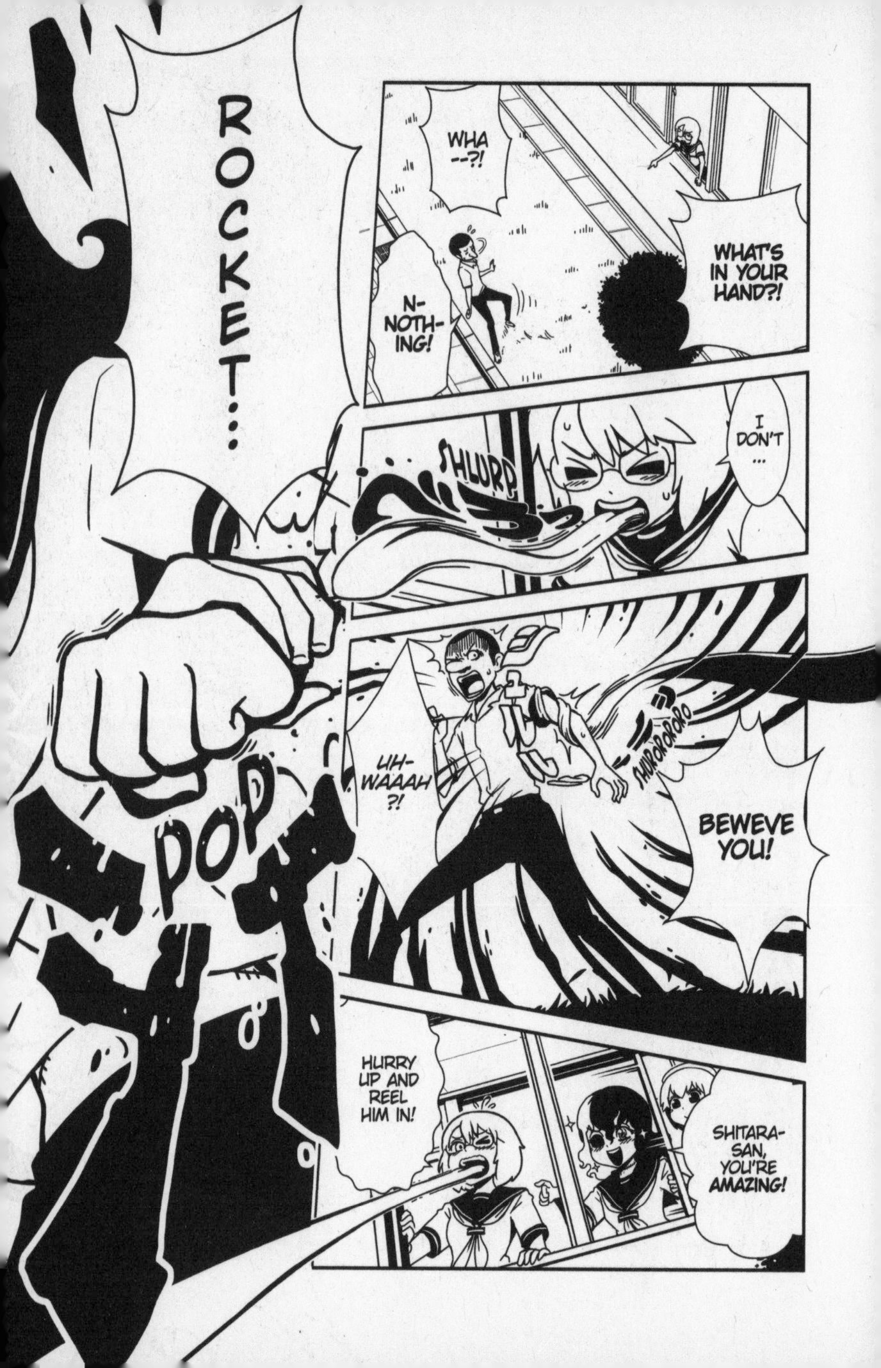
WHAT'S IN YOUR HAND?!
WHA--?!
N-NOTHING!
I DON'T ...
SHLURP
BEWEVE YOU!
SHURORORO
UH-WAAAH?!
SHITARA-SAN, YOU'RE AMAZING!
HURRY UP AND REEL HIM IN!
ROCKET...
POP

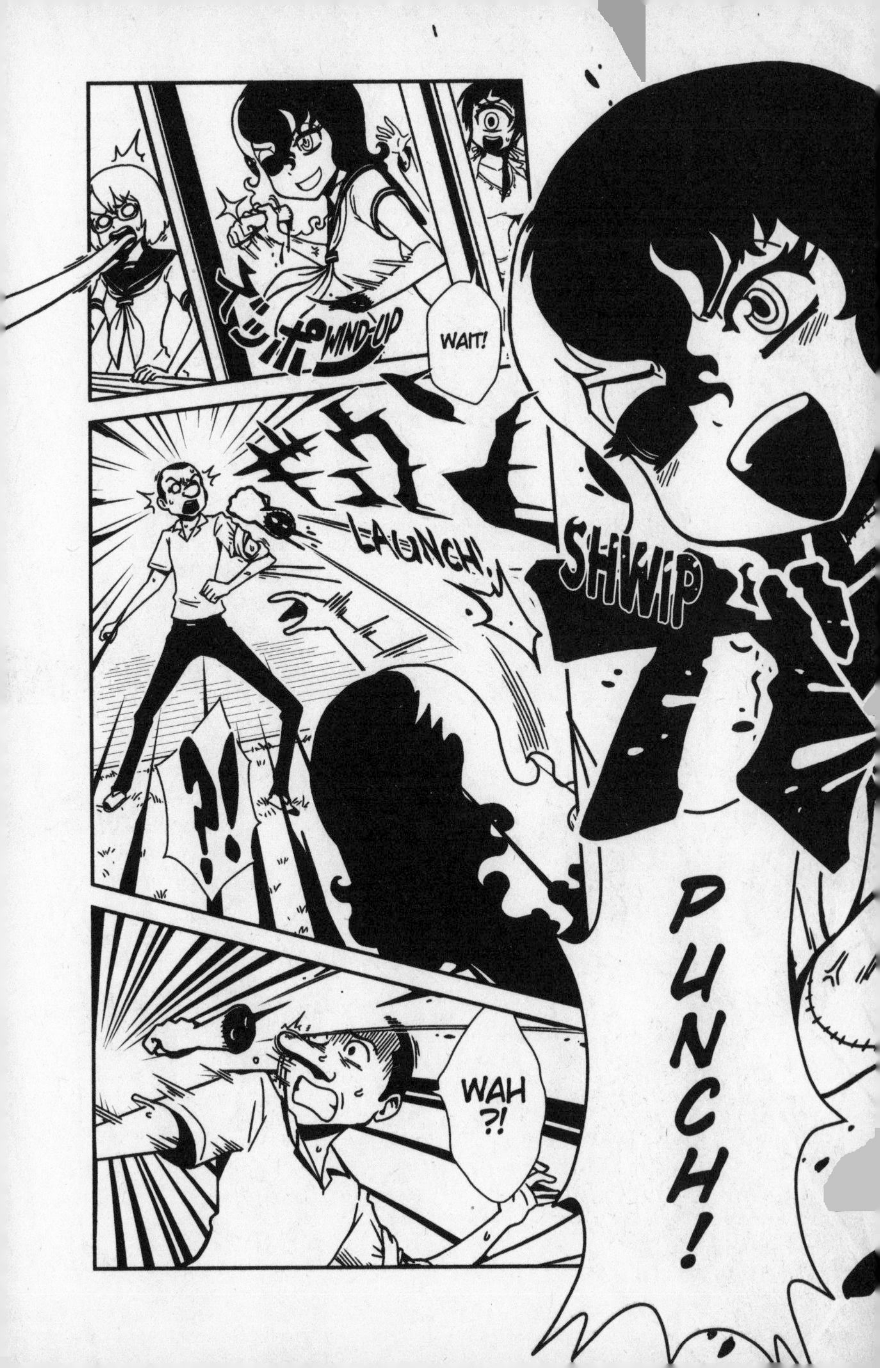
WAIT!
SHWIP
PUNCH!
WIND-UP
LAUNCH!
?!!
WAH ?!

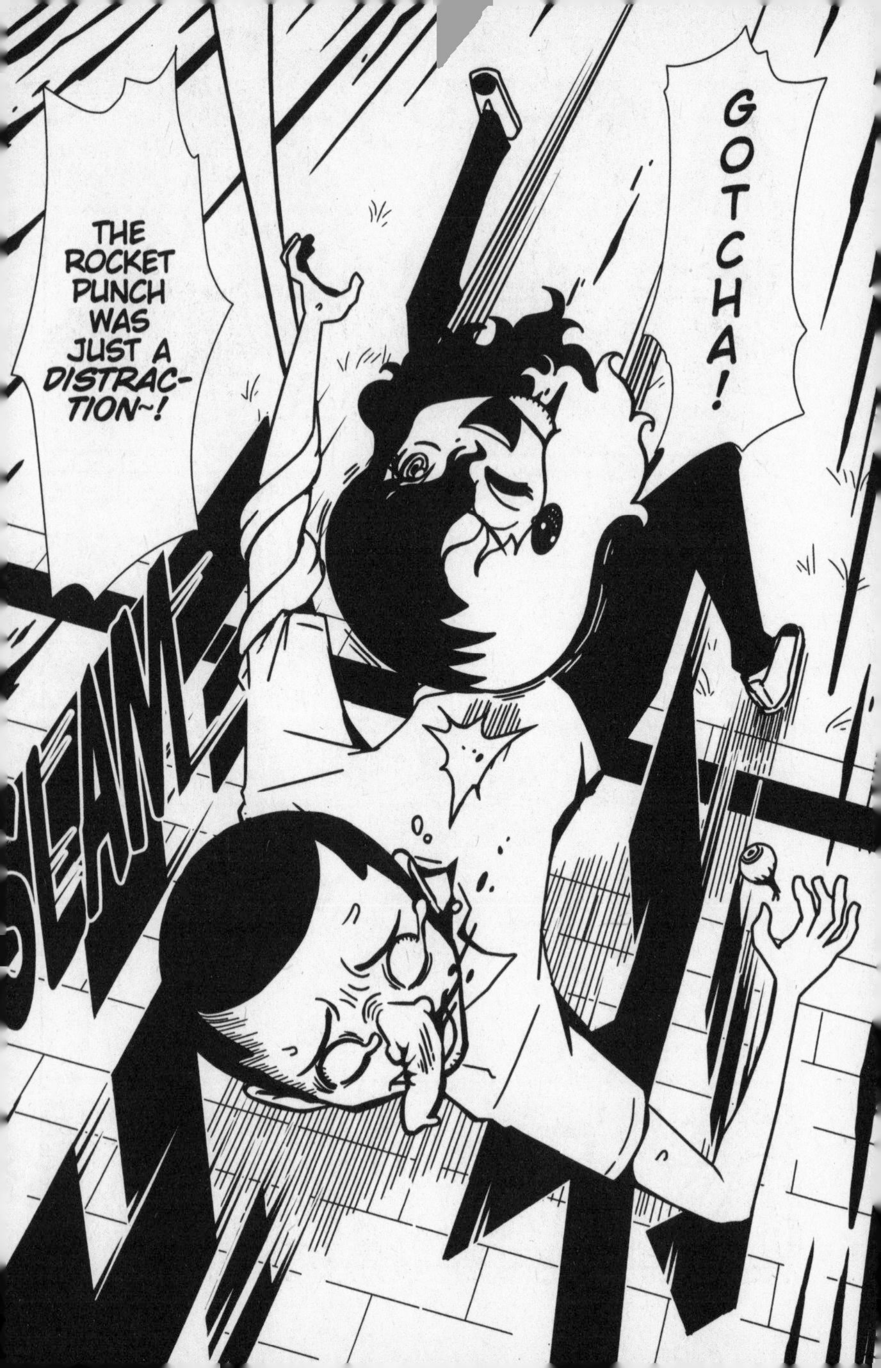
GOTCHA!
THE ROCKET PUNCH WAS JUST A DISTRAC-TION~!
SLAM

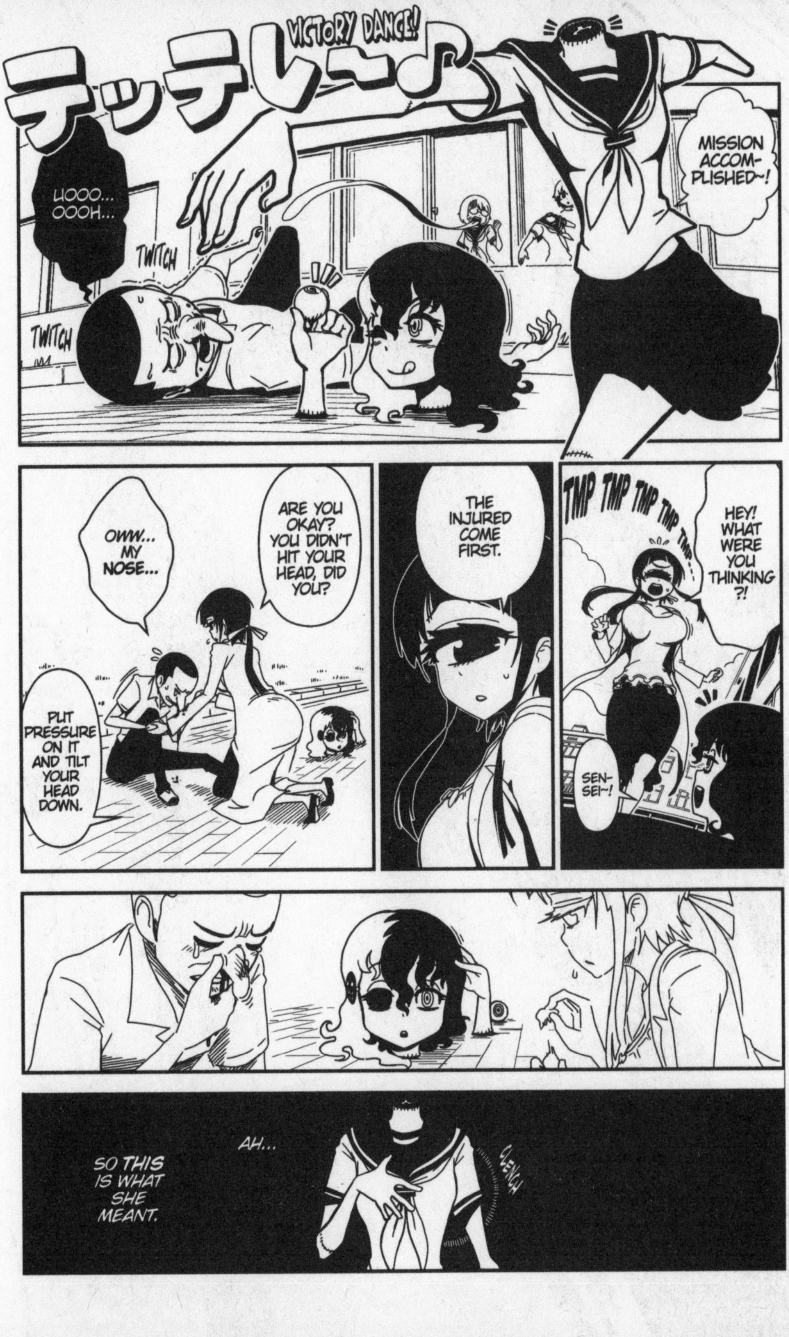
テッテレ～♪
VICTORY DANCE!
MISSION ACCOM-PLISHED~!
UOOO... OOOH...
TWITCH
TWITCH
TMP TMP TMP TMP TMP
HEY! WHAT WERE YOU THINKING?!
SEN-SEI~!
THE INJURED COME FIRST.
ARE YOU OKAY? YOU DIDN'T HIT YOUR HEAD, DID YOU?
OWW... MY NOSE...
PUT PRESSURE ON IT AND TILT YOUR HEAD DOWN.
AH...
CLENCH
SO THIS IS WHAT SHE MEANT.

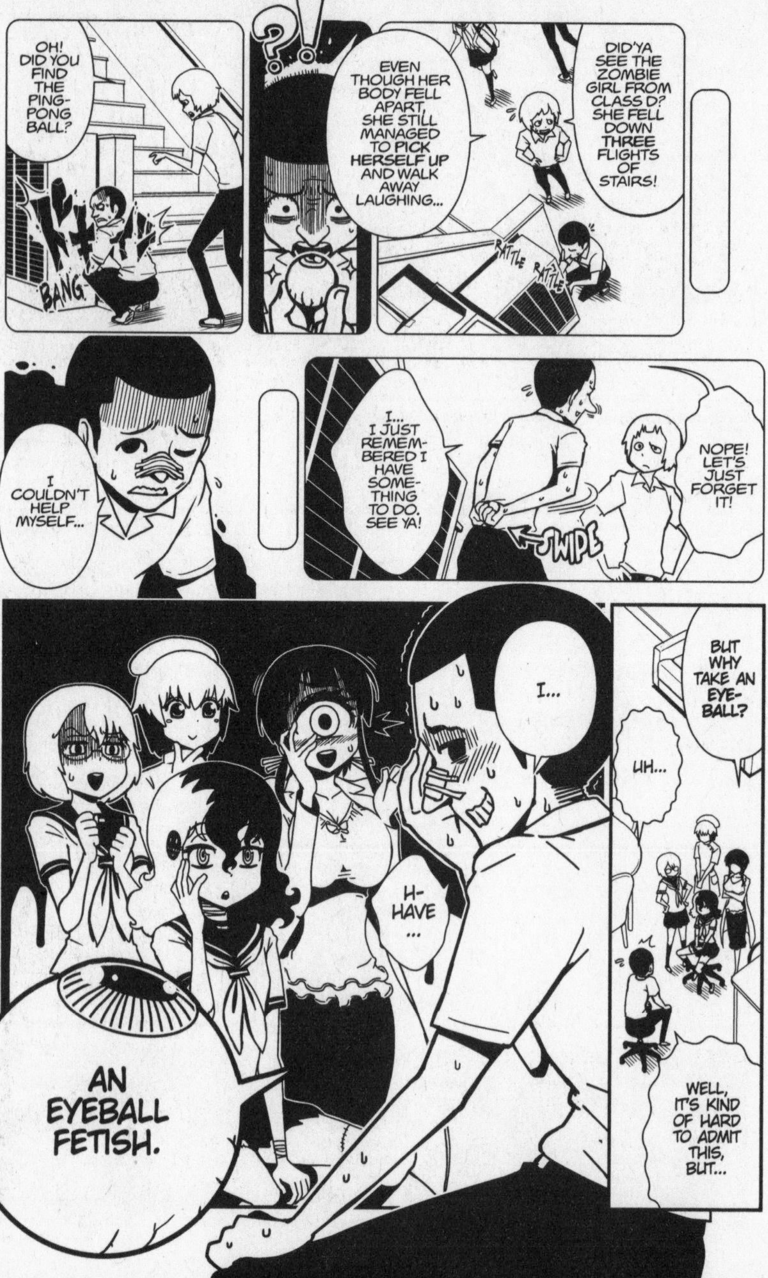
DID'YA SEE THE ZOMBIE GIRL FROM CLASS D? SHE FELL DOWN THREE FLIGHTS OF STAIRS!
RATTLE RATTLE
?!!
EVEN THOUGH HER BODY FELL APART, SHE STILL MANAGED TO PICK HERSELF UP AND WALK AWAY LAUGHING...
OH! DID YOU FIND THE PING-PONG BALL?
BANG
NOPE! LET'S JUST FORGET IT!
I... I JUST REMEMBERED I HAVE SOMETHING TO DO. SEE YA!
SWIPE
I COULDN'T HELP MYSELF...
BUT WHY TAKE AN EYEBALL?
UH...
WELL, IT'S KIND OF HARD TO ADMIT THIS, BUT...
I...
H-HAVE...
AN EYEBALL FETISH.

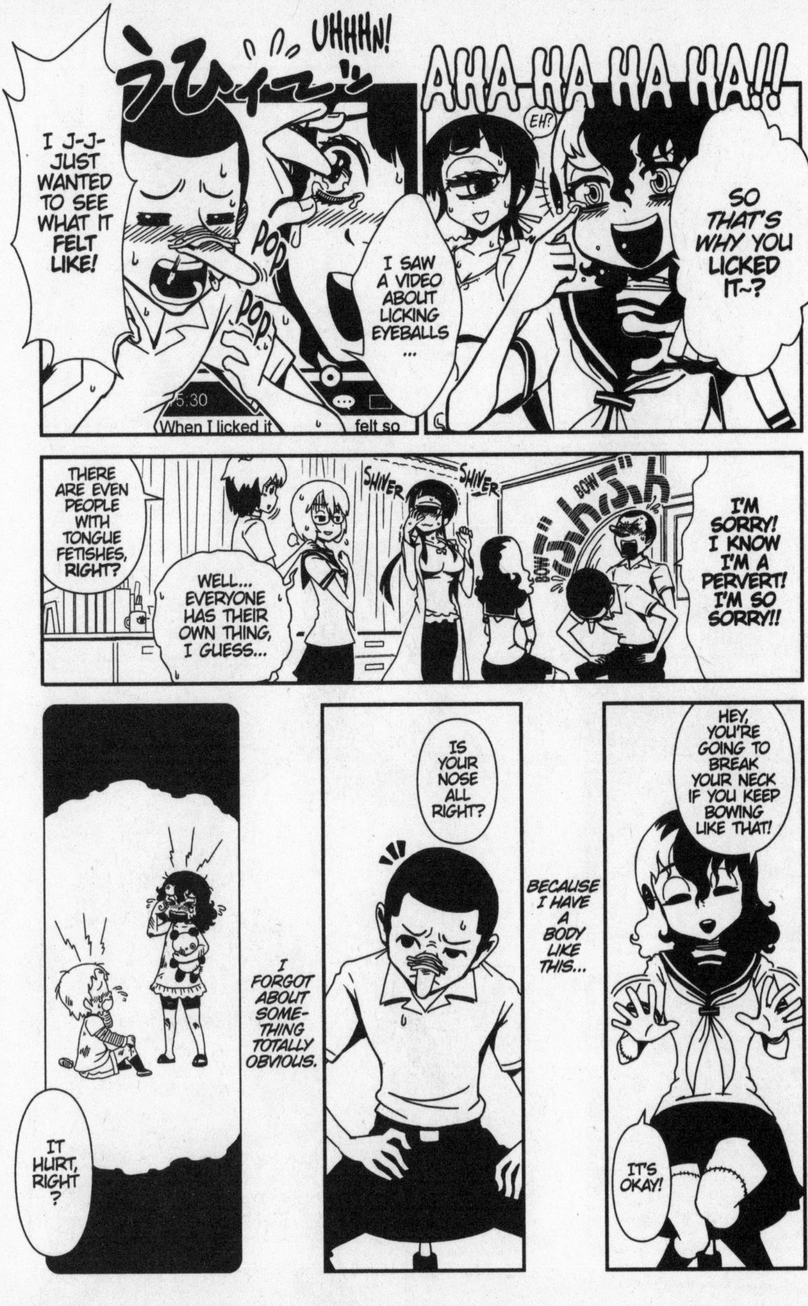
AHA HA HA HA HA!!
EH?
SO THAT'S WHY YOU LICKED IT~?
I SAW A VIDEO ABOUT LICKING EYEBALLS ...
UHHHN!
I J-J-JUST WANTED TO SEE WHAT IT FELT LIKE!
POP
POP
5:30
When I licked it felt so
I'M SORRY! I KNOW I'M A PERVERT! I'M SO SORRY!!
BOW
BOW
SHIVER
SHIVER
WELL... EVERYONE HAS THEIR OWN THING, I GUESS...
THERE ARE EVEN PEOPLE WITH TONGUE FETISHES, RIGHT?
HEY, YOU'RE GOING TO BREAK YOUR NECK IF YOU KEEP BOWING LIKE THAT!
IT'S OKAY!
IS YOUR NOSE ALL RIGHT?
BECAUSE I HAVE A BODY LIKE THIS...
I FORGOT ABOUT SOMETHING TOTALLY OBVIOUS.
IT HURT, RIGHT?

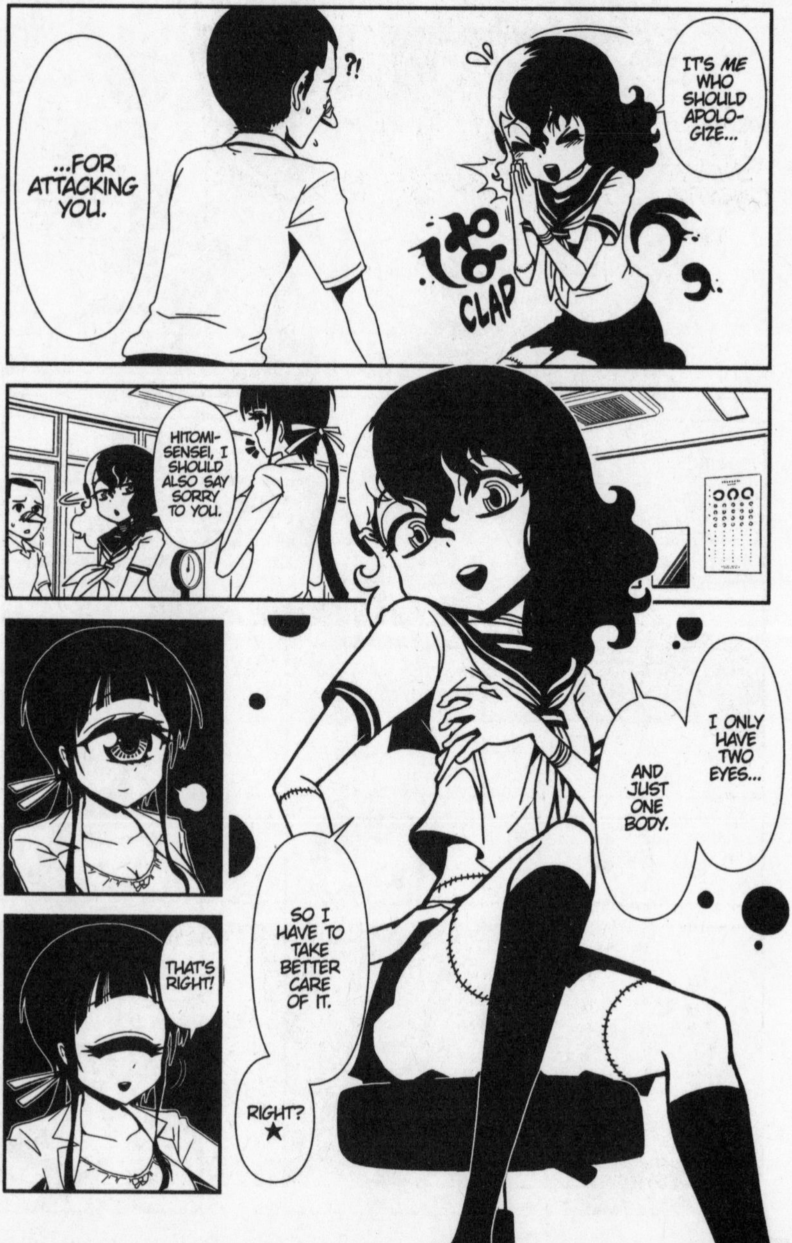
IT'S ME WHO SHOULD APOLOGIZE...
?!
CLAP
...FOR ATTACKING YOU.
HITOMI-SENSEI, I SHOULD ALSO SAY SORRY TO YOU.
I ONLY HAVE TWO EYES...
AND JUST ONE BODY.
SO I HAVE TO TAKE BETTER CARE OF IT.
RIGHT? ★
THAT'S RIGHT!

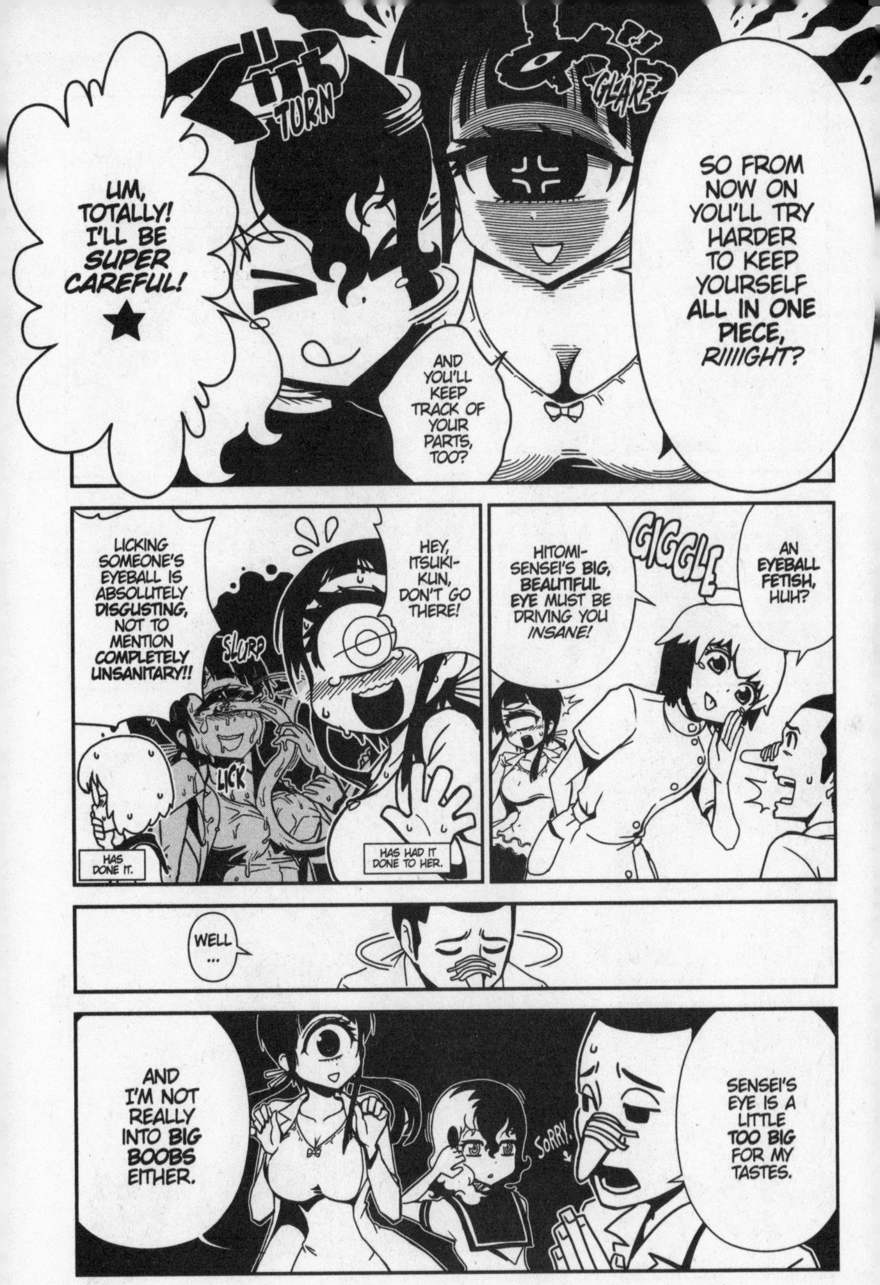
GLARE
SO FROM NOW ON YOU'LL TRY HARDER TO KEEP YOURSELF ALL IN ONE PIECE, RIIIIGHT?
AND YOU'LL KEEP TRACK OF YOUR PARTS, TOO?
TURN
UM, TOTALLY! I'LL BE SUPER CAREFUL! ★
AN EYEBALL FETISH, HUH?
GIGGLE
HITOMI-SENSEI'S BIG, BEAUTIFUL EYE MUST BE DRIVING YOU INSANE!
HEY, ITSUKI-KUN, DON'T GO THERE!
LICKING SOMEONE'S EYEBALL IS ABSOLUTELY DISGUSTING, NOT TO MENTION COMPLETELY UNSANITARY!!
SLURP
LICK
HAS HAD IT DONE TO HER.
HAS DONE IT.
WELL ...
SENSEI'S EYE IS A LITTLE TOO BIG FOR MY TASTES.
SORRY.
AND I'M NOT REALLY INTO BIG BOOBS EITHER.

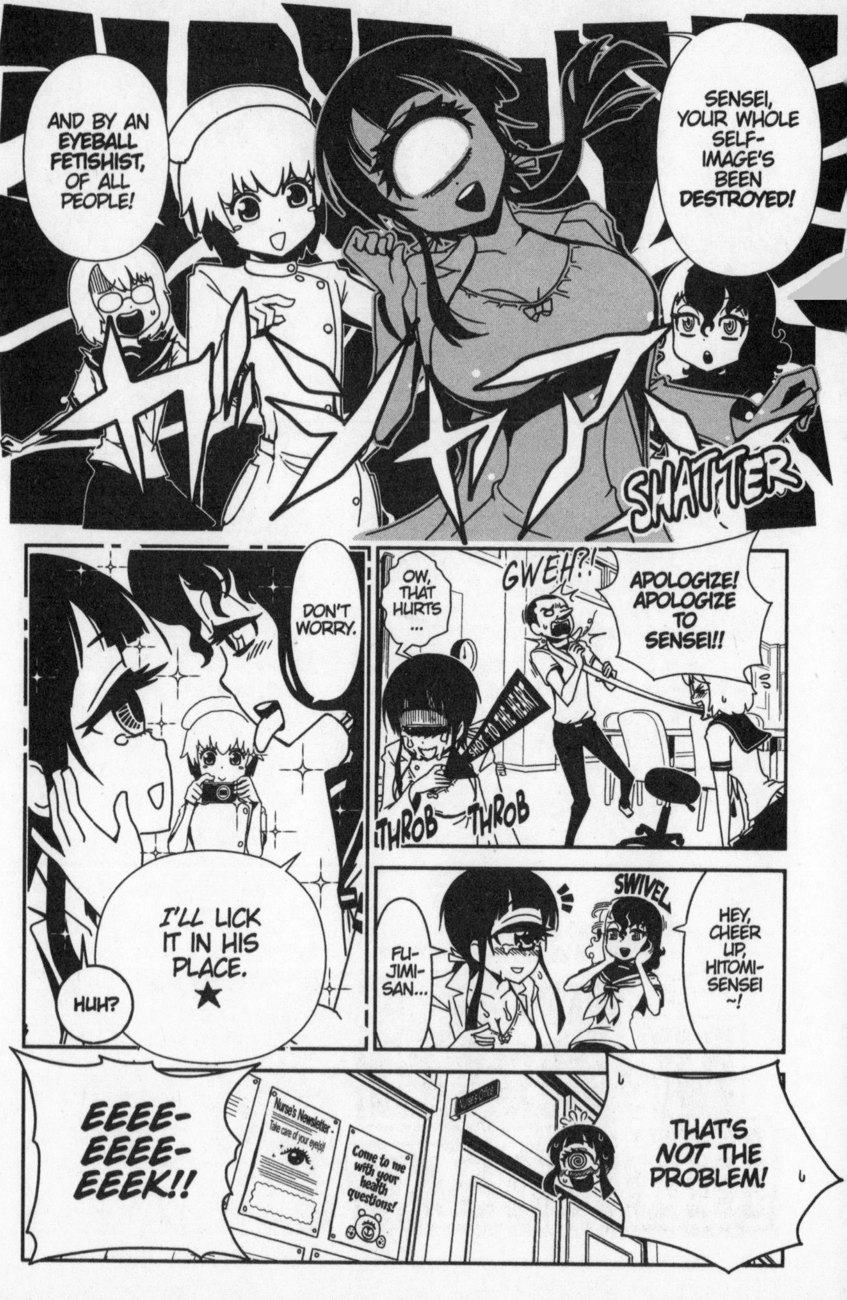
SENSEI, YOUR WHOLE SELF-IMAGE'S BEEN DESTROYED!
AND BY AN EYEBALL FETISHIST, OF ALL PEOPLE!
SHATTER
APOLOGIZE! APOLOGIZE TO SENSEI!!
GWEH?!
OW, THAT HURTS ...
SHOT TO THE HEART
THROB THROB
SWIVEL
HEY, CHEER UP, HITOMI-SENSEI ~!
FUJIMI-SAN...
DON'T WORRY.
I'LL LICK IT IN HIS PLACE. ★
HUH?
THAT'S *NOT* THE PROBLEM!
EEEE-EEEE-EEEK!!
Nurse's Newsletter
Take care of your eye(s)!
Come to me with your health questions!

NURSE HITOMI'S Monster Infirmary

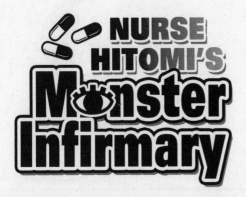

July 201X

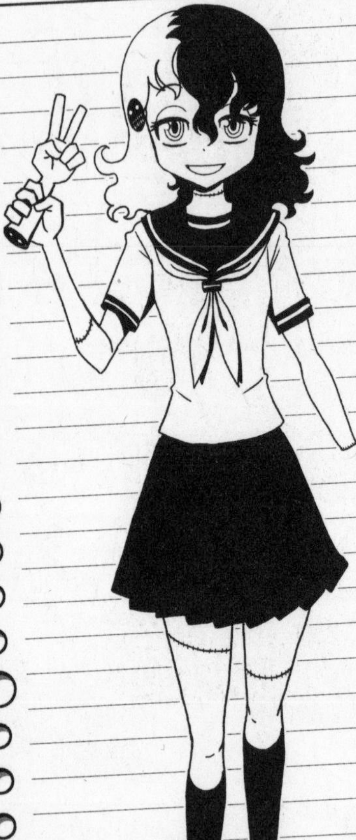

Class 2-D   Fujimi Yomi

Undead Girl

- Has a mix of survivability and healing abilities. Cannot die and has a reckless attitude towards life because of that.

- Even when reassembled, her different parts still don't stick together very well. They become detached frequently and the stitches holding her together heal slowly.

- Fujimi-san is numb to pain and only feels itchiness when her stitches start to open up.

- Likes meat (not human flesh or brains).

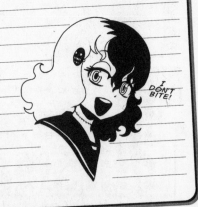

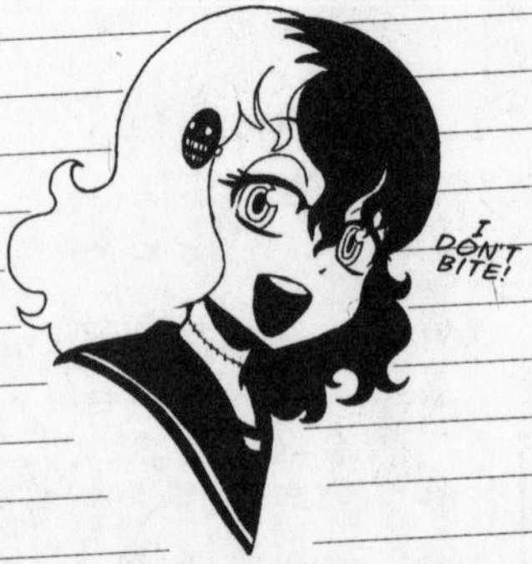
I DON'T BITE!

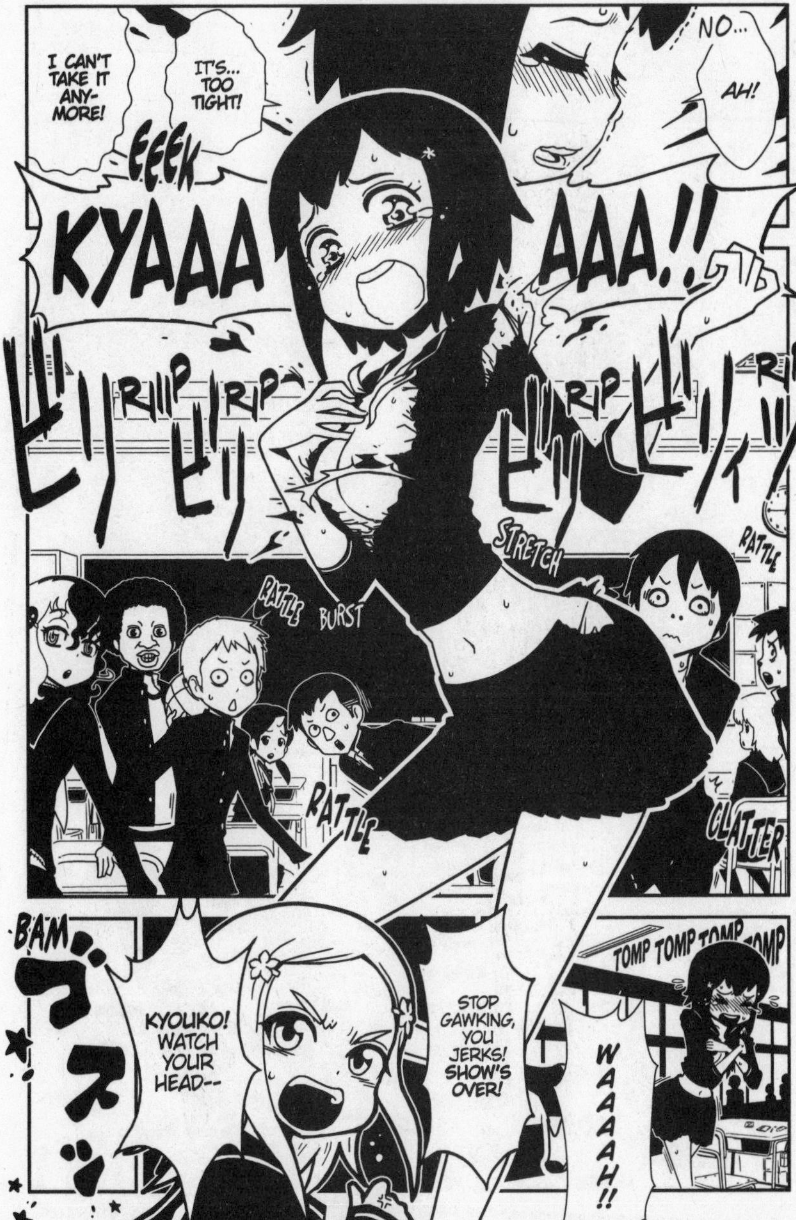
NO...
AH!
IT'S... TOO TIGHT!
I CAN'T TAKE IT ANYMORE!
EEEK
KYAAA AAA!!
RIP
RIP
ビリビリィッ
RIP
RIIIP
ビリ
ビリ
STRETCH
RATTLE
RATTLE
BURST
RATTLE
CLATTER
TOMP TOMP TOMP TOMP
WAAAAAH!!
STOP GAWKING, YOU JERKS! SHOW'S OVER!
KYOUKO! WATCH YOUR HEAD--
BAM
ゴスッ

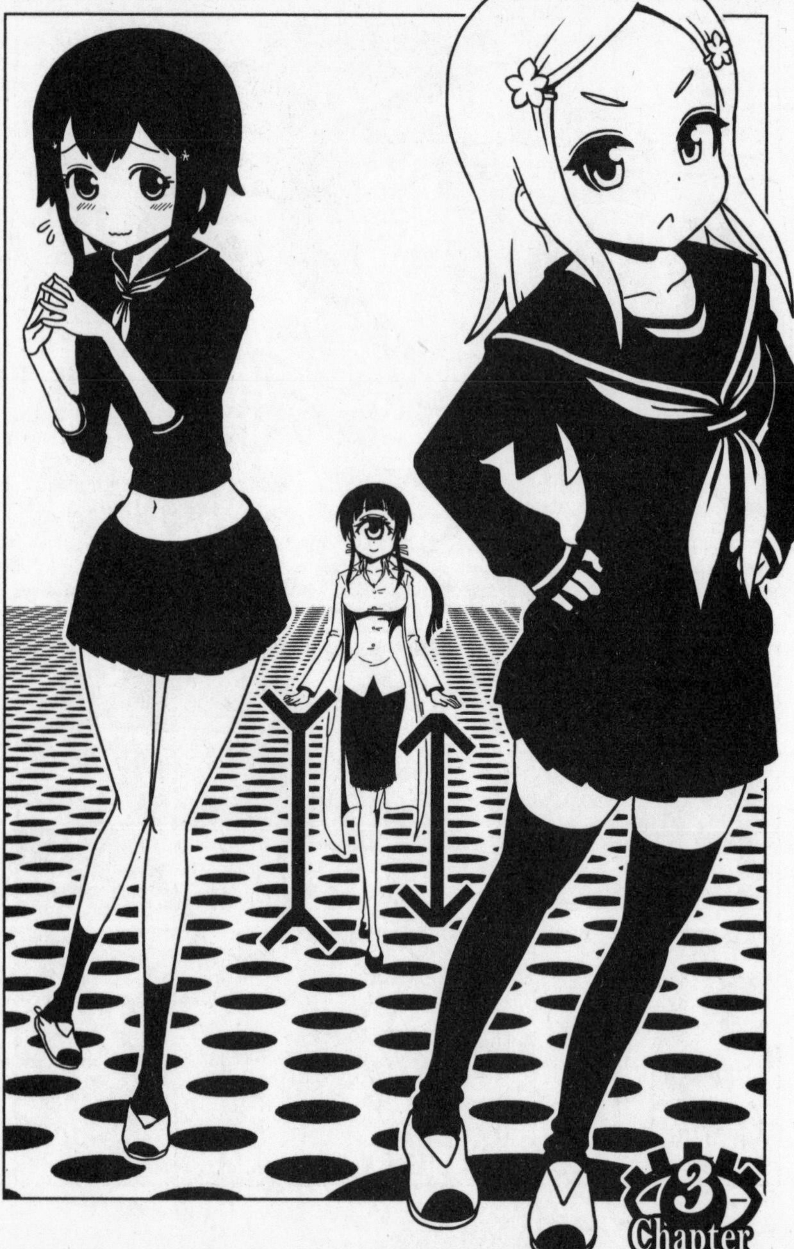
3
Chapter

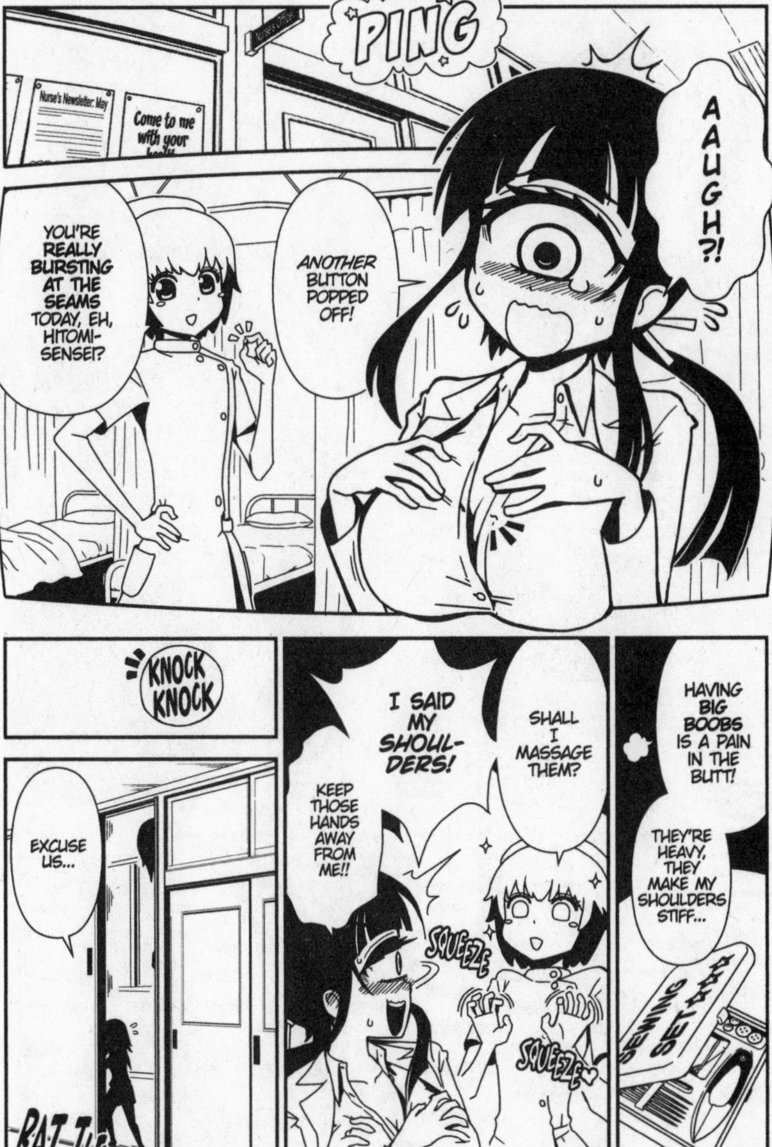
PING
AAUGH?!
Nurse's Office
Nurse's Newsletter: May
Come to me with your
ANOTHER BUTTON POPPED OFF!
YOU'RE REALLY BURSTING AT THE SEAMS TODAY, EH, HITOMI-SENSEI?
HAVING BIG BOOBS IS A PAIN IN THE BUTT!
THEY'RE HEAVY, THEY MAKE MY SHOULDERS STIFF...
SEWING SET
SHALL I MASSAGE THEM?
I SAID MY SHOULDERS!
KEEP THOSE HANDS AWAY FROM ME!!
SQUEEZE
SQUEEZE♥
KNOCK KNOCK
EXCUSE US...
RAT...TLE...

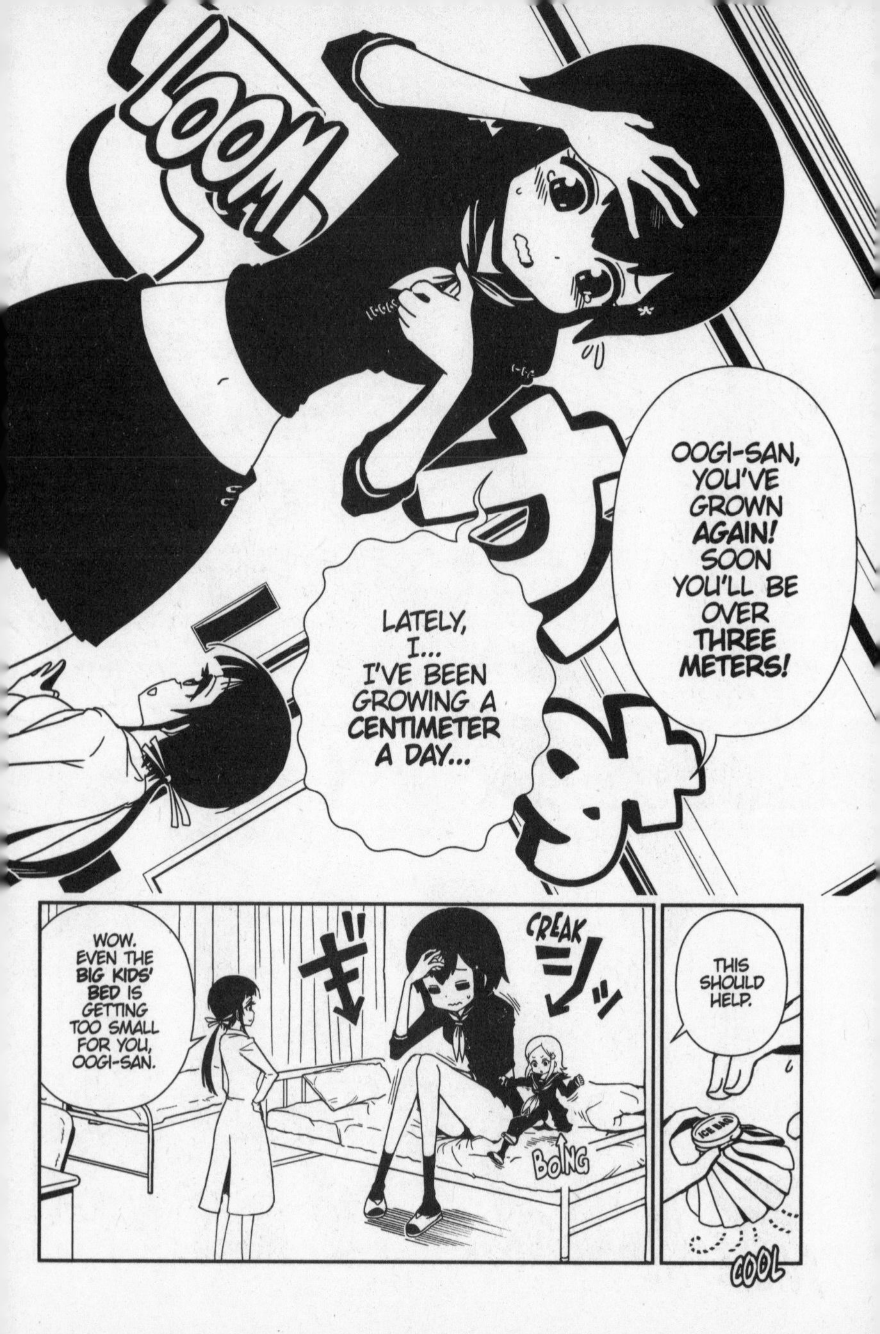
LOOM
OOGI-SAN, YOU'VE GROWN AGAIN! SOON YOU'LL BE OVER THREE METERS!
LATELY, I... I'VE BEEN GROWING A CENTIMETER A DAY...
THIS SHOULD HELP.
ICE BAG
COOL
CREAK
WOW. EVEN THE BIG KIDS' BED IS GETTING TOO SMALL FOR YOU, OOGI-SAN.
BOING

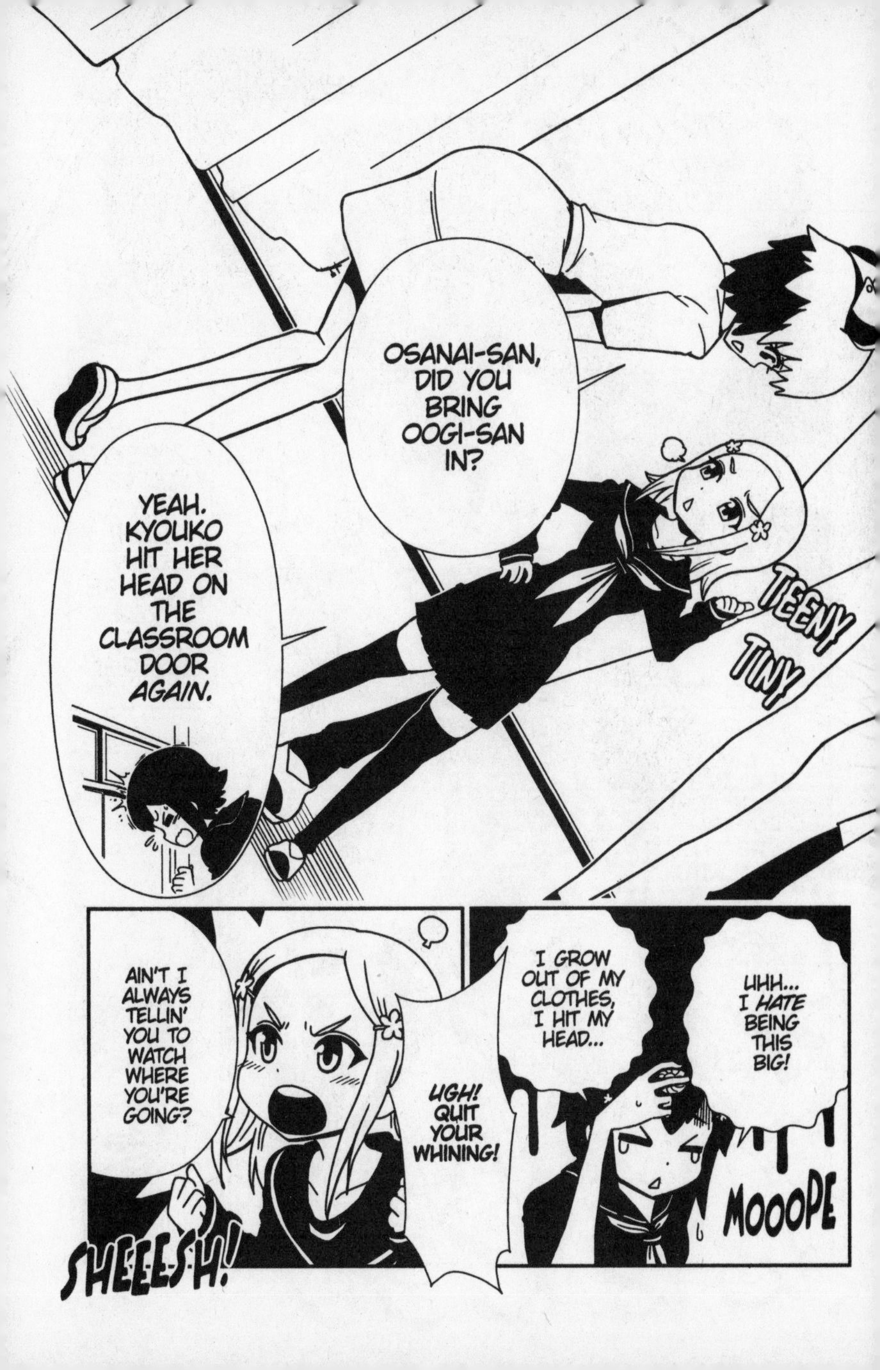
OSANAI-SAN, DID YOU BRING OOGI-SAN IN?
YEAH. KYOUKO HIT HER HEAD ON THE CLASSROOM DOOR *AGAIN.*
TEENY TINY
UHH... I *HATE* BEING THIS BIG!
I GROW OUT OF MY CLOTHES, I HIT MY HEAD...
MOOOPE
UGH! QUIT YOUR WHINING!
AIN'T I ALWAYS TELLIN' YOU TO WATCH WHERE YOU'RE GOING?
SHEEESH!

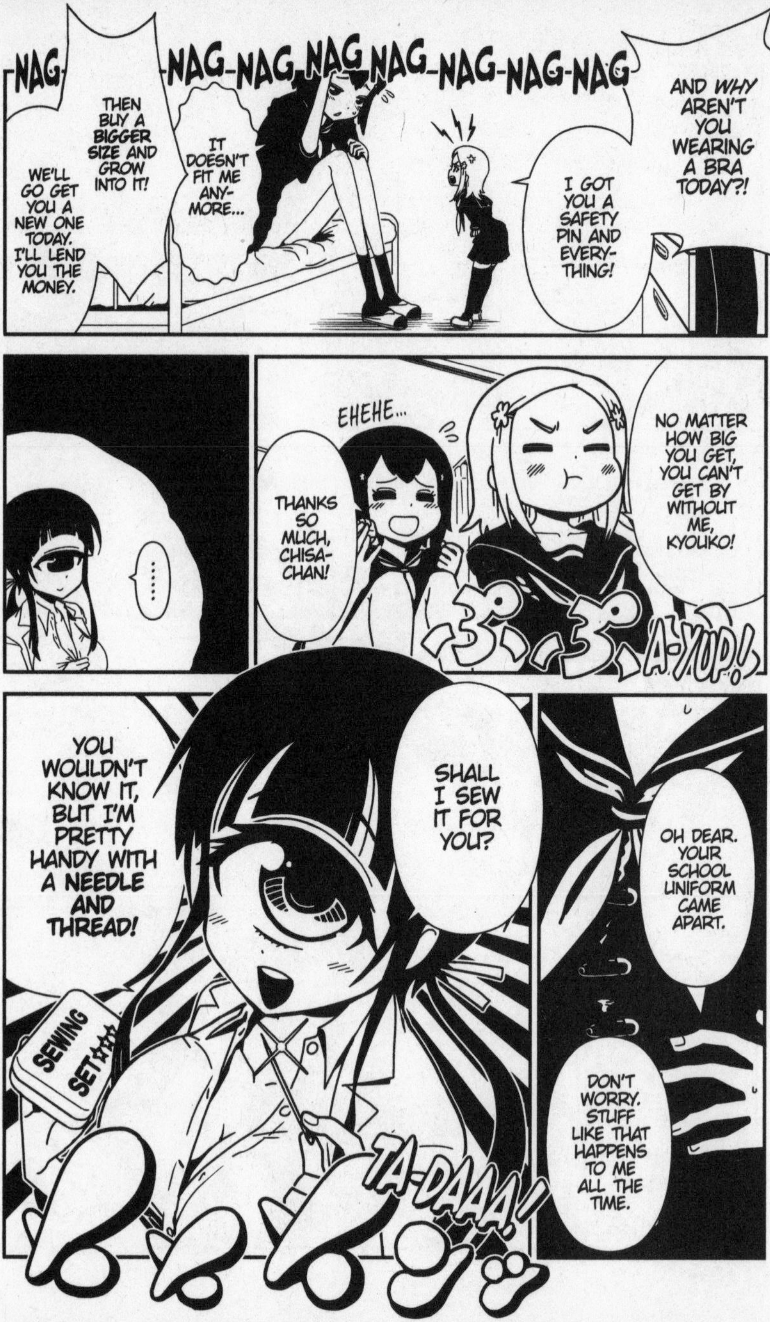

AND WHY AREN'T YOU WEARING A BRA TODAY?!
I GOT YOU A SAFETY PIN AND EVERY-THING!
NAG- -NAG-NAG NAG NAG-NAG-NAG-NAG
IT DOESN'T FIT ME ANY-MORE...
THEN BUY A BIGGER SIZE AND GROW INTO IT!
WE'LL GO GET YOU A NEW ONE TODAY. I'LL LEND YOU THE MONEY.
NO MATTER HOW BIG YOU GET, YOU CAN'T GET BY WITHOUT ME, KYOUKO!
EHEHE...
THANKS SO MUCH, CHISA-CHAN!
3 3 A-YUP!
......
OH DEAR. YOUR SCHOOL UNIFORM CAME APART.
DON'T WORRY. STUFF LIKE THAT HAPPENS TO ME ALL THE TIME.
SHALL I SEW IT FOR YOU?
YOU WOULDN'T KNOW IT, BUT I'M PRETTY HANDY WITH A NEEDLE AND THREAD!
SEWING SET☆☆☆
TA-DAAA!

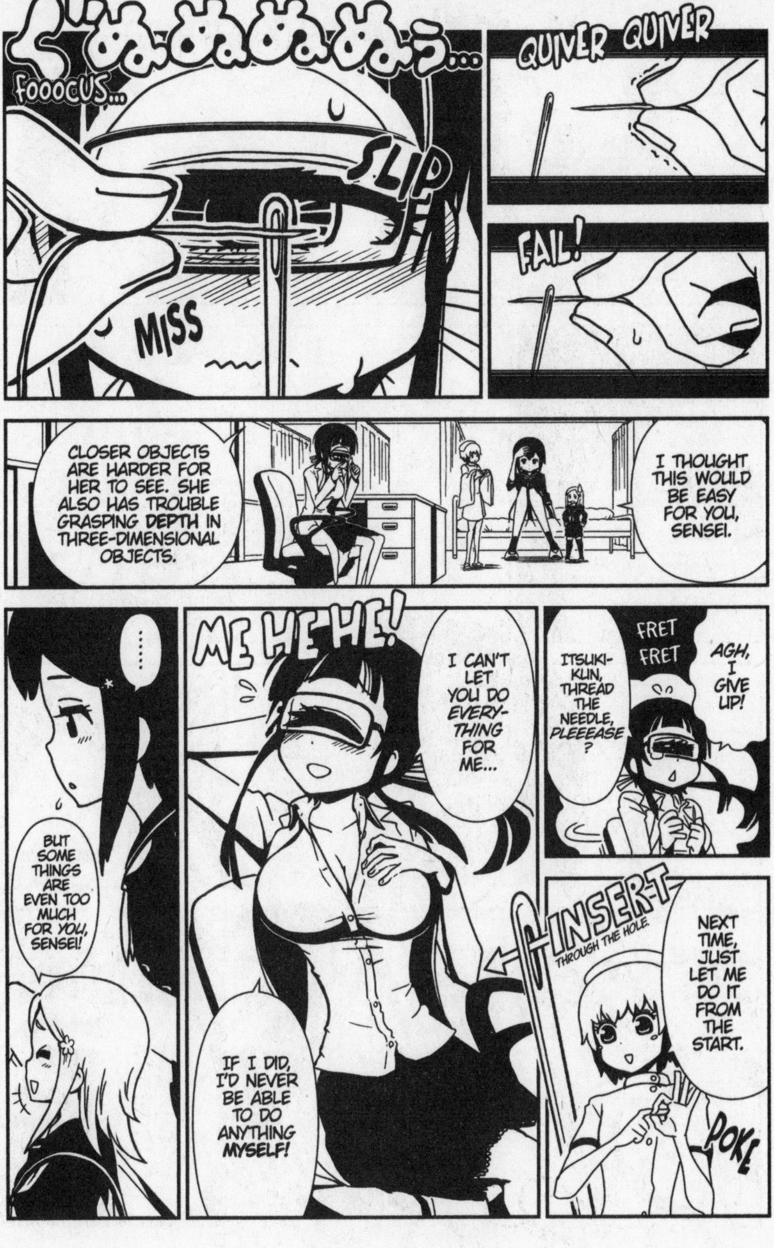
QUIVER QUIVER
FAIL!
ぐぬぬぬぬう…
FOOOCUS...
SLIP
MISS
I THOUGHT THIS WOULD BE EASY FOR YOU, SENSEI.
CLOSER OBJECTS ARE HARDER FOR HER TO SEE. SHE ALSO HAS TROUBLE GRASPING DEPTH IN THREE-DIMENSIONAL OBJECTS.
AGH, I GIVE UP!
FRET FRET
ITSUKI-KUN, THREAD THE NEEDLE, PLEEEASE?
NEXT TIME, JUST LET ME DO IT FROM THE START.
INSERT-T
THROUGH THE HOLE.
POKE
I CAN'T LET YOU DO EVERYTHING FOR ME...
ME HE HE!
IF I DID, I'D NEVER BE ABLE TO DO ANYTHING MYSELF!
......
BUT SOME THINGS ARE EVEN TOO MUCH FOR YOU, SENSEI!

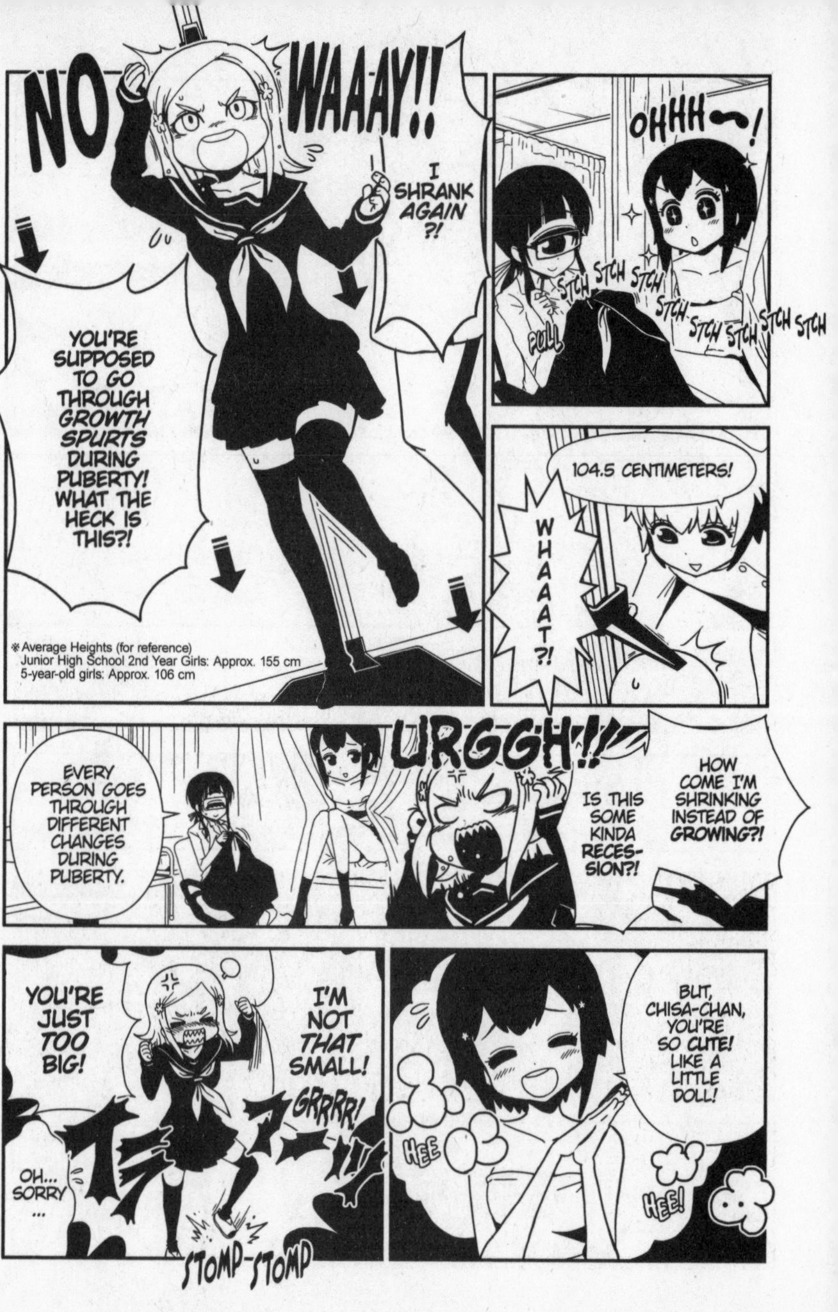
OHHH~!
STCH STCH STCH STCH STCH STCH STCH STCH
PULL
104.5 CENTIMETERS!
WHAAAAT?!
NO WAAAY!!
I SHRANK AGAIN?!
YOU'RE SUPPOSED TO GO THROUGH GROWTH SPURTS DURING PUBERTY! WHAT THE HECK IS THIS?!
※Average Heights (for reference)
Junior High School 2nd Year Girls: Approx. 155 cm
5-year-old girls: Approx. 106 cm
HOW COME I'M SHRINKING INSTEAD OF GROWING?!
IS THIS SOME KINDA RECES-SION?!
URGGH!!
EVERY PERSON GOES THROUGH DIFFERENT CHANGES DURING PUBERTY.
BUT, CHISA-CHAN, YOU'RE SO CUTE! LIKE A LITTLE DOLL!
HEE
HEE!
I'M NOT THAT SMALL!
GRRRR!
YOU'RE JUST TOO BIG!
OH... SORRY ...
STOMP-STOMP

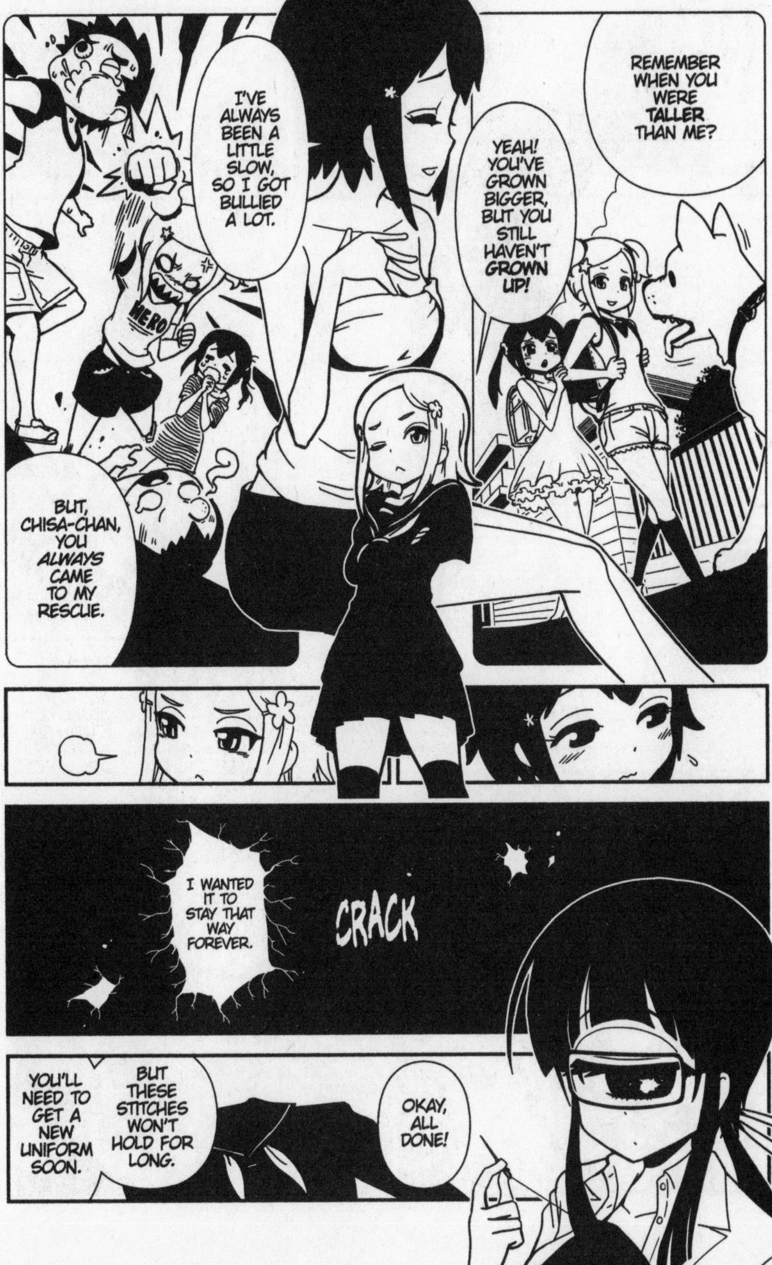
REMEMBER WHEN YOU WERE TALLER THAN ME?
YEAH! YOU'VE GROWN BIGGER, BUT YOU STILL HAVEN'T GROWN UP!
I'VE ALWAYS BEEN A LITTLE SLOW, SO I GOT BULLIED A LOT.
HERO
BUT, CHISA-CHAN, YOU ALWAYS CAME TO MY RESCUE.
CRACK
I WANTED IT TO STAY THAT WAY FOREVER.
OKAY, ALL DONE!
BUT THESE STITCHES WON'T HOLD FOR LONG.
YOU'LL NEED TO GET A NEW UNIFORM SOON.

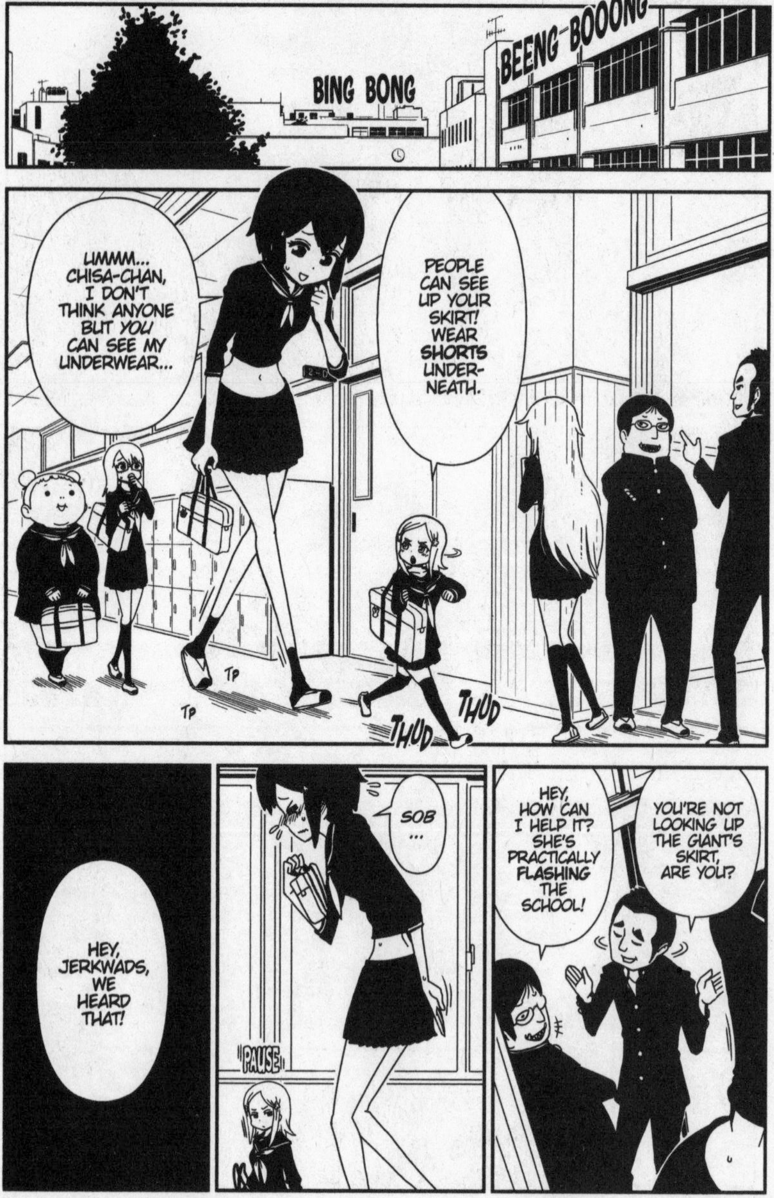
BEENG BOOONG
BING BONG
PEOPLE CAN SEE UP YOUR SKIRT! WEAR SHORTS UNDERNEATH.
UMMM... CHISA-CHAN, I DON'T THINK ANYONE BUT YOU CAN SEE MY UNDERWEAR...
THUD
THUD
TP
TP
YOU'RE NOT LOOKING UP THE GIANT'S SKIRT, ARE YOU?
HEY, HOW CAN I HELP IT? SHE'S PRACTICALLY FLASHING THE SCHOOL!
SOB ...
PAUSE
HEY, JERKWADS, WE HEARD THAT!

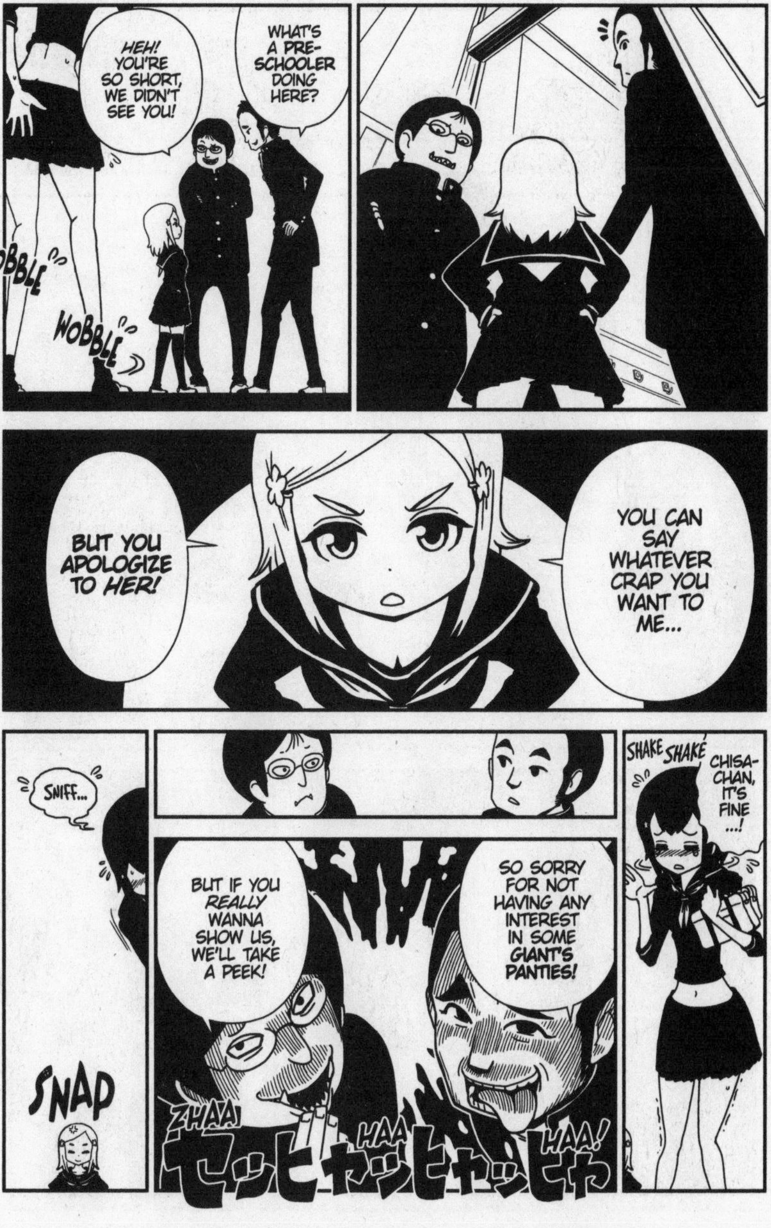
WHAT'S A PRE-SCHOOLER DOING HERE?
HEH! YOU'RE SO SHORT, WE DIDN'T SEE YOU!
WOBBLE
WOBBLE
YOU CAN SAY WHATEVER CRAP YOU WANT TO ME...
BUT YOU APOLOGIZE TO HER!
SHAKE SHAKE
CHISA-CHAN, IT'S FINE...!
SO SORRY FOR NOT HAVING ANY INTEREST IN SOME GIANT'S PANTIES!
BUT IF YOU REALLY WANNA SHOW US, WE'LL TAKE A PEEK!
ZHAA HAA HAA!
SNIFF...
SNAP

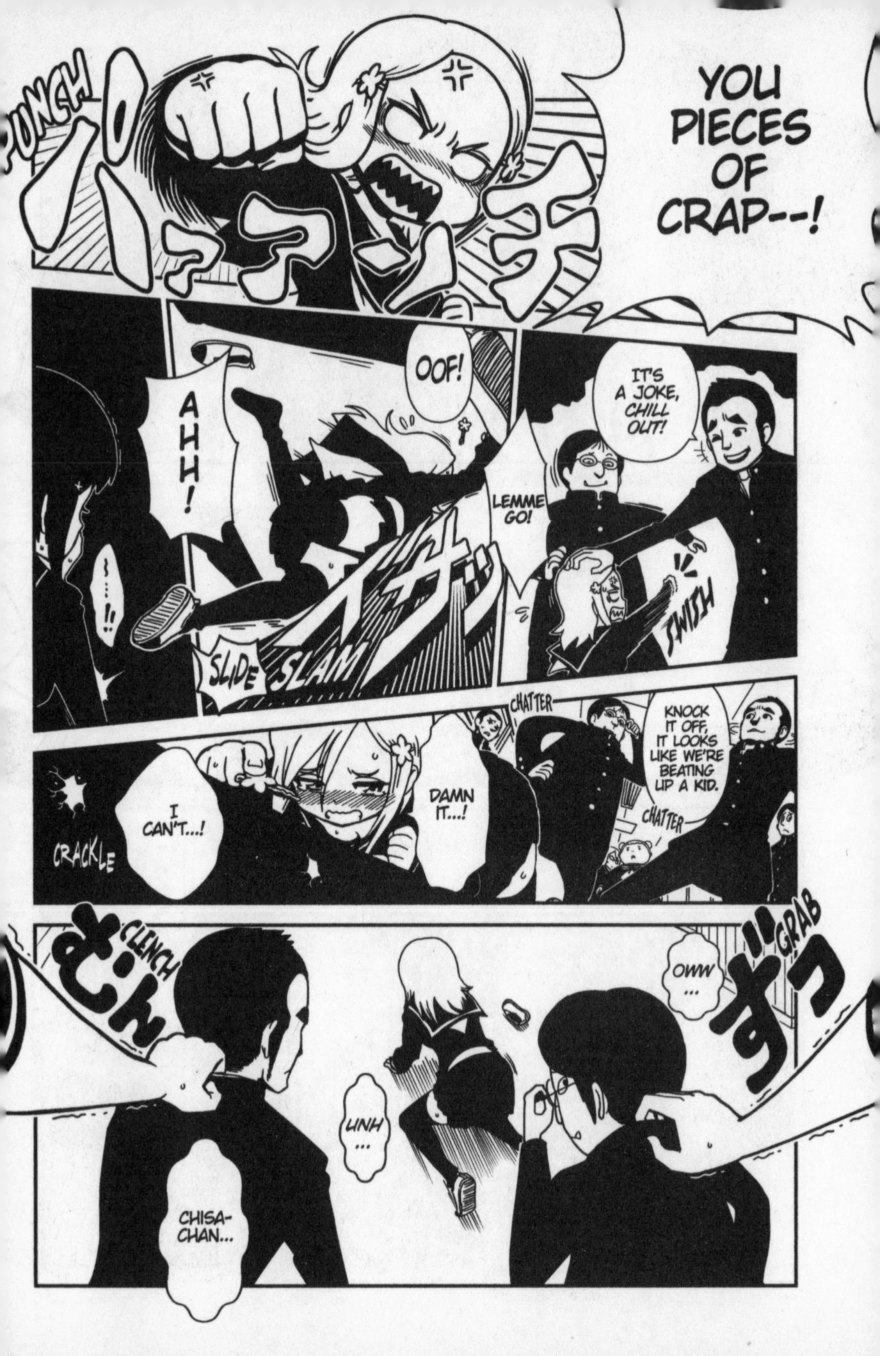
YOU PIECES OF CRAP--!
PUNCH
IT'S A JOKE, CHILL OUT!
LEMME GO!
SWISH
OOF!
AHH!
SLIDE
SLAM
...!!
KNOCK IT OFF, IT LOOKS LIKE WE'RE BEATING UP A KID.
CHATTER
CHATTER
DAMN IT...!
I CAN'T...!
CRACKLE
GRAB
OWW ...
UNH ...
CLENCH
CHISA-CHAN...

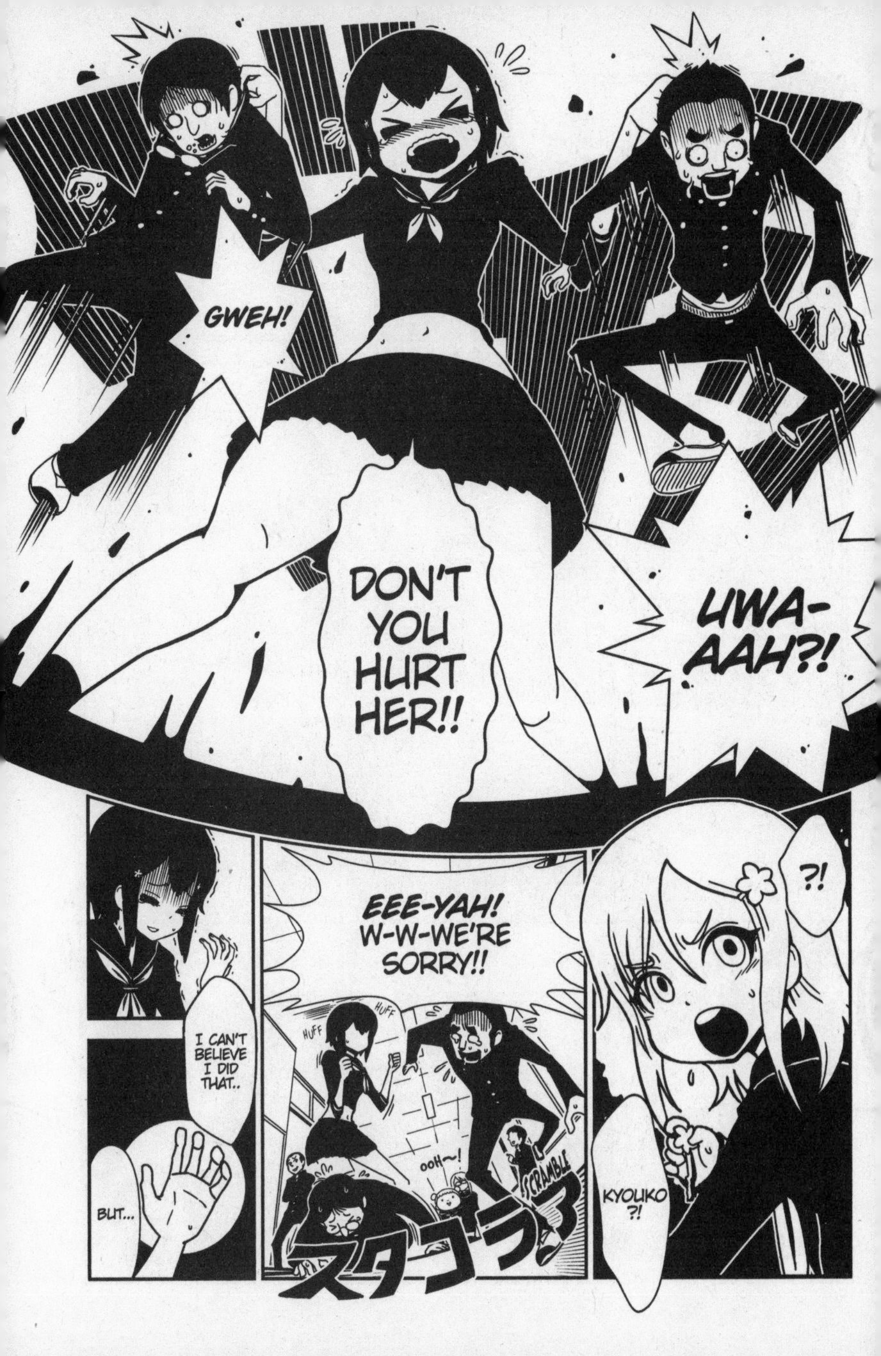
DON'T YOU HURT HER!!
GWEH!
UWA-AAH?!
?!
KYOUKO ?!
EEE-YAH! W-W-WE'RE SORRY!!
HUFF
HUFF
OOH~!
SCRAMBLE
スタコラ
I CAN'T BELIEVE I DID THAT..
BUT...

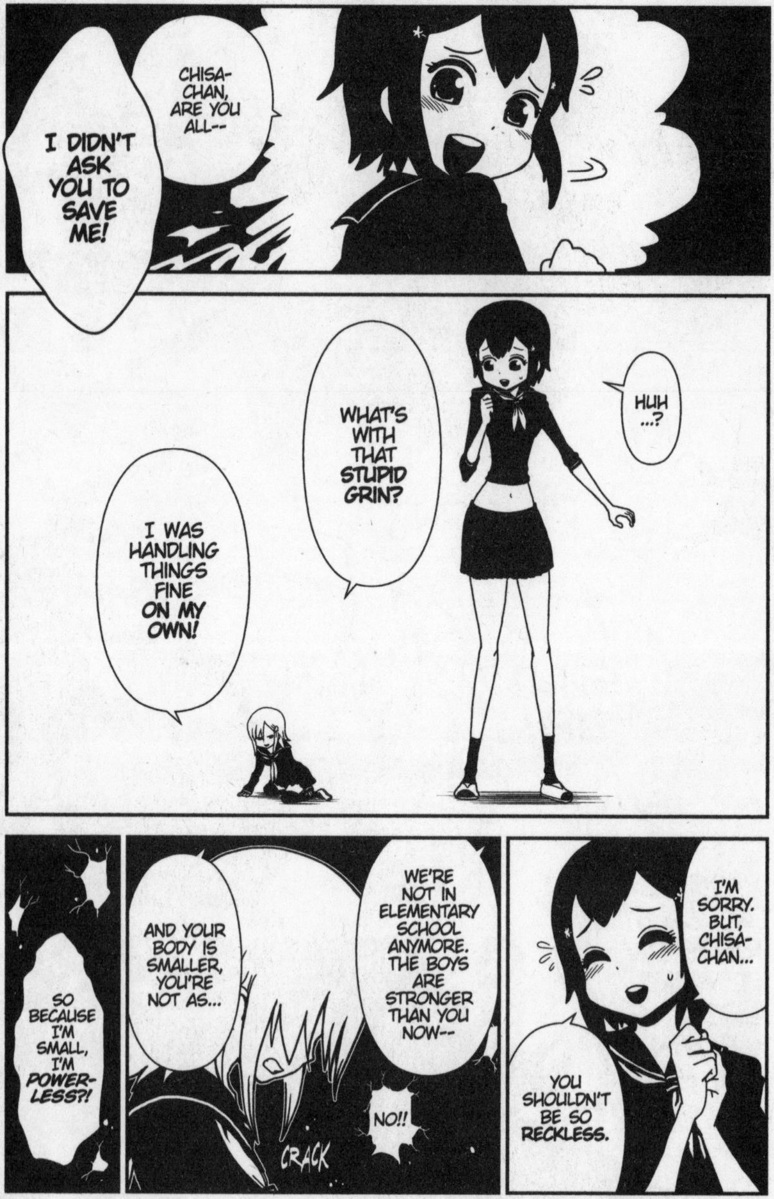
CHISA-CHAN, ARE YOU ALL--
I DIDN'T ASK YOU TO SAVE ME!
HUH ...?
WHAT'S WITH THAT STUPID GRIN?
I WAS HANDLING THINGS FINE ON MY OWN!
I'M SORRY. BUT, CHISA-CHAN...
YOU SHOULDN'T BE SO RECKLESS.
WE'RE NOT IN ELEMENTARY SCHOOL ANYMORE. THE BOYS ARE STRONGER THAN YOU NOW--
AND YOUR BODY IS SMALLER, YOU'RE NOT AS...
NO!!
CRACK
SO BECAUSE I'M SMALL, I'M POWER-LESS?!

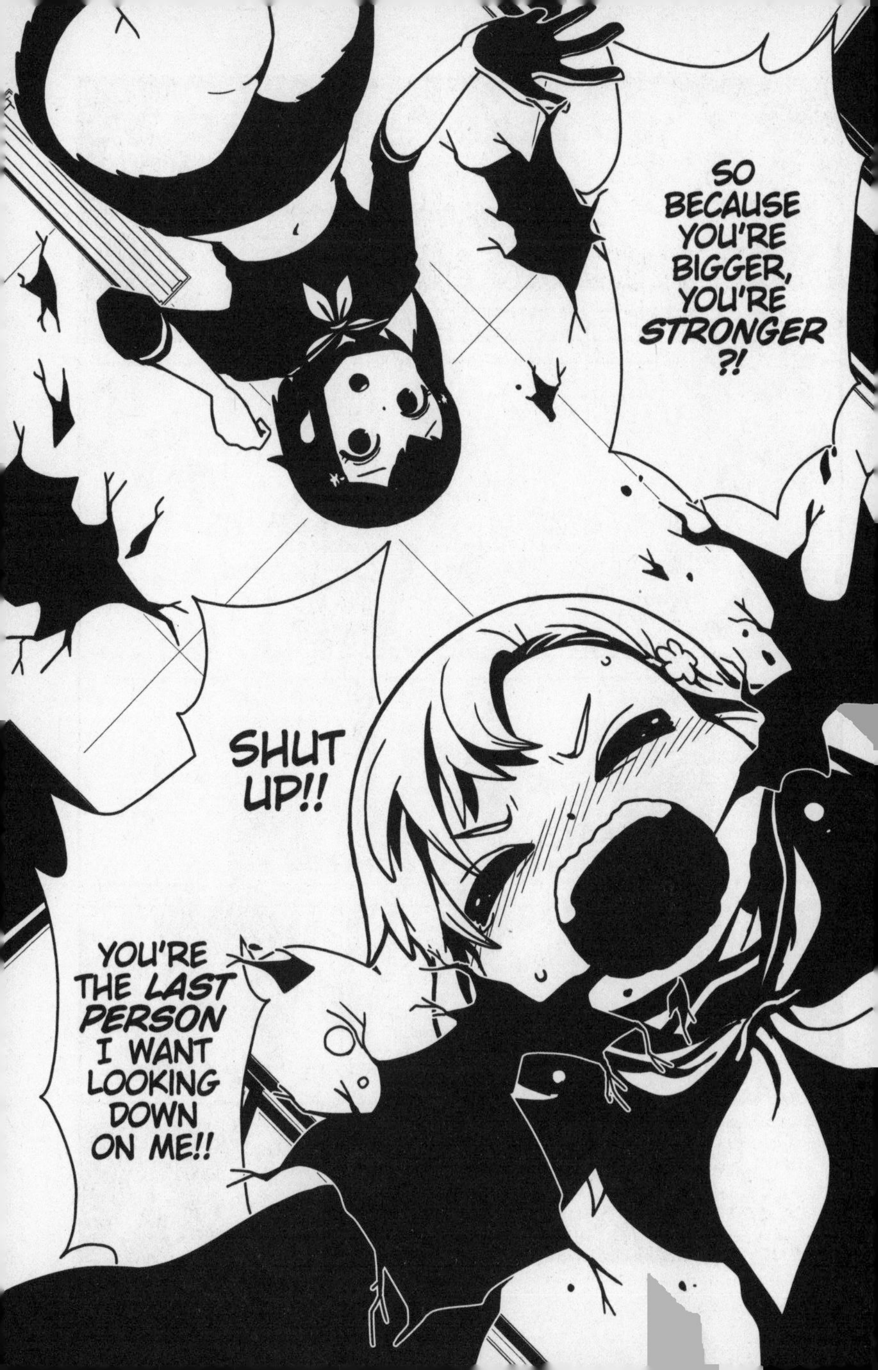
SO BECAUSE YOU'RE BIGGER, YOU'RE STRONGER?!
SHUT UP!!
YOU'RE THE LAST PERSON I WANT LOOKING DOWN ON ME!!

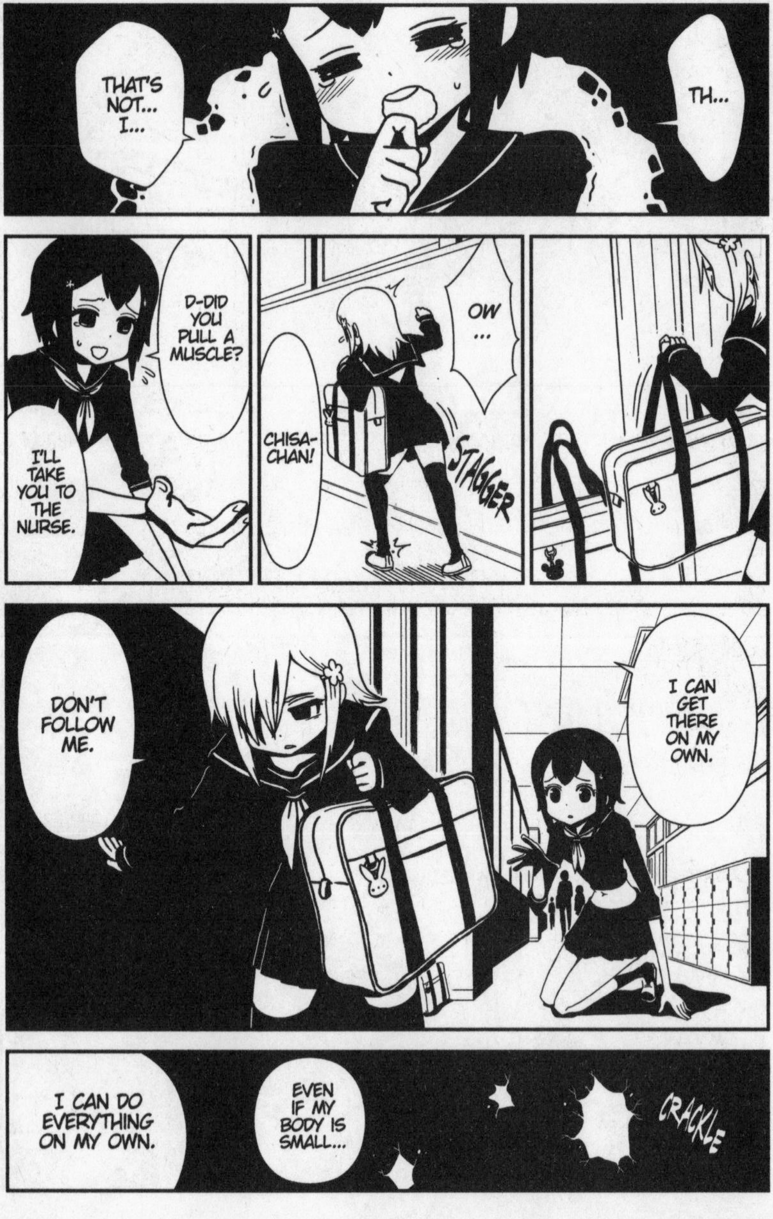
TH...
THAT'S NOT... I...
OW ...
STAGGER
CHISA-CHAN!
D-DID YOU PULL A MUSCLE?
I'LL TAKE YOU TO THE NURSE.
I CAN GET THERE ON MY OWN.
DON'T FOLLOW ME.
CRACKLE
EVEN IF MY BODY IS SMALL...
I CAN DO EVERYTHING ON MY OWN.

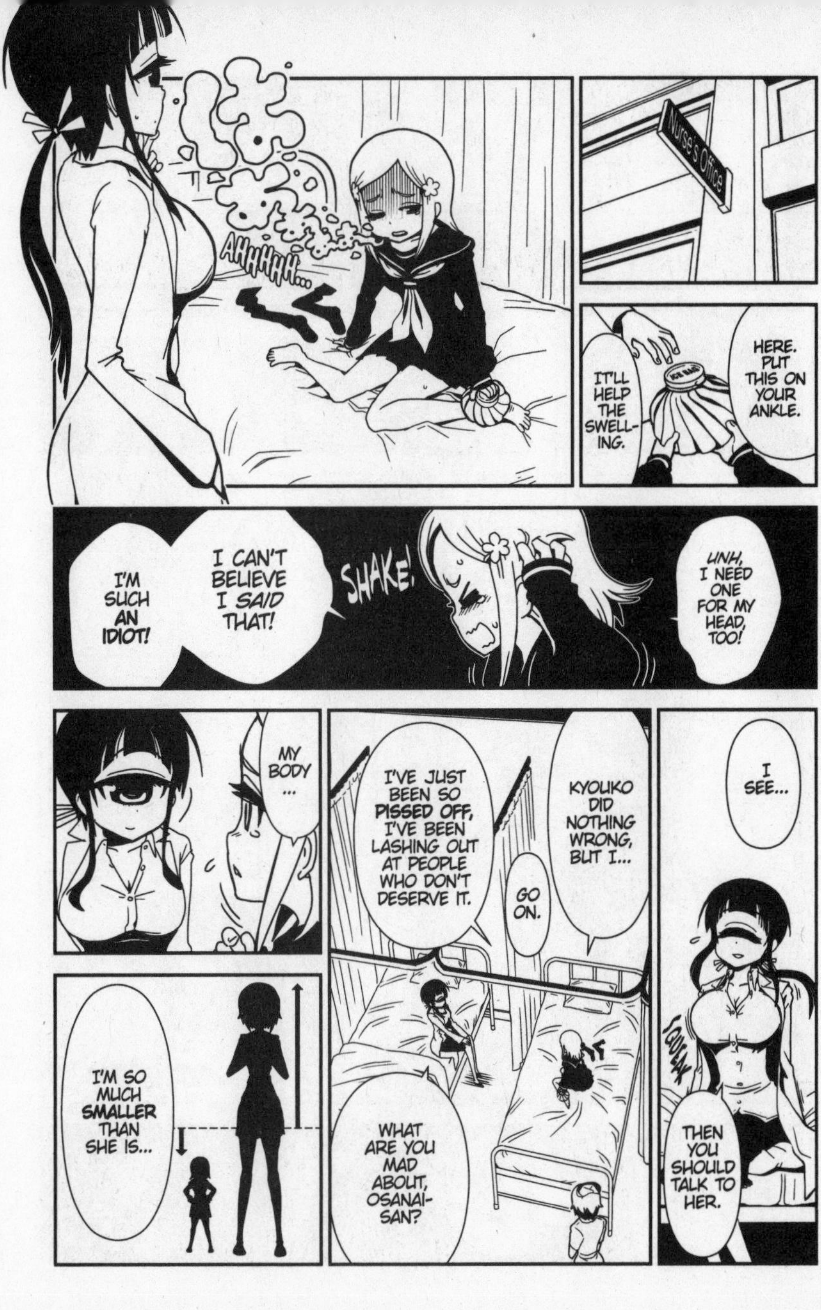
Nurse's Office
HERE. PUT THIS ON YOUR ANKLE.
IT'LL HELP THE SWELLING.
ICE BAG
AHHHHH...
UNH, I NEED ONE FOR MY HEAD, TOO!
SHAKE!
I CAN'T BELIEVE I *SAID* THAT!
I'M SUCH AN IDIOT!
I SEE...
THEN YOU SHOULD TALK TO HER.
KYOUKO DID NOTHING WRONG, BUT I...
GO ON.
I'VE JUST BEEN SO **PISSED OFF**, I'VE BEEN LASHING OUT AT PEOPLE WHO DON'T DESERVE IT.
WHAT ARE YOU MAD ABOUT, OSANAI-SAN?
MY BODY ...
I'M SO MUCH **SMALLER** THAN SHE IS...

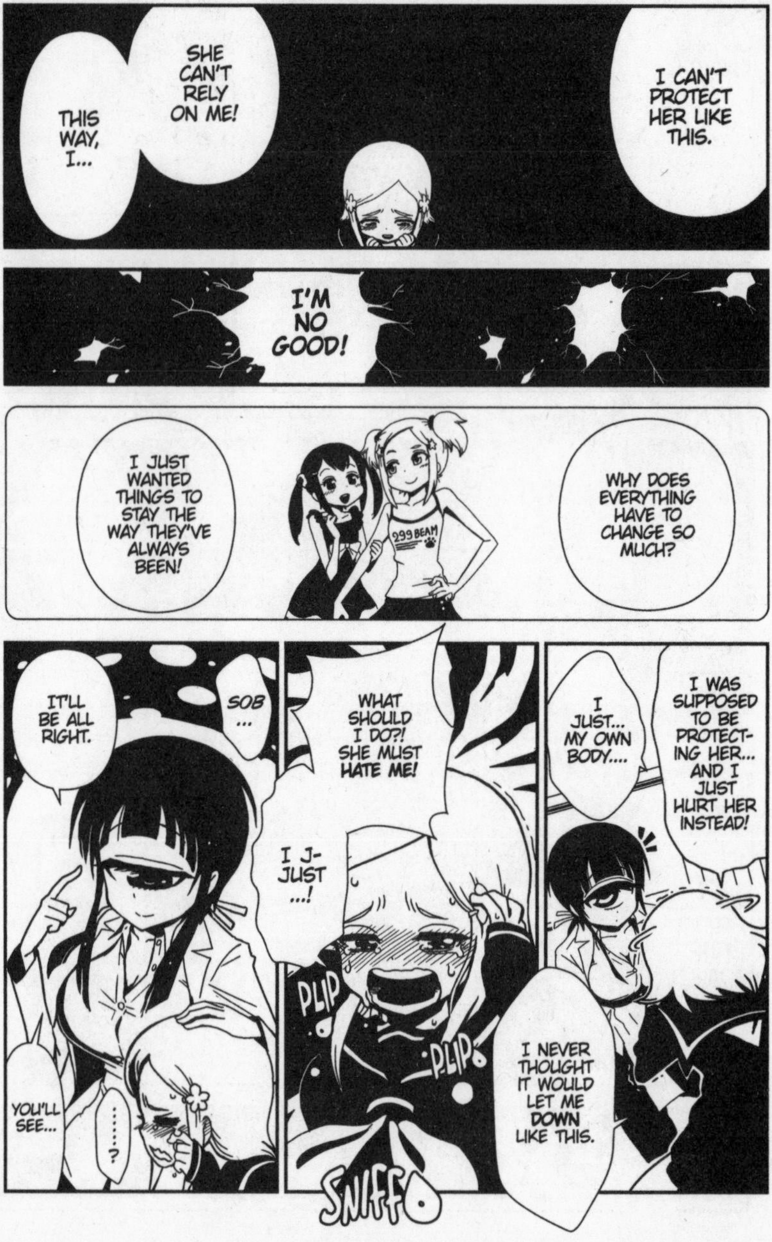
I CAN'T PROTECT HER LIKE THIS.
SHE CAN'T RELY ON ME!
THIS WAY, I...
I'M NO GOOD!
WHY DOES EVERYTHING HAVE TO CHANGE SO MUCH?
299 BEAM
I JUST WANTED THINGS TO STAY THE WAY THEY'VE ALWAYS BEEN!
I WAS SUPPOSED TO BE PROTECTING HER... AND I JUST HURT HER INSTEAD!
I JUST... MY OWN BODY....
I NEVER THOUGHT IT WOULD LET ME DOWN LIKE THIS.
WHAT SHOULD I DO?! SHE MUST HATE ME!
I J-JUST ...!
PLIP
PLIP
SNIFF
SOB ...
IT'LL BE ALL RIGHT.
......?
YOU'LL SEE...

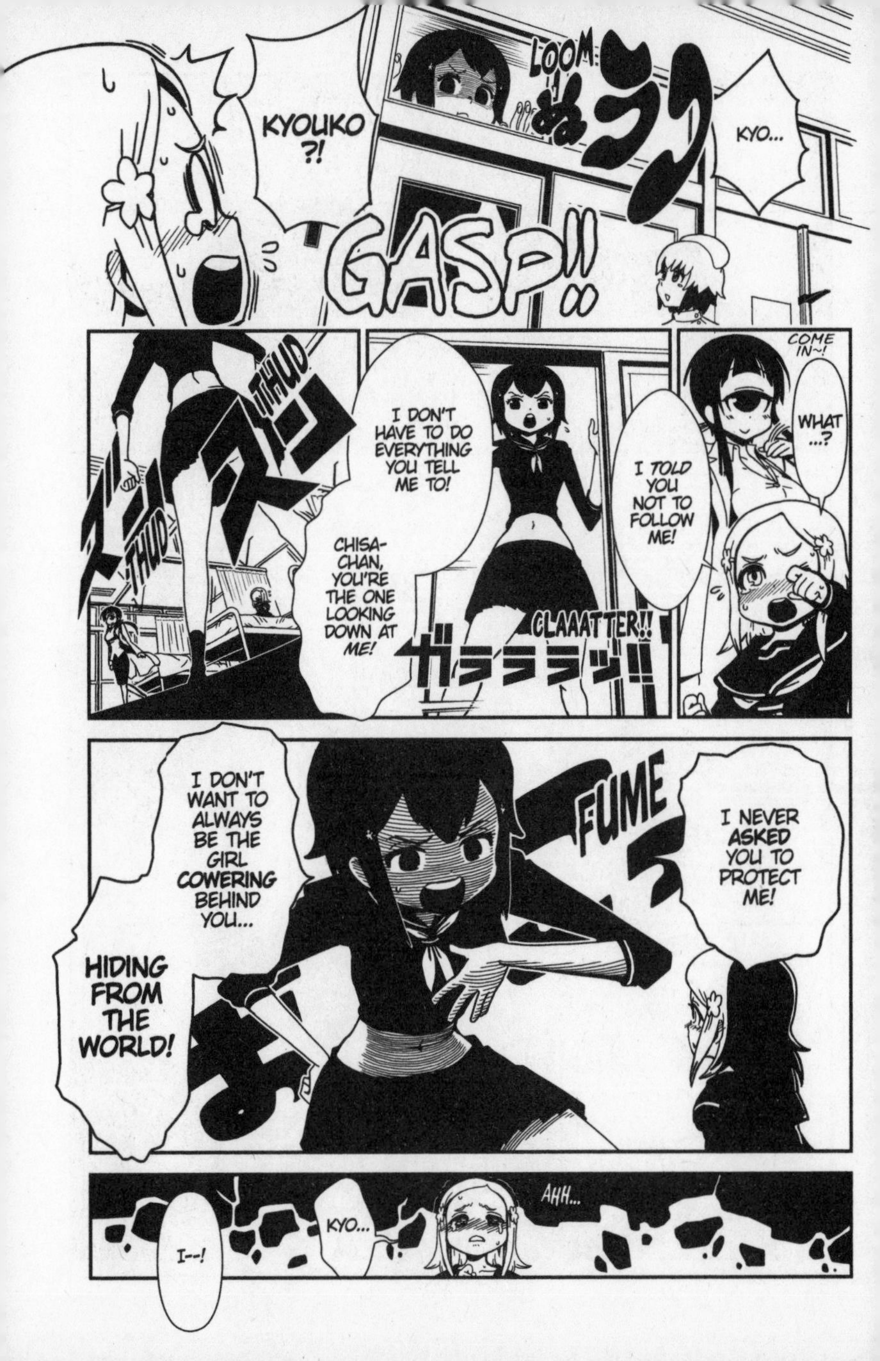
KYO...
LOOM
ぬうう
KYOUKO ?!
GASP!!
COME IN~!
WHAT ...?
I TOLD YOU NOT TO FOLLOW ME!
I DON'T HAVE TO DO EVERYTHING YOU TELL ME TO!
CHISA-CHAN, YOU'RE THE ONE LOOKING DOWN AT ME!
CLAAATTER!!
ガラララッ!!
THUD
THUD
I NEVER ASKED YOU TO PROTECT ME!
FUME
I DON'T WANT TO ALWAYS BE THE GIRL COWERING BEHIND YOU...
HIDING FROM THE WORLD!
AHH...
KYO...
I--!

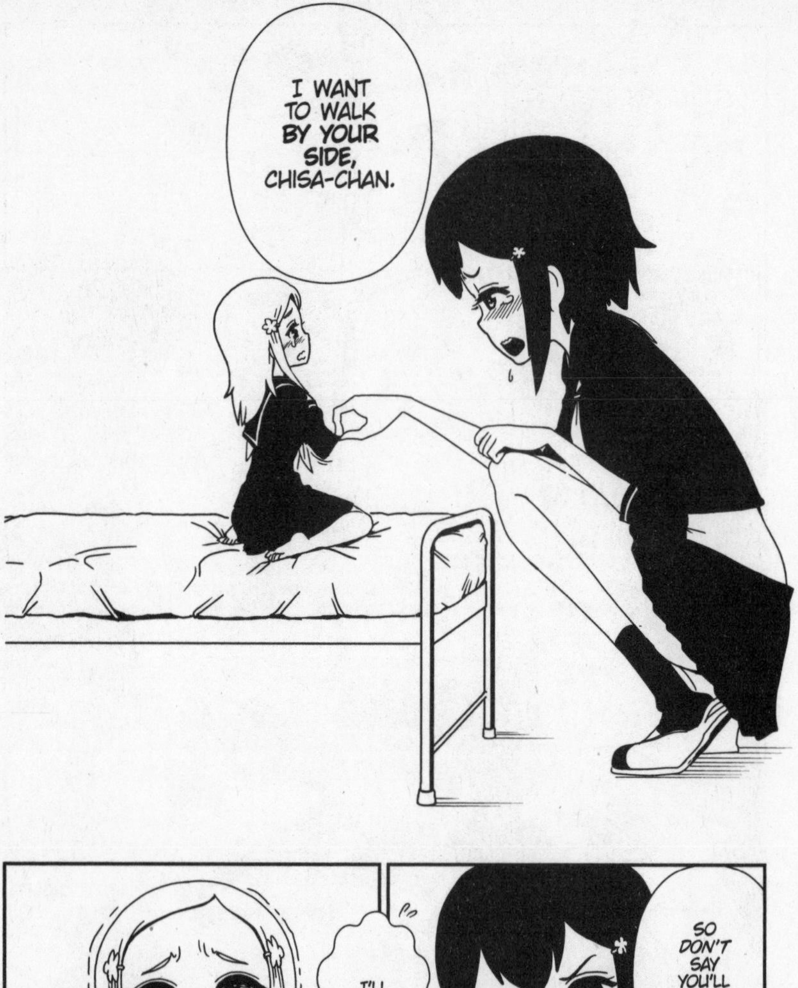
I WANT TO WALK BY YOUR SIDE, CHISA-CHAN.

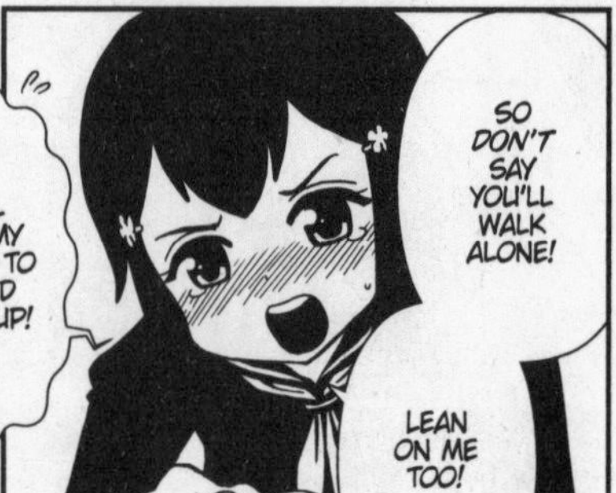
SO DON'T SAY YOU'LL WALK ALONE!
LEAN ON ME TOO!
I'LL DO MY BEST TO HOLD YOU UP!

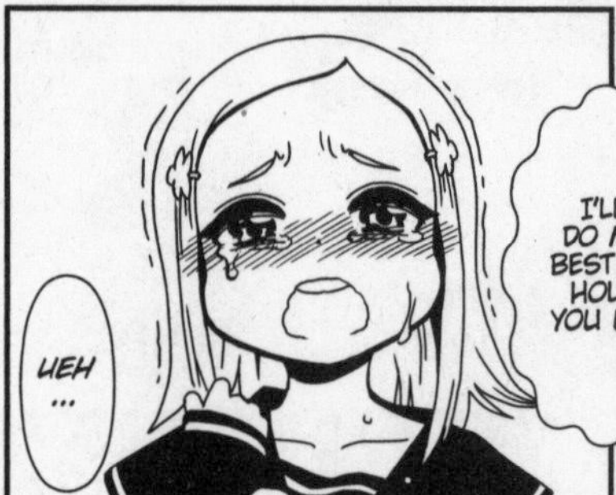
UEH ...

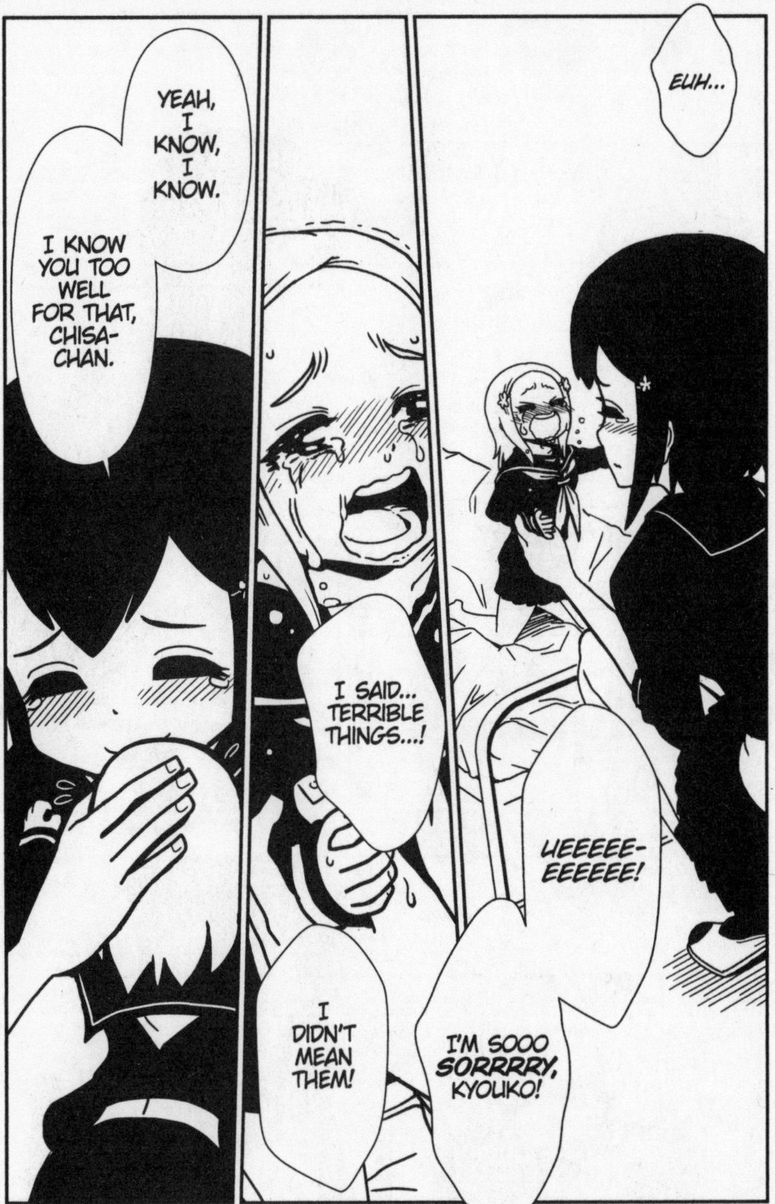
EUH...
UEEEEE-EEEEEE!
I'M SOOO SORRRRY, KYOUKO!
I SAID... TERRIBLE THINGS...!
I DIDN'T MEAN THEM!
YEAH, I KNOW, I KNOW.
I KNOW YOU TOO WELL FOR THAT, CHISA-CHAN.

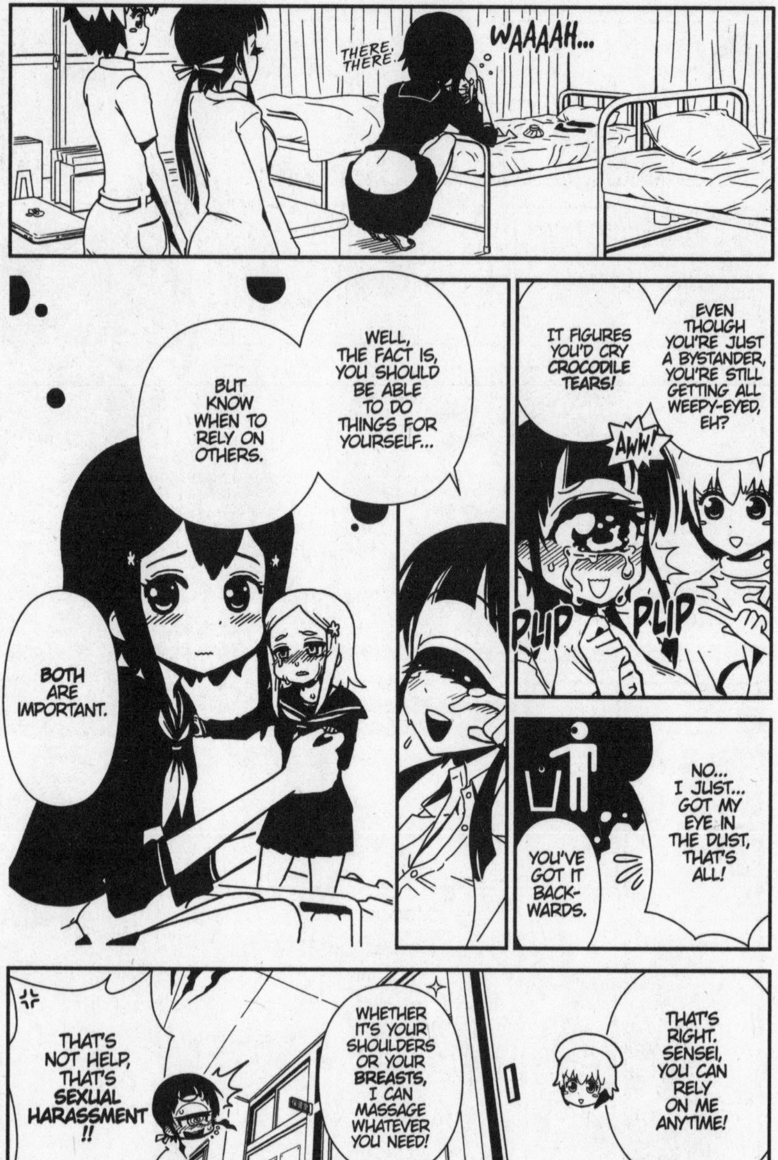
WAAAAH...
THERE, THERE.
EVEN THOUGH YOU'RE JUST A BYSTANDER, YOU'RE STILL GETTING ALL WEEPY-EYED, EH?
AWW!
IT FIGURES YOU'D CRY CROCODILE TEARS!
PLIP
PLIP
NO... I JUST... GOT MY EYE IN THE DUST, THAT'S ALL!
YOU'VE GOT IT BACK-WARDS.
WELL, THE FACT IS, YOU SHOULD BE ABLE TO DO THINGS FOR YOURSELF...
BUT KNOW WHEN TO RELY ON OTHERS.
BOTH ARE IMPORTANT.
THAT'S RIGHT. SENSEI, YOU CAN RELY ON ME ANYTIME!
WHETHER IT'S YOUR SHOULDERS OR YOUR BREASTS, I CAN MASSAGE WHATEVER YOU NEED!
THAT'S NOT HELP, THAT'S SEXUAL HARASSMENT !!

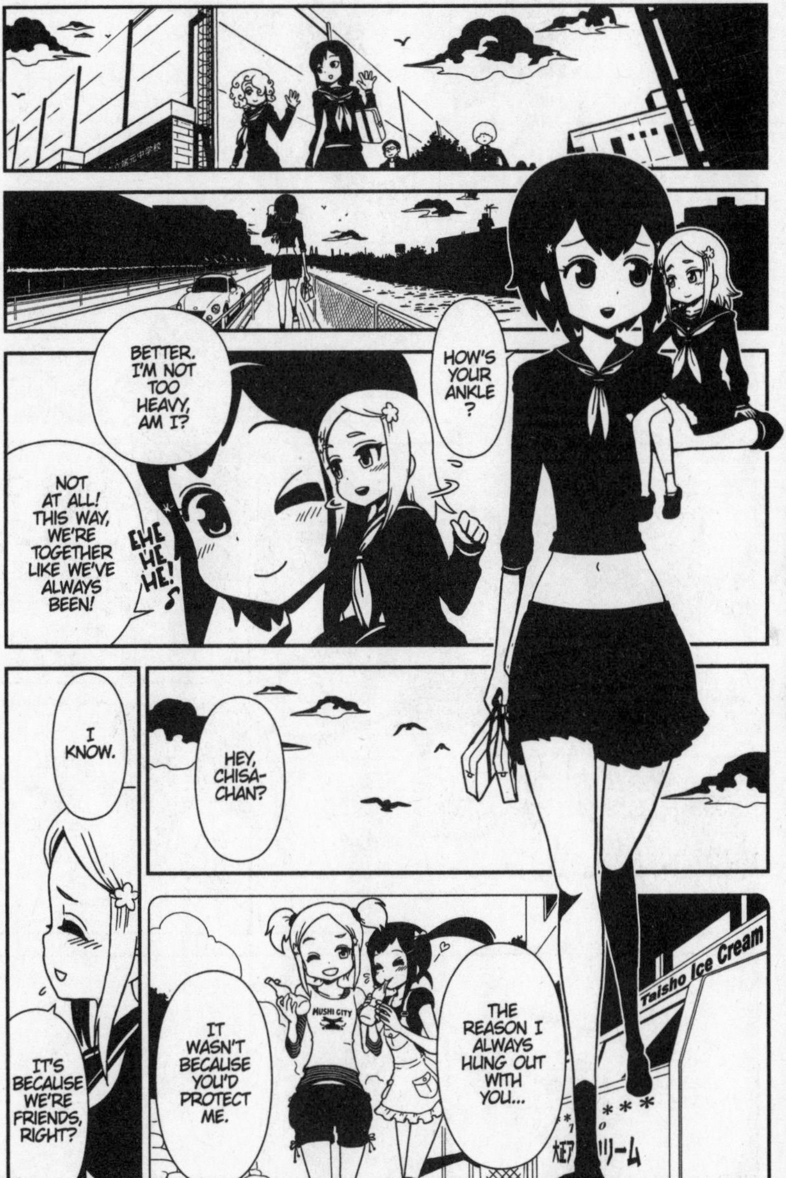
HOW'S YOUR ANKLE?
BETTER. I'M NOT TOO HEAVY, AM I?
NOT AT ALL! THIS WAY, WE'RE TOGETHER LIKE WE'VE ALWAYS BEEN!
EHE HE HE! ♪
HEY, CHISA-CHAN?
Taisho Ice Cream
THE REASON I ALWAYS HUNG OUT WITH YOU...
MUSHI CITY
IT WASN'T BECAUSE YOU'D PROTECT ME.
I KNOW.
IT'S BECAUSE WE'RE FRIENDS, RIGHT?

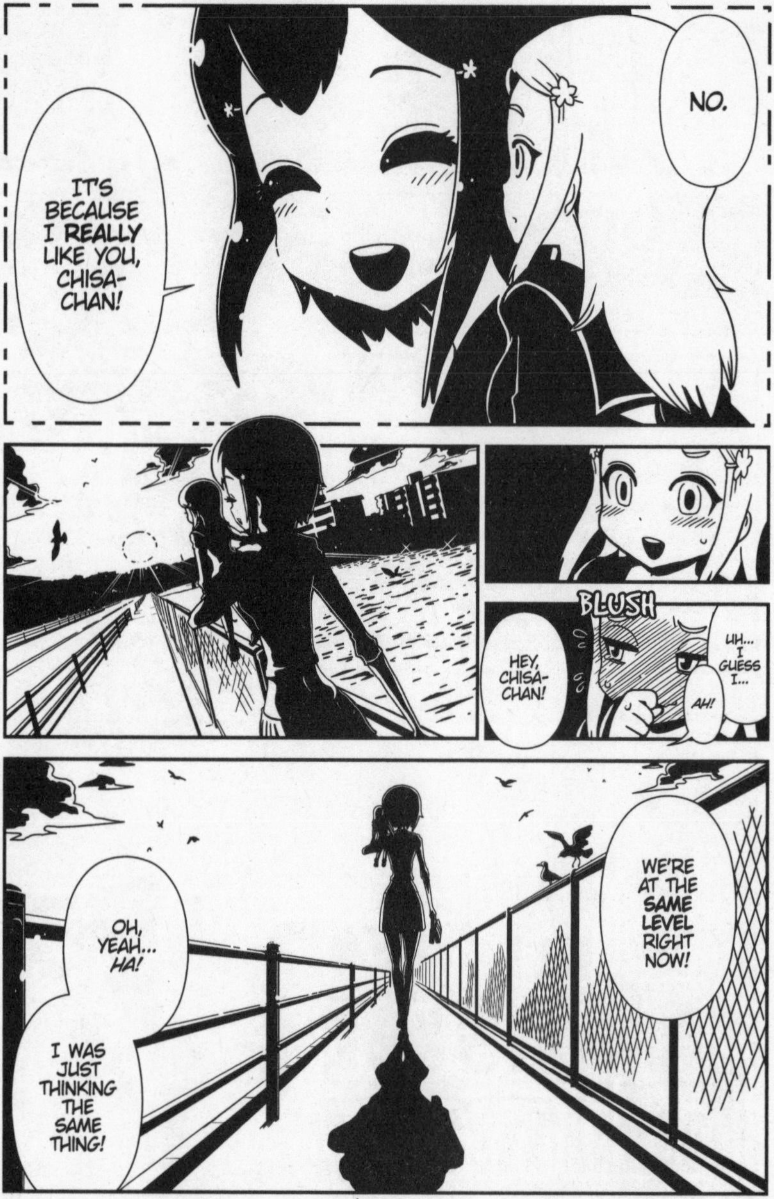
NO.
IT'S BECAUSE I REALLY LIKE YOU, CHISA-CHAN!
BLUSH
UH... I GUESS I...
AH!
HEY, CHISA-CHAN!
WE'RE AT THE SAME LEVEL RIGHT NOW!
OH, YEAH... HA!
I WAS JUST THINKING THE SAME THING!

NURSE HITOMI'S Monster Infirmary

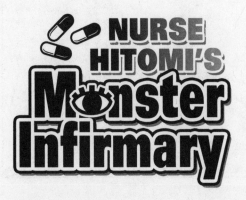

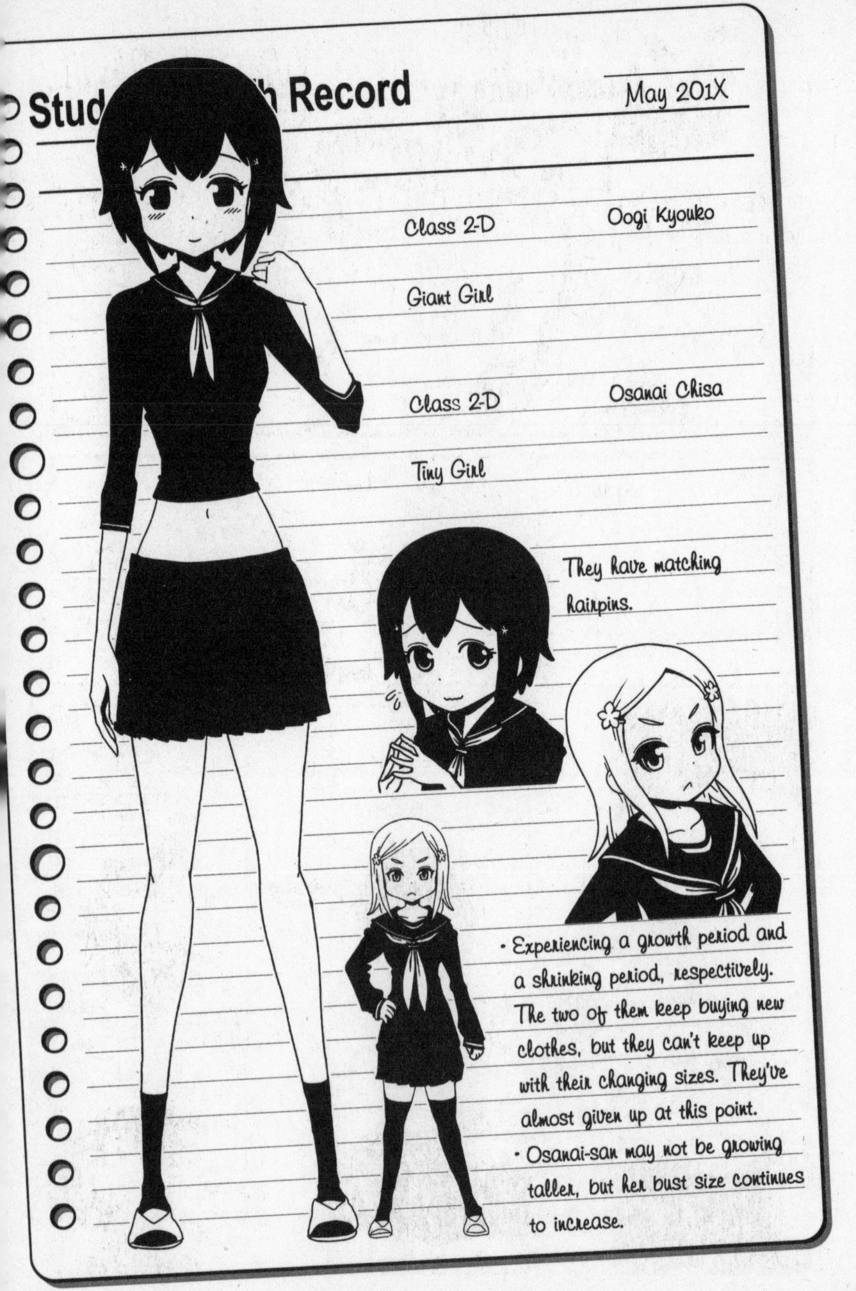
Stud
h Record
May 201X
Class 2-D
Oogi Kyouko
Giant Girl
Class 2-D
Osanai Chisa
Tiny Girl
They have matching hairpins.
· Experiencing a growth period and a shrinking period, respectively. The two of them keep buying new clothes, but they can't keep up with their changing sizes. They've almost given up at this point.
· Osanai-san may not be growing taller, but her bust size continues to increase.

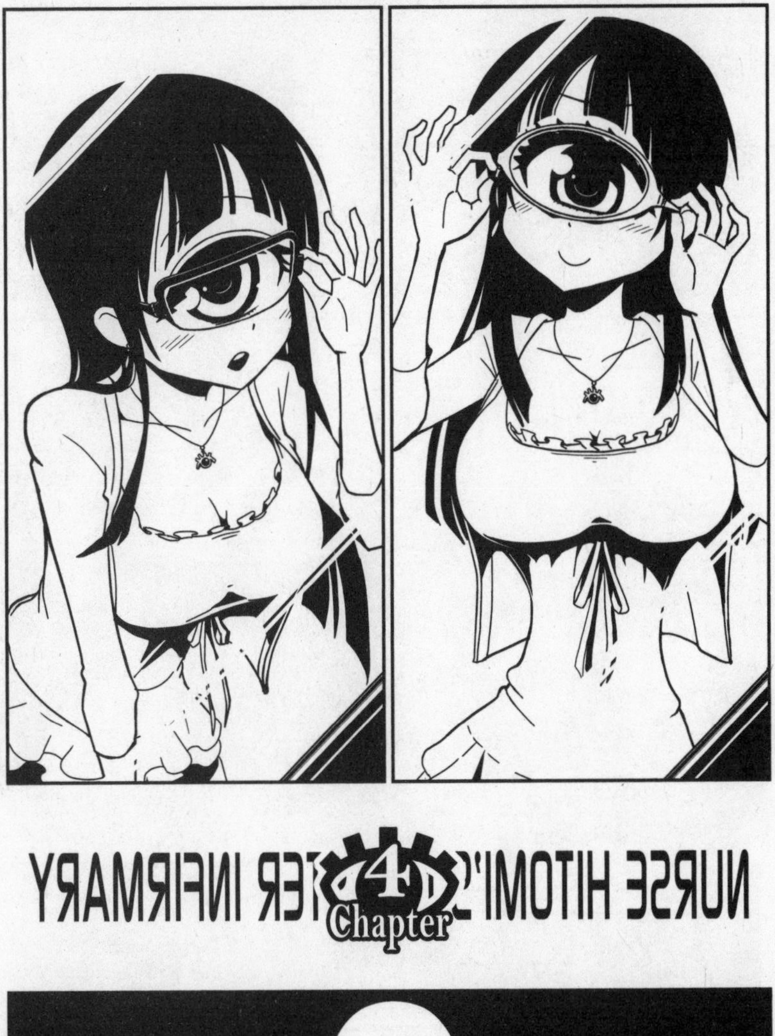
Chapter 4
NURSE HITOMI'S
TER INFIRMARY
HMMM. WHICH ONE DO YOU LIKE BETTER?

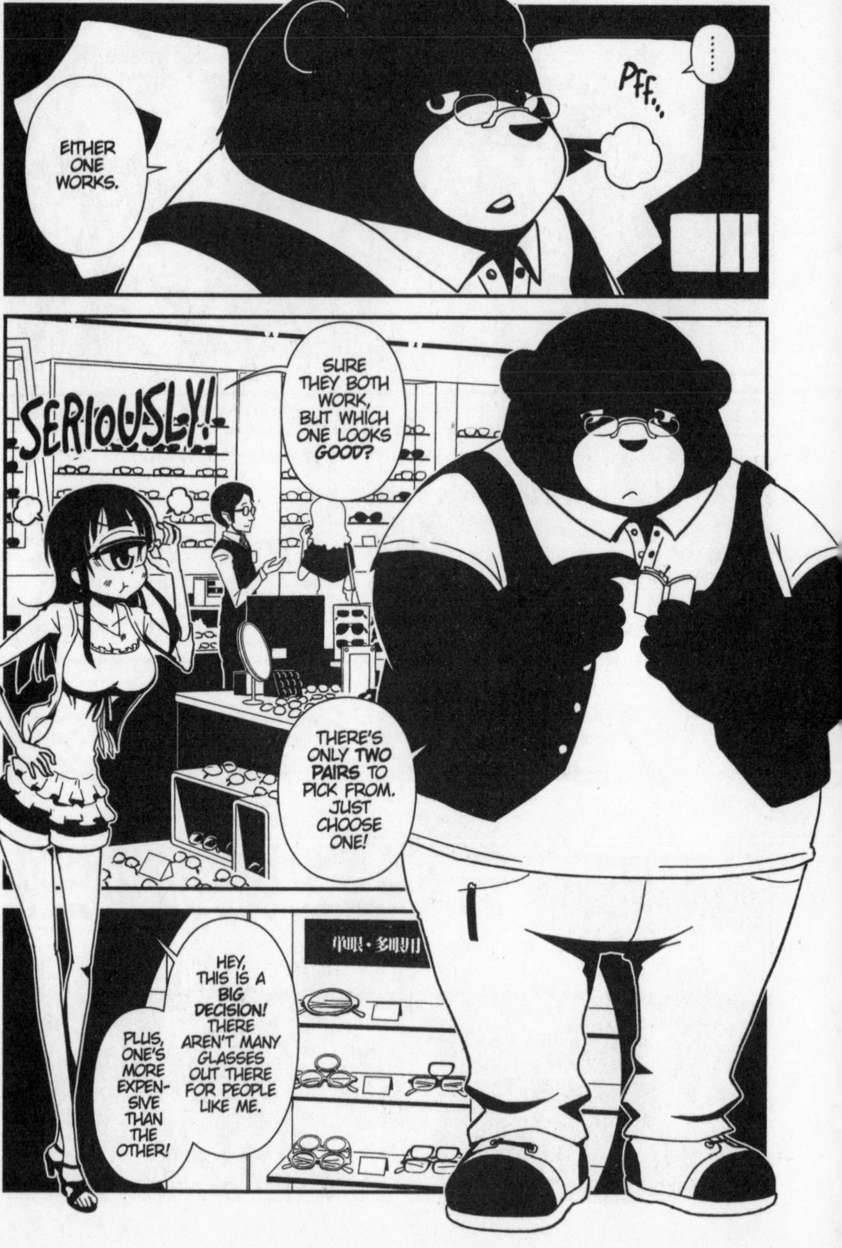
……
PFF...
EITHER ONE WORKS.
SURE THEY BOTH WORK, BUT WHICH ONE LOOKS GOOD?
SERIOUSLY!
THERE'S ONLY TWO PAIRS TO PICK FROM. JUST CHOOSE ONE!
HEY, THIS IS A BIG DECISION! THERE AREN'T MANY GLASSES OUT THERE FOR PEOPLE LIKE ME.
PLUS, ONE'S MORE EXPEN-SIVE THAN THE OTHER!

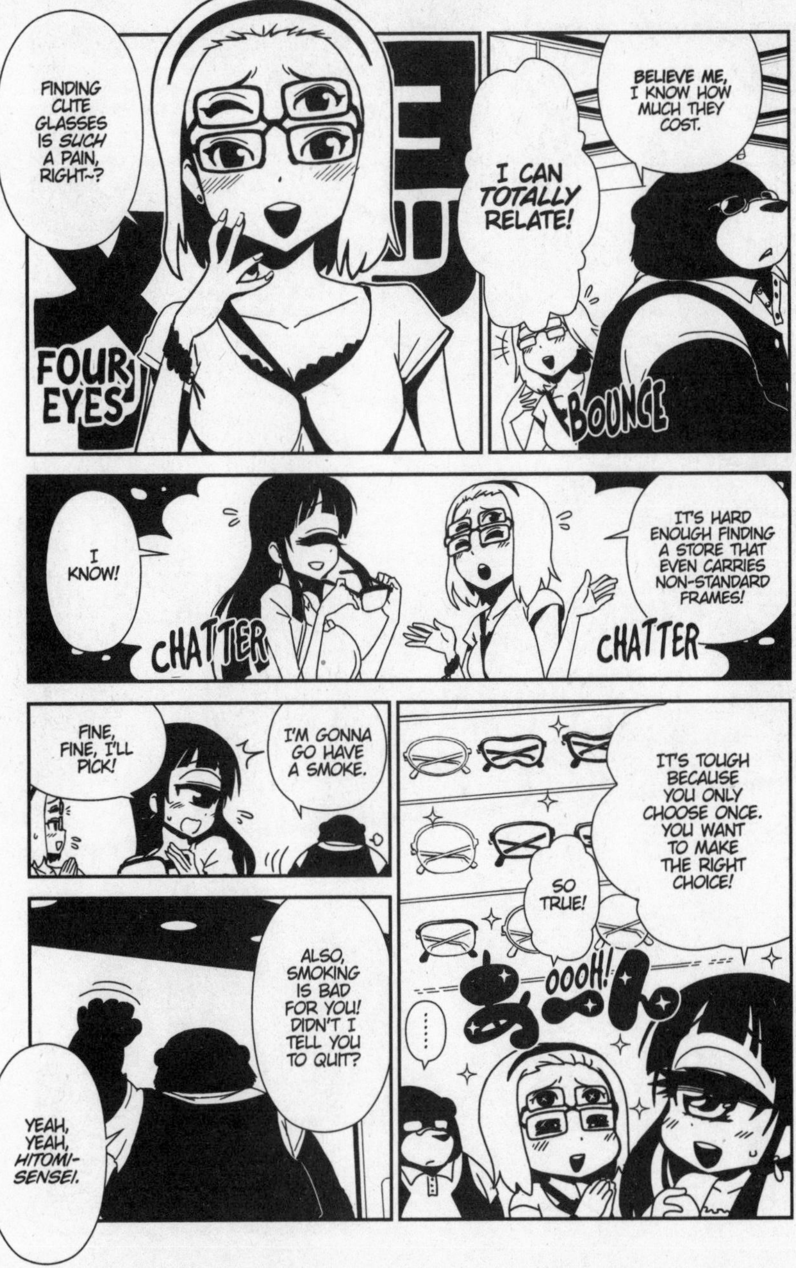
BELIEVE ME, I KNOW HOW MUCH THEY COST.
I CAN *TOTALLY* RELATE!
BOUNCE
FINDING CUTE GLASSES IS *SUCH* A PAIN, RIGHT~?
FOUR EYES
IT'S HARD ENOUGH FINDING A STORE THAT EVEN CARRIES NON-STANDARD FRAMES!
CHATTER
I KNOW!
CHATTER
IT'S TOUGH BECAUSE YOU ONLY CHOOSE ONCE. YOU WANT TO MAKE THE RIGHT CHOICE!
SO TRUE!
OOOH!
あ〜ん
......
I'M GONNA GO HAVE A SMOKE.
FINE, FINE, I'LL PICK!
ALSO, SMOKING IS BAD FOR YOU! DIDN'T I TELL YOU TO QUIT?
YEAH, YEAH, *HITOMI-SENSEI.*

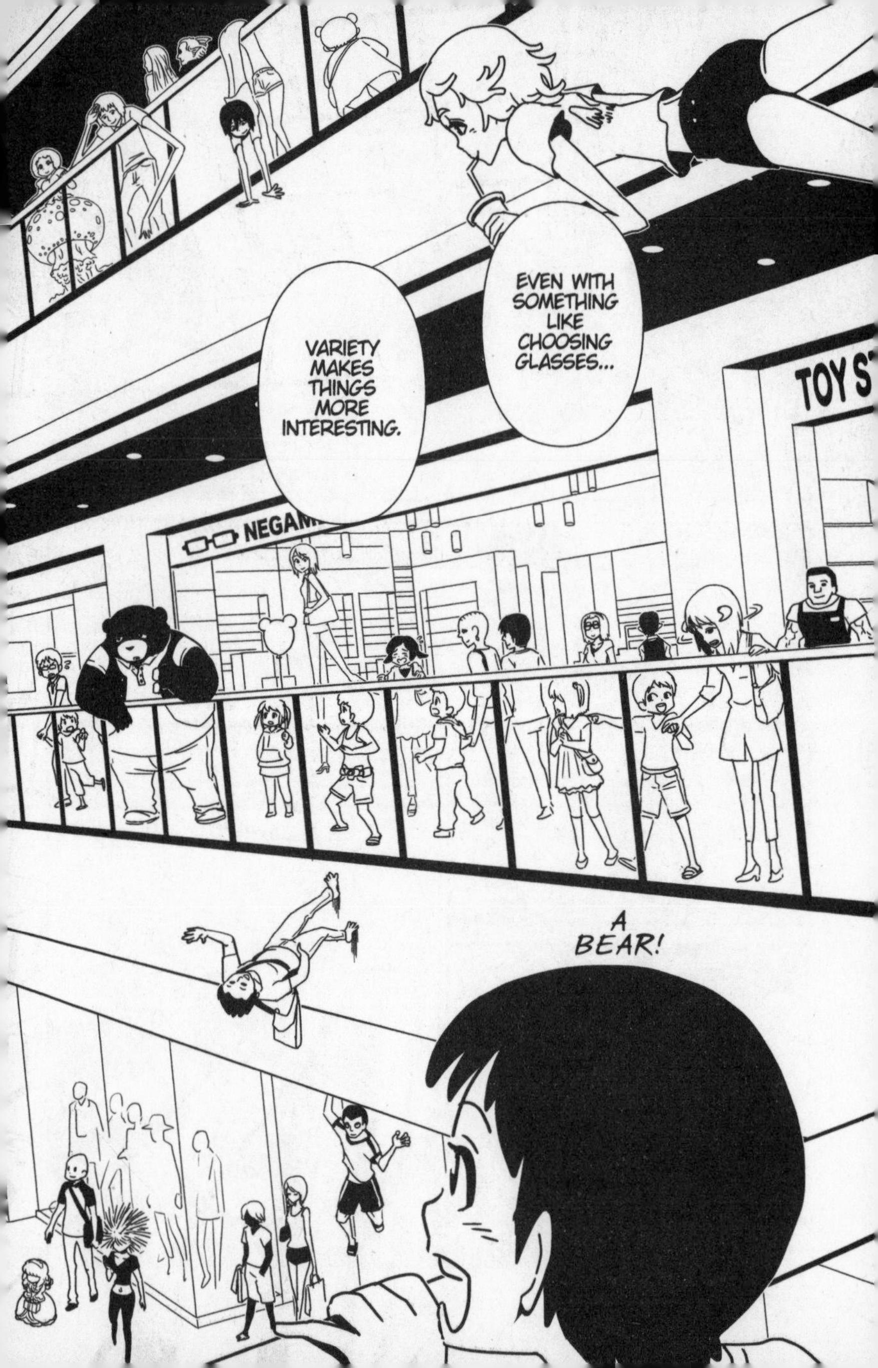
EVEN WITH SOMETHING LIKE CHOOSING GLASSES...
VARIETY MAKES THINGS MORE INTERESTING.
TOY ST
NEGAM
A BEAR!

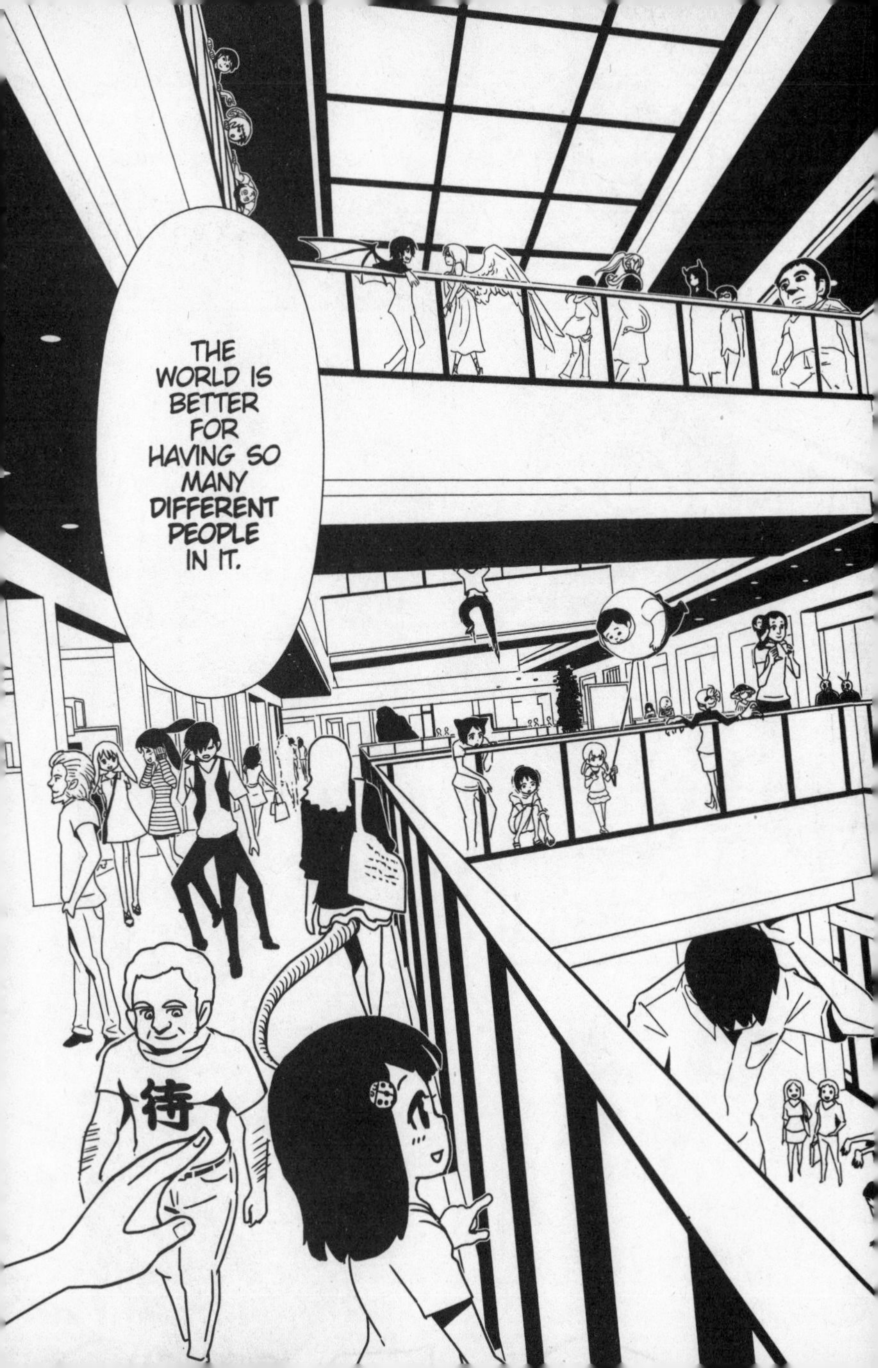
THE WORLD IS BETTER FOR HAVING SO MANY DIFFERENT PEOPLE IN IT.
待

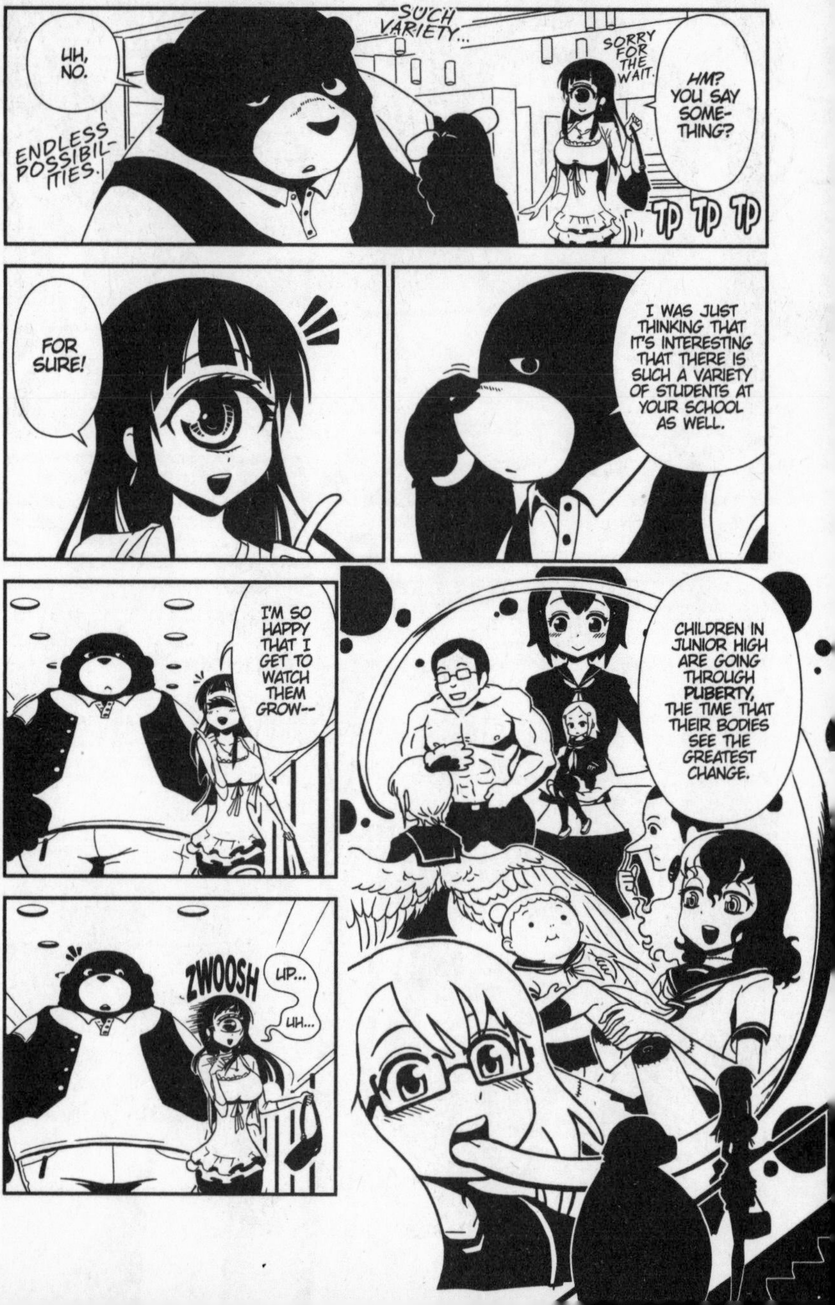
HM? YOU SAY SOME-THING?
SORRY FOR THE WAIT.
TP TP TP
SUCH VARIETY...
UH, NO.
ENDLESS POSSIBIL-ITIES.
I WAS JUST THINKING THAT IT'S INTERESTING THAT THERE IS SUCH A VARIETY OF STUDENTS AT YOUR SCHOOL AS WELL.
FOR SURE!
CHILDREN IN JUNIOR HIGH ARE GOING THROUGH PUBERTY, THE TIME THAT THEIR BODIES SEE THE GREATEST CHANGE.
I'M SO HAPPY THAT I GET TO WATCH THEM GROW--
UP...
UH...
ZWOOSH

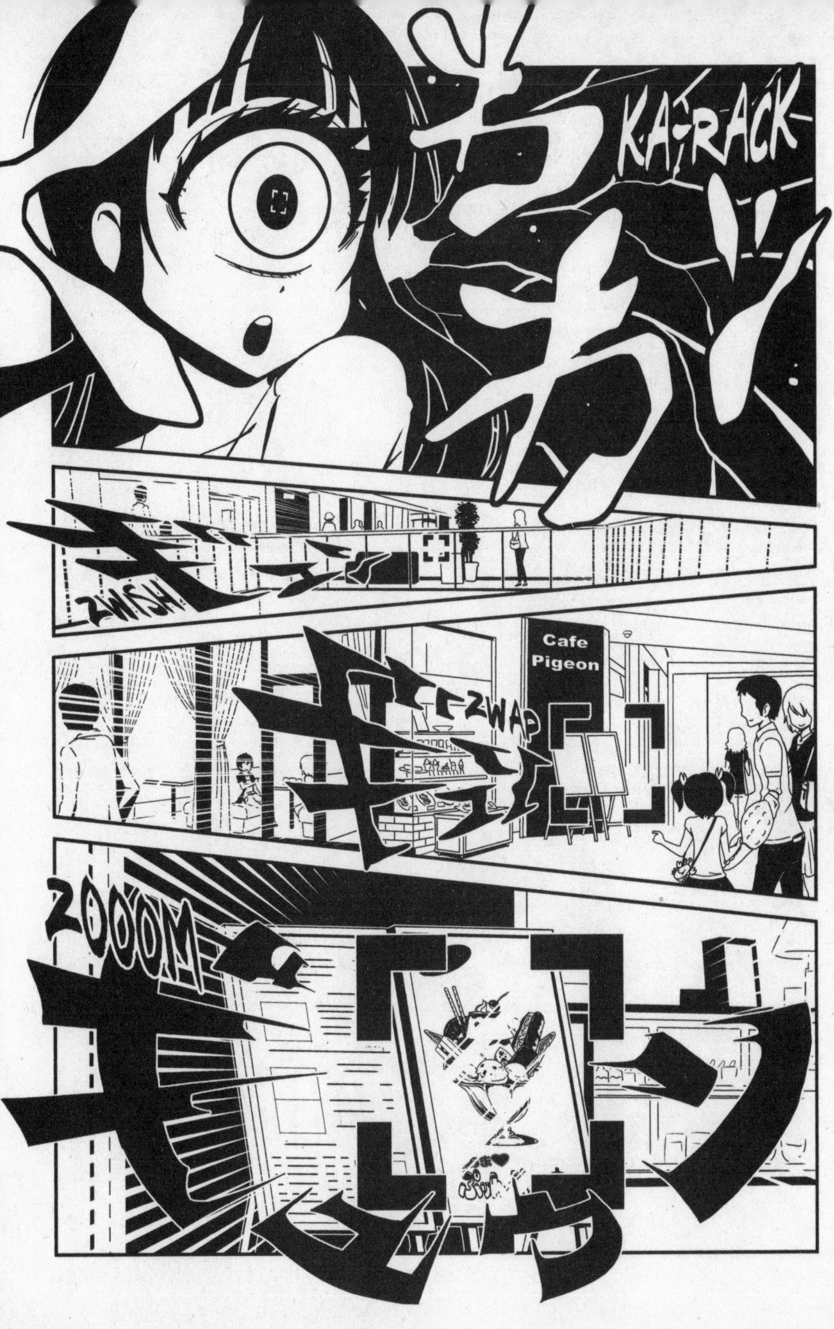
KA-RACK
ZWISH
Cafe
Pigeon
ZWAP
ZOOM

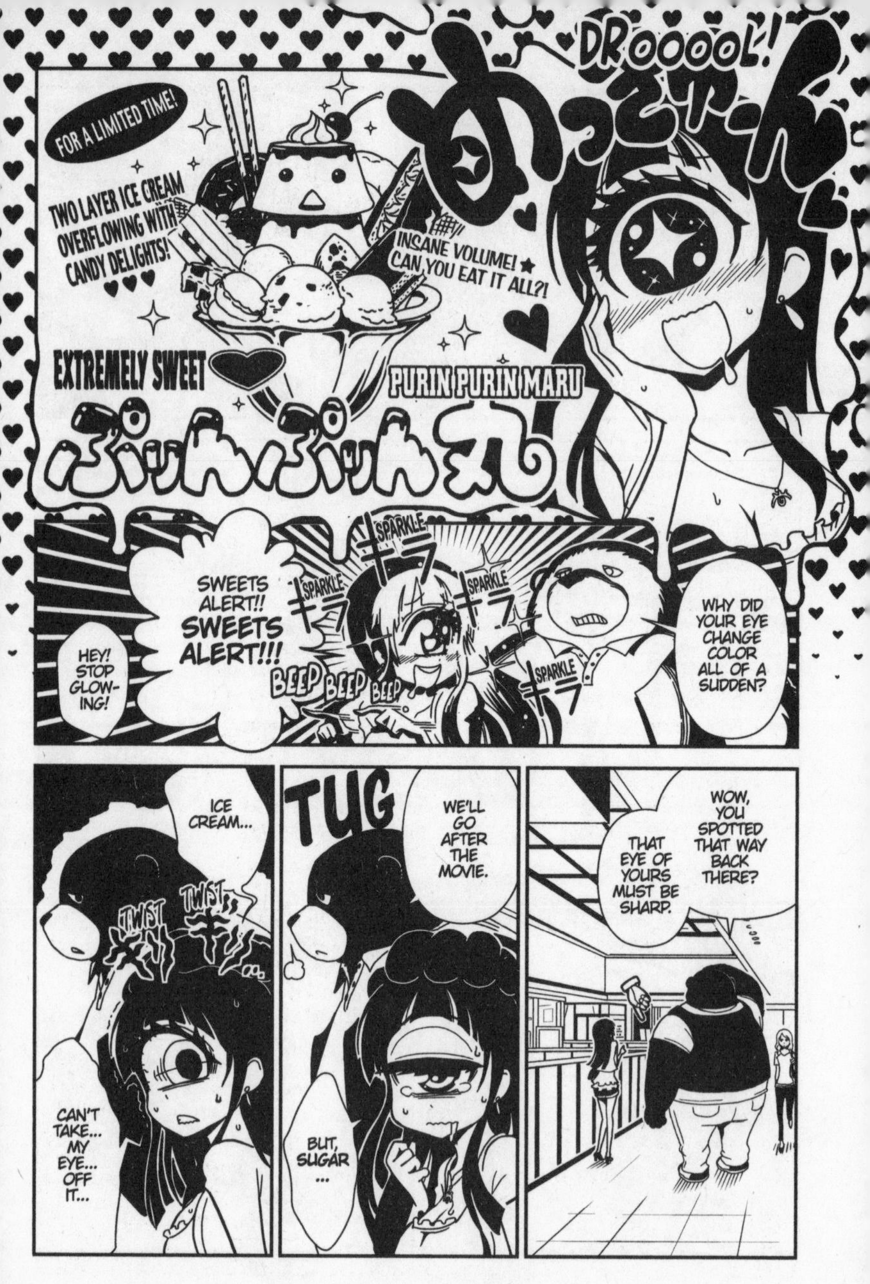
DROOOOL!
FOR A LIMITED TIME!
TWO LAYER ICE CREAM OVERFLOWING WITH CANDY DELIGHTS!
INSANE VOLUME! ★ CAN YOU EAT IT ALL?!
EXTREMELY SWEET
PURIN PURIN MARU
WHY DID YOUR EYE CHANGE COLOR ALL OF A SUDDEN?
SPARKLE
SPARKLE
SPARKLE
SPARKLE
SWEETS ALERT!! SWEETS ALERT!!!
BEEP BEEP BEEP
HEY! STOP GLOWING!
WOW, YOU SPOTTED THAT WAY BACK THERE?
THAT EYE OF YOURS MUST BE SHARP.
TUG
WE'LL GO AFTER THE MOVIE.
BUT, SUGAR...
ICE CREAM...
TWIST
TWIST
CAN'T TAKE... MY EYE... OFF IT...

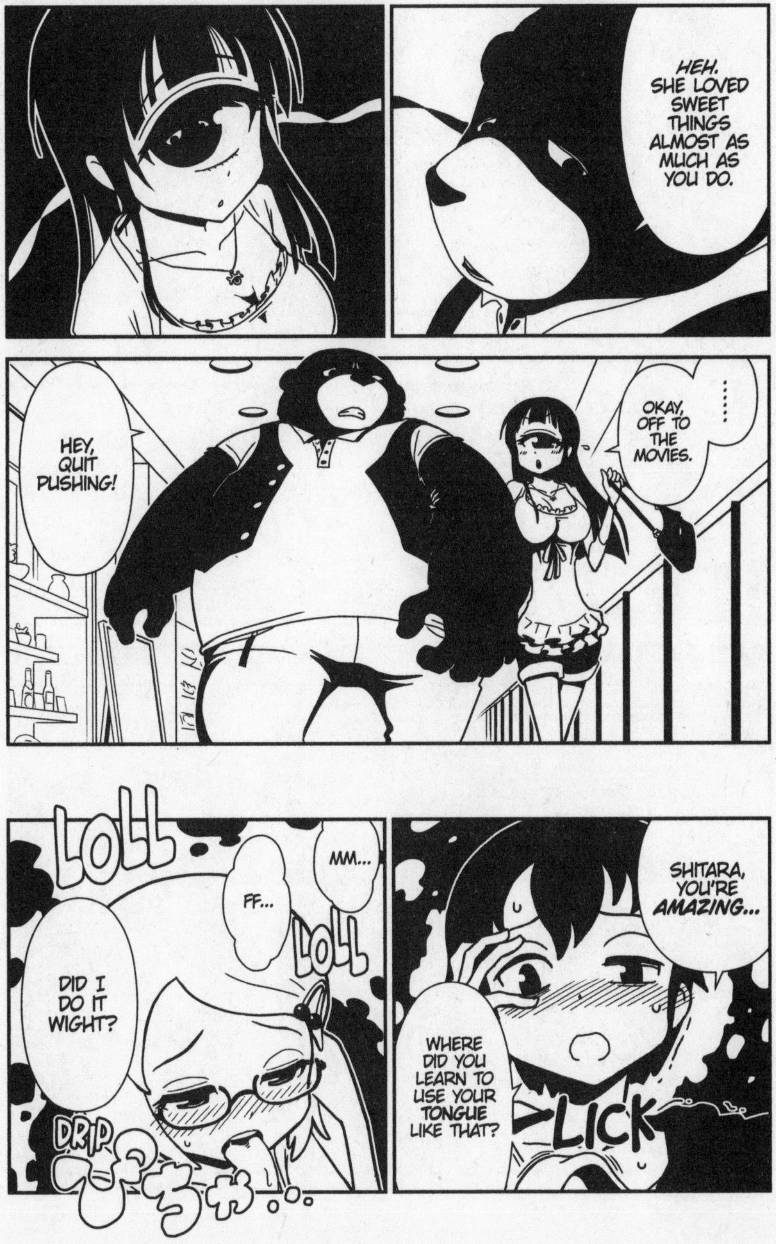
HEH. SHE LOVED SWEET THINGS ALMOST AS MUCH AS YOU DO.
......
OKAY, OFF TO THE MOVIES.
HEY, QUIT PUSHING!
SHITARA, YOU'RE AMAZING...
WHERE DID YOU LEARN TO USE YOUR TONGUE LIKE THAT?
LICK
MM...
FF...
LOLL
LOLL
DID I DO IT WIGHT?
DRIP

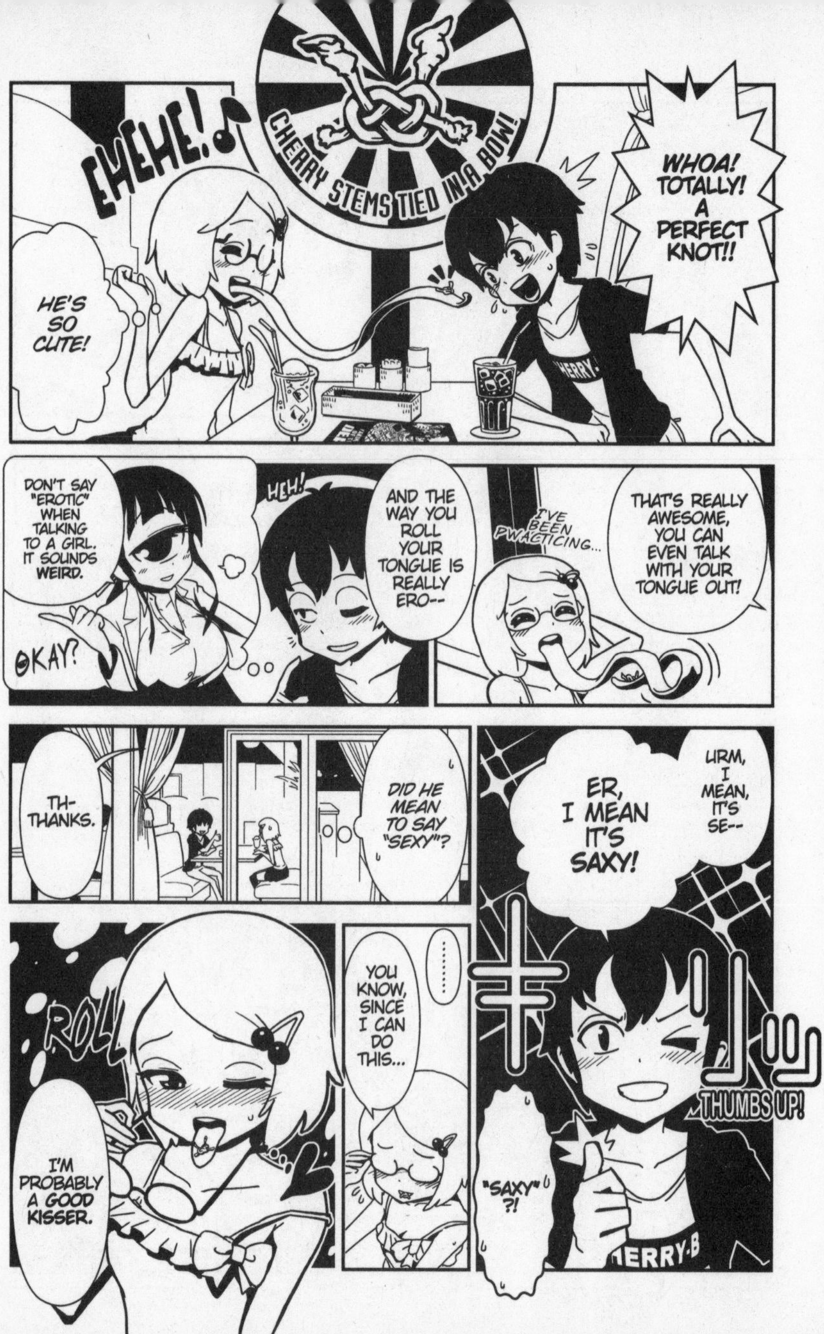
WHOA! TOTALLY! A PERFECT KNOT!!
CHERRY STEMS TIED IN A BOW!
EHEHE!♪
HE'S SO CUTE!
THAT'S REALLY AWESOME, YOU CAN EVEN TALK WITH YOUR TONGUE OUT!
I'VE BEEN PWACTICING...
AND THE WAY YOU ROLL YOUR TONGUE IS REALLY ERO--
HEH!
DON'T SAY "EROTIC" WHEN TALKING TO A GIRL. IT SOUNDS WEIRD.
OKAY?
URM, I MEAN, IT'S SE--
ER, I MEAN IT'S SAXY!
THUMBS UP!
"SAXY" ?!
DID HE MEAN TO SAY "SEXY"?
TH-THANKS.
......
YOU KNOW, SINCE I CAN DO THIS...
ROLL
I'M PROBABLY A GOOD KISSER.

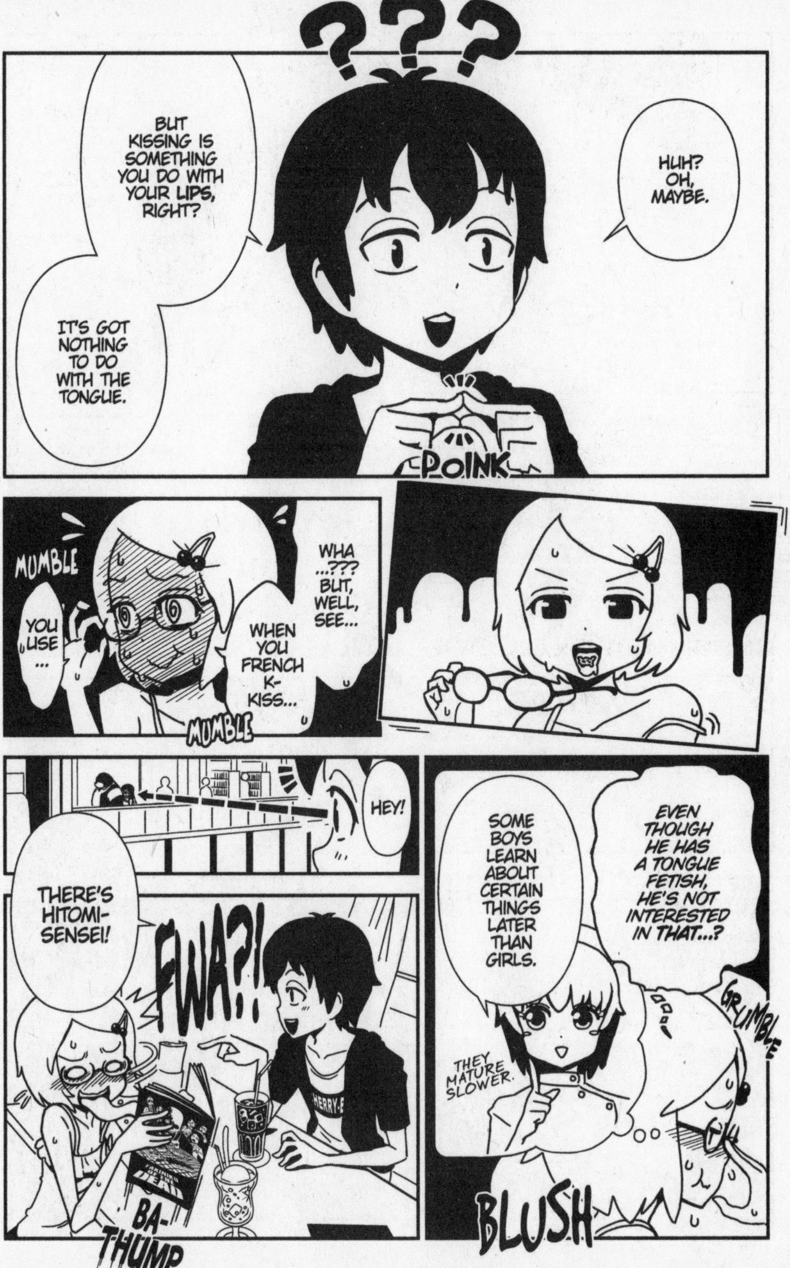
???
HUH? OH, MAYBE.
BUT KISSING IS SOMETHING YOU DO WITH YOUR LIPS, RIGHT?
IT'S GOT NOTHING TO DO WITH THE TONGUE.
POINK
WHA ...??? BUT, WELL, SEE...
WHEN YOU FRENCH K-KISS...
MUMBLE
YOU USE ...
MUMBLE
EVEN THOUGH HE HAS A TONGUE FETISH, HE'S NOT INTERESTED IN THAT...?
SOME BOYS LEARN ABOUT CERTAIN THINGS LATER THAN GIRLS.
THEY MATURE SLOWER.
GRUMBLE
BLUSH
HEY!
THERE'S HITOMI-SENSEI!
FWA?!
BA-THUMP

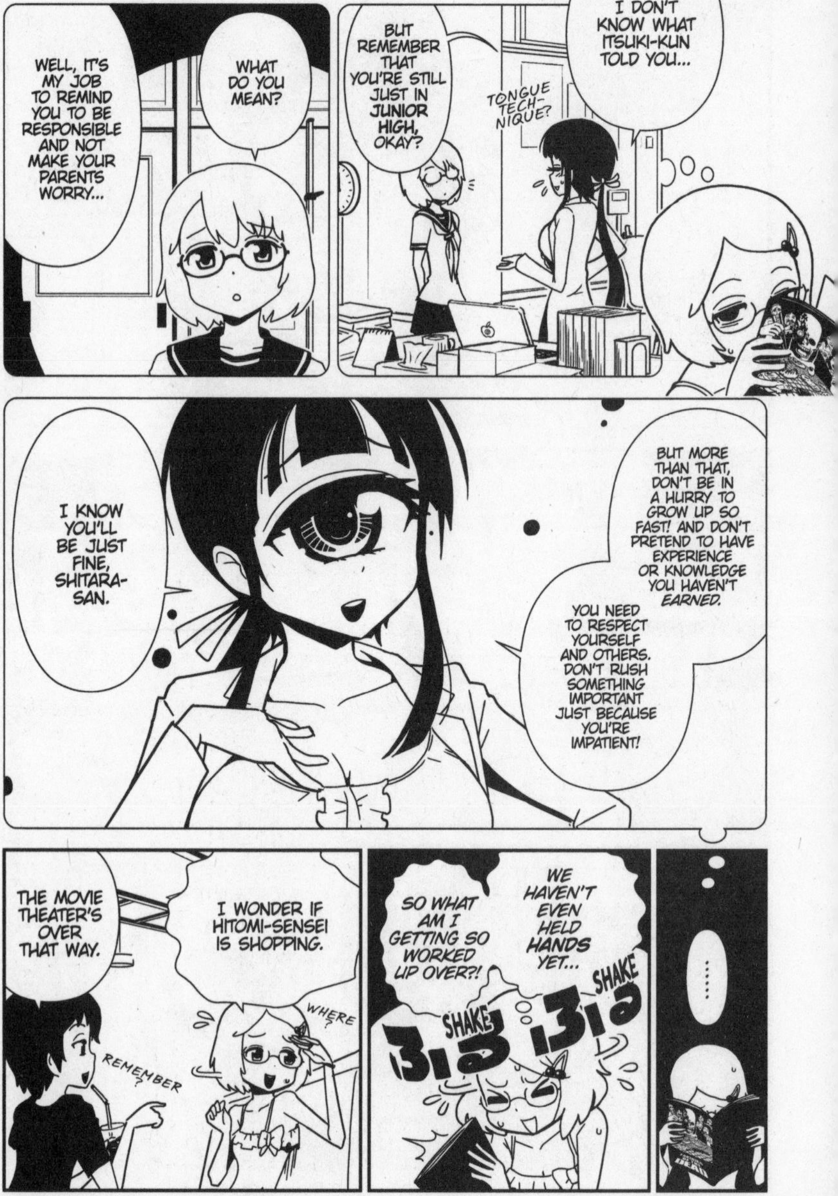
I DON'T KNOW WHAT ITSUKI-KUN TOLD YOU...
TONGUE TECHNIQUE?
BUT REMEMBER THAT YOU'RE STILL JUST IN JUNIOR HIGH, OKAY?
WHAT DO YOU MEAN?
WELL, IT'S MY JOB TO REMIND YOU TO BE RESPONSIBLE AND NOT MAKE YOUR PARENTS WORRY...
BUT MORE THAN THAT, DON'T BE IN A HURRY TO GROW UP SO FAST! AND DON'T PRETEND TO HAVE EXPERIENCE OR KNOWLEDGE YOU HAVEN'T EARNED.
YOU NEED TO RESPECT YOURSELF AND OTHERS. DON'T RUSH SOMETHING IMPORTANT JUST BECAUSE YOU'RE IMPATIENT!
I KNOW YOU'LL BE JUST FINE, SHITARA-SAN.
......
WE HAVEN'T EVEN HELD HANDS YET...
SO WHAT AM I GETTING SO WORKED UP OVER?!
SHAKE
SHAKE
I WONDER IF HITOMI-SENSEI IS SHOPPING.
THE MOVIE THEATER'S OVER THAT WAY.
WHERE?
REMEMBER?

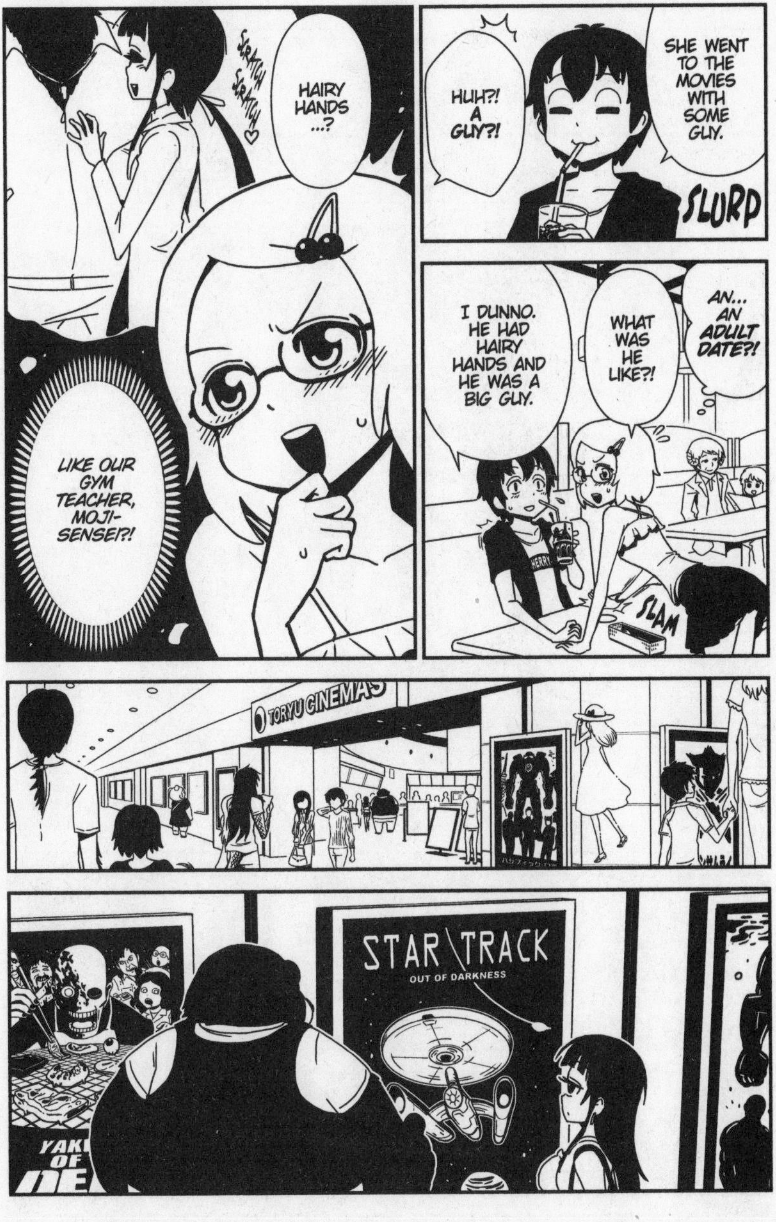
SHE WENT TO THE MOVIES WITH SOME GUY.
HUH?! A GUY?!
SLURP
AN... AN ADULT DATE?!
WHAT WAS HE LIKE?!
I DUNNO. HE HAD HAIRY HANDS AND HE WAS A BIG GUY.
SLAM
SCRATCH SCRATCH ♡
HAIRY HANDS ...?
LIKE OUR GYM TEACHER, MOJI-SENSEI?!
TORYU CINEMAS
STAR TRACK
OUT OF DARKNESS

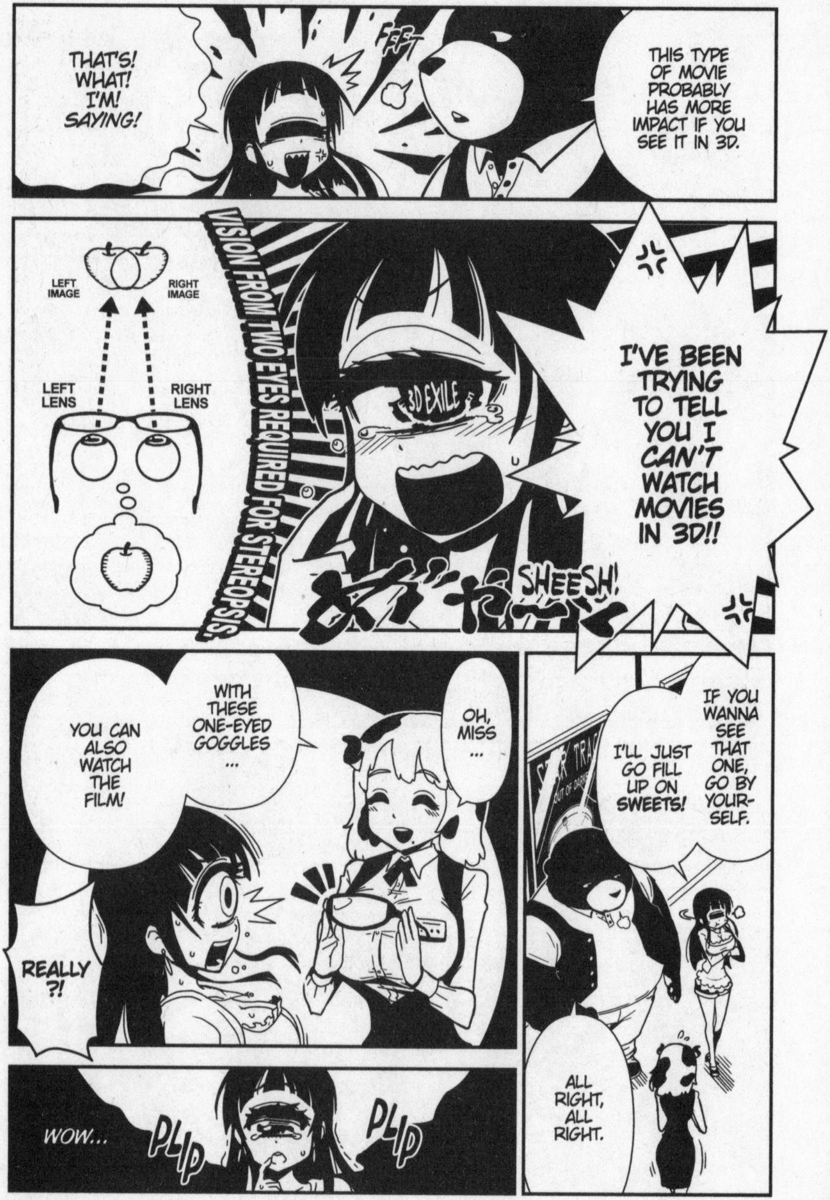
THIS TYPE OF MOVIE PROBABLY HAS MORE IMPACT IF YOU SEE IT IN 3D.
FFFT
THAT'S! WHAT! I'M! SAYING!
I'VE BEEN TRYING TO TELL YOU I CAN'T WATCH MOVIES IN 3D!!
SHEESH!
3D EXILE
VISION FROM TWO EYES REQUIRED FOR STEREOPSIS.
LEFT IMAGE
RIGHT IMAGE
LEFT LENS
RIGHT LENS
IF YOU WANNA SEE THAT ONE, GO BY YOURSELF.
I'LL JUST GO FILL UP ON SWEETS!
ALL RIGHT, ALL RIGHT.
OH, MISS...
WITH THESE ONE-EYED GOGGLES...
YOU CAN ALSO WATCH THE FILM!
REALLY?!
PLIP
PLIP
WOW...

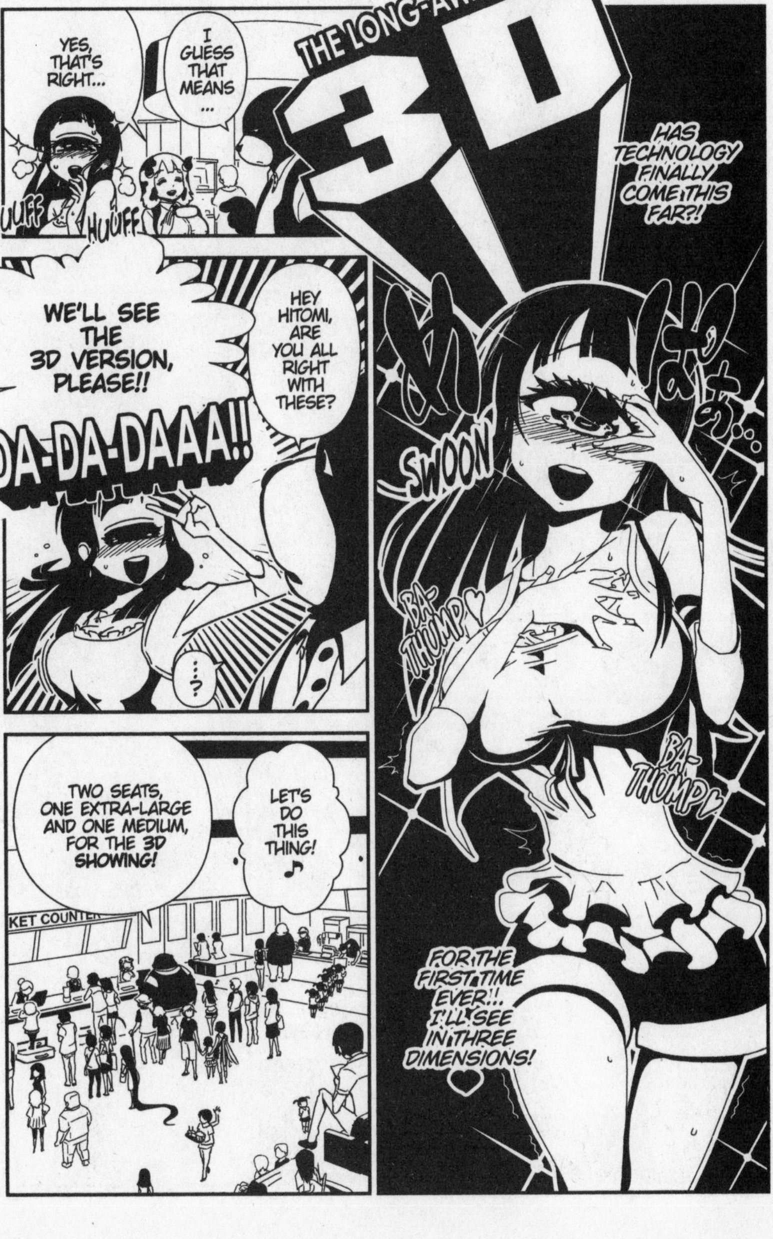
THE LONG-AWAITED 3D
HAS TECHNOLOGY FINALLY COME THIS FAR?!
SWOON
BA-THUMP♥
BA-THUMP♥
FOR THE FIRST TIME EVER!! I'LL SEE IN THREE DIMENSIONS! ♥
I GUESS THAT MEANS ...
YES, THAT'S RIGHT...
HUUFF
HUUFF
HEY HITOMI, ARE YOU ALL RIGHT WITH THESE?
WE'LL SEE THE 3D VERSION, PLEASE!!
DA-DA-DAAA!!
...?
LET'S DO THIS THING! ♪
TWO SEATS, ONE EXTRA-LARGE AND ONE MEDIUM, FOR THE 3D SHOWING!
KET COUNTE

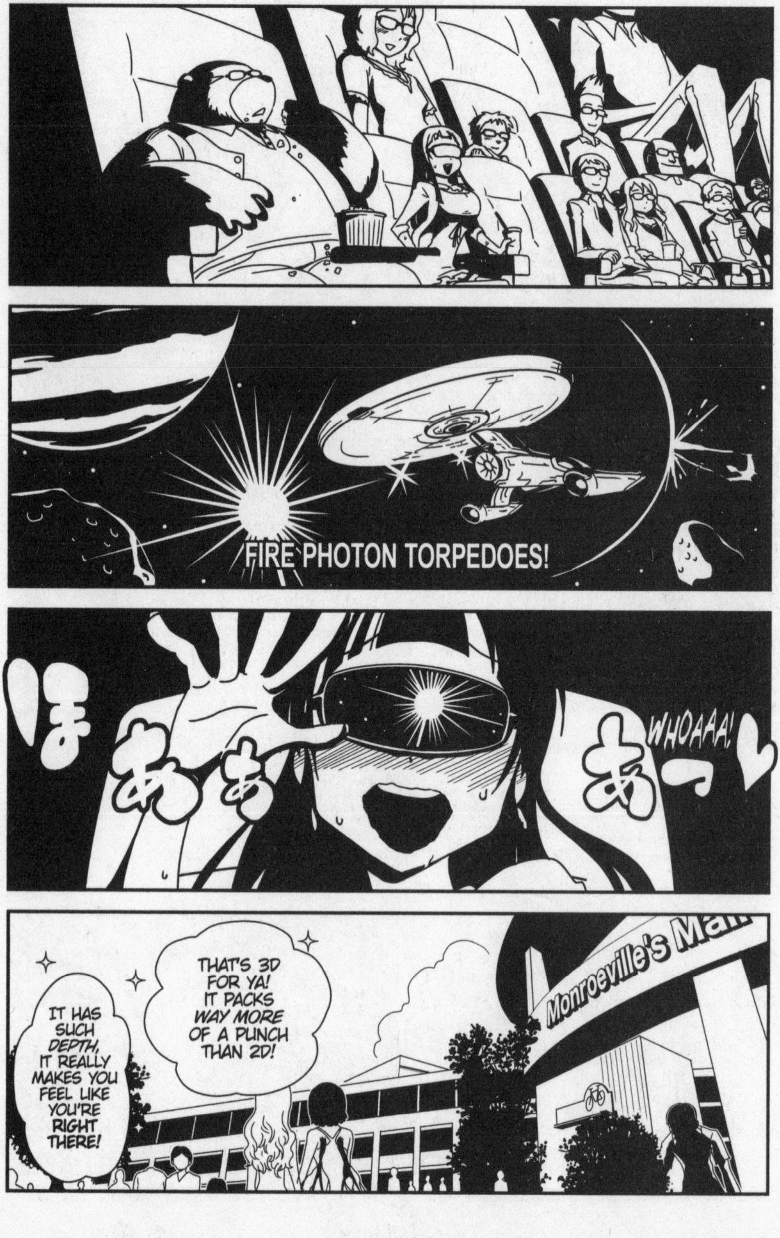
FIRE PHOTON TORPEDOES!
あっ
WHOAAA!
ま
ああ
Monroeville's Ma
THAT'S 3D FOR YA! IT PACKS WAY MORE OF A PUNCH THAN 2D!
IT HAS SUCH DEPTH, IT REALLY MAKES YOU FEEL LIKE YOU'RE RIGHT THERE!

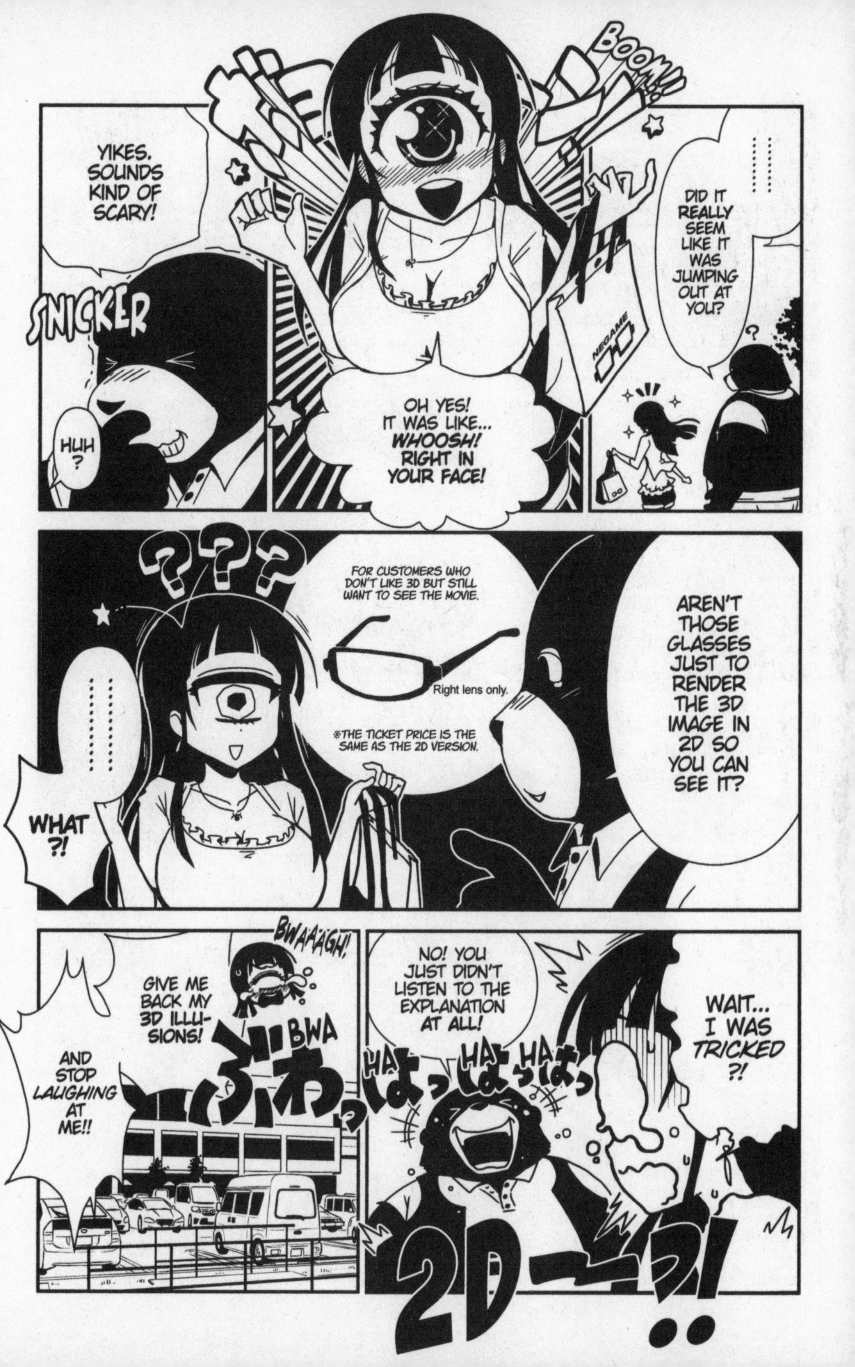
......
DID IT REALLY SEEM LIKE IT WAS JUMPING OUT AT YOU?
?
BOOM!!
OH YES! IT WAS LIKE... WHOOSH! RIGHT IN YOUR FACE!
NEGAME
YIKES. SOUNDS KIND OF SCARY!
SNICKER
HUH?
AREN'T THOSE GLASSES JUST TO RENDER THE 3D IMAGE IN 2D SO YOU CAN SEE IT?
FOR CUSTOMERS WHO DON'T LIKE 3D BUT STILL WANT TO SEE THE MOVIE.
Right lens only.
※THE TICKET PRICE IS THE SAME AS THE 2D VERSION.
???
......
WHAT?!
WAIT... I WAS TRICKED?!
NO! YOU JUST DIDN'T LISTEN TO THE EXPLANATION AT ALL!
BWA HA HA HA
2D—!!
BWAAAGH!
GIVE ME BACK MY 3D ILLUSIONS!
AND STOP LAUGHING AT ME!!

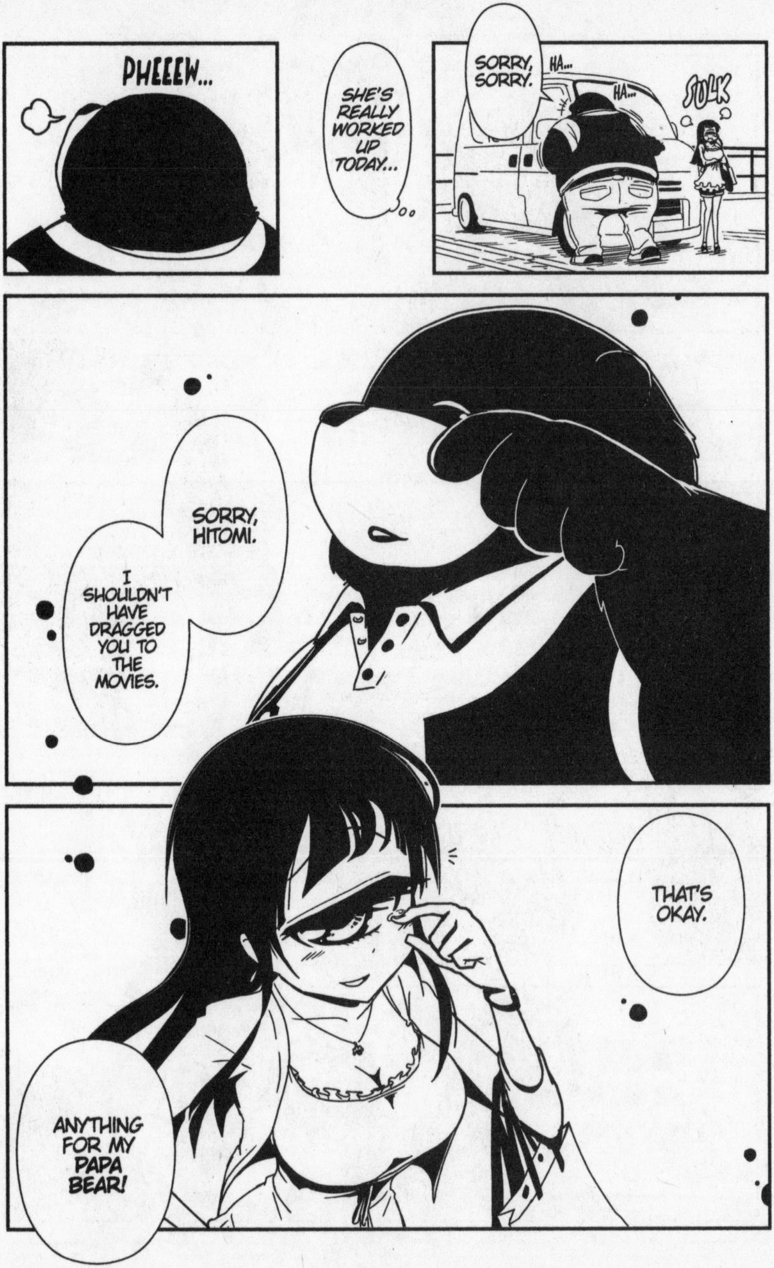
SORRY, SORRY.
HA...
HA...
SULK
SHE'S REALLY WORKED UP TODAY...
PHEEEW...
SORRY, HITOMI.
I SHOULDN'T HAVE DRAGGED YOU TO THE MOVIES.
THAT'S OKAY.
ANYTHING FOR MY PAPA BEAR!

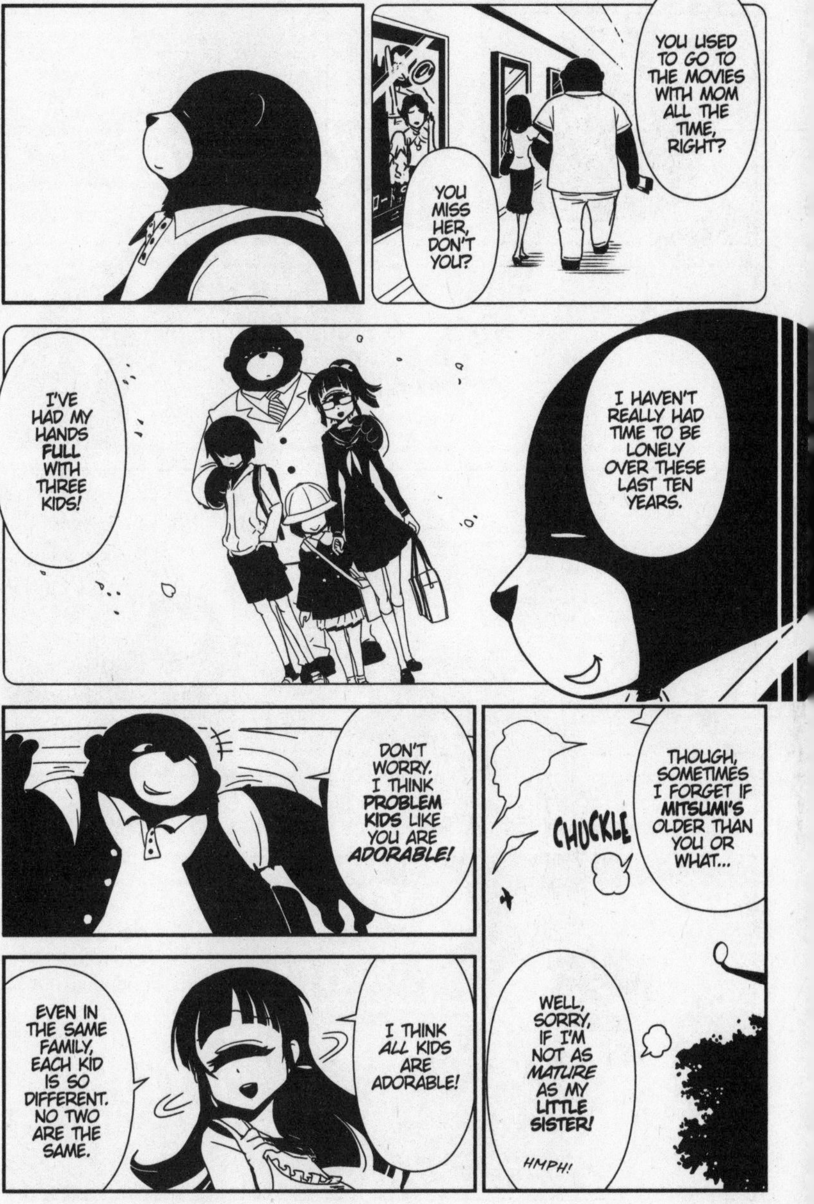
YOU USED TO GO TO THE MOVIES WITH MOM ALL THE TIME, RIGHT?
YOU MISS HER, DON'T YOU?
I HAVEN'T REALLY HAD TIME TO BE LONELY OVER THESE LAST TEN YEARS.
I'VE HAD MY HANDS FULL WITH THREE KIDS!
THOUGH, SOMETIMES I FORGET IF MITSUMI'S OLDER THAN YOU OR WHAT...
CHUCKLE
WELL, SORRY, IF I'M NOT AS *MATURE* AS MY LITTLE SISTER!
HMPH!
DON'T WORRY. I THINK PROBLEM KIDS LIKE YOU ARE *ADORABLE!*
I THINK *ALL* KIDS ARE ADORABLE!
EVEN IN THE SAME FAMILY, EACH KID IS SO DIFFERENT. NO TWO ARE THE SAME.

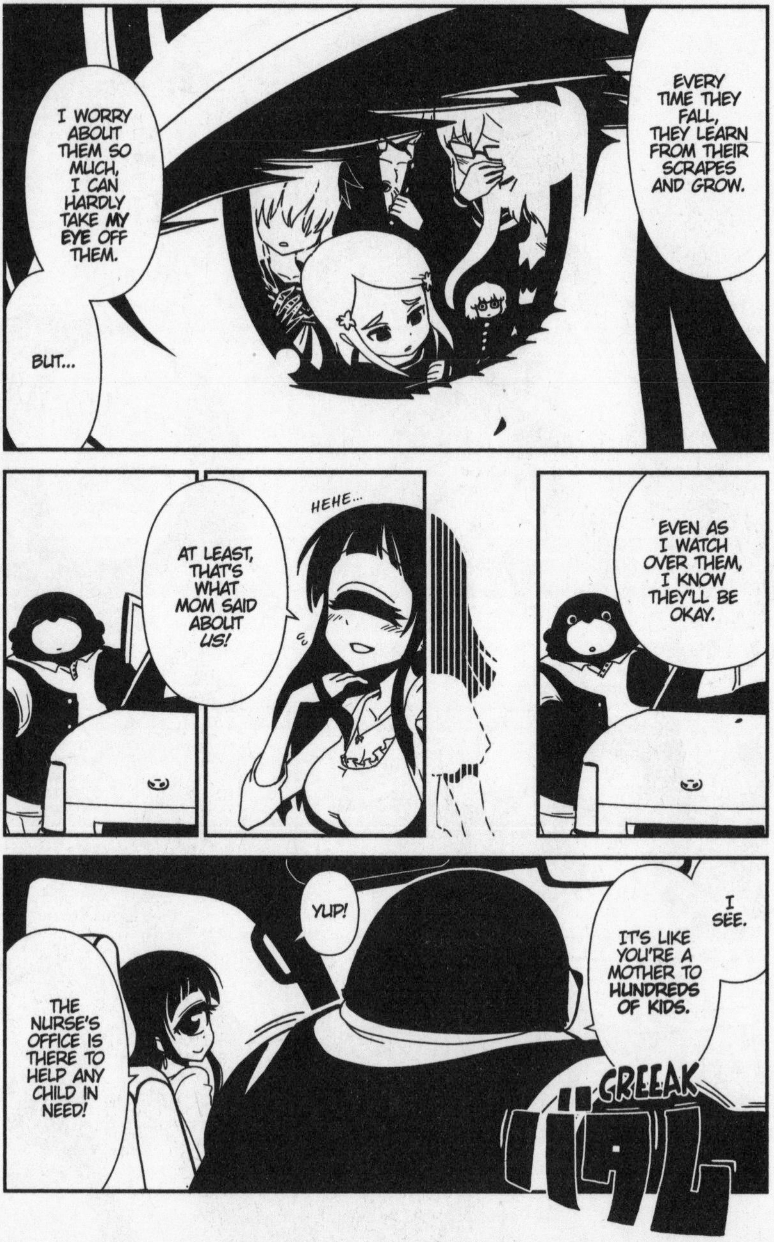
EVERY TIME THEY FALL, THEY LEARN FROM THEIR SCRAPES AND GROW.
I WORRY ABOUT THEM SO MUCH, I CAN HARDLY TAKE MY EYE OFF THEM.
BUT...
EVEN AS I WATCH OVER THEM, I KNOW THEY'LL BE OKAY.
HEHE...
AT LEAST, THAT'S WHAT MOM SAID ABOUT US!
I SEE.
IT'S LIKE YOU'RE A MOTHER TO HUNDREDS OF KIDS.
CREEAK
YUP!
THE NURSE'S OFFICE IS THERE TO HELP ANY CHILD IN NEED!

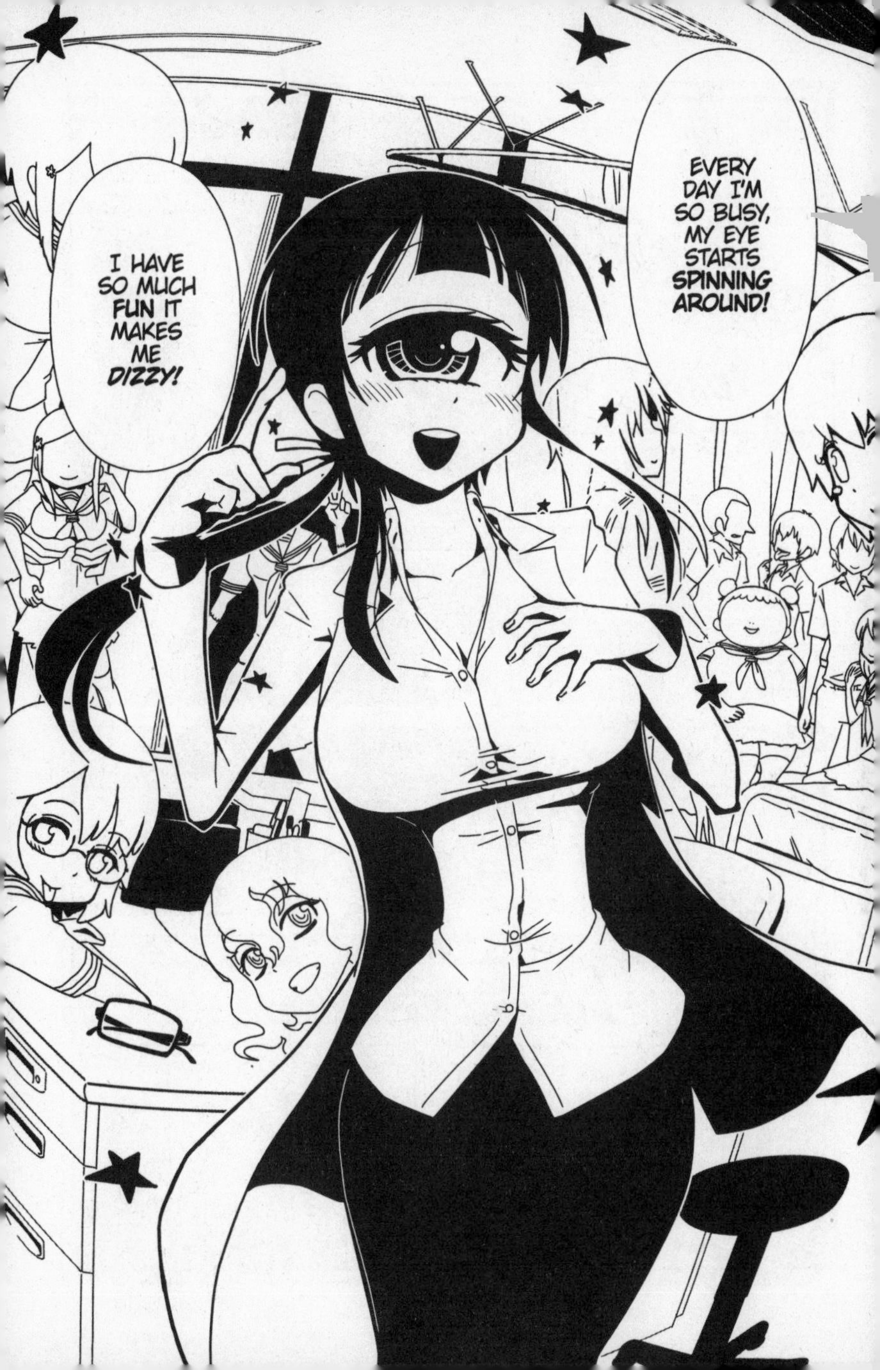
EVERY DAY I'M SO BUSY, MY EYE STARTS SPINNING AROUND!
I HAVE SO MUCH FUN IT MAKES ME *DIZZY!*

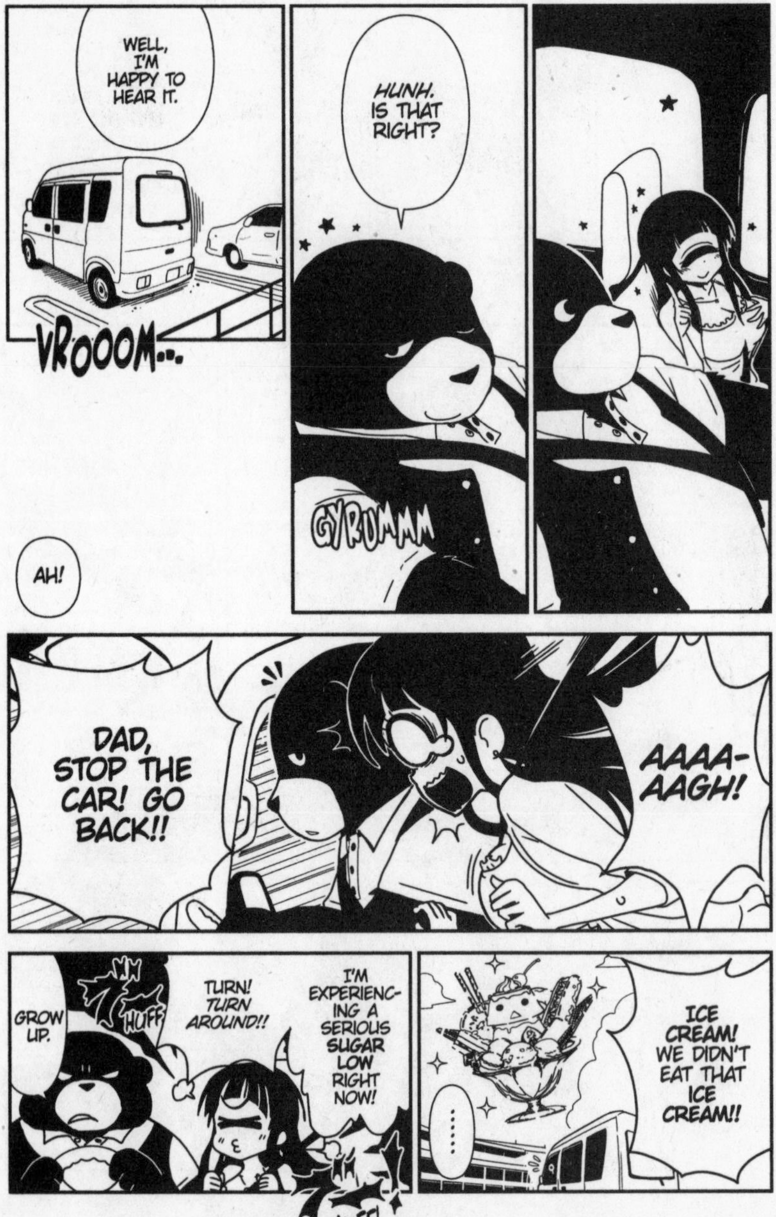
HUNH. IS THAT RIGHT?
GYRUMMM
WELL, I'M HAPPY TO HEAR IT.
VROOOM...
AH!
AAAA-AAGH!
DAD, STOP THE CAR! GO BACK!!
ICE CREAM! WE DIDN'T EAT THAT ICE CREAM!!
......
I'M EXPERIENCING A SERIOUS SUGAR LOW RIGHT NOW!
TURN! TURN AROUND!!
HUFF
GROW UP.
HUFF!

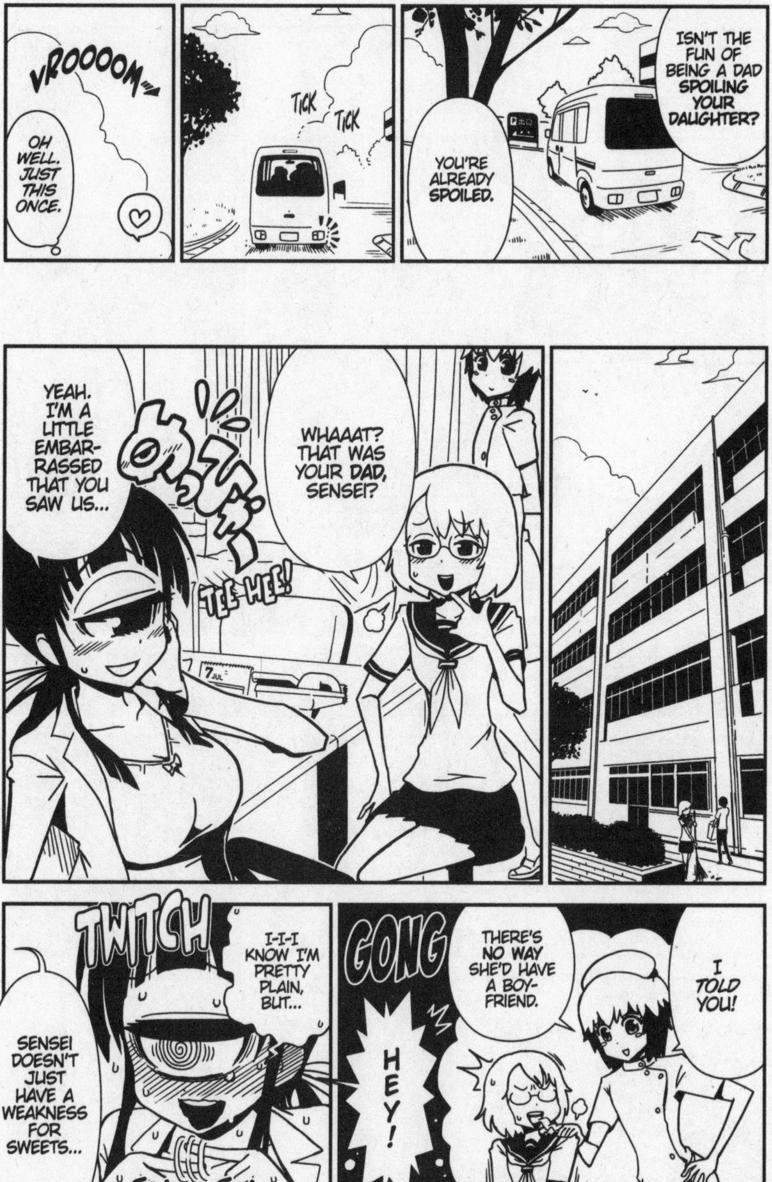
ISN'T THE FUN OF BEING A DAD SPOILING YOUR DAUGHTER?
YOU'RE ALREADY SPOILED.
TICK
TICK
VROOOOM
OH WELL. JUST THIS ONCE.
WHAAAT? THAT WAS YOUR DAD, SENSEI?
TEE-HEE!
YEAH. I'M A LITTLE EMBAR-RASSED THAT YOU SAW US...
I TOLD YOU!
THERE'S NO WAY SHE'D HAVE A BOY-FRIEND.
GONG
HEY!
I-I-I KNOW I'M PRETTY PLAIN, BUT...
TWITCH
SENSEI DOESN'T JUST HAVE A WEAKNESS FOR SWEETS...
SPIN
SPIN

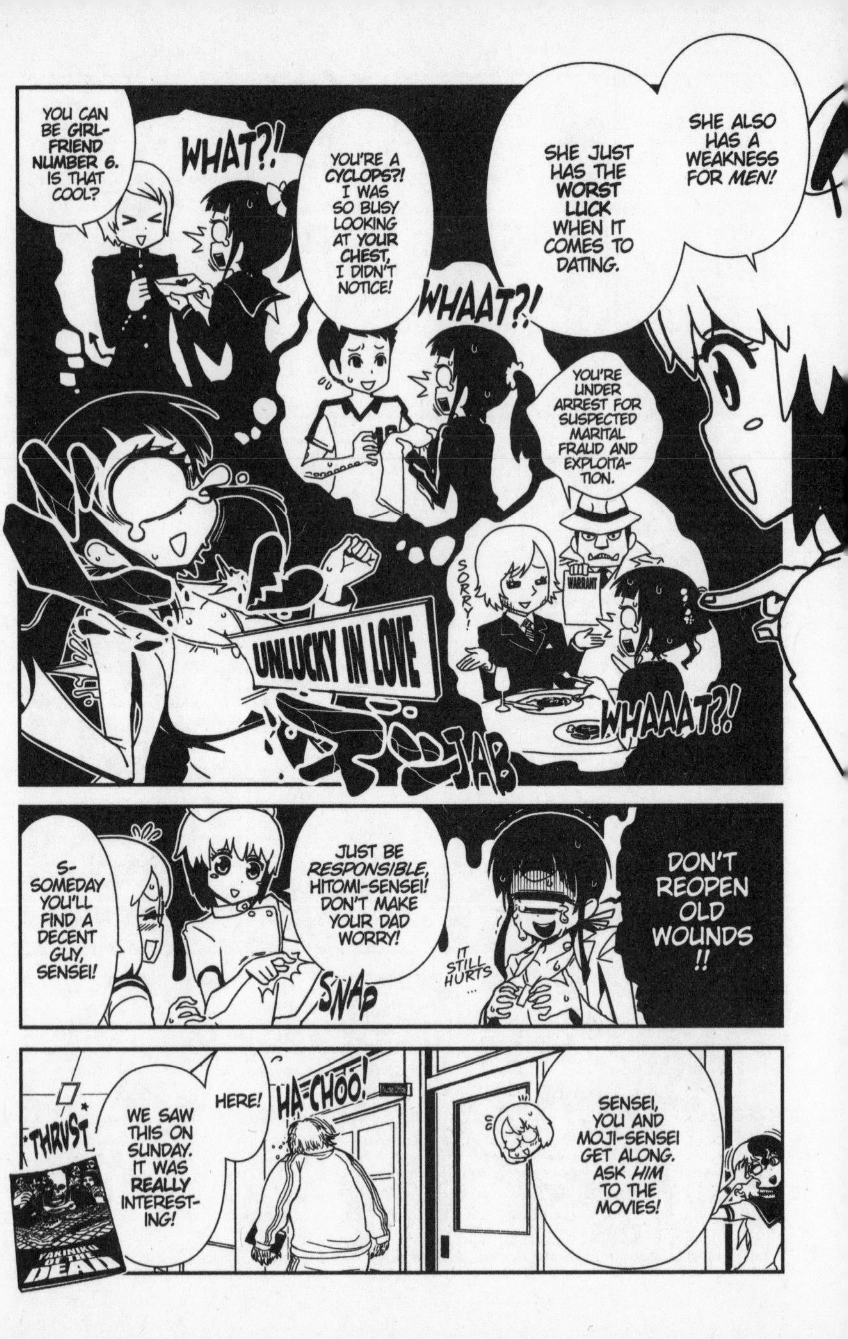
SHE ALSO HAS A WEAKNESS FOR MEN!
SHE JUST HAS THE WORST LUCK WHEN IT COMES TO DATING.
YOU'RE A CYCLOPS?! I WAS SO BUSY LOOKING AT YOUR CHEST, I DIDN'T NOTICE!
WHAAT?!
YOU CAN BE GIRL-FRIEND NUMBER 6. IS THAT COOL?
WHAT?!
YOU'RE UNDER ARREST FOR SUSPECTED MARITAL FRAUD AND EXPLOITA-TION.
WARRANT
SORRY!
WHAAAT?!
UNLUCKY IN LOVE
JAB
DON'T REOPEN OLD WOUNDS !!
IT STILL HURTS ...
JUST BE RESPONSIBLE, HITOMI-SENSEI! DON'T MAKE YOUR DAD WORRY!
SNAP
S-SOMEDAY YOU'LL FIND A DECENT GUY, SENSEI!
SENSEI, YOU AND MOJI-SENSEI GET ALONG. ASK HIM TO THE MOVIES!
HA-CHOO!
HERE!
WE SAW THIS ON SUNDAY. IT WAS REALLY INTEREST-ING!
THRUST
YAKINIKU OF THE DEAD

NURSE HITOMI'S Monster Infirmary

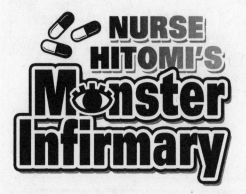

OMAKE DELETED SCENE FROM CHAPTER 04!

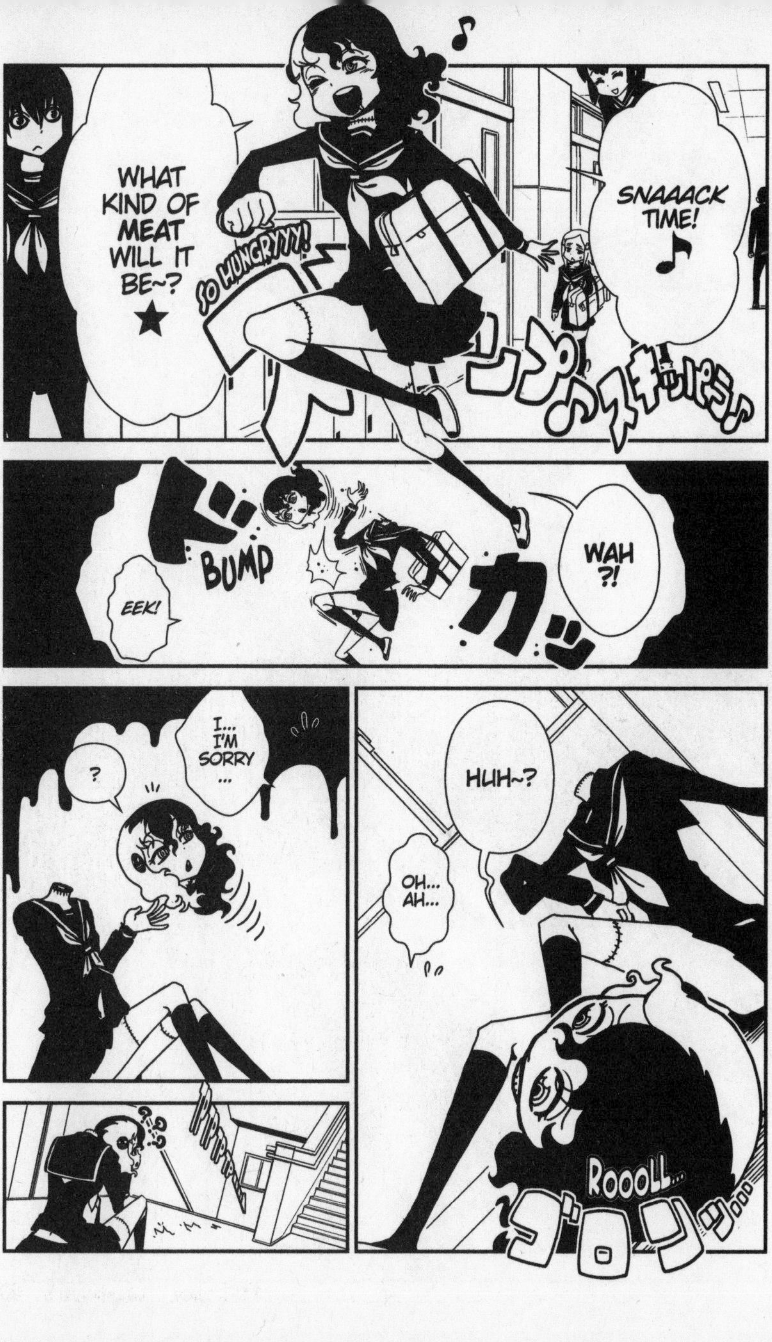
SNAAACK TIME! ♪
WHAT KIND OF MEAT WILL IT BE~? ★
SO HUNGRYYY!
WAH ?!
カッ
BUMP
EEK!
HUH~?
OH... AH...
ROOOLL...
I... I'M SORRY ...
?

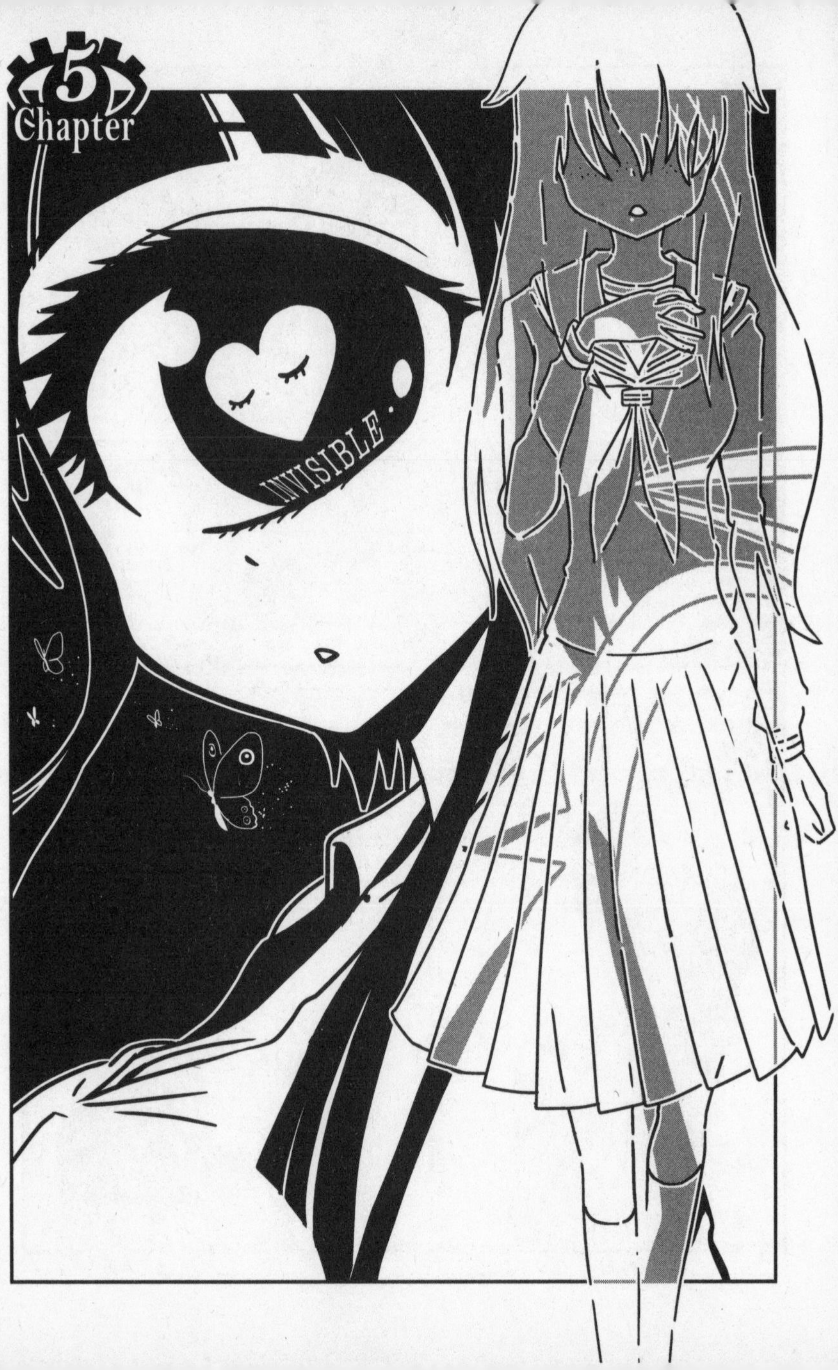
5
Chapter
INVISIBLE.

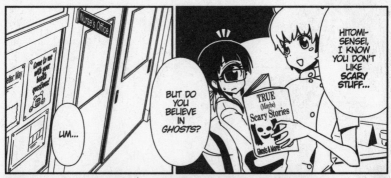

HITOMI-SENSEI, I KNOW YOU DON'T LIKE SCARY STUFF...
BUT DO YOU BELIEVE IN GHOSTS?
TRUE (Maybe) Scary Stories
Ghosts & More!
Nurse's Office
Come to me with your health questions!
etter: May
UM...
I DON'T REALLY WANT TO THINK ABOUT WHETHER GHOSTS EXIST...
BUT I DO BELIEVE THERE ARE THINGS THAT SOME PEOPLE CAN SEE THAT OTHERS CAN'T.
KNOCK KNOCK...
RAAAT...
TTTLLLE...

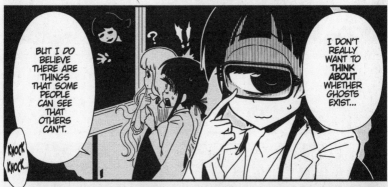

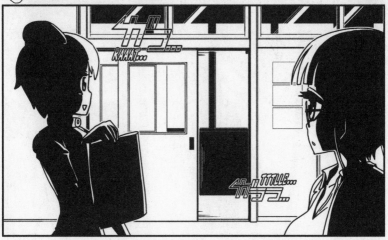

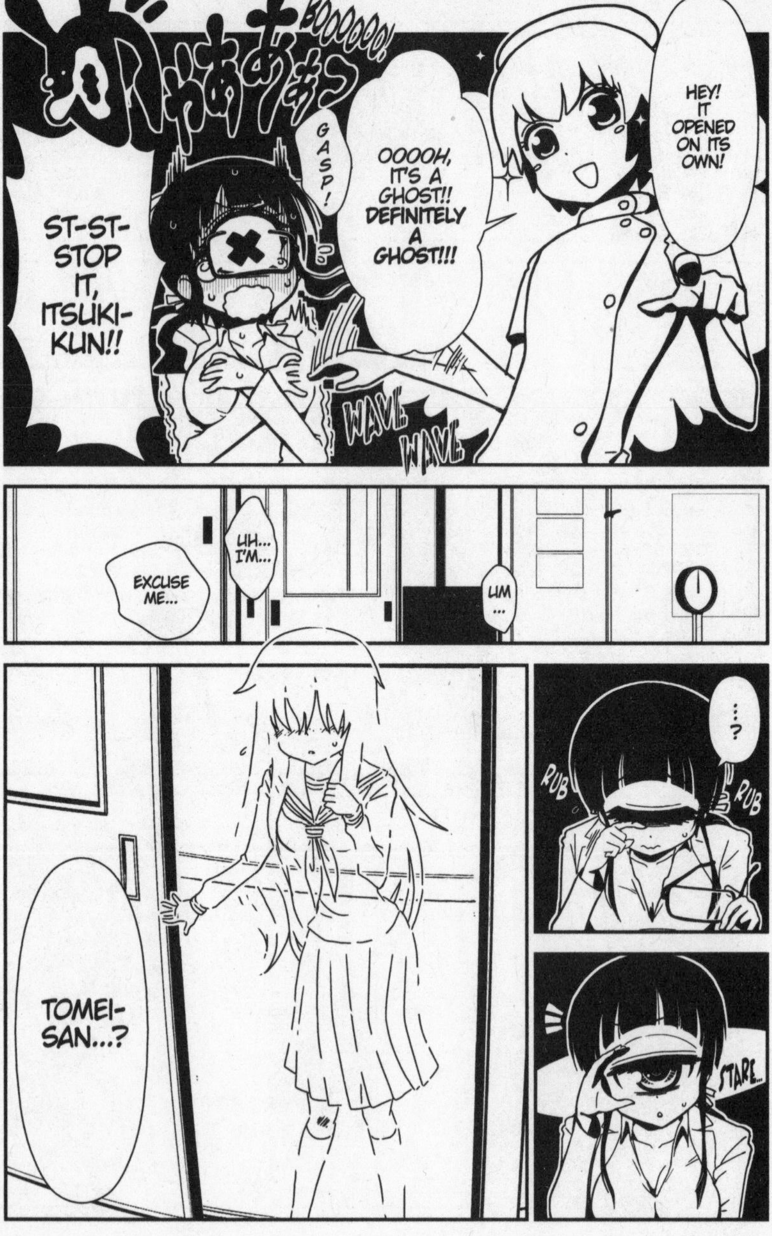
HEY! IT OPENED ON ITS OWN!
OOOOH, IT'S A GHOST!! DEFINITELY A GHOST!!!
GASP!
BOOOOOO!
ST-ST-STOP IT, ITSUKI-KUN!!
WAVE
WAVE
UM ...
UH... I'M...
EXCUSE ME...
...?
RUB
RUB
STARE...
TOMEI-SAN...?

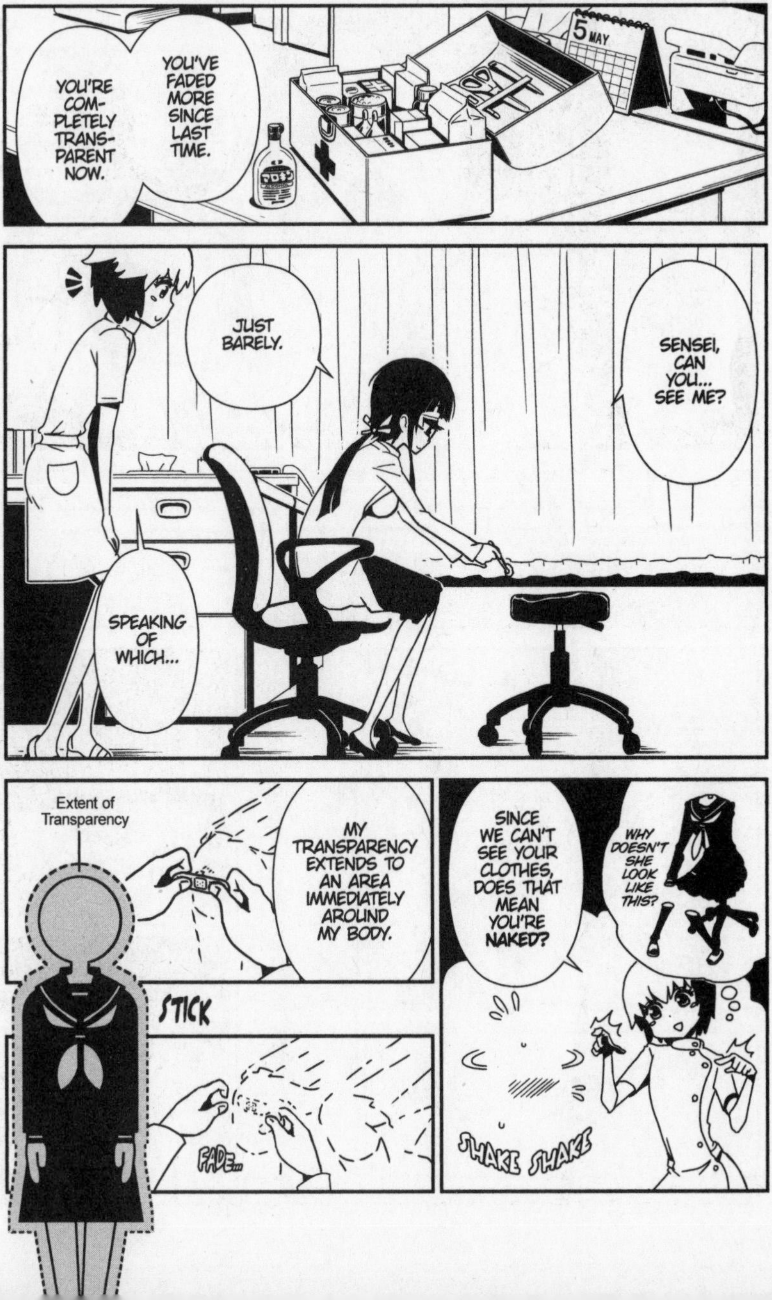
YOU'VE FADED MORE SINCE LAST TIME.
YOU'RE COM-PLETELY TRANS-PARENT NOW.
5 MAY
SENSEI, CAN YOU... SEE ME?
JUST BARELY.
SPEAKING OF WHICH...
SINCE WE CAN'T SEE YOUR CLOTHES, DOES THAT MEAN YOU'RE NAKED?
WHY DOESN'T SHE LOOK LIKE THIS?
SHAKE SHAKE
MY TRANSPARENCY EXTENDS TO AN AREA IMMEDIATELY AROUND MY BODY.
Extent of Transparency
STICK
FADE...

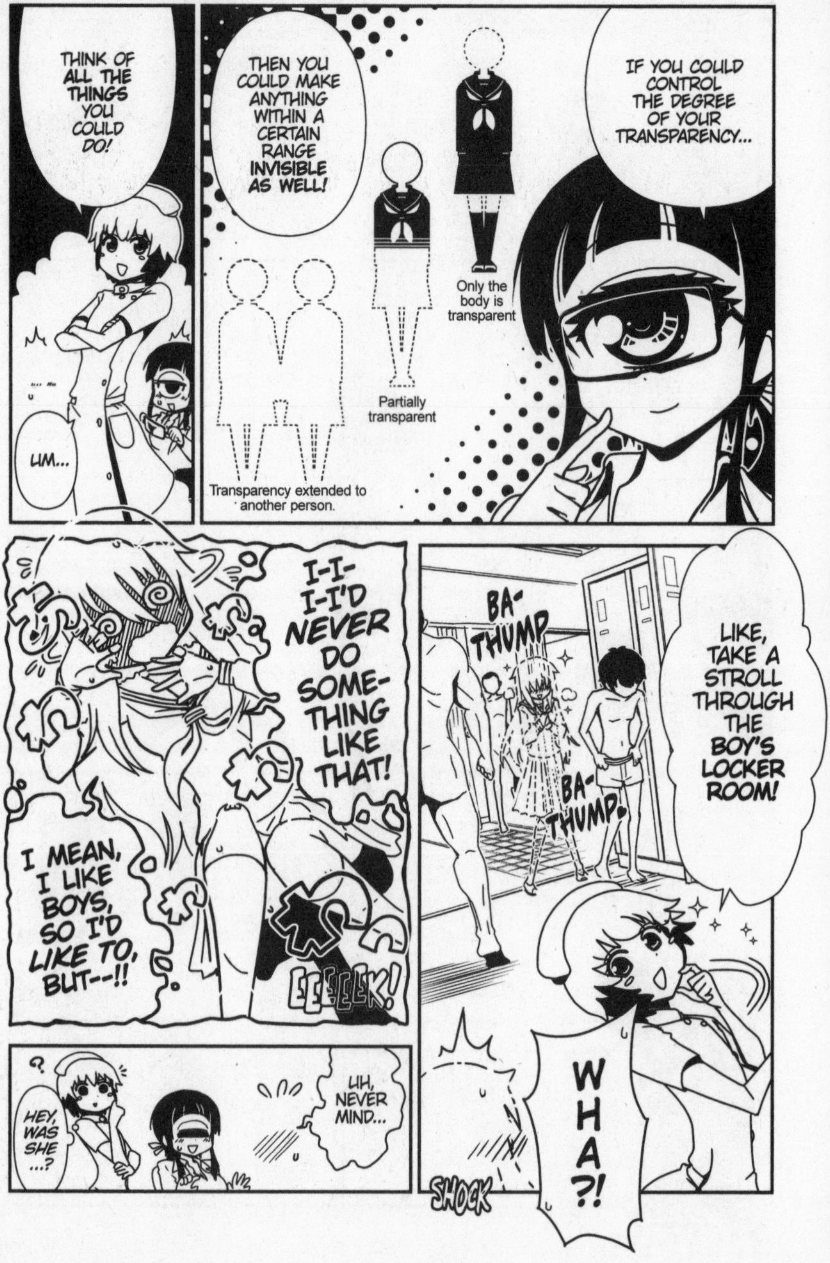
IF YOU COULD CONTROL THE DEGREE OF YOUR TRANSPARENCY...
Only the body is transparent
Partially transparent
Transparency extended to another person.
THEN YOU COULD MAKE ANYTHING WITHIN A CERTAIN RANGE INVISIBLE AS WELL!
THINK OF ALL THE THINGS YOU COULD DO!
UM...
LIKE, TAKE A STROLL THROUGH THE BOY'S LOCKER ROOM!
BA-THUMP
BA-THUMP
WHA?!
SHOCK
I-I-I-I'D NEVER DO SOMETHING LIKE THAT!
I MEAN, I LIKE BOYS, SO I'D LIKE TO, BUT--!!
EEEEEEK!
UH, NEVER MIND...
HEY, WAS SHE ...?

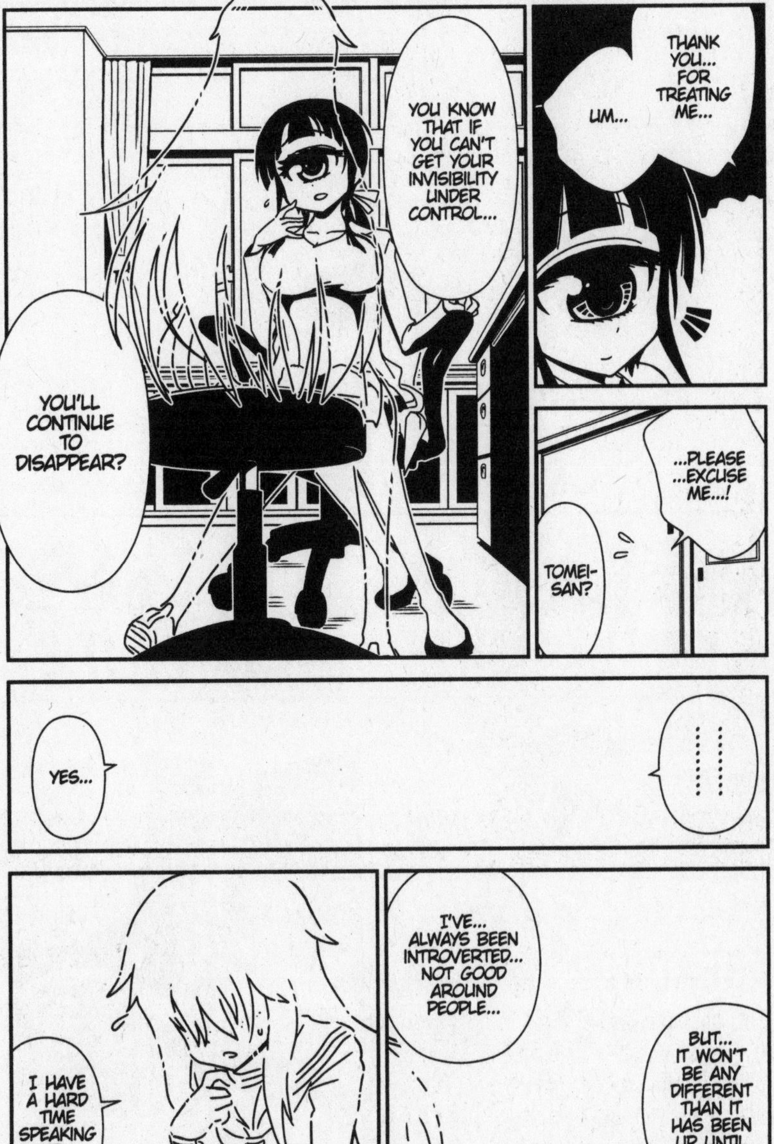
UM...
THANK YOU... FOR TREATING ME...
...PLEASE ...EXCUSE ME...!
TOMEI-SAN?
YOU KNOW THAT IF YOU CAN'T GET YOUR INVISIBILITY UNDER CONTROL...
YOU'LL CONTINUE TO DISAPPEAR?
......
YES...
I'VE... ALWAYS BEEN INTROVERTED... NOT GOOD AROUND PEOPLE...
BUT... IT WON'T BE ANY DIFFERENT THAN IT HAS BEEN UP UNTIL NOW.
I HAVE A HARD TIME SPEAKING UP...

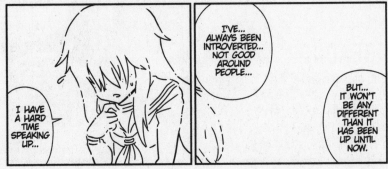

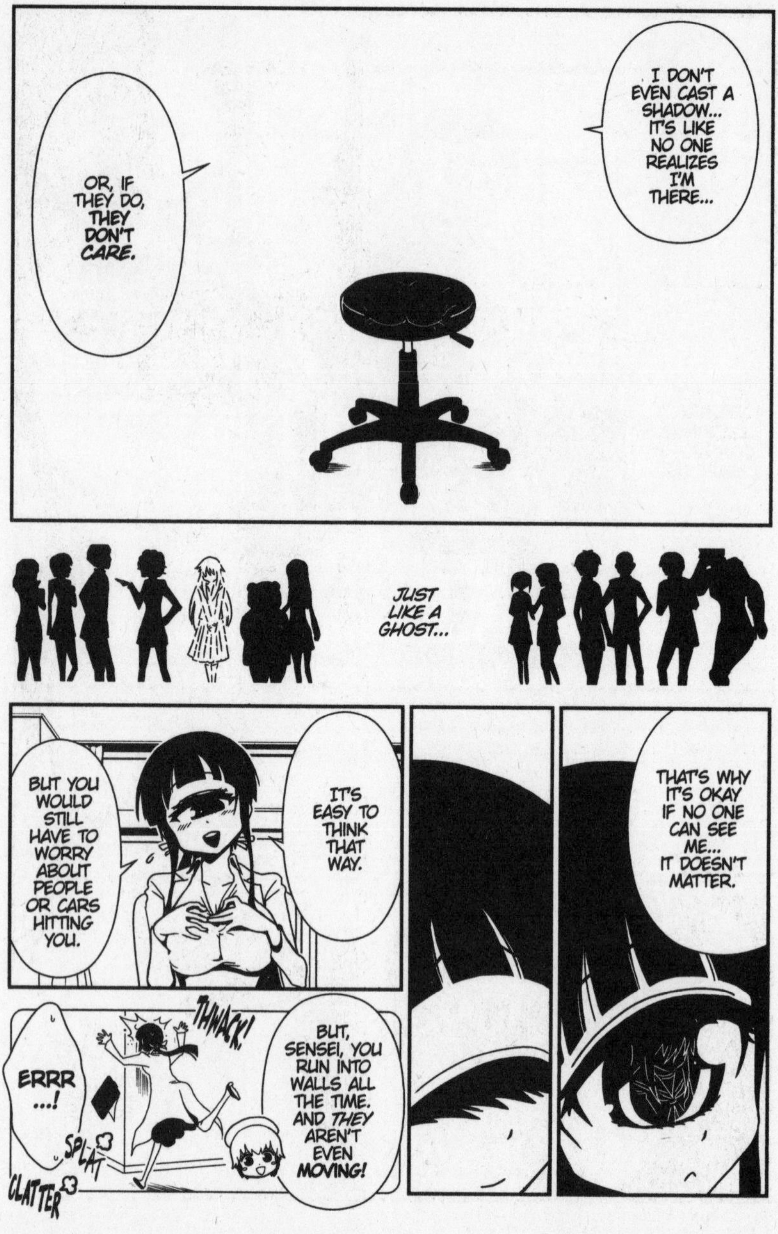
I DON'T EVEN CAST A SHADOW... IT'S LIKE NO ONE REALIZES I'M THERE...
OR, IF THEY DO, THEY DON'T CARE.
JUST LIKE A GHOST...
THAT'S WHY IT'S OKAY IF NO ONE CAN SEE ME... IT DOESN'T MATTER.
IT'S EASY TO THINK THAT WAY.
BUT YOU WOULD STILL HAVE TO WORRY ABOUT PEOPLE OR CARS HITTING YOU.
BUT, SENSEI, YOU RUN INTO WALLS ALL THE TIME. AND THEY AREN'T EVEN MOVING!
THWACK!
ERRR ...!
SPLAT
CLATTER

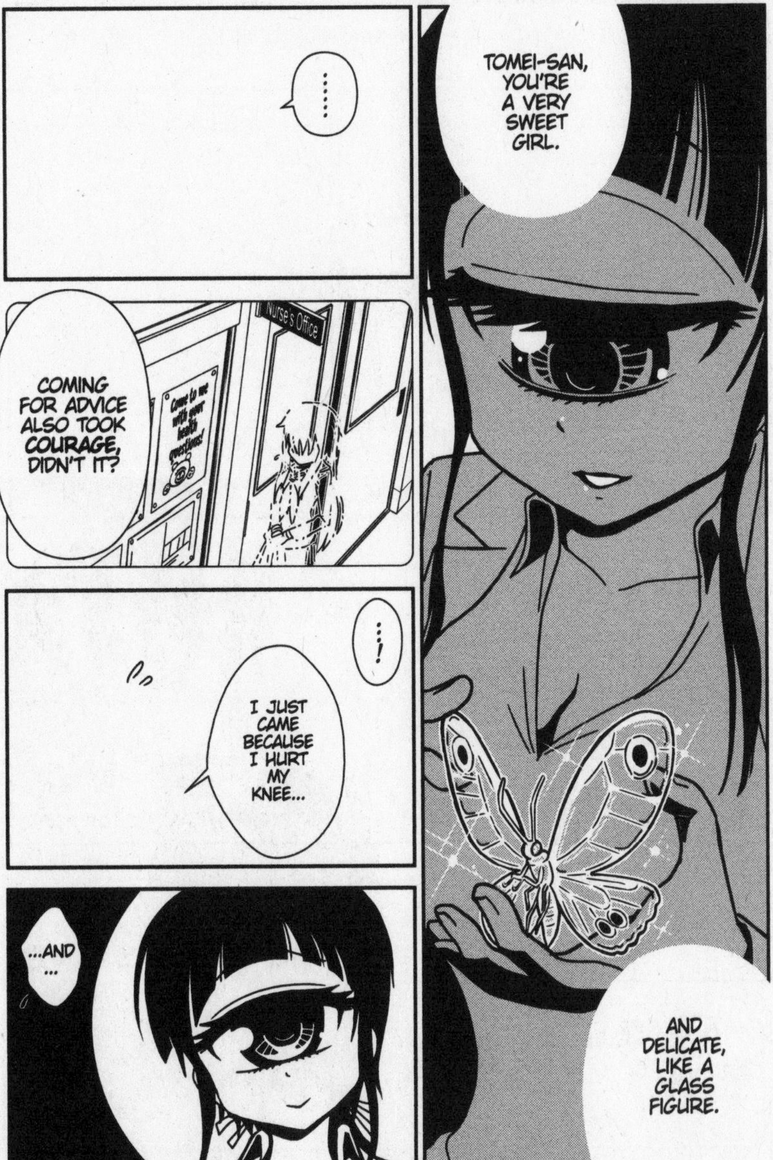
TOMEI-SAN, YOU'RE A VERY SWEET GIRL.
AND DELICATE, LIKE A GLASS FIGURE.
......
Nurse's Office
Come to me with your health questions!
COMING FOR ADVICE ALSO TOOK COURAGE, DIDN'T IT?
...!
I JUST CAME BECAUSE I HURT MY KNEE...
...AND ...

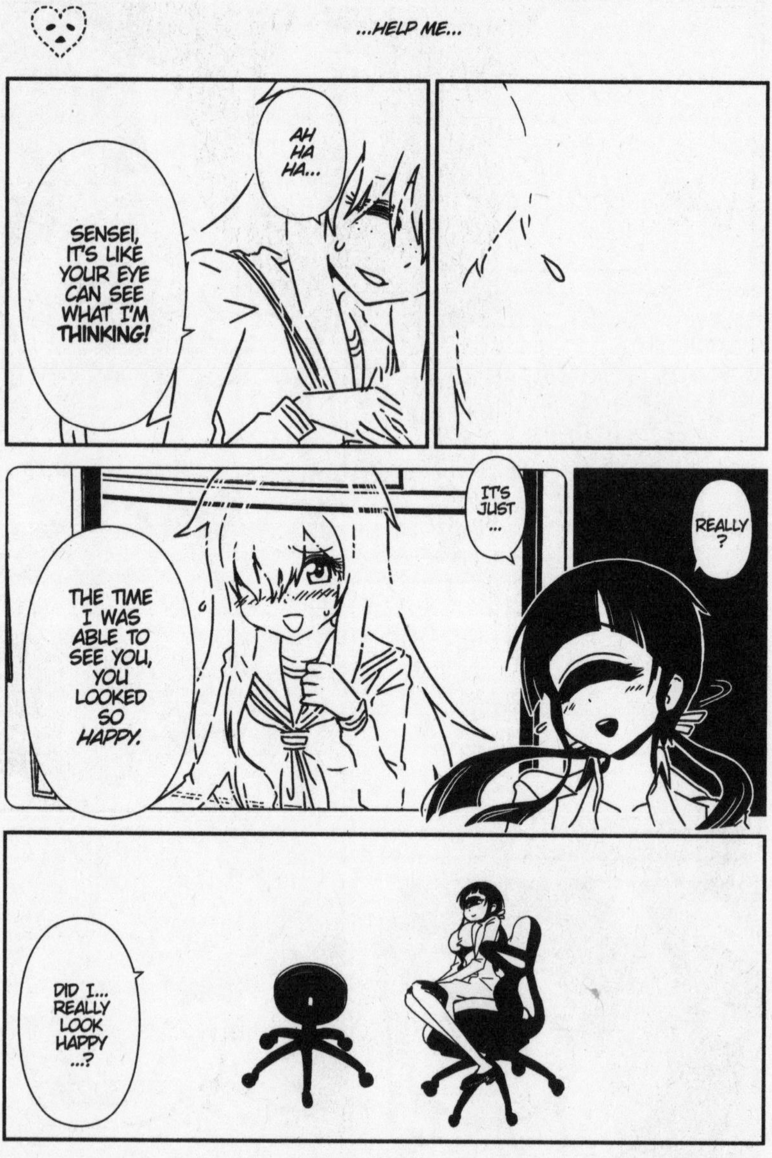
...HELP ME...
AH HA HA...
SENSEI, IT'S LIKE YOUR EYE CAN SEE WHAT I'M THINKING!
REALLY?
IT'S JUST...
THE TIME I WAS ABLE TO SEE YOU, YOU LOOKED SO *HAPPY.*
DID I... REALLY LOOK HAPPY...?

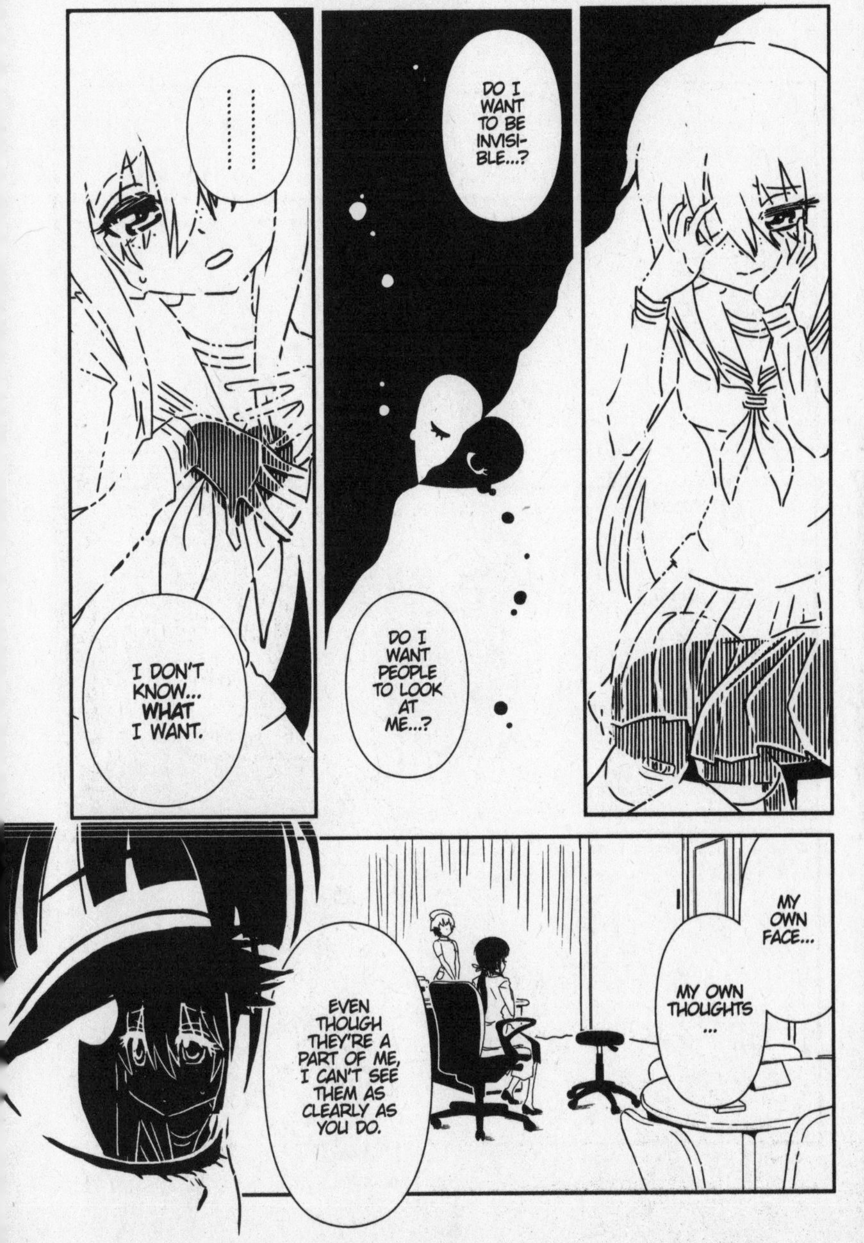
DO I WANT TO BE INVISIBLE...?
DO I WANT PEOPLE TO LOOK AT ME...?
......
I DON'T KNOW... WHAT I WANT.
MY OWN FACE...
MY OWN THOUGHTS ...
EVEN THOUGH THEY'RE A PART OF ME, I CAN'T SEE THEM AS CLEARLY AS YOU DO.

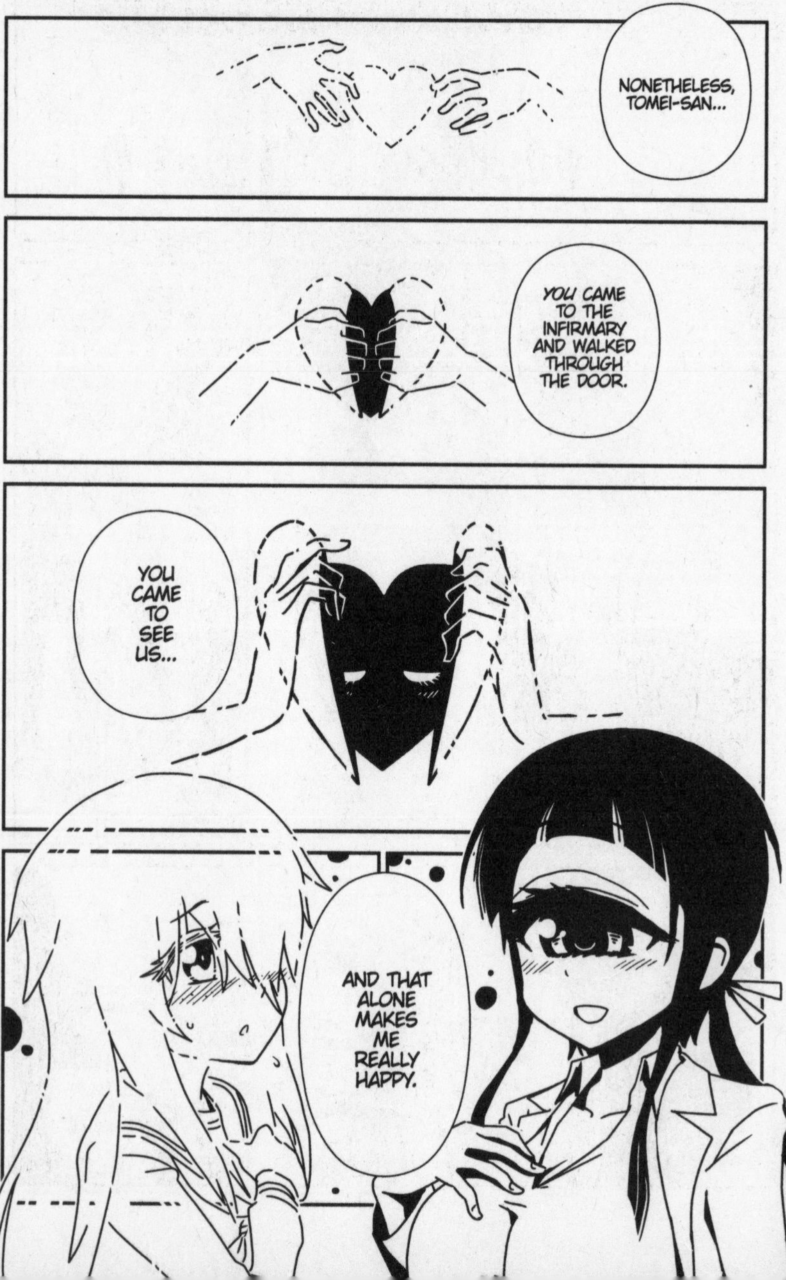
NONETHELESS, TOMEI-SAN...
YOU CAME TO THE INFIRMARY AND WALKED THROUGH THE DOOR.
YOU CAME TO SEE US...
AND THAT ALONE MAKES ME REALLY HAPPY.

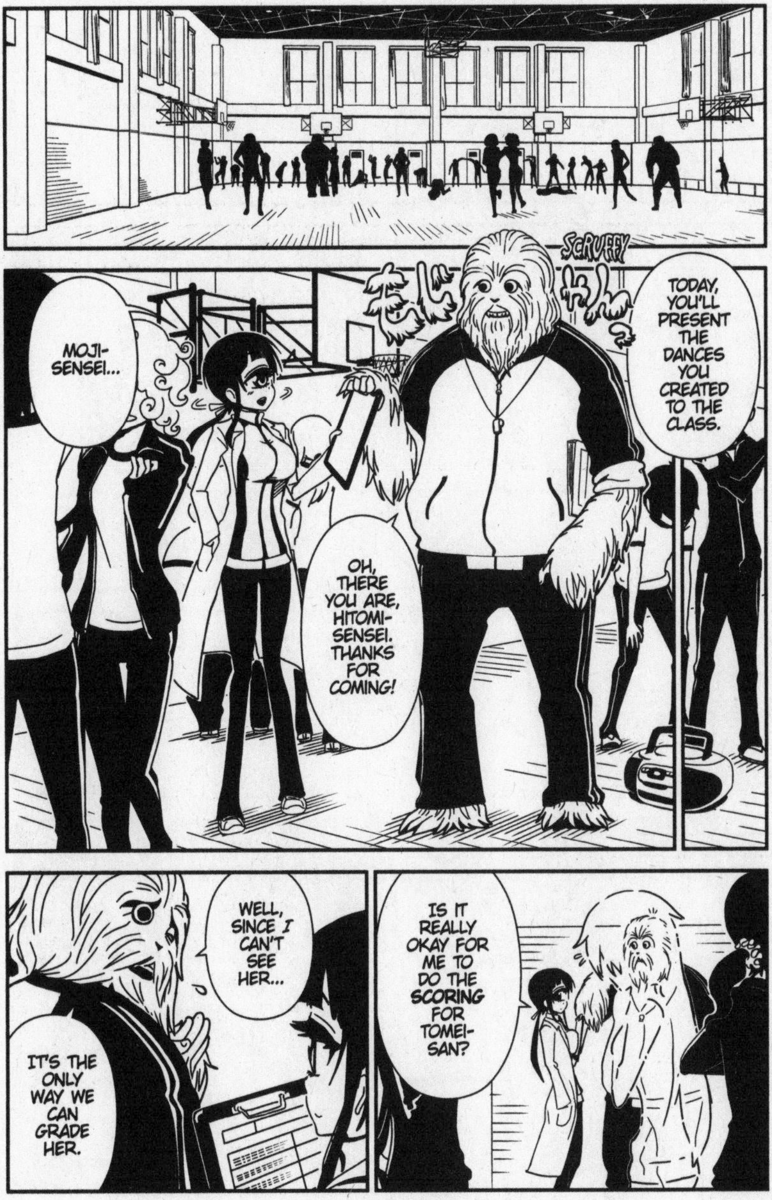
TODAY, YOU'LL PRESENT THE DANCES YOU CREATED TO THE CLASS.
SCRUFFY
MOJI-SENSEI...
OH, THERE YOU ARE, HITOMI-SENSEI. THANKS FOR COMING!
IS IT REALLY OKAY FOR ME TO DO THE SCORING FOR TOMEI-SAN?
WELL, SINCE I CAN'T SEE HER...
IT'S THE ONLY WAY WE CAN GRADE HER.

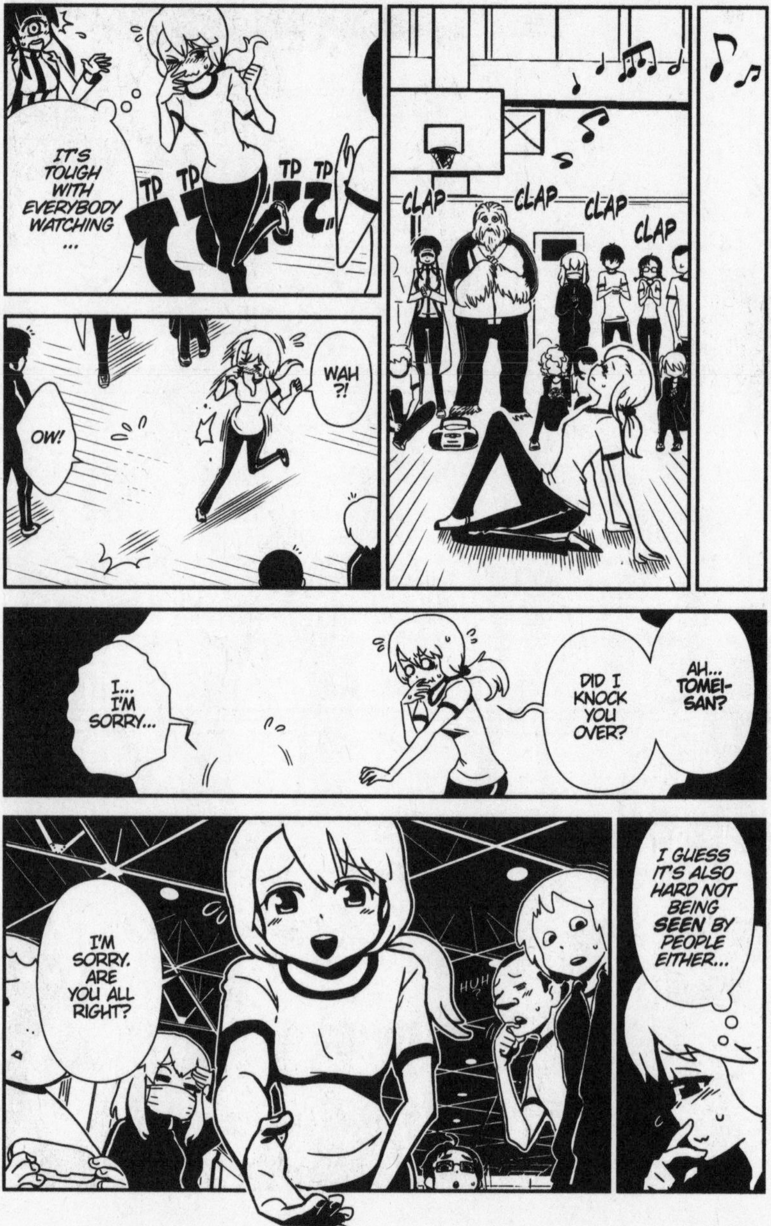
CLAP
CLAP
CLAP
CLAP
IT'S TOUGH WITH EVERYBODY WATCHING ...
TP TP
TP TP
WAH ?!
OW!
AH... TOMEI-SAN?
DID I KNOCK YOU OVER?
I... I'M SORRY...
I GUESS IT'S ALSO HARD NOT BEING SEEN BY PEOPLE EITHER...
I'M SORRY. ARE YOU ALL RIGHT?
HUH?

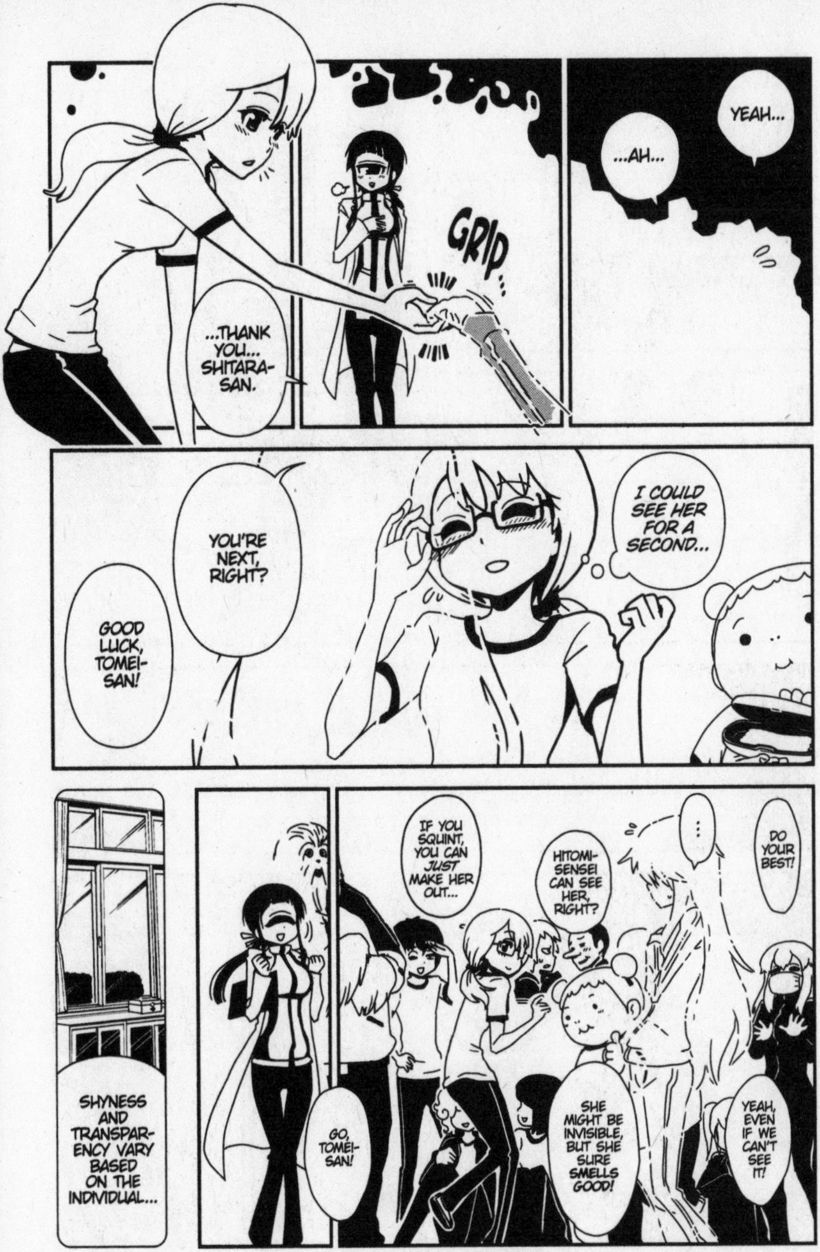
YEAH...
...AH...
GRIP
...THANK YOU... SHITARA-SAN.
I COULD SEE HER FOR A SECOND...
YOU'RE NEXT, RIGHT?
GOOD LUCK, TOMEI-SAN!
DO YOUR BEST!
...
HITOMI-SENSEI CAN SEE HER, RIGHT?
IF YOU SQUINT, YOU CAN JUST MAKE HER OUT...
YEAH, EVEN IF WE CAN'T SEE IT!
SHE MIGHT BE INVISIBLE, BUT SHE SURE SMELLS GOOD!
GO, TOMEI-SAN!
SHYNESS AND TRANSPARENCY VARY BASED ON THE INDIVIDUAL...

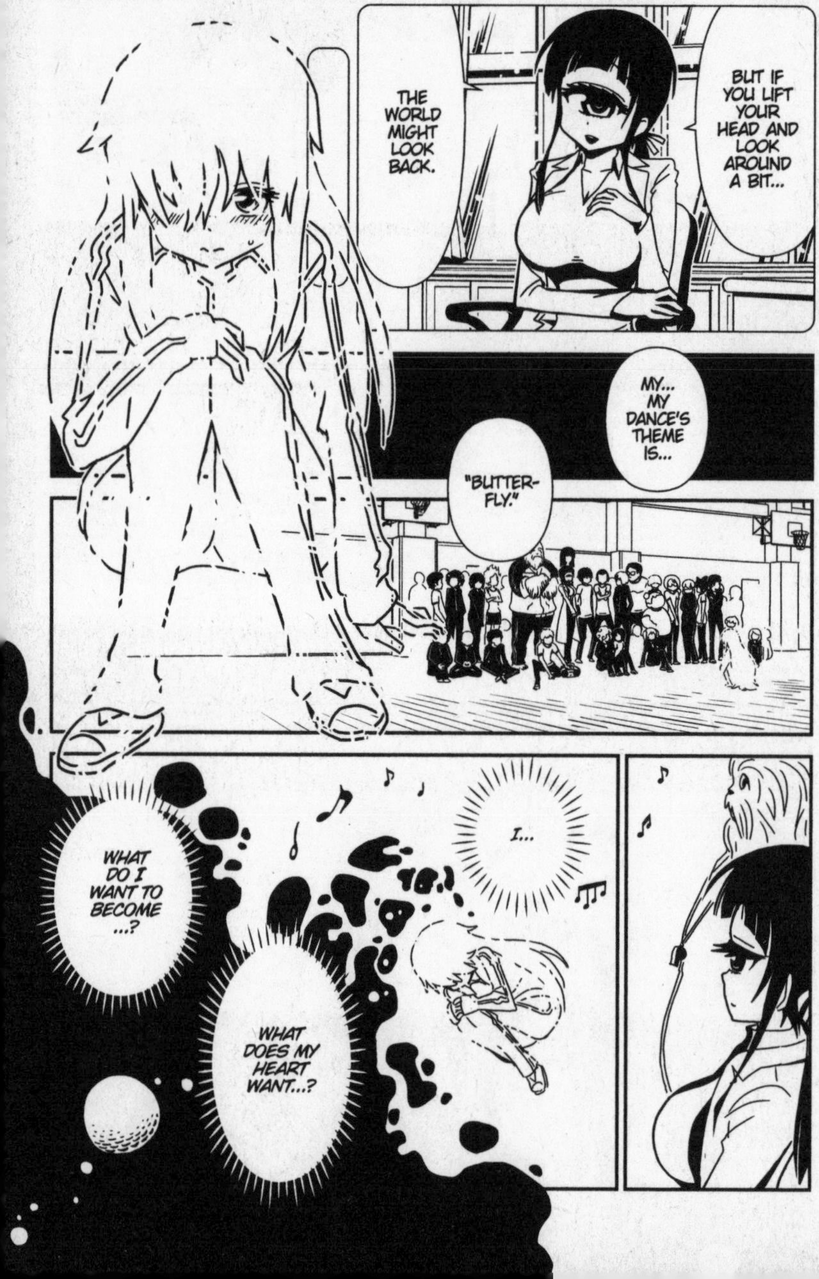
BUT IF YOU LIFT YOUR HEAD AND LOOK AROUND A BIT...
THE WORLD MIGHT LOOK BACK.
MY... MY DANCE'S THEME IS...
"BUTTER-FLY."
I...
WHAT DO I WANT TO BECOME ...?
WHAT DOES MY HEART WANT...?

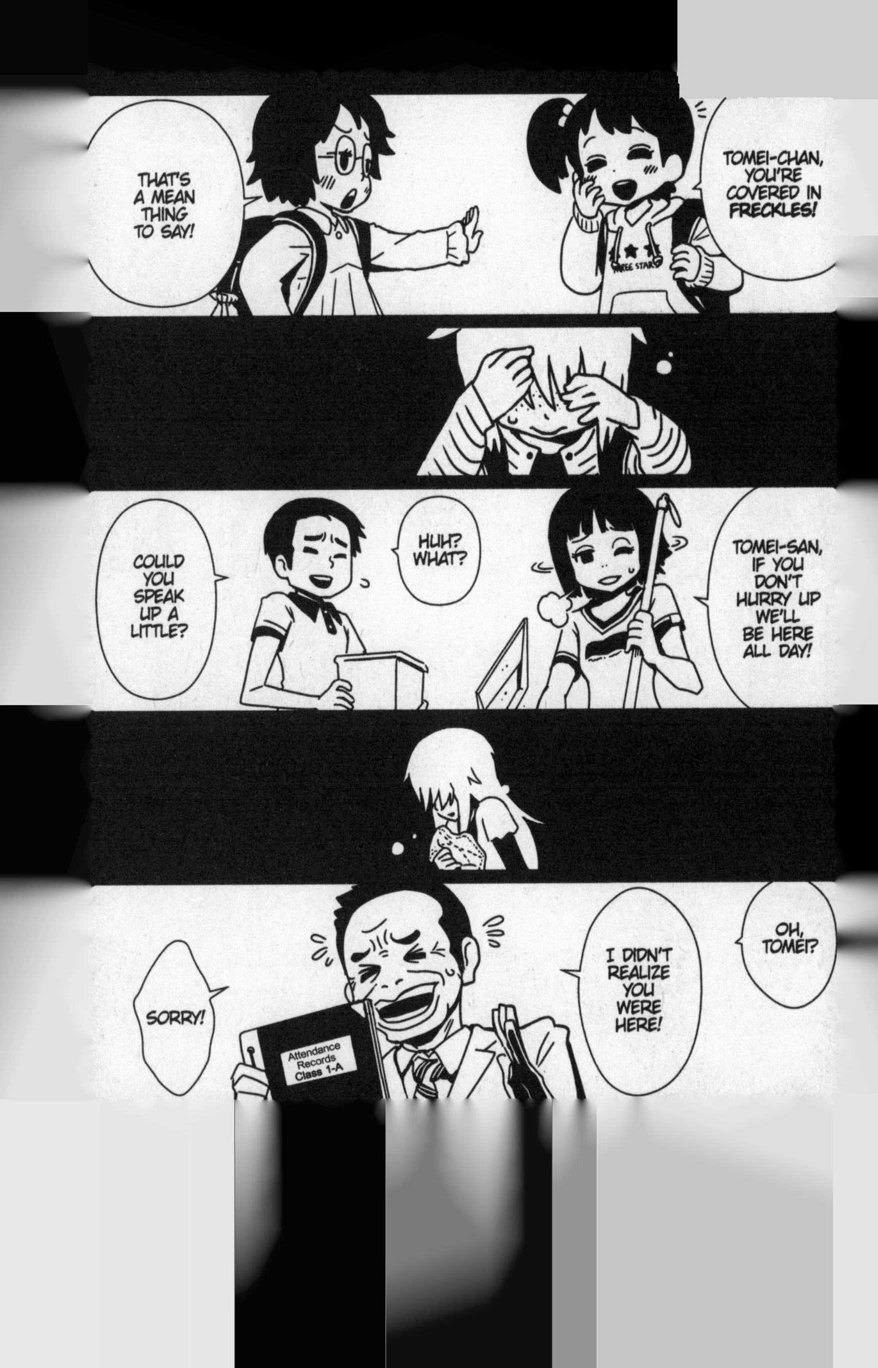
TOMEI-CHAN, YOU'RE COVERED IN FRECKLES!
THAT'S A MEAN THING TO SAY!
TOMEI-SAN, IF YOU DON'T HURRY UP WE'LL BE HERE ALL DAY!
HUH? WHAT?
COULD YOU SPEAK UP A LITTLE?
OH, TOMEI?
I DIDN'T REALIZE YOU WERE HERE!
SORRY!
Attendance Records Class 1-A

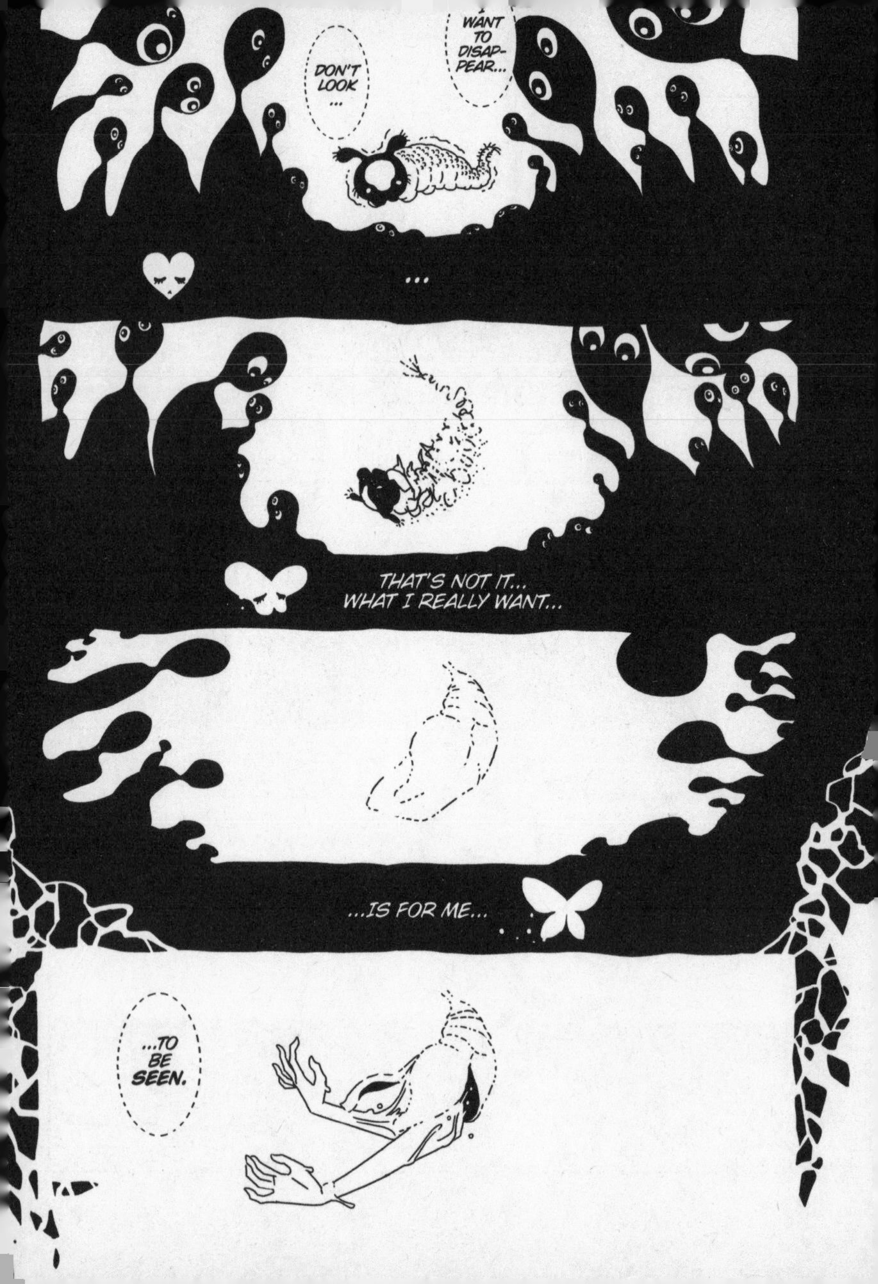
I WANT TO DISAP-PEAR...
DON'T LOOK...
...
THAT'S NOT IT... WHAT I REALLY WANT...
...IS FOR ME...
...TO BE SEEN.

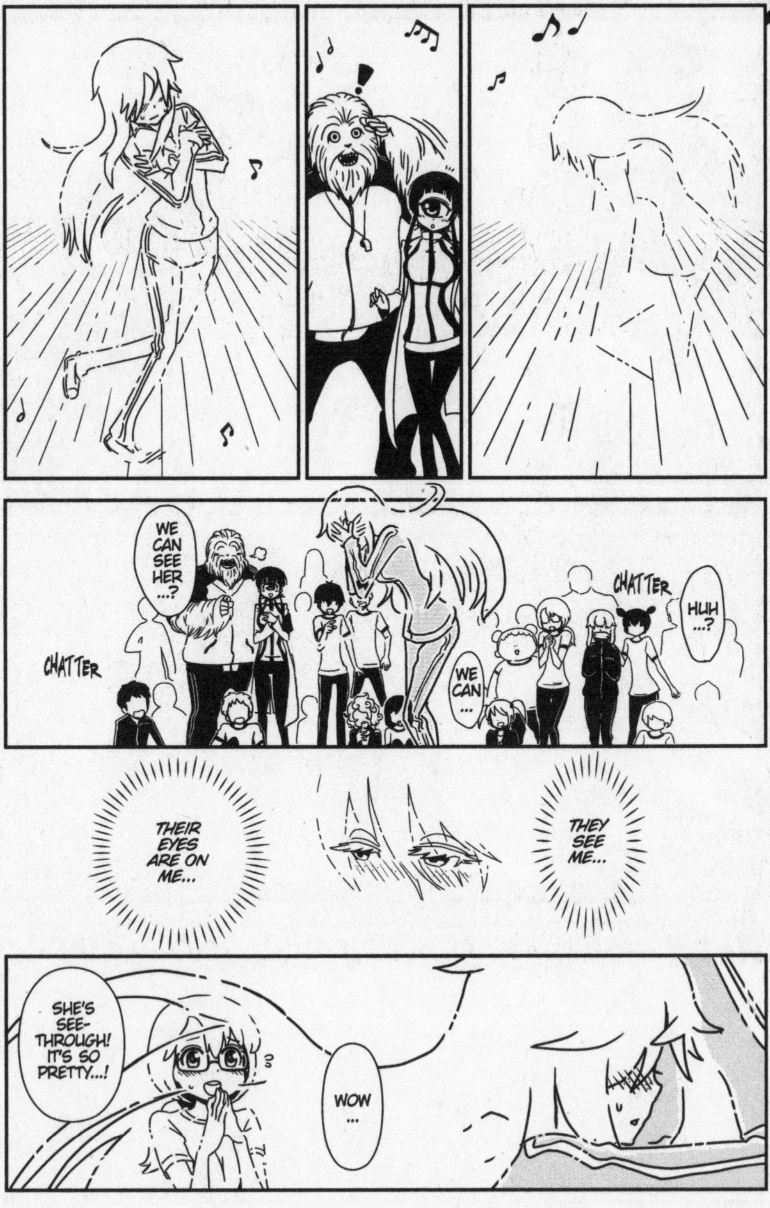
HUH ...?
CHATTER
WE CAN ...
WE CAN SEE HER ...?
CHATTER
THEY SEE ME...
THEIR EYES ARE ON ME...
WOW ...
SHE'S SEE-THROUGH! IT'S SO PRETTY...!

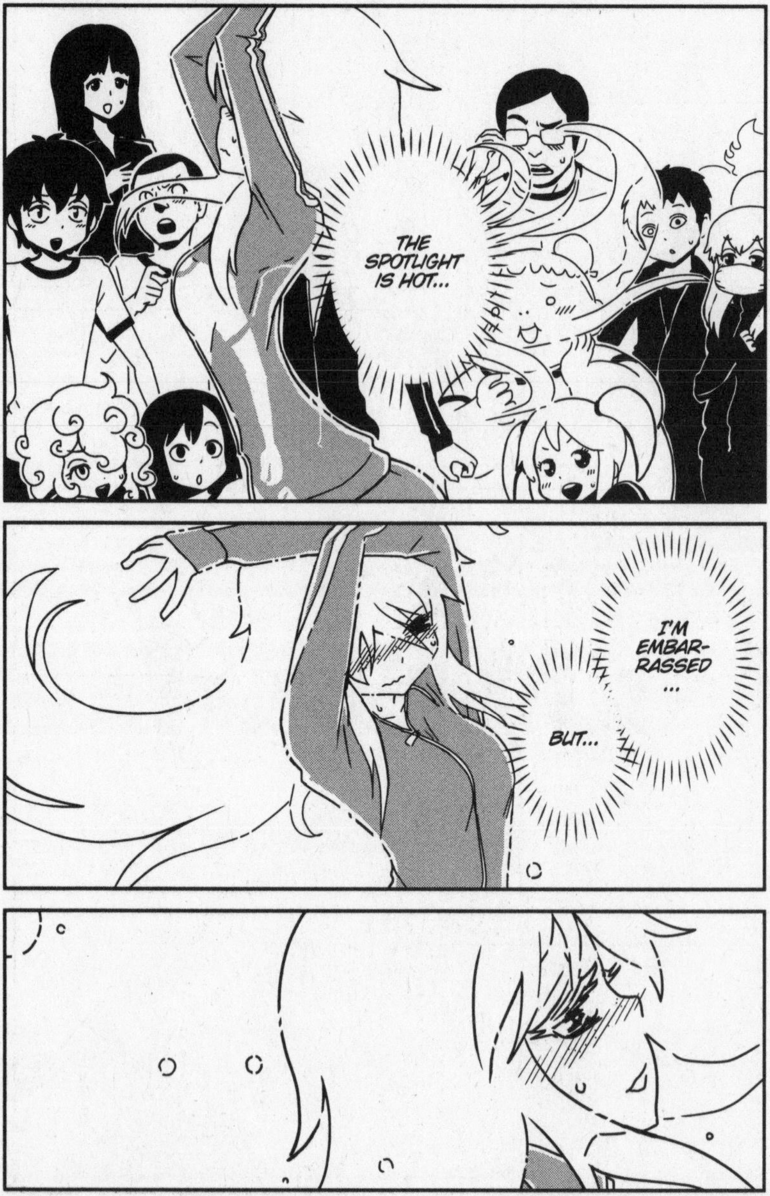
THE SPOTLIGHT IS HOT...
I'M EMBAR-RASSED ...
BUT...

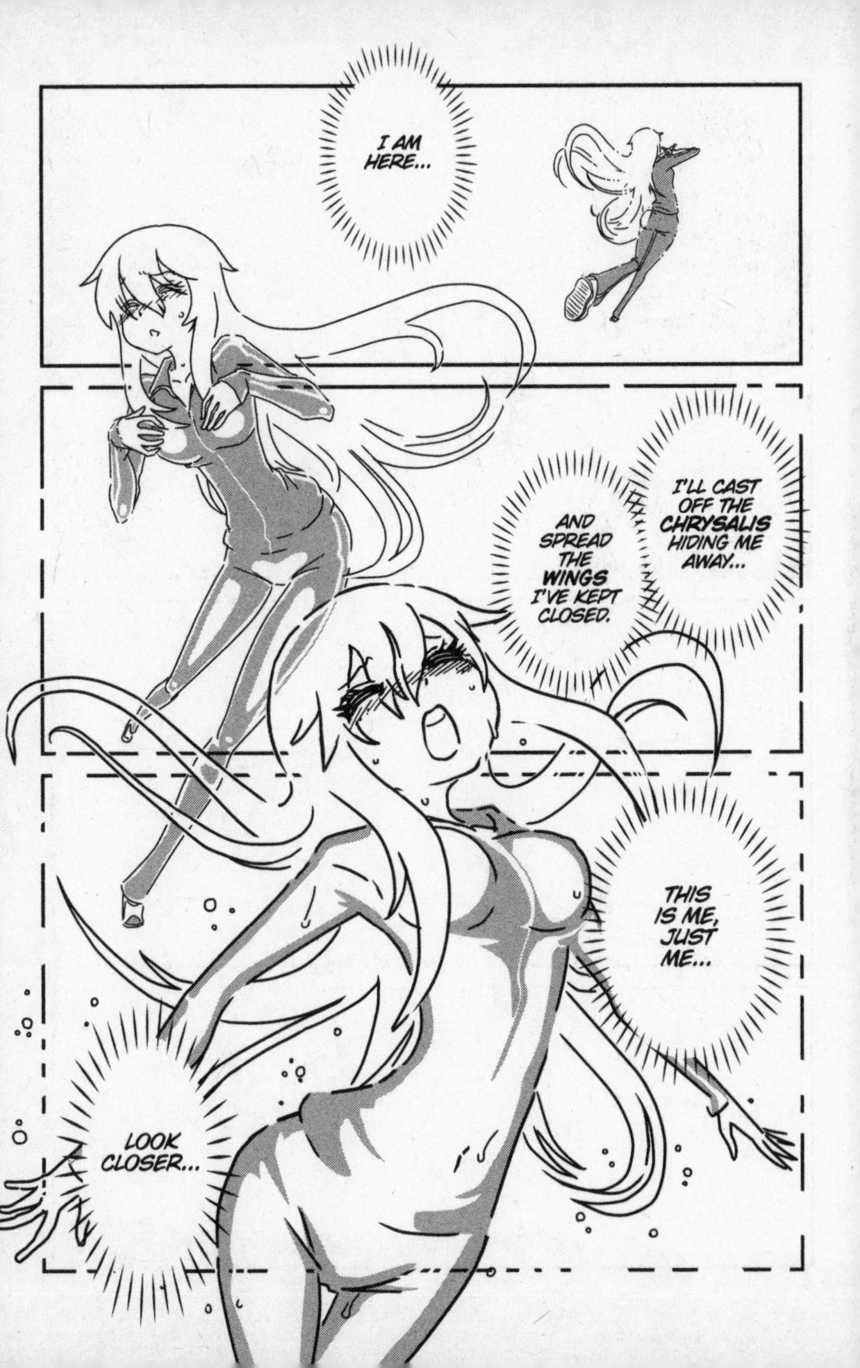
I AM HERE...
I'LL CAST OFF THE CHRYSALIS HIDING ME AWAY...
AND SPREAD THE WINGS I'VE KEPT CLOSED.
THIS IS ME, JUST ME...
LOOK CLOSER...

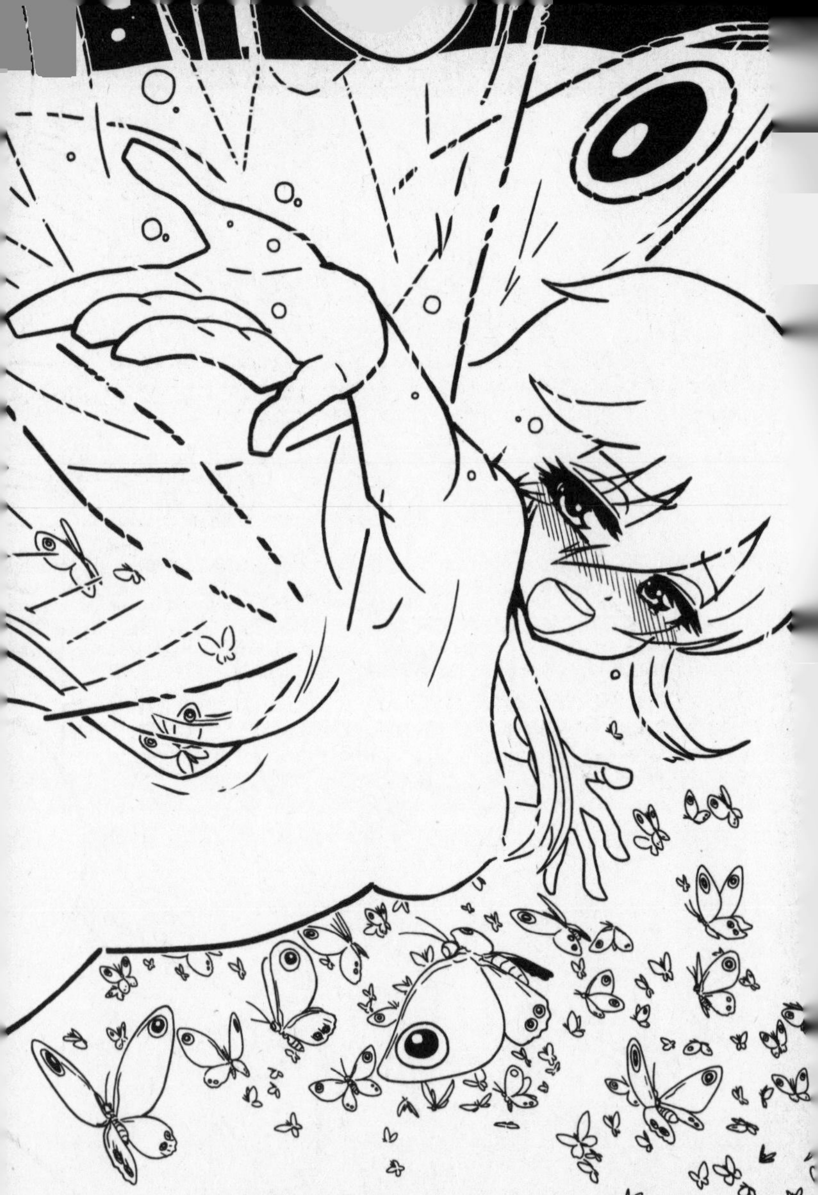

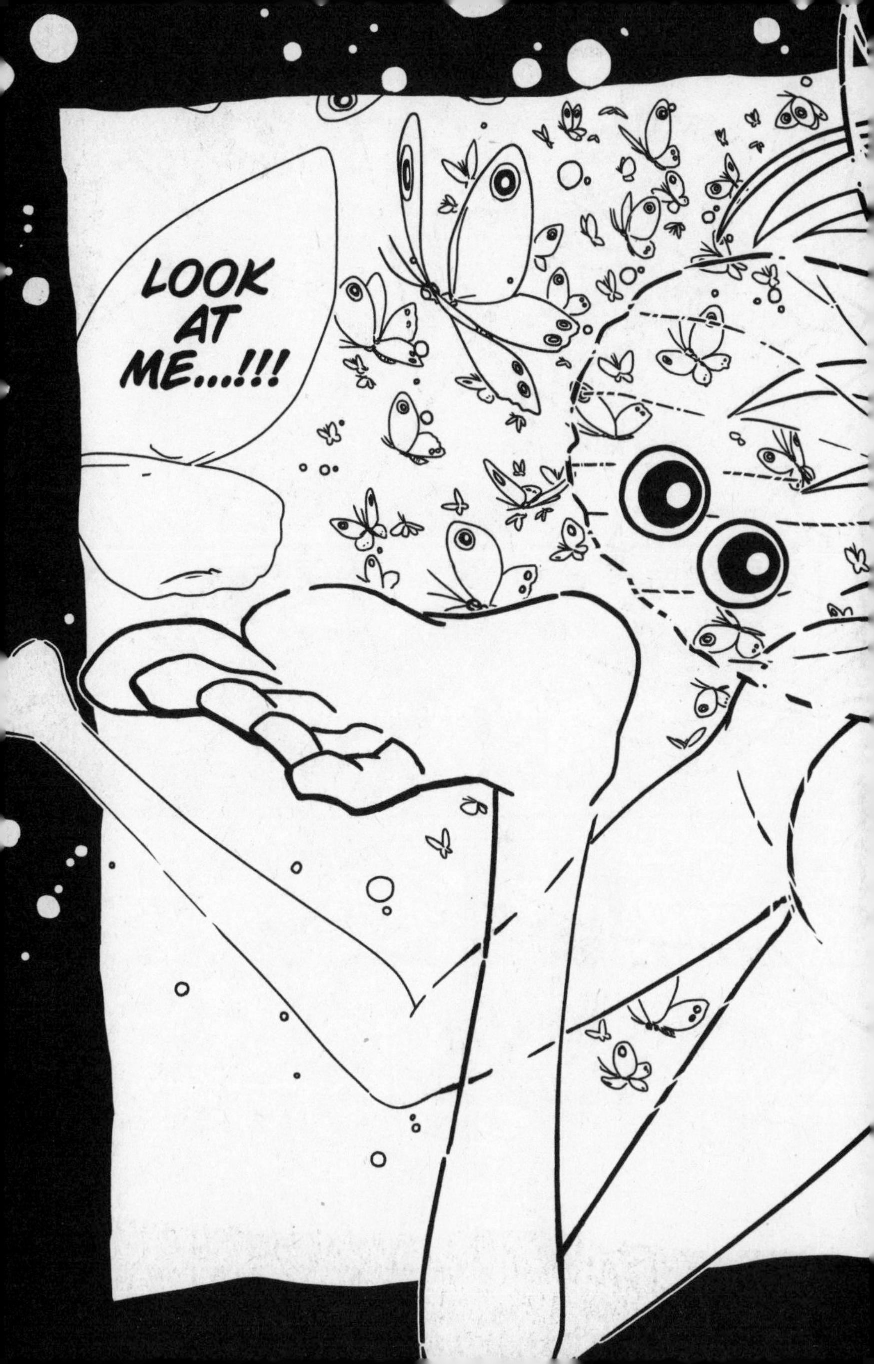
LOOK AT ME...!!!

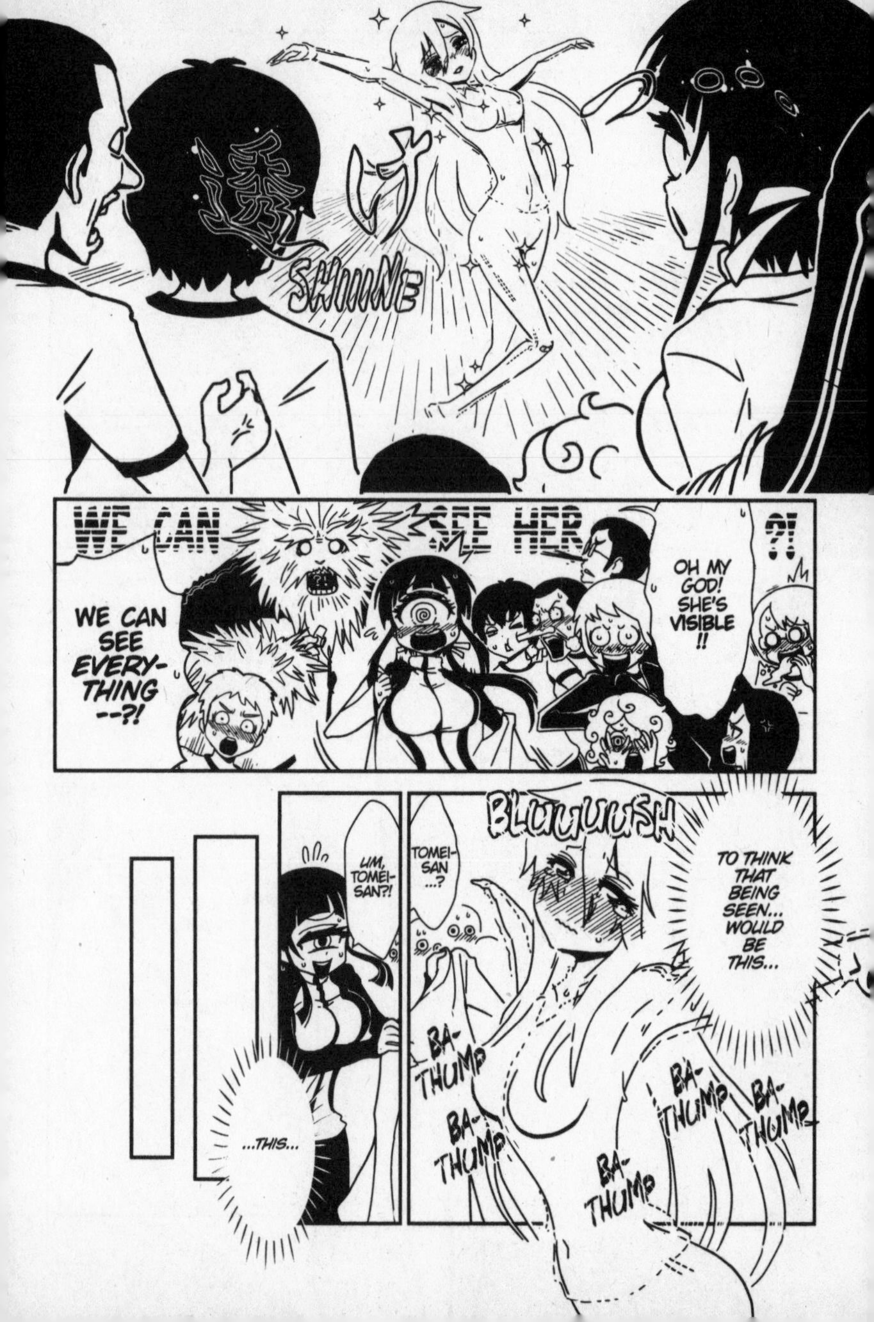
SHIIIINE
WE CAN SEE HER ?!
OH MY GOD! SHE'S VISIBLE !!
WE CAN SEE EVERY-THING --?!
BLUUUUUSH
TO THINK THAT BEING SEEN... WOULD BE THIS...
TOMEI-SAN ...?
BA-THUMP
BA-THUMP
BA-THUMP
BA-THUMP
BA-THUMP
UM, TOMEI-SAN?!
...THIS...

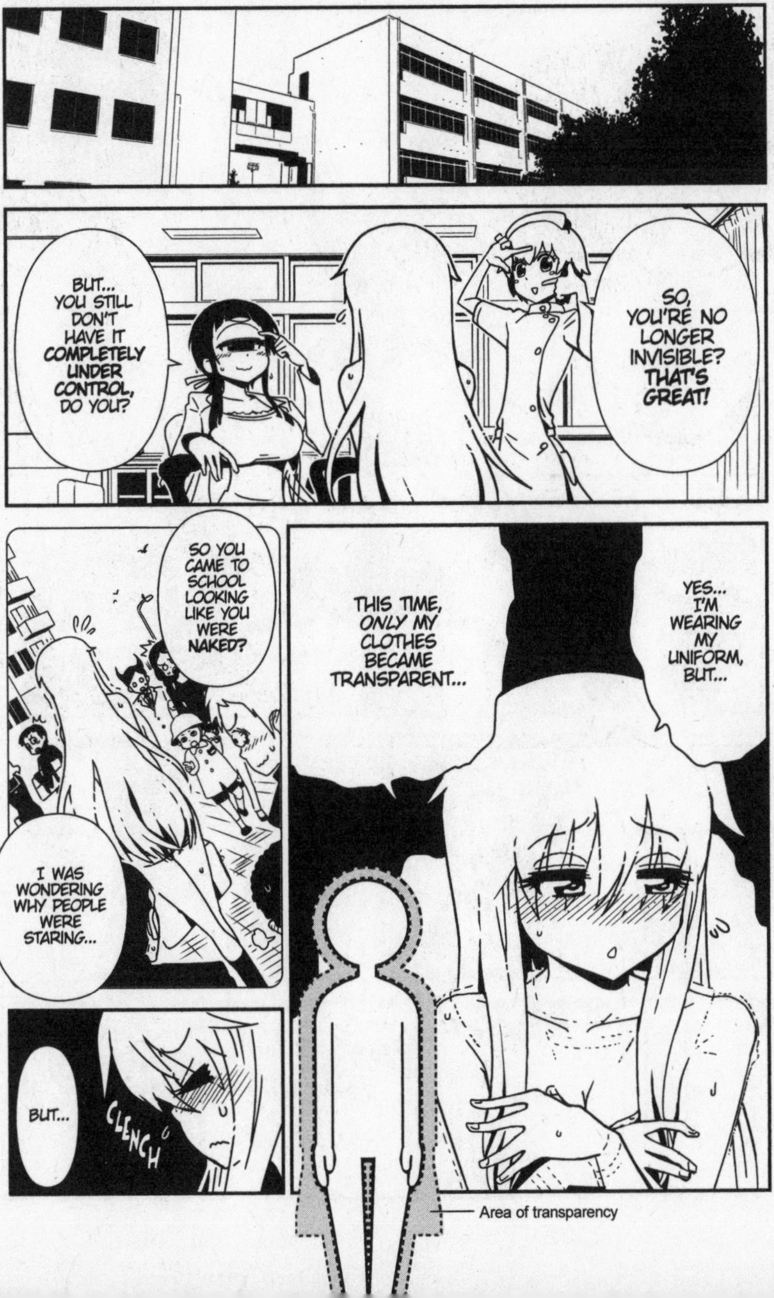
SO, YOU'RE NO LONGER INVISIBLE? THAT'S GREAT!
BUT... YOU STILL DON'T HAVE IT COMPLETELY UNDER CONTROL, DO YOU?
YES... I'M WEARING MY UNIFORM, BUT...
THIS TIME, *ONLY MY* CLOTHES BECAME TRANSPARENT...
Area of transparency
SO YOU CAME TO SCHOOL LOOKING LIKE YOU WERE NAKED?
I WAS WONDERING WHY PEOPLE WERE STARING...
BUT...
CLENCH

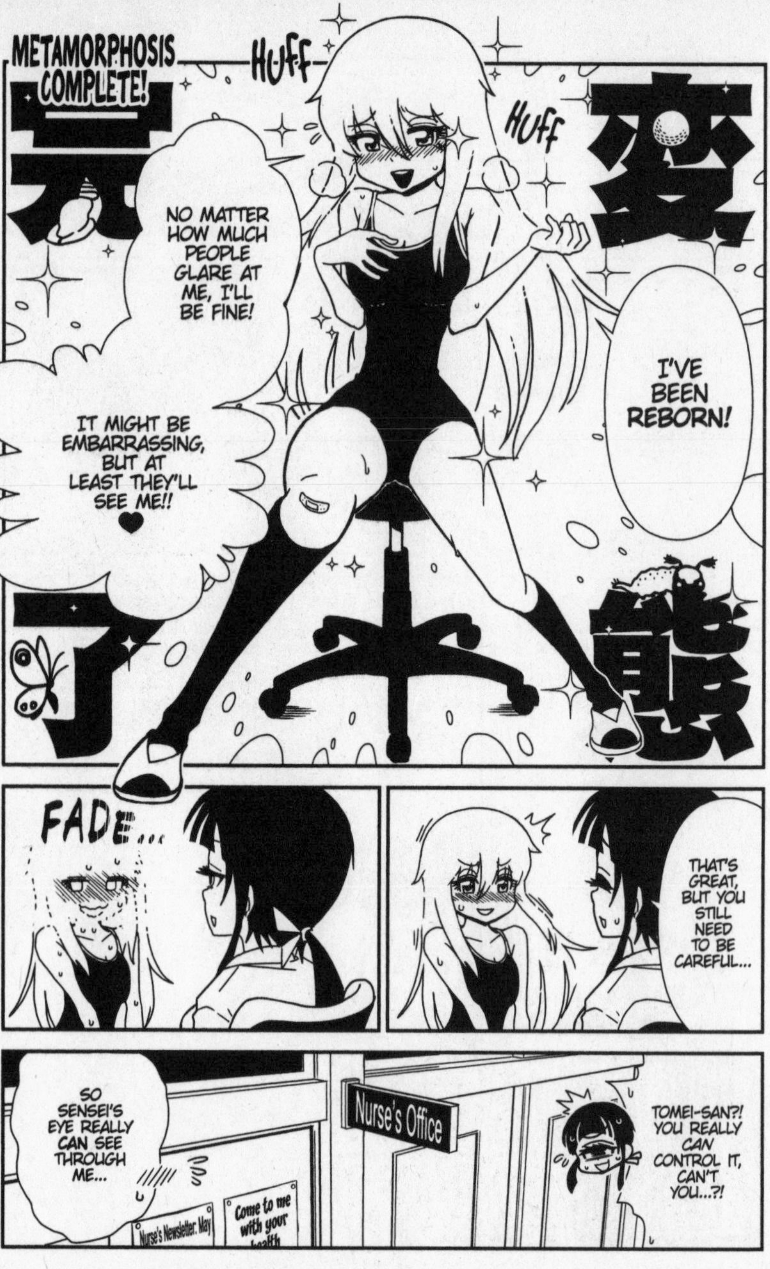
変態
HUFF
I'VE BEEN REBORN!
HUFF
NO MATTER HOW MUCH PEOPLE GLARE AT ME, I'LL BE FINE!
IT MIGHT BE EMBARRASSING, BUT AT LEAST THEY'LL SEE ME!! ♥
METAMORPHOSIS COMPLETE!
完了
THAT'S GREAT, BUT YOU STILL NEED TO BE CAREFUL...
FADE...
TOMEI-SAN?! YOU REALLY CAN CONTROL IT, CAN'T YOU...?!
Nurse's Office
SO SENSEI'S EYE REALLY CAN SEE THROUGH ME...
Come to me with your health
Nurse's Newsletter. May

NURSE HITOMI'S
Monster Infirmary

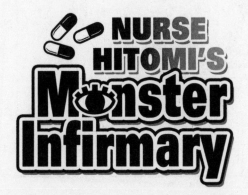

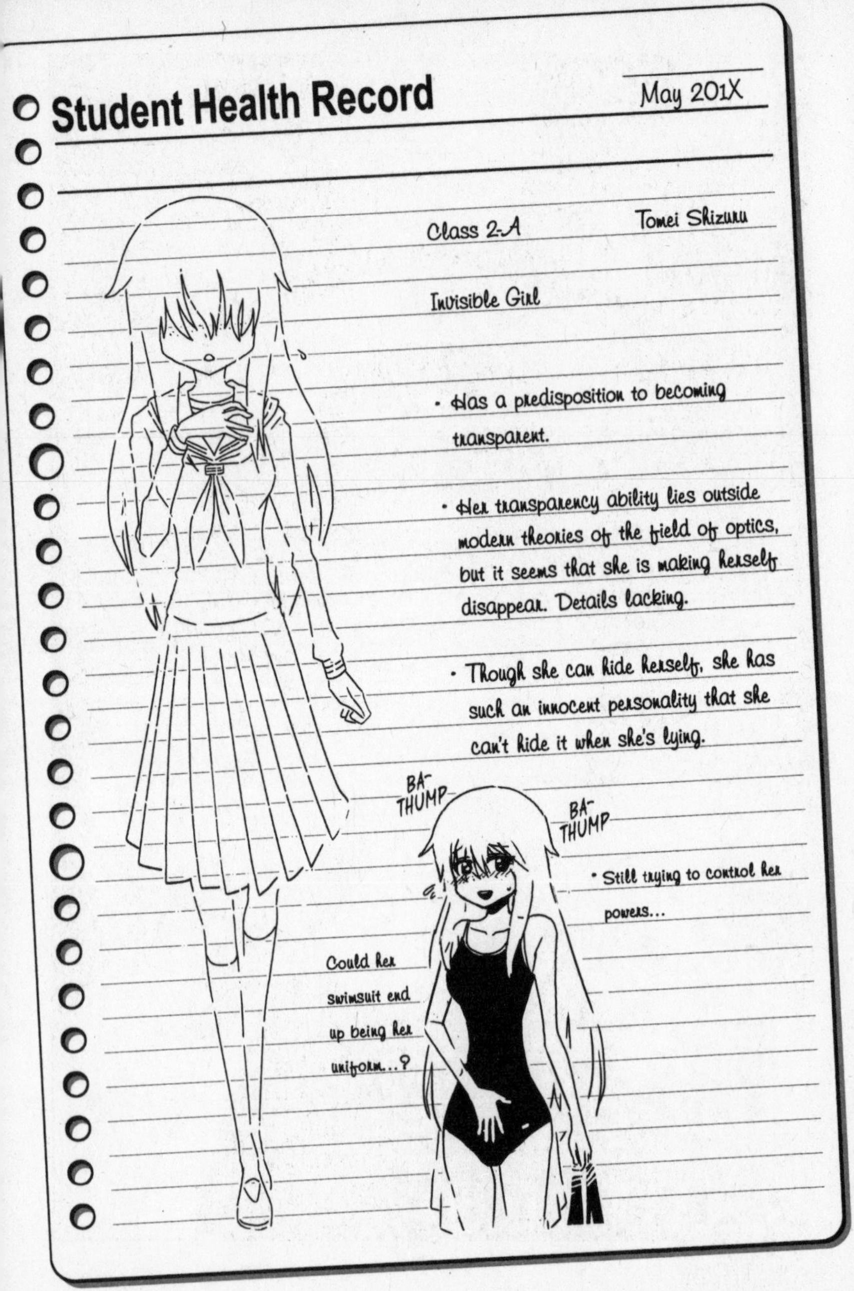
Student Health Record
May 201X
Class 2-A
Tomei Shizuru
Invisible Girl
• Has a predisposition to becoming transparent.
• Her transparency ability lies outside modern theories of the field of optics, but it seems that she is making herself disappear. Details lacking.
• Though she can hide herself, she has such an innocent personality that she can't hide it when she's lying.
BA-THUMP
BA-THUMP
• Still trying to control her powers...
Could her swimsuit end up being her uniform...?

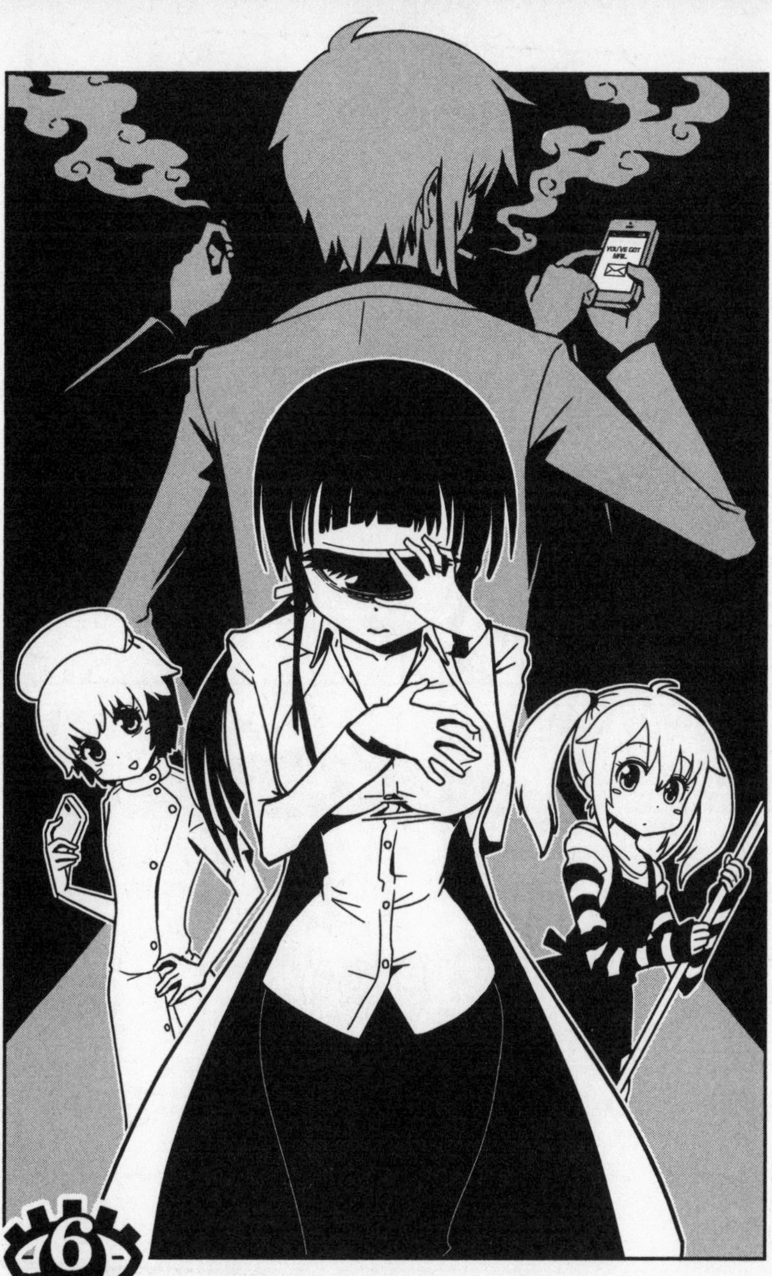
YOU'VE GOT MAIL.
6
Chapter

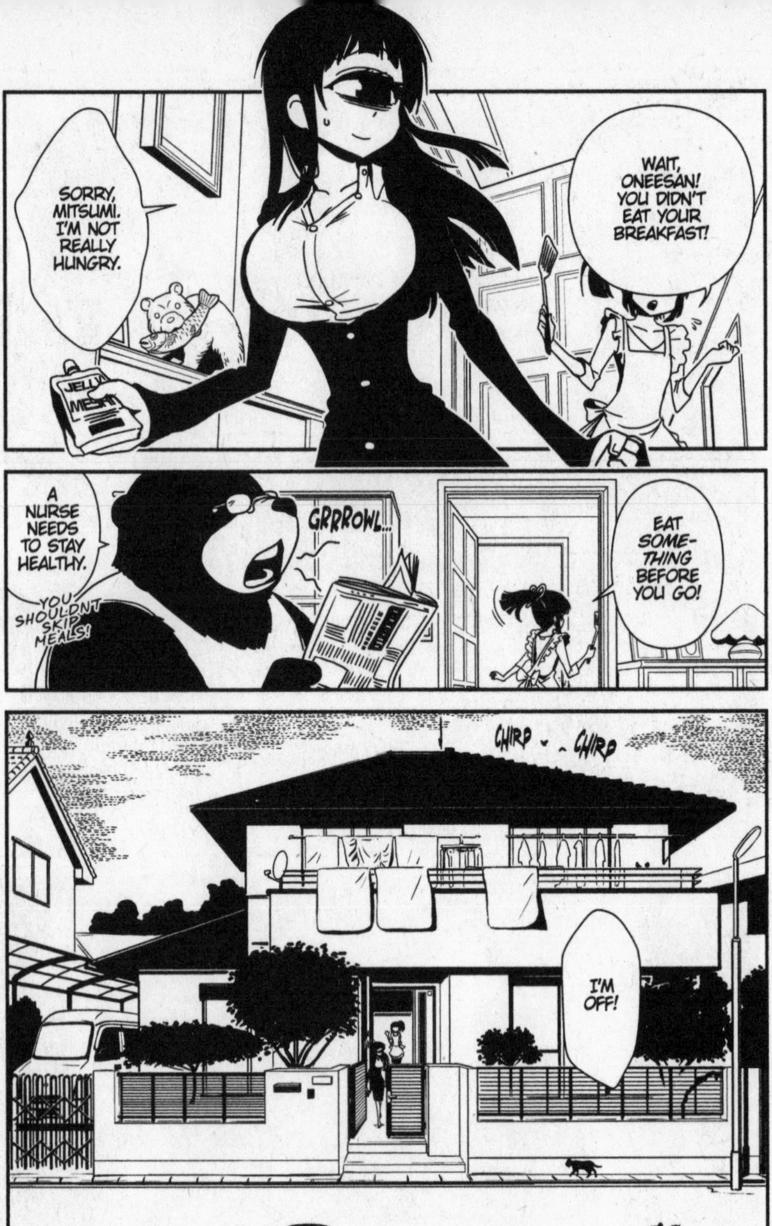
WAIT, ONEESAN! YOU DIDN'T EAT YOUR BREAKFAST!
SORRY, MITSUMI. I'M NOT REALLY HUNGRY.
EAT SOME-THING BEFORE YOU GO!
GRRROWL...
A NURSE NEEDS TO STAY HEALTHY.
YOU SHOULDNT SKIP MEALS!
CHIRP .. CHIRP
I'M OFF!

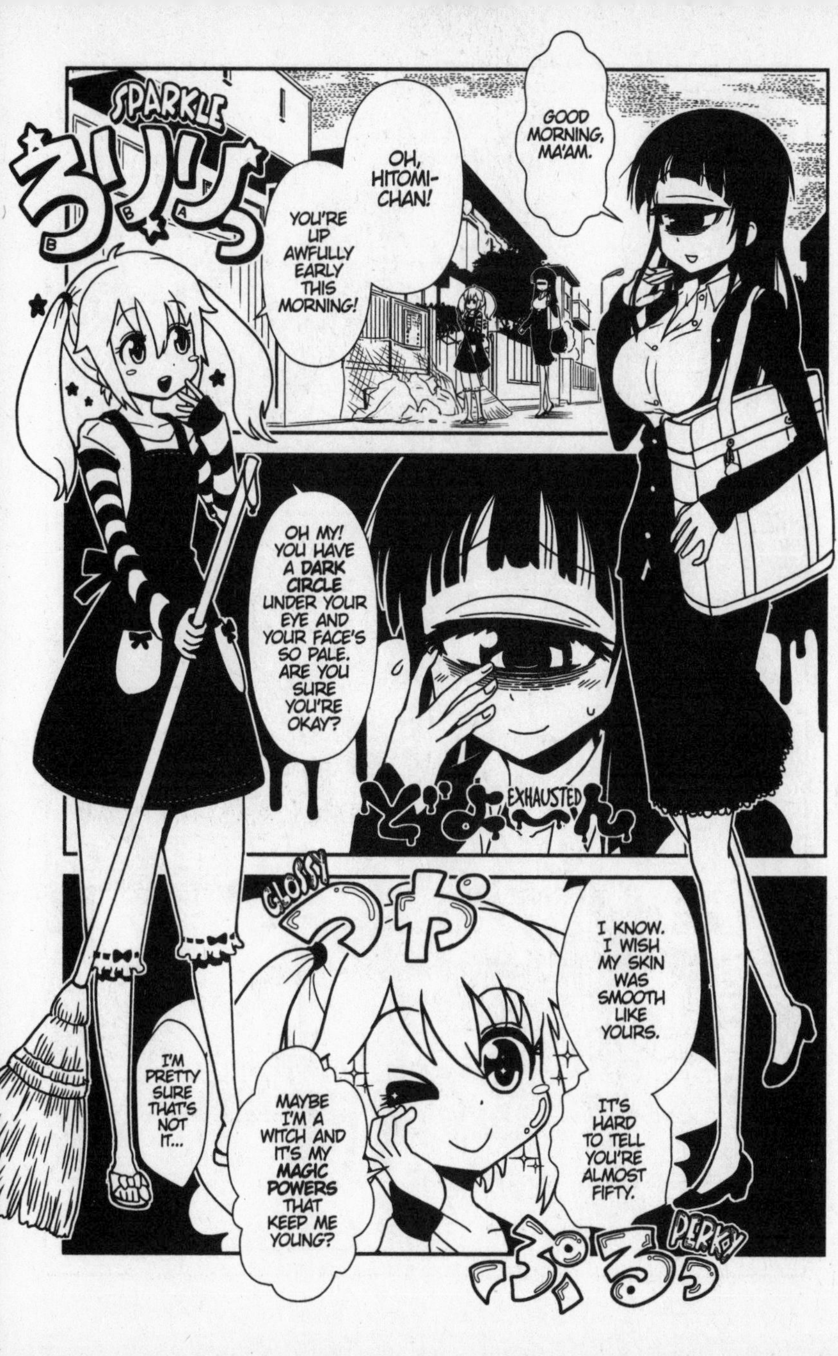
GOOD MORNING, MA'AM.
OH, HITOMI-CHAN!
YOU'RE UP AWFULLY EARLY THIS MORNING!
SPARKLE
OH MY! YOU HAVE A DARK CIRCLE UNDER YOUR EYE AND YOUR FACE'S SO PALE. ARE YOU SURE YOU'RE OKAY?
EXHAUSTED
I KNOW. I WISH MY SKIN WAS SMOOTH LIKE YOURS.
IT'S HARD TO TELL YOU'RE ALMOST FIFTY.
GLOSSY
MAYBE I'M A WITCH AND IT'S MY MAGIC POWERS THAT KEEP ME YOUNG?
I'M PRETTY SURE THAT'S NOT IT...
PERKY

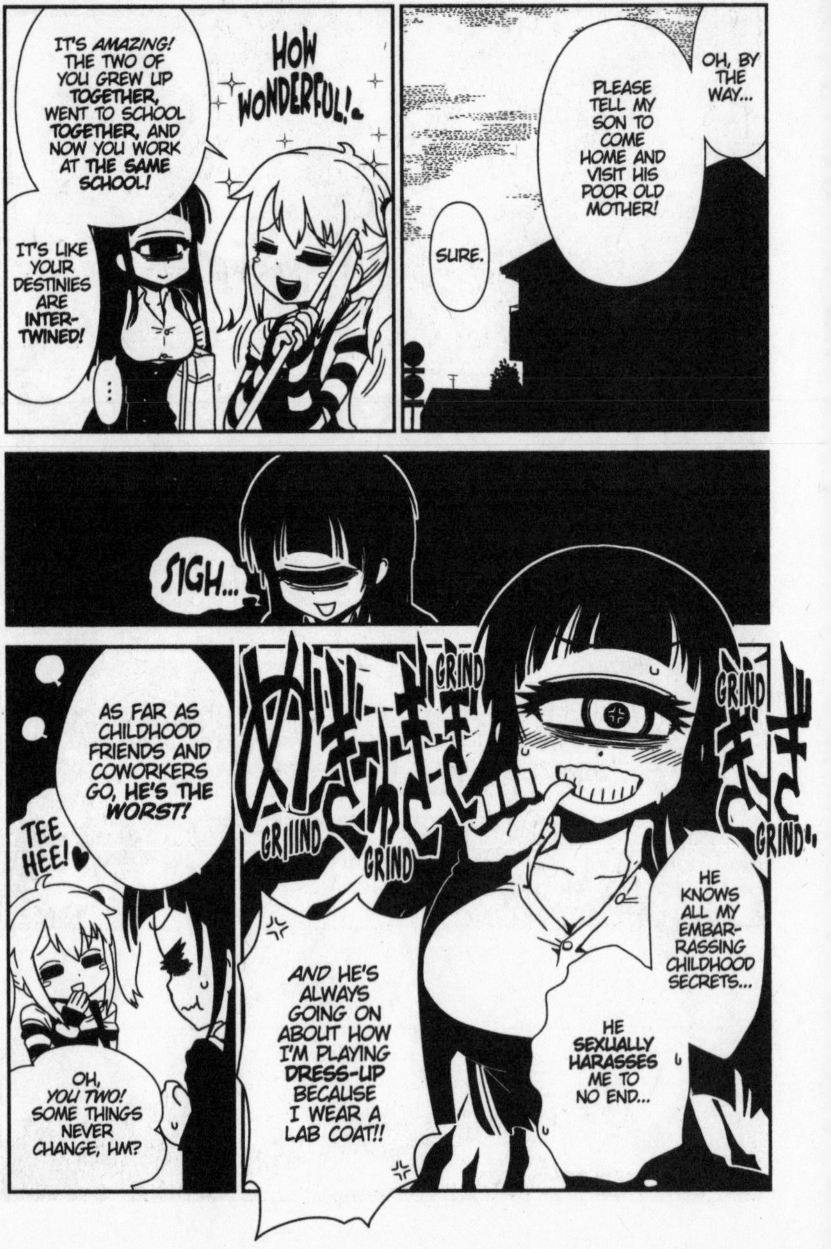
OH, BY THE WAY...
PLEASE TELL MY SON TO COME HOME AND VISIT HIS POOR OLD MOTHER!
SURE.
HOW WONDERFUL!♥
IT'S *AMAZING*! THE TWO OF YOU GREW UP **TOGETHER**, WENT TO SCHOOL **TOGETHER**, AND NOW YOU WORK **AT THE SAME SCHOOL**!
IT'S LIKE YOUR DESTINIES ARE INTER-TWINED!
...
SIGH...
GRIND
GRIND
GRIND
GRIIIND
GRIND
HE KNOWS ALL MY EMBAR-RASSING CHILDHOOD SECRETS...
HE SEXUALLY HARASSES ME TO NO END...
AND HE'S ALWAYS GOING ON ABOUT HOW I'M PLAYING **DRESS-UP** BECAUSE I WEAR A LAB COAT!!
AS FAR AS CHILDHOOD FRIENDS AND COWORKERS GO, HE'S THE ***WORST***!
TEE HEE!♥
OH, *YOU TWO*! SOME THINGS NEVER CHANGE, HM?

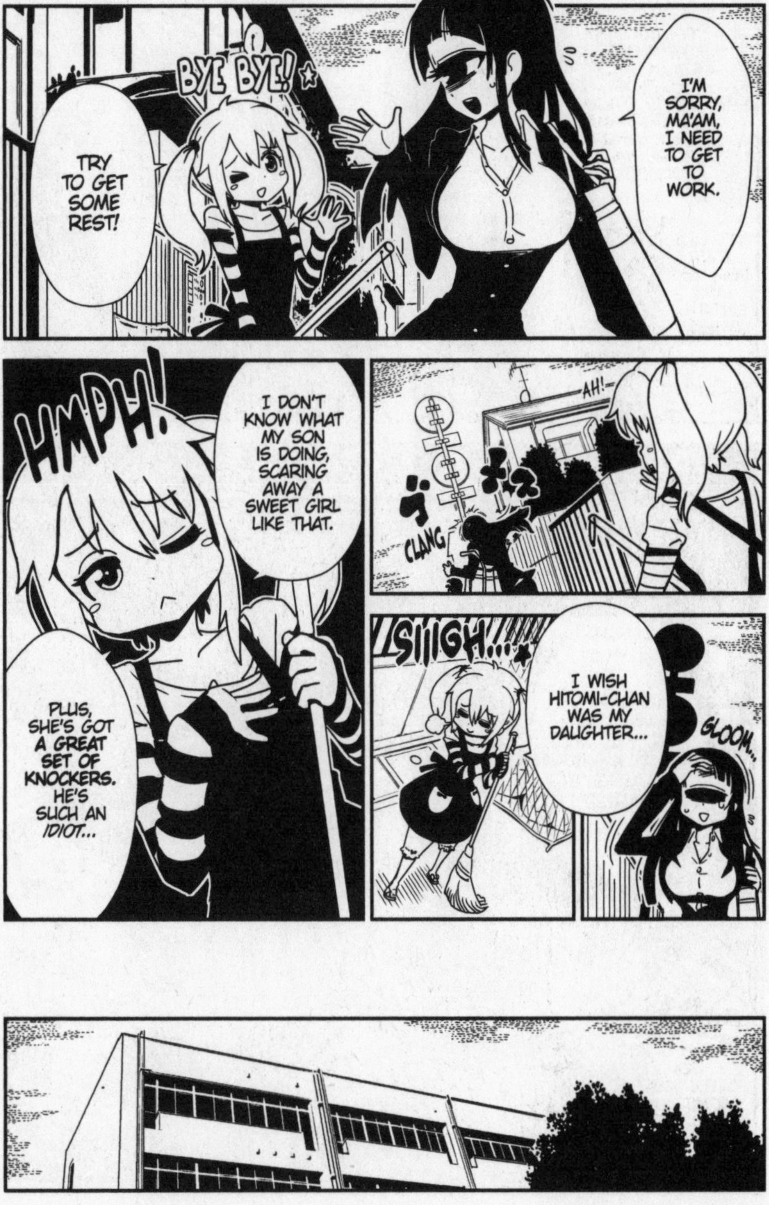
I'M SORRY, MA'AM, I NEED TO GET TO WORK.
BYE BYE! ☆
TRY TO GET SOME REST!
AH!
CLANG
GLOOM...
SIIIGH...!!!
I WISH HITOMI-CHAN WAS MY DAUGHTER...
I DON'T KNOW WHAT MY SON IS DOING, SCARING AWAY A SWEET GIRL LIKE THAT.
HMPH!
PLUS, SHE'S GOT A GREAT SET OF KNOCKERS. HE'S SUCH AN IDIOT...

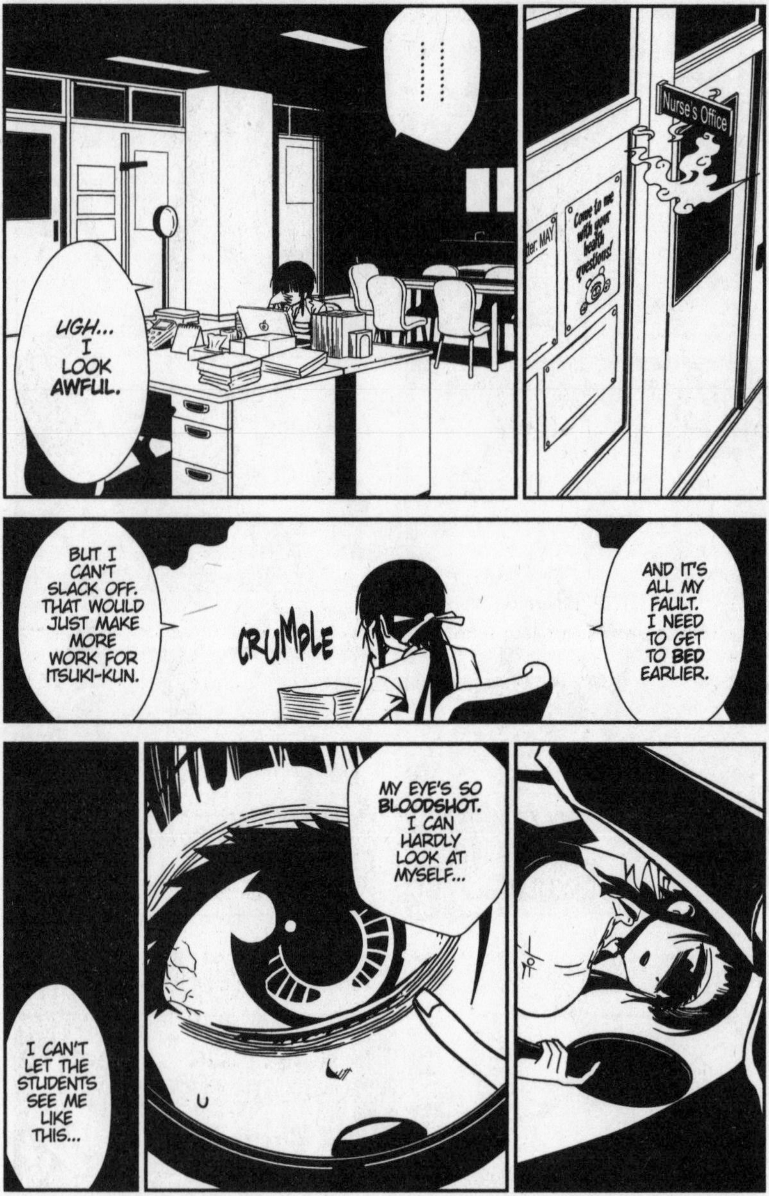
Nurse's Office
Come to me with your health questions!
......
UGH... I LOOK AWFUL.
AND IT'S ALL MY FAULT. I NEED TO GET TO BED EARLIER.
CRUMPLE
BUT I CAN'T SLACK OFF. THAT WOULD JUST MAKE MORE WORK FOR ITSUKI-KUN.
MY EYE'S SO BLOODSHOT. I CAN HARDLY LOOK AT MYSELF...
I CAN'T LET THE STUDENTS SEE ME LIKE THIS...

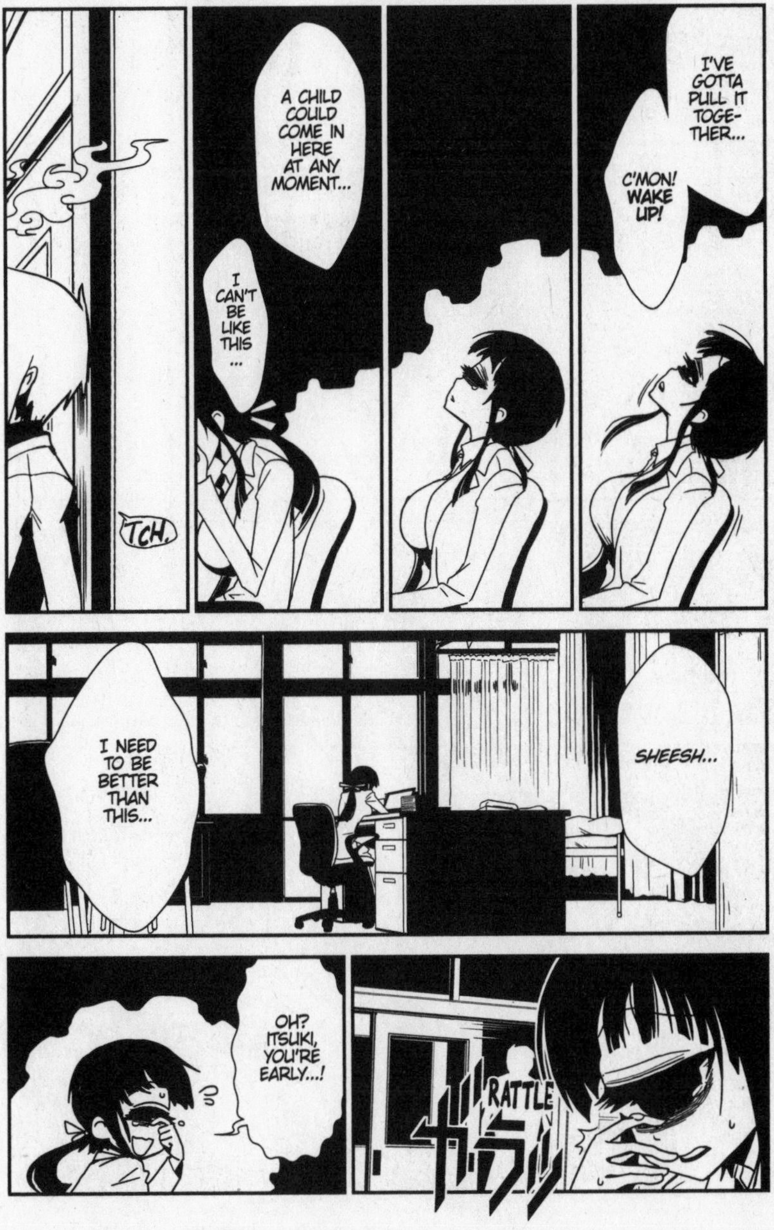
I'VE GOTTA PULL IT TOGE-THER...
C'MON! WAKE UP!
A CHILD COULD COME IN HERE AT ANY MOMENT...
I CAN'T BE LIKE THIS ...
TCH.
SHEESH...
I NEED TO BE BETTER THAN THIS...
RATTLE
OH? ITSUKI, YOU'RE EARLY...!

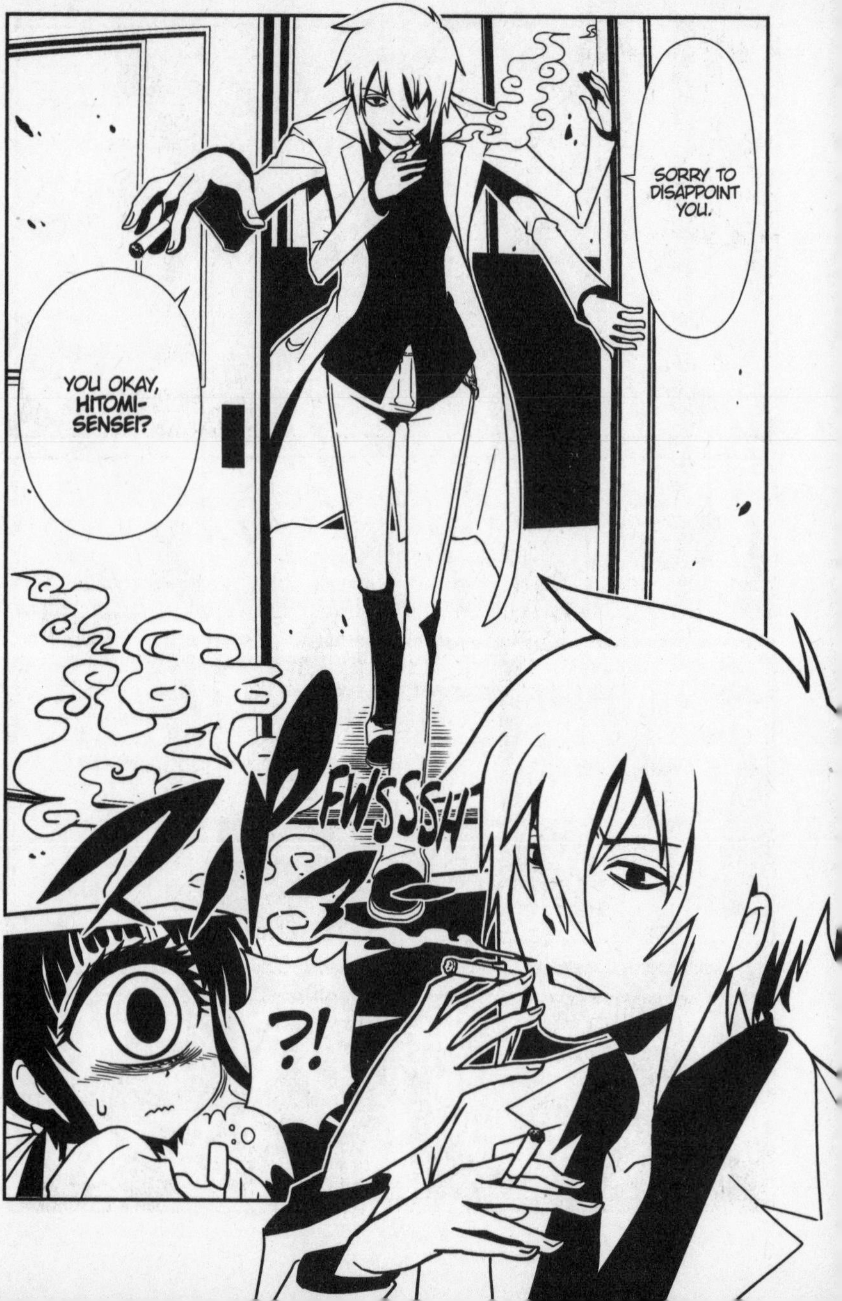
SORRY TO DISAPPOINT YOU.
YOU OKAY, HITOMI-SENSEI?
FWSSSH
?!

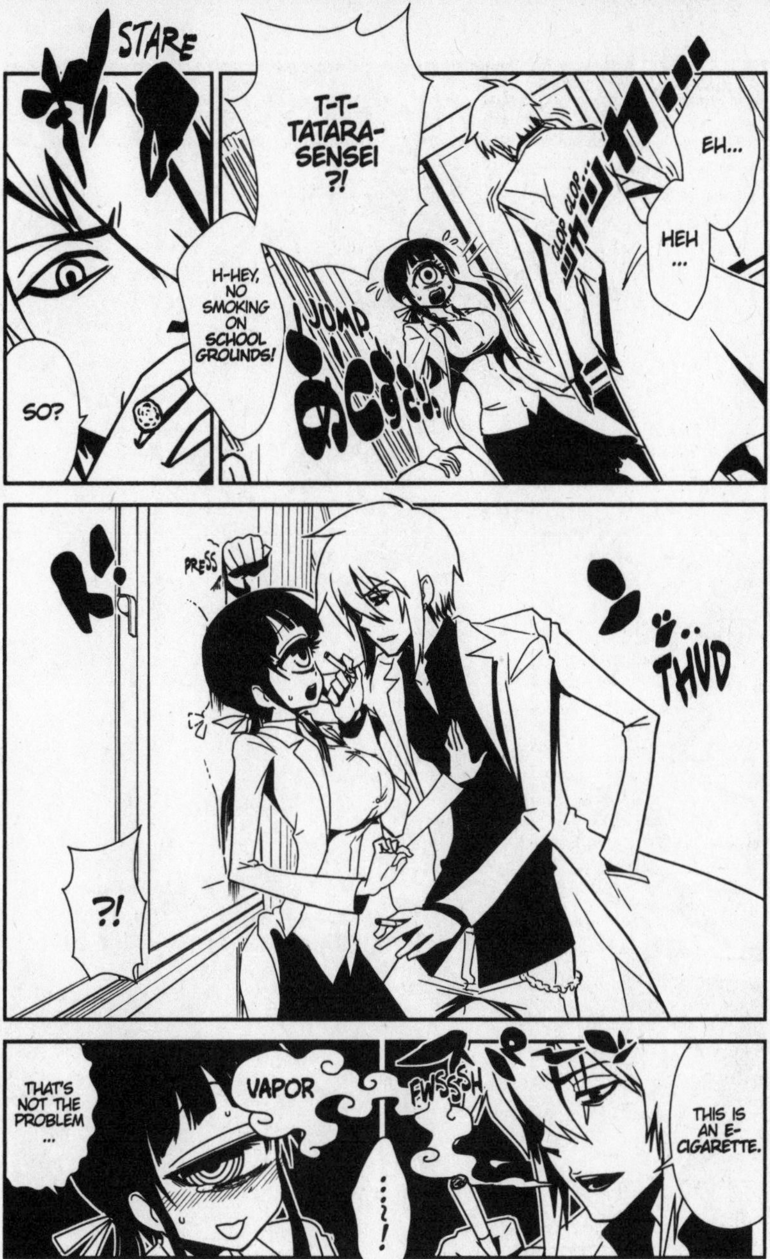
EH...
HEH...
CLOP CLOP...
T-T-TATARA-SENSEI?!
JUMP
STARE
H-HEY, NO SMOKING ON SCHOOL GROUNDS!
SO?
THUD
PRESS
?!
THIS IS AN E-CIGARETTE.
FWSSSH
...?!
VAPOR
THAT'S NOT THE PROBLEM...

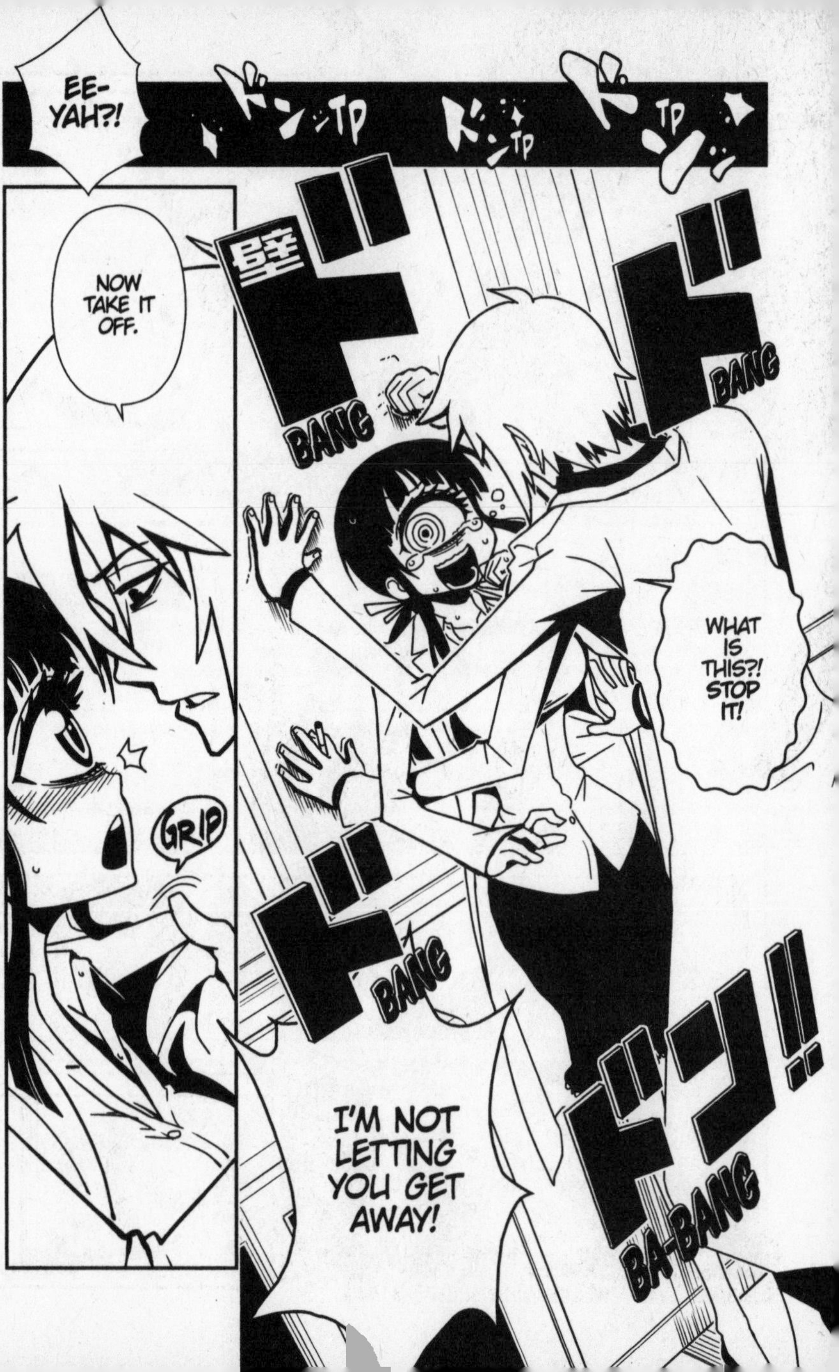
ドTP
ドンTP
ドンTP
EE-YAH?!
ドBANG
壁ドBANG
WHAT IS THIS?! STOP IT!
ドBANG
ドーン!!
BA-BANG
I'M NOT LETTING YOU GET AWAY!
NOW TAKE IT OFF.
GRIP

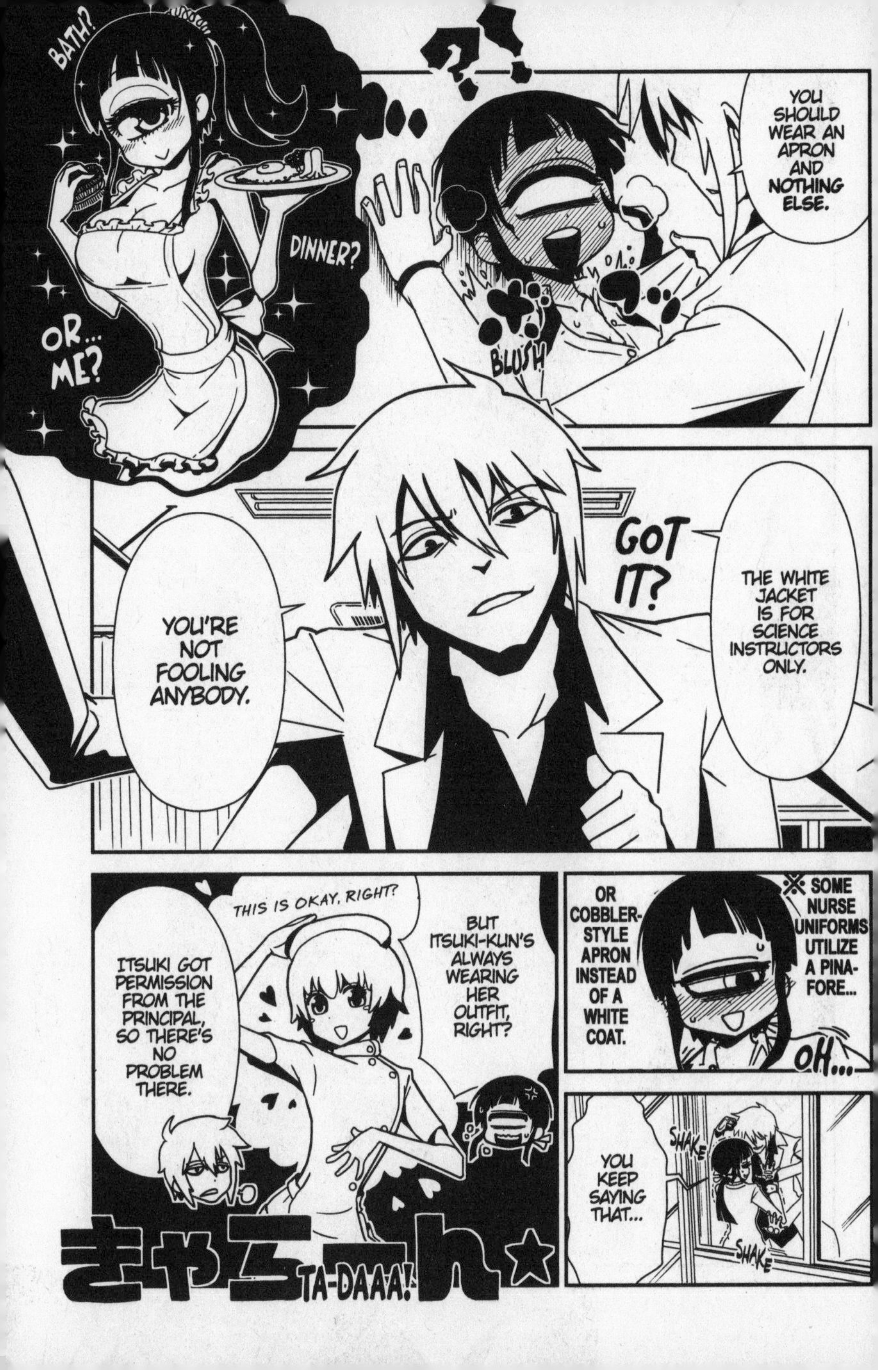
?!
YOU SHOULD WEAR AN APRON AND NOTHING ELSE.
...
BATH?
DINNER?
BLUSH
OR... ME?
THE WHITE JACKET IS FOR SCIENCE INSTRUCTORS ONLY.
GOT IT?
YOU'RE NOT FOOLING ANYBODY.
※SOME NURSE UNIFORMS UTILIZE A PINAFORE...
OR COBBLER-STYLE APRON INSTEAD OF A WHITE COAT.
OH...
SHAKE
YOU KEEP SAYING THAT...
SHAKE
BUT ITSUKI-KUN'S ALWAYS WEARING HER OUTFIT, RIGHT?
THIS IS OKAY, RIGHT?
ITSUKI GOT PERMISSION FROM THE PRINCIPAL, SO THERE'S NO PROBLEM THERE.
きゃるーん☆
TA-DAAA!

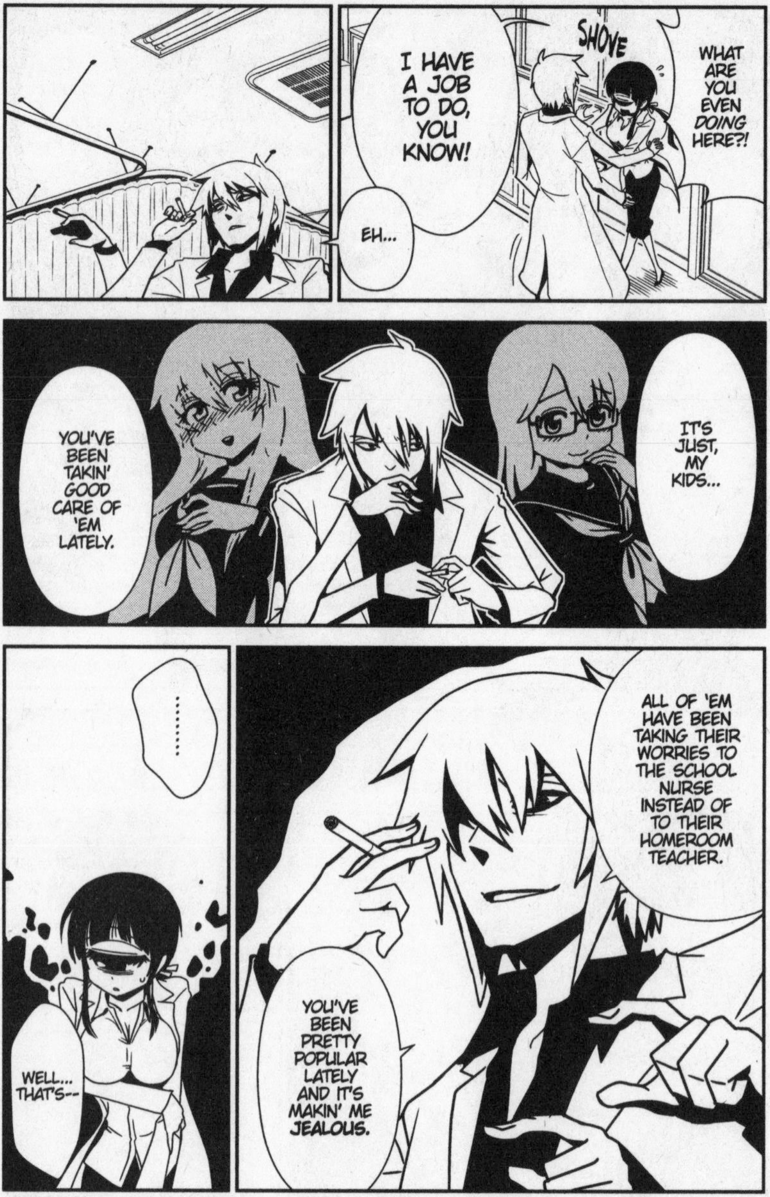
WHAT ARE YOU EVEN DOING HERE?!
SHOVE
I HAVE A JOB TO DO, YOU KNOW!
EH...
IT'S JUST, MY KIDS...
YOU'VE BEEN TAKIN' GOOD CARE OF 'EM LATELY.
ALL OF 'EM HAVE BEEN TAKING THEIR WORRIES TO THE SCHOOL NURSE INSTEAD OF TO THEIR HOMEROOM TEACHER.
YOU'VE BEEN PRETTY POPULAR LATELY AND IT'S MAKIN' ME JEALOUS.
......
WELL... THAT'S--

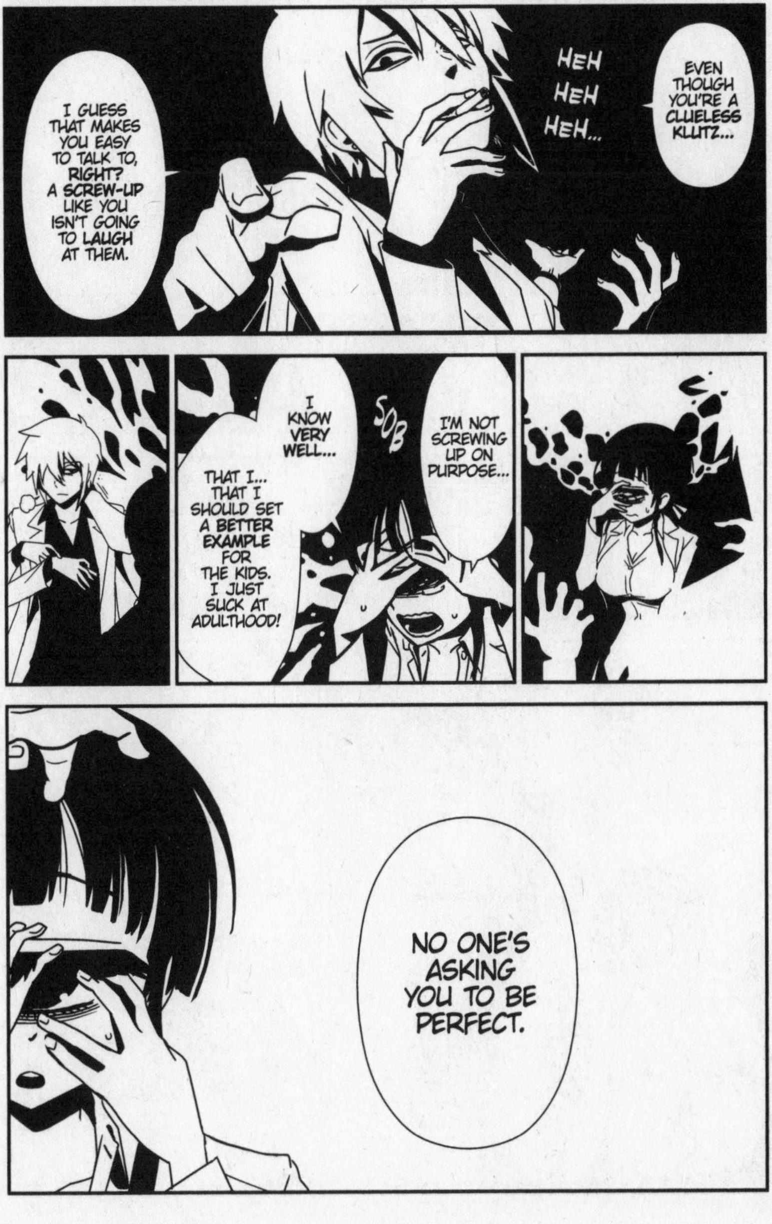
EVEN THOUGH YOU'RE A CLUELESS KLUTZ...
HEH HEH HEH...
I GUESS THAT MAKES YOU EASY TO TALK TO, RIGHT? A SCREW-UP LIKE YOU ISN'T GOING TO LAUGH AT THEM.
I'M NOT SCREWING UP ON PURPOSE...
SOB
I KNOW VERY WELL...
THAT I... THAT I SHOULD SET A BETTER EXAMPLE FOR THE KIDS. I JUST SUCK AT ADULTHOOD!
NO ONE'S ASKING YOU TO BE PERFECT.

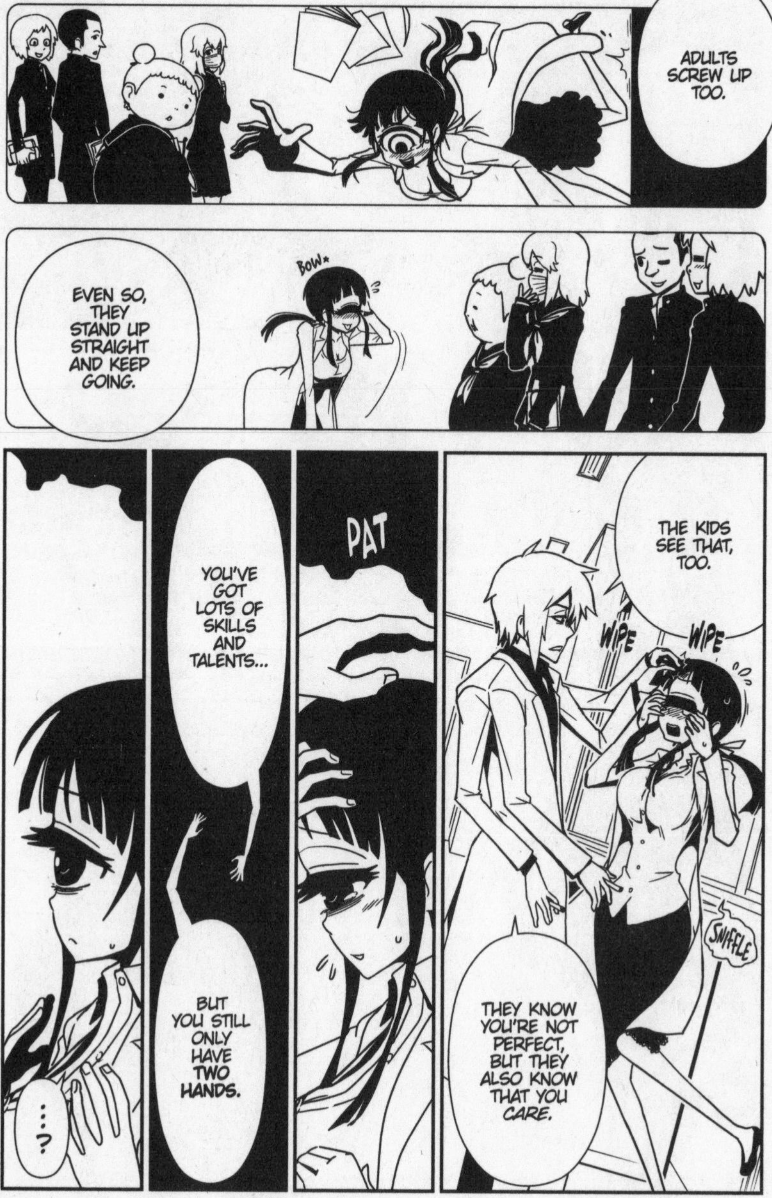

ADULTS SCREW UP TOO.
BOW★
EVEN SO, THEY STAND UP STRAIGHT AND KEEP GOING.
THE KIDS SEE THAT, TOO.
WIPE
WIPE
SNIFFLE
THEY KNOW YOU'RE NOT PERFECT, BUT THEY ALSO KNOW THAT YOU CARE.
PAT
YOU'VE GOT LOTS OF SKILLS AND TALENTS...
BUT YOU STILL ONLY HAVE TWO HANDS.
...?

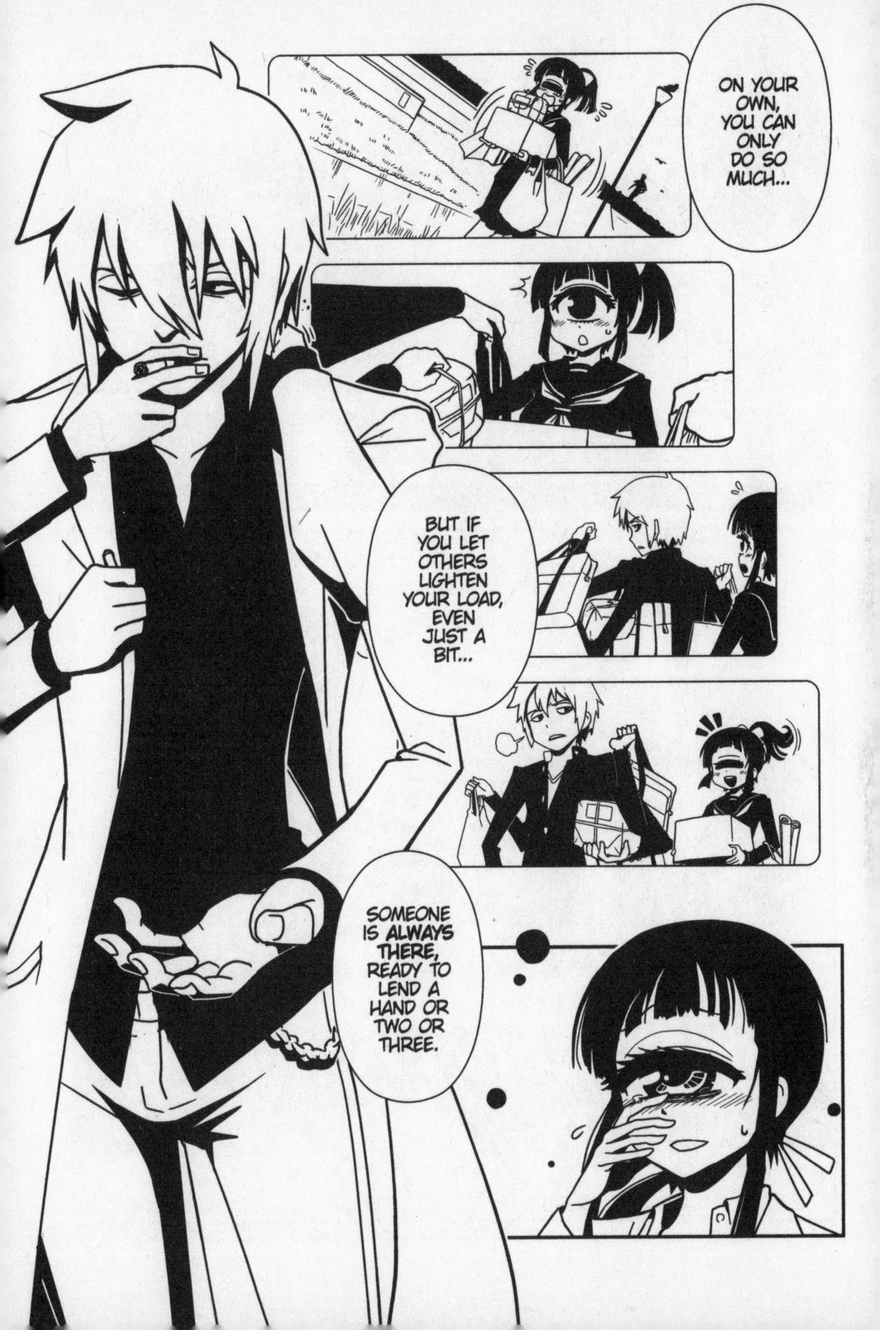
ON YOUR OWN, YOU CAN ONLY DO SO MUCH...
BUT IF YOU LET OTHERS LIGHTEN YOUR LOAD, EVEN JUST A BIT...
SOMEONE IS ALWAYS THERE, READY TO LEND A HAND OR TWO OR THREE.

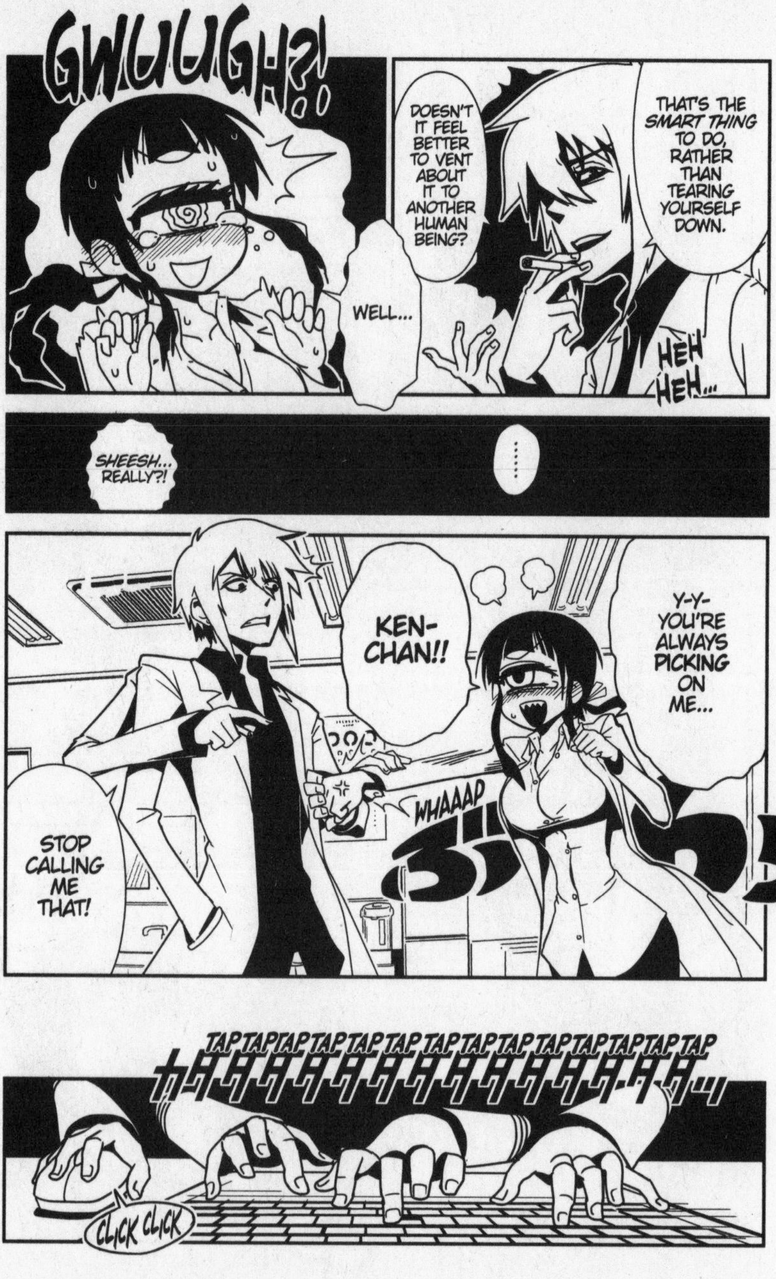
THAT'S THE SMART THING TO DO, RATHER THAN TEARING YOURSELF DOWN.
DOESN'T IT FEEL BETTER TO VENT ABOUT IT TO ANOTHER HUMAN BEING?
HEH HEH...
WELL...
GWUUGH?!
......
SHEESH... REALLY?!
Y-Y-YOU'RE ALWAYS PICKING ON ME...
KEN-CHAN!!
WHAAAP
STOP CALLING ME THAT!
TAP TAP TAP TAP TAP TAP TAP TAP TAP TAP TAP TAP TAP TAP
CLICK CLICK

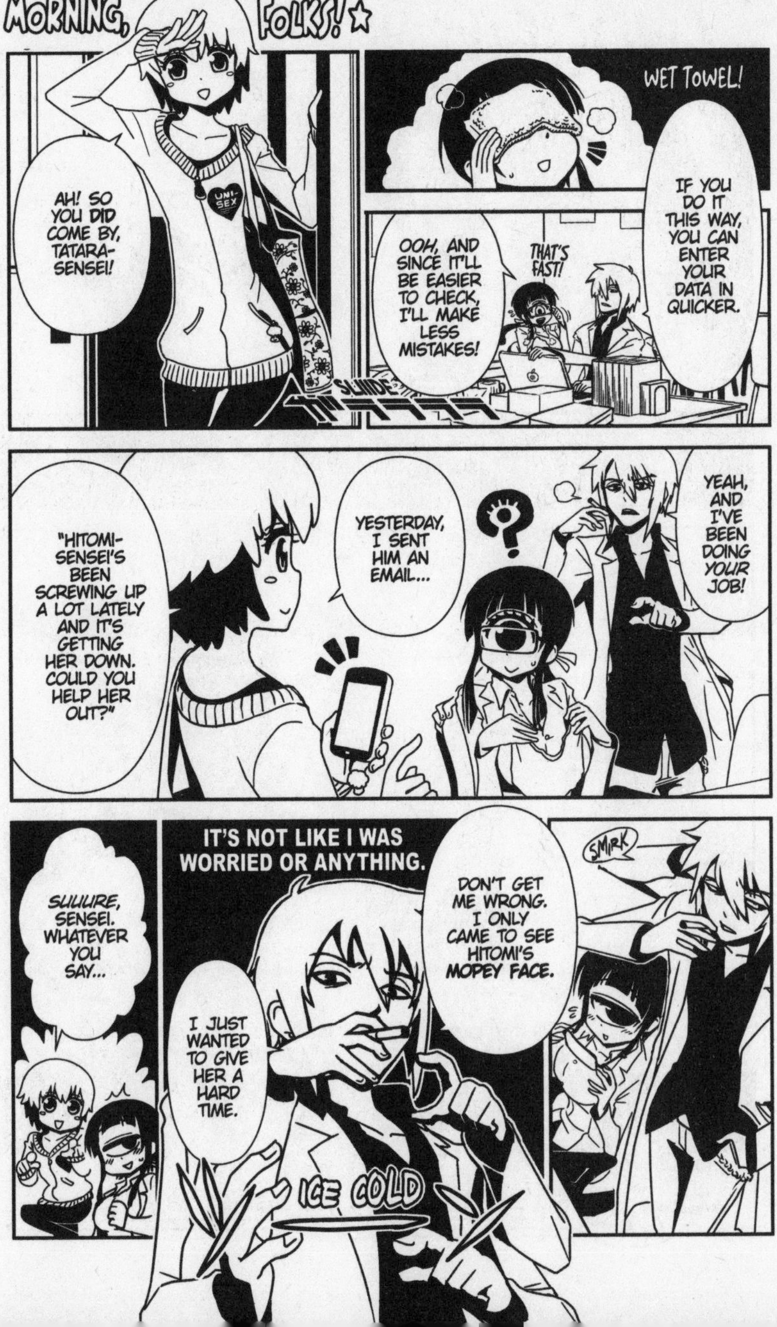
MORNING, FOLKS!☆
WET TOWEL!
IF YOU DO IT THIS WAY, YOU CAN ENTER YOUR DATA IN QUICKER.
THAT'S FAST!
OOH, AND SINCE IT'LL BE EASIER TO CHECK, I'LL MAKE LESS MISTAKES!
SLIIIDE
AH! SO YOU DID COME BY, TATARA-SENSEI!
YEAH, AND I'VE BEEN DOING YOUR JOB!
YESTERDAY, I SENT HIM AN EMAIL...
"HITOMI-SENSEI'S BEEN SCREWING UP A LOT LATELY AND IT'S GETTING HER DOWN. COULD YOU HELP HER OUT?"
SMIRK
DON'T GET ME WRONG. I ONLY CAME TO SEE HITOMI'S MOPEY FACE.
IT'S NOT LIKE I WAS WORRIED OR ANYTHING.
I JUST WANTED TO GIVE HER A HARD TIME.
ICE COLD
SUUURE, SENSEI. WHATEVER YOU SAY...

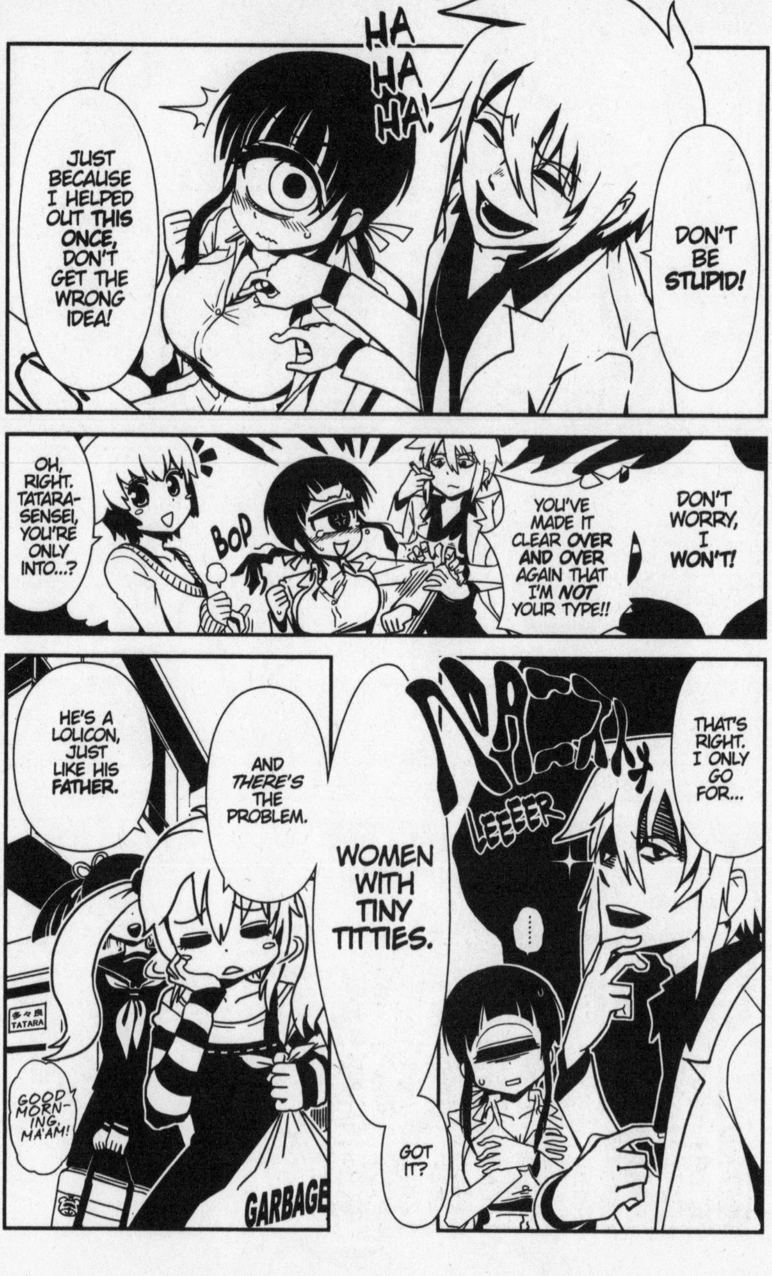
HA HA HA!
DON'T BE STUPID!
JUST BECAUSE I HELPED OUT THIS ONCE, DON'T GET THE WRONG IDEA!
DON'T WORRY, I WON'T!
YOU'VE MADE IT CLEAR OVER AND OVER AGAIN THAT I'M *NOT* YOUR TYPE!!
BOP
OH, RIGHT. TATARA-SENSEI, YOU'RE ONLY INTO...?
THAT'S RIGHT. I ONLY GO FOR...
LEEEER
WOMEN WITH TINY TITTIES.
......
GOT IT?
AND *THERE'S* THE PROBLEM.
HE'S A LOLICON, JUST LIKE HIS FATHER.
多々良 TATARA
GOOD MORNING, MA'AM!
GARBAGE

NURSE HITOMI'S Monster Infirmary

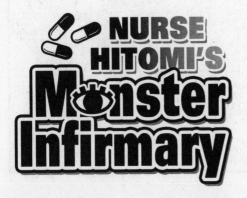

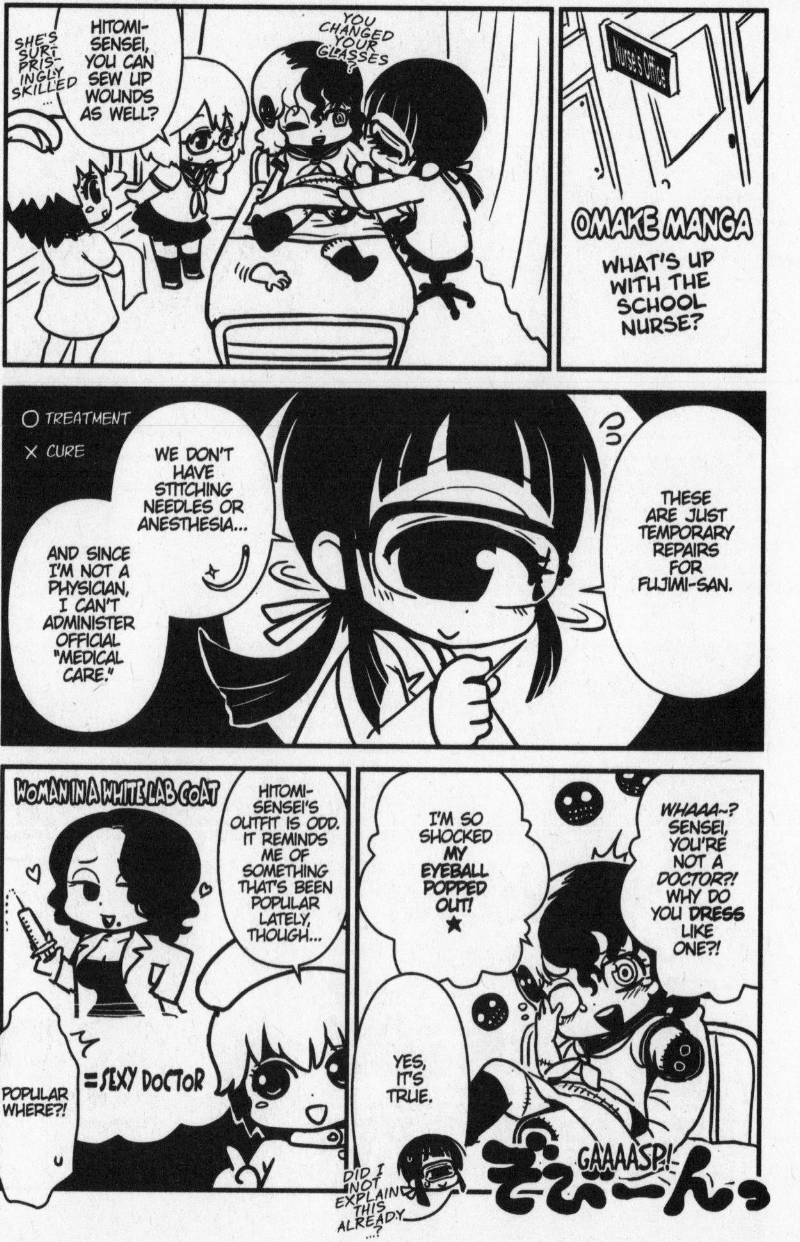

Nurse's Office
OMAKE MANGA
WHAT'S UP WITH THE SCHOOL NURSE?
YOU CHANGED YOUR GLASSES?
HITOMI-SENSEI, YOU CAN SEW UP WOUNDS AS WELL?
SHE'S SURPRISINGLY SKILLED...
THESE ARE JUST TEMPORARY REPAIRS FOR FUJIMI-SAN.
WE DON'T HAVE STITCHING NEEDLES OR ANESTHESIA...
AND SINCE I'M NOT A PHYSICIAN, I CAN'T ADMINISTER OFFICIAL "MEDICAL CARE."
O TREATMENT
X CURE
WHAAA~? SENSEI, YOU'RE NOT A DOCTOR?! WHY DO YOU DRESS LIKE ONE?!
I'M SO SHOCKED MY EYEBALL POPPED OUT! ★
YES, IT'S TRUE.
GAAAASP!
ぞひーんっ
DID I NOT EXPLAIN THIS ALREADY...?
HITOMI-SENSEI'S OUTFIT IS ODD. IT REMINDS ME OF SOMETHING THAT'S BEEN POPULAR LATELY, THOUGH...
WOMAN IN A WHITE LAB COAT
=SEXY DOCTOR
POPULAR WHERE?!

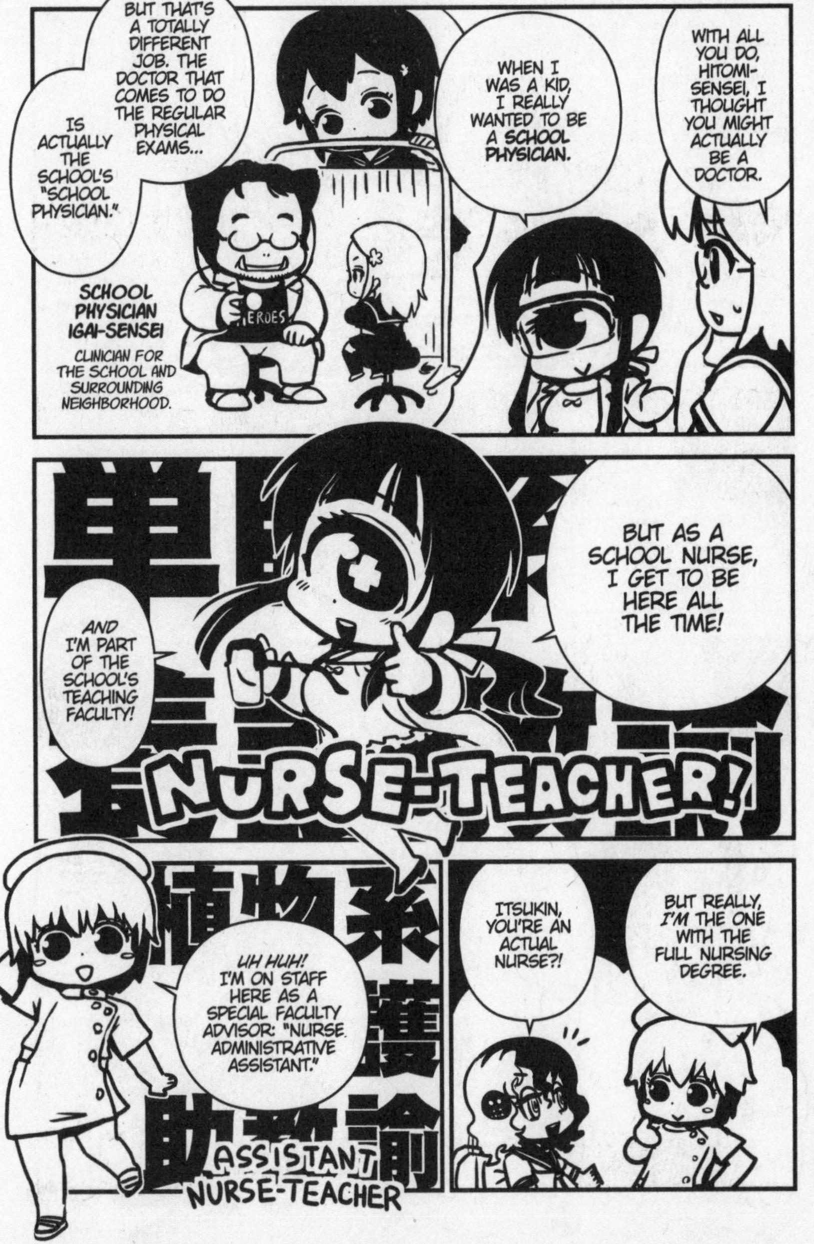
WITH ALL YOU DO, HITOMI-SENSEI, I THOUGHT YOU MIGHT ACTUALLY BE A DOCTOR.
WHEN I WAS A KID, I REALLY WANTED TO BE A SCHOOL PHYSICIAN.
BUT THAT'S A TOTALLY DIFFERENT JOB. THE DOCTOR THAT COMES TO DO THE REGULAR PHYSICAL EXAMS...
IS ACTUALLY THE SCHOOL'S "SCHOOL PHYSICIAN."
SCHOOL PHYSICIAN IGAI-SENSEI
CLINICIAN FOR THE SCHOOL AND SURROUNDING NEIGHBORHOOD.
HEROES
BUT AS A SCHOOL NURSE, I GET TO BE HERE ALL THE TIME!
AND I'M PART OF THE SCHOOL'S TEACHING FACULTY!
NURSE-TEACHER!
BUT REALLY, I'M THE ONE WITH THE FULL NURSING DEGREE.
ITSUKIN, YOU'RE AN ACTUAL NURSE?!
UH HUH! I'M ON STAFF HERE AS A SPECIAL FACULTY ADVISOR: "NURSE ADMINISTRATIVE ASSISTANT."
ASSISTANT NURSE-TEACHER

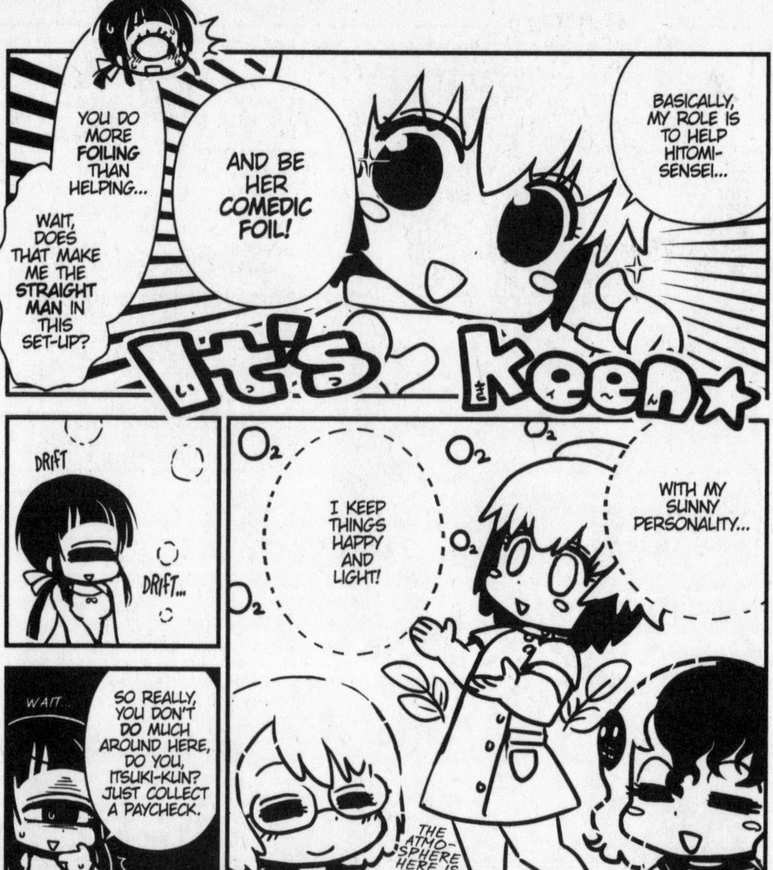
BASICALLY, MY ROLE IS TO HELP HITOMI-SENSEI...
AND BE HER COMEDIC FOIL!
YOU DO MORE FOILING THAN HELPING...
WAIT, DOES THAT MAKE ME THE STRAIGHT MAN IN THIS SET-UP?
It's keen★
WITH MY SUNNY PERSONALITY...
I KEEP THINGS HAPPY AND LIGHT!
THE ATMOSPHERE HERE IS PRETTY CHILL...
DRIFT
DRIFT...
WAIT...
SO REALLY, YOU DON'T DO MUCH AROUND HERE, DO YOU, ITSUKI-KUN? JUST COLLECT A PAYCHECK.
THE END!

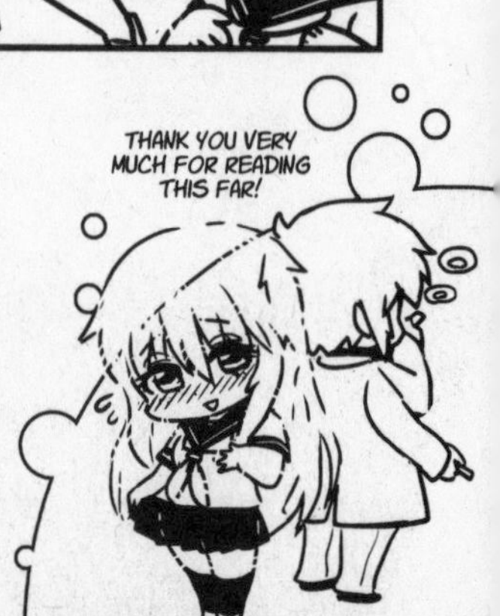
THANK YOU VERY MUCH FOR READING THIS FAR!

WARNING:
THIS IS A WORK OF FICTION AND SHOULD NOT BE VIEWED AS CONTAINING ANY ACTUAL MEDICAL ADVICE. VOID WHERE PROHIBITED.

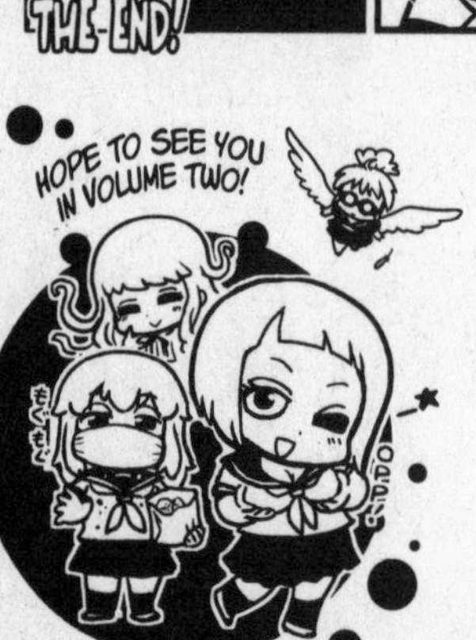
HOPE TO SEE YOU IN VOLUME TWO!
もぐもぐ

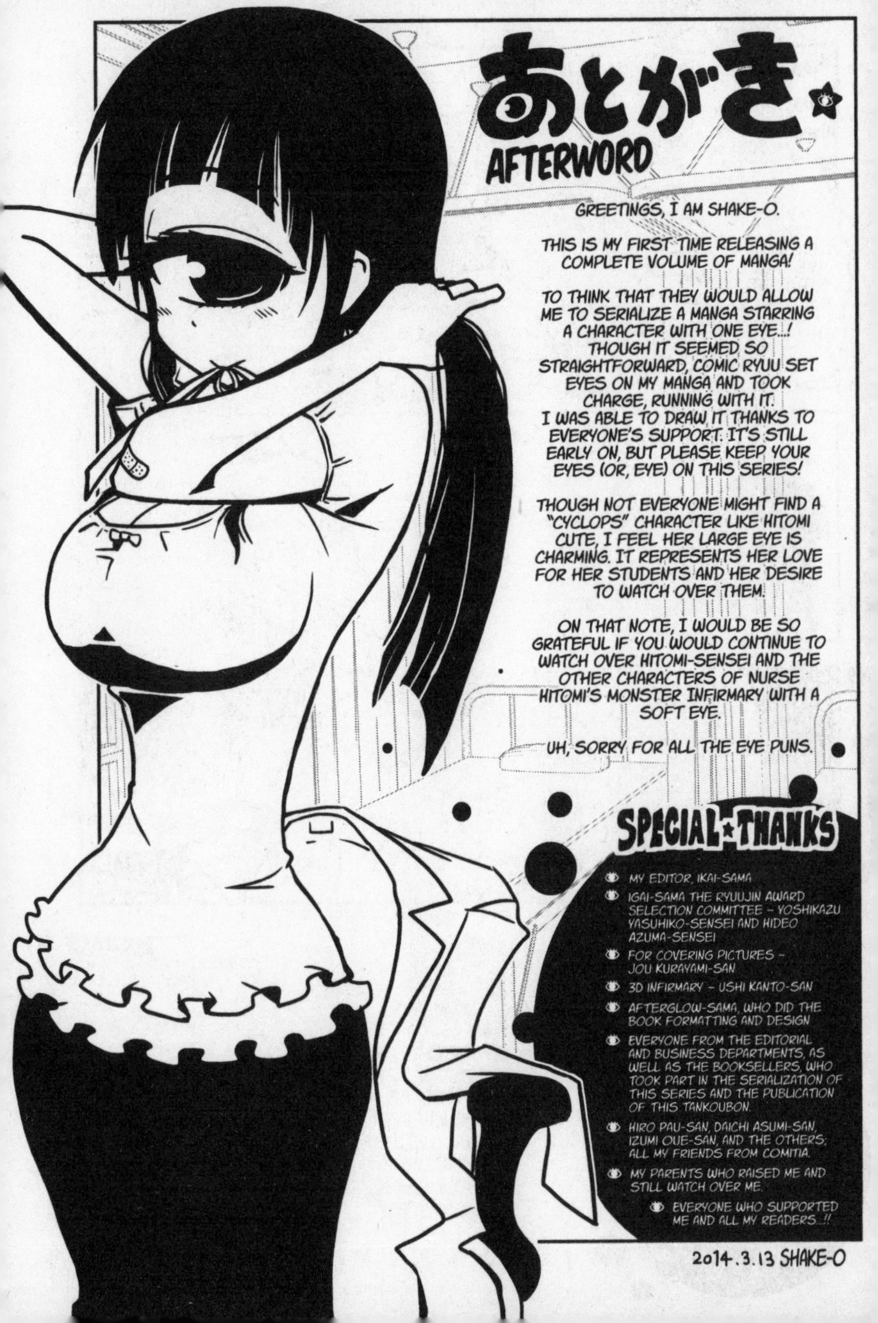

あとがき
AFTERWORD

GREETINGS, I AM SHAKE-O.

THIS IS MY FIRST TIME RELEASING A COMPLETE VOLUME OF MANGA!

TO THINK THAT THEY WOULD ALLOW ME TO SERIALIZE A MANGA STARRING A CHARACTER WITH ONE EYE...! THOUGH IT SEEMED SO STRAIGHTFORWARD, COMIC RYUU SET EYES ON MY MANGA AND TOOK CHARGE, RUNNING WITH IT. I WAS ABLE TO DRAW IT THANKS TO EVERYONE'S SUPPORT. IT'S STILL EARLY ON, BUT PLEASE KEEP YOUR EYES (OR, EYE) ON THIS SERIES!

THOUGH NOT EVERYONE MIGHT FIND A "CYCLOPS" CHARACTER LIKE HITOMI CUTE, I FEEL HER LARGE EYE IS CHARMING. IT REPRESENTS HER LOVE FOR HER STUDENTS AND HER DESIRE TO WATCH OVER THEM.

ON THAT NOTE, I WOULD BE SO GRATEFUL IF YOU WOULD CONTINUE TO WATCH OVER HITOMI-SENSEI AND THE OTHER CHARACTERS OF NURSE HITOMI'S MONSTER INFIRMARY WITH A SOFT EYE.

UH, SORRY FOR ALL THE EYE PUNS.

SPECIAL★THANKS

- MY EDITOR, IKAI-SAMA
- IGAI-SAMA THE RYUUJIN AWARD SELECTION COMMITTEE - YOSHIKAZU YASUHIKO-SENSEI AND HIDEO AZUMA-SENSEI
- FOR COVERING PICTURES - JOU KURAYAMI-SAN
- 3D INFIRMARY - USHI KANTO-SAN
- AFTERGLOW-SAMA, WHO DID THE BOOK FORMATTING AND DESIGN
- EVERYONE FROM THE EDITORIAL AND BUSINESS DEPARTMENTS, AS WELL AS THE BOOKSELLERS, WHO TOOK PART IN THE SERIALIZATION OF THIS SERIES AND THE PUBLICATION OF THIS TANKOUBON.
- HIRO PAU-SAN, DAICHI ASUMI-SAN, IZUMI OUE-SAN, AND THE OTHERS; ALL MY FRIENDS FROM COMITIA.
- MY PARENTS WHO RAISED ME AND STILL WATCH OVER ME.
- EVERYONE WHO SUPPORTED ME AND ALL MY READERS...!!

2014.3.13 SHAKE-O

HEIGHT COMPARISON DIAGRAM

As adolescent bodies are growing and changing daily, this comparison roughly reflects the figures (in units of centimeters) for May.

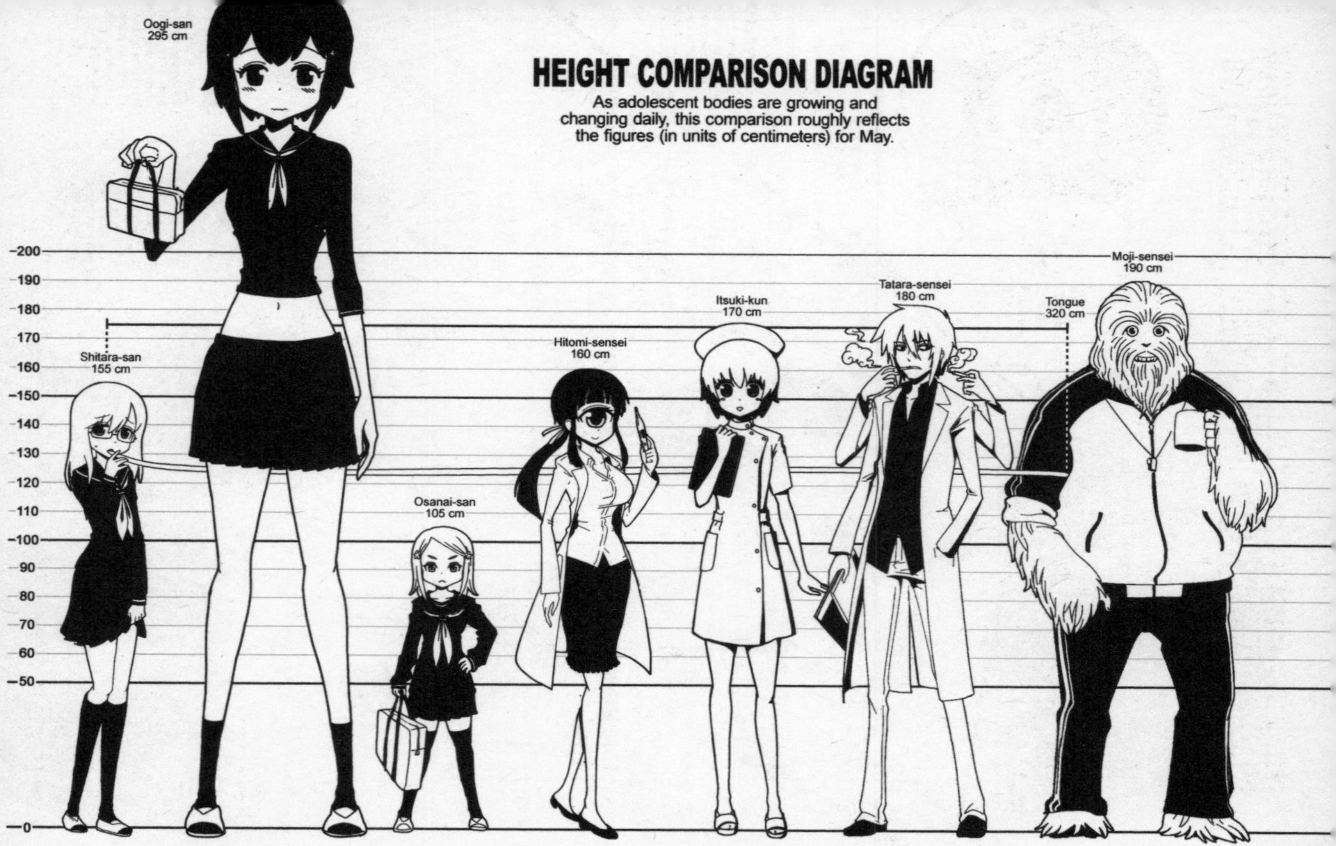

Oogi-san
295 cm
Shitara-san
155 cm
Osanai-san
105 cm
Hitomi-sensei
160 cm
Itsuki-kun
170 cm
Tatara-sensei
180 cm
Tongue
320 cm
Moji-sensei
190 cm
200
190
180
170
160
150
140
130
120
110
100
90
80
70
60
50
0

SEVEN SEAS ENTERTAINMENT PRESENTS

NURSE HITOMI'S
Monster Infirmary

story by and art by SHAKE-O   **VOLUME 1**

TRANSLATION
Amber Tamosaitis

ADAPTATION
Shannon Fay

LETTERING
Roland Amago

LAYOUT
Bambi Eloriaga-Amago

LOGO DESIGN
Lissa Pattillo

COVER DESIGN
Nicky Lim

PROOFREADER
Shanti Whitesides
Lee Otter

MANAGING EDITOR
Adam Arnold

PUBLISHER
Jason DeAngelis

HITOMI-SENSEI NO HOKENSHITSU VOLUME 1
© SHAKE-O 2014
Originally published in Japan in 2014 by TOKUMA SHOTEN PUBLISHING
CO., LTD., Tokyo. English translation rights arranged with TOKUMA SHOTEN
PUBLISHING CO., LTD., Tokyo, through TOHAN CORPORATION, Tokyo.

No portion of this book may be reproduced or transmitted in any form without
written permission from the copyright holders. This is a work of fiction. Names,
characters, places, and incidents are the products of the author's imagination
or are used fictitiously. Any resemblance to actual events, locals, or persons,
living or dead, is entirely coincidental.

Seven Seas books may be purchased in bulk for educational, business, or
promotional use. For information on bulk purchases, please contact Macmillan
Corporate & Premium Sales Department at 1-800-221-7945 (ext 5442)
or write specialmarkets@macmillan.com.

Seven Seas and the Seven Seas logo are trademarks of
Seven Seas Entertainment, LLC. All rights reserved.

ISBN: 978-1-626921-47-4

Printed in Canada

First Printing: February 2015

10 9 8 7 6 5 4 3 2

FOLLOW US ONLINE: *www.gomanga.com*

READING DIRECTIONS

This book reads from *right to left*, Japanese style.
If this is your first time reading manga, you start
reading from the top right panel on each page and
take it from there. If you get lost, just follow the
numbered diagram here. It may seem backwards at
first, but you'll get the hang of it! Have fun!!

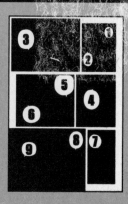

NURSE HITOMI'S MONSTER INFIRMARY

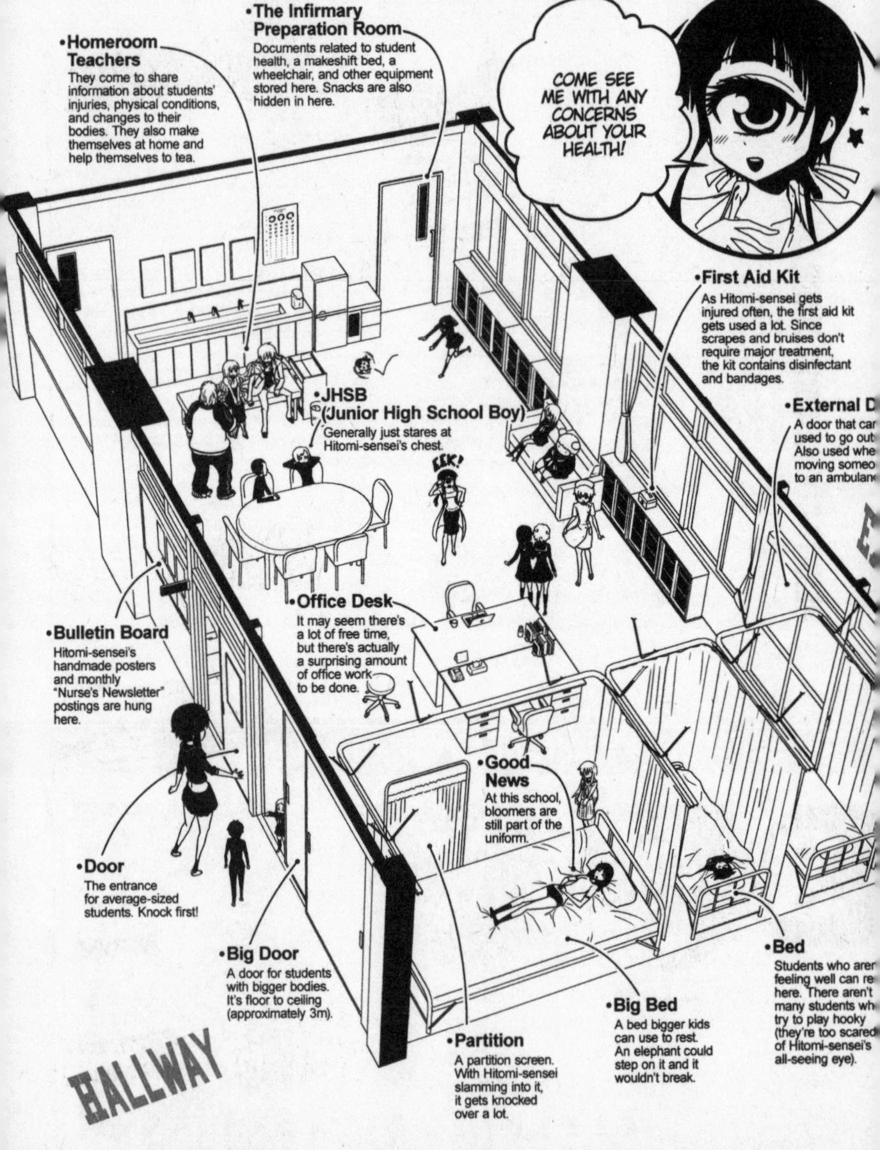

COME SEE ME WITH ANY CONCERNS ABOUT YOUR HEALTH!
•The Infirmary Preparation Room
Documents related to student health, a makeshift bed, a wheelchair, and other equipment stored here. Snacks are also hidden in here.
•Homeroom Teachers
They come to share information about students' injuries, physical conditions, and changes to their bodies. They also make themselves at home and help themselves to tea.
•First Aid Kit
As Hitomi-sensei gets injured often, the first aid kit gets used a lot. Since scrapes and bruises don't require major treatment, the kit contains disinfectant and bandages.
•External D
A door that car
used to go out
Also used whe
moving someo
to an ambulan
•JHSB (Junior High School Boy)
Generally just stares at Hitomi-sensei's chest.
EEK!
•Office Desk
It may seem there's a lot of free time, but there's actually a surprising amount of office work to be done.
•Bulletin Board
Hitomi-sensei's handmade posters and monthly "Nurse's Newsletter" postings are hung here.
•Good News
At this school, bloomers are still part of the uniform.
•Door
The entrance for average-sized students. Knock first!
•Bed
Students who aren
feeling well can re
here. There aren't
many students wh
try to play hooky
(they're too scared
of Hitomi-sensei's
all-seeing eye).
•Big Door
A door for students with bigger bodies. It's floor to ceiling (approximately 3m).
•Big Bed
A bed bigger kids can use to rest. An elephant could step on it and it wouldn't break.
•Partition
A partition screen. With Hitomi-sensei slamming into it, it gets knocked over a lot.
HALLWAY